scott kauffman

IN DEEPEST CONSEQUENCES

PRESS®

Gold Imprint
Medallion Press, Inc.
Printed in USA

scott kauffman

IN DEEPEST CONSEQUENCES

DEDICATION:

For Adin, Betty, and Elizabeth,
In Deepest Appreciation.

Published 2006 by Medallion Press, Inc.

The MEDALLION PRESS LOGO
is a registered tradmark of Medallion Press, Inc.

If you purchased this book without a cover, you should be aware that this book is stolen property. It was reported as "unsold and destroyed" to the publisher, and neither the author nor the publisher has received any payment from this "stripped book."

Copyright © 2006 by Scott Kauffman
Cover Illustration by Adam Mock

All rights reserved. No part of this book may be reproduced or transmitted in any form or by any electronic or mechanical means, including photocopying, recording, or by any information storage and retrieval system, without written permission of the publisher, except where permitted by law.

Names, characters, places, and incidents are the products of the author's imagination or are used fictionally. Any resemblance to actual events, locales, or persons, living or dead, is entirely coincidental.

Typeset in Perpetua

Printed in the United States of America

10 9 8 7 6 5 4 3 2 1
First Edition

Oftentimes, to win us to our harm,
The instruments of darkness tell us truths;
Win us with honest trifles, to betray's
In deepest consequence.

——Macbeth

CHAPTER 1
ACT 1

1992

WHEN DEATH CAME, she was at her bedroom window, standing in the moonlight and looking out as she brushed her crow-black hair that fell to the small of her back, shimmering faintly as does the quicksilver drizzle of winter rain at midnight. She must have seen something in the window because she stopped her brushing in mid-stroke and peered out into the darkness. But she never saw anything more. Before she died her killer had seared her eyes shut, charring their sockets as waxy black as extinguished votive candles. Burned and coagulated blood tear-dropped down her cheeks, and her porcelain-white throat lay open, wide and agape, as though she wore a new smile to greet an old lover.

Calvin Samuels eased open the door and slipped inside, letting the door swing shut behind him, its swish as quiet as death's whisper on the night of his wife's murder. He stood listening with his back to the door, his lost, stray-dog eyes graying the darkness. Save for the flame in the fireplace, the only light in the judge's chambers fell through a tall Moorish window opposite him. Beside the window in a corner stood a three-foot, spindly Christmas tree, decorated with colored-paper ornaments like those made by a child in art class. A clock ticked somewhere. Outside the chamber's door, a white-haired Negro and his wife made their way up the hall as they swept and polished the courthouse, office by office.

After a long minute, Calvin crossed the parquet floor, feeling his way with scarred fingertips, until he came to a desk of English walnut, behind which slept a snoring, open-mouthed judge still dressed in his robes. Calvin sat in one of two visitor's chairs, its leather upholstery so old and parched it crackled like ripping silk as he lowered himself. He leaned back and assumed a posture akin to a poker player who has drawn his last card and now awaits the showing of hands. The judge yawned and opened his eyes, unaware.

"Judge Benjamin Thompson," Calvin said, his voice sharp, pugnacious.

Thompson's mouth snapped shut in mid yawn.

"You *still* sleeping on the job?"

Thompson's eyes flicked to the chamber's door and slowly came back to the man in silhouette seated across his desk. He fumbled for the steel-rimmed glasses resting on his forehead and leaned forward.

"Calvin? Calvin Samuels? Is that you?"

"You better hope it is."

"Well, I'll just be goddamned."

"No doubt we both are."

"Well, then, I'll just be doubly goddamned."

"Must've been a real hard day of judging if you're napping in the middle of the afternoon."

Thompson shook his head and chuckled. "No, not really. But I've promised a ruling before I leave for the day, and my clerk's girlfriend dropped by and kidnapped him for the afternoon. Probably the evening and night, too. I think she's in a hurry to get herself in a family way so the dumb sonnuvabitch will think he has to marry her."

He reached down and lifted the spine-broken reporter straddling his lap and dropped it on top of the pleadings and motions scattered across his desktop. "Never could stay awake while reading these old cases. Not even in law school."

The two sat there and just looked at one another, Thompson still shaking his head, but grinning, and after a minute, he stood and walked to the front corner of his desk.

"Well, God damn it, Calvin. How the hell are you?

When did you get back into Hanna?"

Calvin looked toward the window, giving his chin a slight sideways turn, as might a man considering his possible answers, the possible consequences that could come of them.

"Calvin?"

Calvin turned back, thinning his lips in what would not quite pass for a smile. "Renate's office was closed downstairs when I walked by. It's still hers, isn't it?"

"Sure is. She just left early to pick up supplies for tonight."

"Tonight?"

"You know, New Year's Eve and all."

Calvin leaned forward and squinted at the calendar behind Thompson's desk. "Is it?"

"And we were engaged on New Year's, so this is sort of an anniversary for us."

Calvin looked down into the glass well of his hands.

"Doesn't stop with just your wedding anniversary, old boy," Thompson said. "It's your engagement anniversary and your first-date anniversary and all that goes with it. More anniversaries than Catholic saint days."

He walked back behind his desk and across to the window where he looked up and down the snow drifted street, his hands clasped behind him. "But you know how sentimental the ladies are."

When Calvin didn't answer, Thompson turned back around. Calvin was staring into the fireplace, as though buried in the gray ash was some long-forgotten work the two of

6

them had left there to anneal, and he had begun to shiver in an odd quiver, like an old dog brought in from a freezing rain.

"What in the world are you doing out in this weather without a coat?" Thompson said. "You look half frozen. Pull that chair up closer to the fire, why don't you?"

Calvin again didn't answer.

"Calvin?"

"Yeah," Calvin said, and stood and picked up his chair and carried it closer. "I will, thank you."

Thompson looked out his window once more, and then he too walked to the fireplace. "Actually, Renate should've been back by now."

"Oh?"

"Yeah. It looks ugly out there. How's the driving?"

Calvin shrugged. "Couldn't tell you."

"Why can't you tell me?"

"Because I walked in."

"You walked in?"

"Yeah."

Thompson frowned. "In this weather?"

Calvin nodded.

"You walked in from where?"

Calvin closed his eyes and pressed his fingertips against them. "I hitched a ride partway in from Route 154."

"You hitched?"

"Yeah, but they dropped me off a couple of miles out." He let his hands drop into his lap. "But that explains it."

"Explains what?"

"New Year's Eve. The driver was all over the road."

Thompson looked back to the window. He looked down at Calvin.

"Have a seat, why don't you?" Calvin said.

Thompson went to pull up the other chair, but he stopped short. He raised his palm to his mouth, as a man about to gag, and swallowed it back down. It had been more than just a few days since Calvin had bathed. He stepped back out of the firelight so that it fell on Calvin and studied him for the first time. It had been even longer than a few days since Calvin had shaved. His straggled greasy hair had not been cut in months. His rag of a shirt was coming apart at the stitches down the yoke of its back, and food stains ran down the front in dried trickles of red and brown and yellow. His leaden, red-rimmed eyes looked into the fire, sullen. Depthless.

Thompson lowered his hand. "You want some coffee to warm you up? I made it this morning and it'll most likely eat the lining out of your stomach, but it's still hot, I think."

"No, but I'll take a drink if you have it."

Thompson nodded. "I think I could use one too."

He walked to the bookcase opposite the fireplace and removed several *Ohio State Reporters* and reached in and came out holding a spider-webbed bottle of Jameson. In the back of a bottom desk drawer, he found two yellowed tumblers. He held them up to the window light and eyed them and blew out brown clouds of acrid dust and cleaned them with the hem of his robes.

"I keep the hooch back behind to keep it away from the cleaning crew."

"I don't recall Clarence being much of a drinker."

"No, but with an election coming up again next November, I don't need any rumors floating around about the judge drinking in chambers."

He glanced at Calvin as he poured. "Normally I don't before six, but it's the season, after all."

"I guess."

"And with your visit, now we've good cause if not just cause, hey?"

He filled both glasses two fingers full and held one out. A car passed beneath the chamber's window as Calvin reached up, and Thompson turned to look, not seeing Calvin slosh half the whiskey out of his glass.

"Not Renate," Thompson said. He turned back and raised his drink. "To your health. And a happy New Year."

But even before Thompson finished his toast, Calvin had already drained what whiskey he hadn't spilled. He held his glass back up, his hand still trembling. Thompson at first grinned, as if Calvin was only showing off as if it were the old days, but when he looked into Calvin's eyes, he set down his own glass and poured again, this time filling Calvin's to the rim. He corked the bottle and held the drink out. When Calvin reached up, Thompson saw his hands and grimaced. "What happened to your fingers?"

"Roofing accident."

"Where?"

"At work."

"Since when did lawyers begin roofing?"

Calvin drank the glass half empty and sat back. "So you're now the Common Pleas Court judge for Creek County, Ohio."

Thompson, still staring at Calvin's fingers, nodded.

Calvin's eyes swept over the three walls lined floor to ceiling with shelves of codes and reporters. "Damnation. And the Commissioners even gave you Judge Biltmore's old chambers to boot."

"Yeah, they did. Ran the year Bilty decided not to stand again."

"How do you like it? Being judge and all."

"Not nearly as exciting as prosecuting, I'll tell you that straight out."

"No, I suppose not."

"Oh, once, maybe twice a year we'll fill up the gallery."

"Yeah?"

"But most days it's guilty pleas and settlements. Uncontested divorces. Most days nothing much memorable happens. You remember how it used to be."

Calvin nodded. He looked down at what remained of his whiskey and swirled it around the bottom, regarding his own dark self in the amber ring of his glass.

"But it gives me more time with my kids."

Calvin looked up. "Kids?"

"Yeah. Kids. Rumor has it you were one yourself once."

"You and Renate?"

"Me and Renate."

"How many?"

"We've a son, Donald, and a daughter, Sara, now."

"Congratulations."

"Hard to imagine, isn't it? Me," Thompson said, and half-turned toward the Christmas tree. "It's time to take it down now. Getting to be a firetrap. But ever since she's been four or so, Sara's insisted I have one in chambers. Says otherwise Daddy comes home all grumpy and ruins Christmas for everyone else."

He turned back to Calvin. "So? How long's it been now? Eight years?"

"Ten. Ten last August."

"Ten? Yeah, I guess that's right. You left not long after the Alexander trial. You and . . ."

"Yeah, we did."

Thompson pursed his lips. He looked toward his door. After a minute he said, "I'm sorry, Calvin. I didn't mean to . . ."

"Forget it."

"I can't tell you how badly I felt when I heard. Renate, too."

Calvin nodded.

"What happened?"

Calvin didn't answer. The fire ticked.

"I apologize," Thompson said. "I've no right."

11

"No. You've every right. That's why I'm back."

"Back?"

Calvin emptied his glass. He pushed himself up from the chair and walked to the window, the snow now falling so thick the storefronts across the village square had all but disappeared.

"She's nowhere now," Calvin said. "Just a wandering voice that still calls to me."

Thompson said nothing.

"Can't even see Cemetery Hill any more."

Calvin looked back from the window. "You know, I've never even been up to her grave."

"She's buried behind your granddad."

"I see."

"Next to John Rogers."

Calvin looked back out the window.

"Never did find Rogers's killer, in case you've wondered. Renate still asks me every once in a while if anything has ever come up."

"You might be surprised someday."

"What do you mean?"

It was a long while before Calvin spoke again, his soft voice corrupted by a bottomless anger. "It was in Judge Biltmore's courtroom. Just outside. You prosecuted Alexander, and I, I defended him. Do you remember?"

"I remember."

"Ten years ago last summer. You and I duked it out for over a week."

Calvin again looked back from the window. "She was murdered just five months ago."

"Yes."

"Seems more like five years."

Thompson pulled at his whiskey. He tapped the rim of his glass with the gold band on his finger.

A car passed by the chamber's window, and Calvin followed it until its two glowing taillights disappeared into the falling snow.

"It was late morning," he said. "Got a call at the house we were roofing. Said she still hadn't shown up. Asked me if there was a problem because she'd never been late, you know, never even missed a day. After her supervisor hung up, I knew something was wrong. Bad wrong. Her job as a buyer was just too important to her to miss without calling in. Even on the day after she had her abortion, she still went in to work."

"Abortion?"

"Wasn't mine."

"Wasn't . . ."

"She all but collapsed inside the door when she got home from the clinic that night, blood loss I guess, but she still went in the next day just the same. The same as if nothing had happened. The same as if she'd done nothing. After I stopped being a lawyer, well, her job and her traveling that went with it seemed to be all she cared about."

Thompson set his whiskey glass on the fireplace mantle,

his own hands now unsteady. He sat down and leaned forward, his elbows resting on his knees. "Calvin, how long's it been since you were in to see your doctor?"

"Of course, I immediately called home, but no one answered. Figured her car most likely had broken down on the freeway. Probably hadn't yet reached a payphone, but I was worried all the same. Worried because soon after we moved out there, a girl's car was found not far from our exit. Her car was found, but she wasn't. No one saw her. No witnesses. Nothing. Then for two years her face was up on the billboard, her eyes looking down at me whenever I drove by. After a while, I didn't even notice her."

Calvin walked back to Thompson's desk. He picked up the Jamesons and drank the quarter-bottle remaining and dropped it into the wastebasket, wiping his lips with his shirtsleeve.

"Nothing I could do but begin at home and follow her usual route. When I pulled into our driveway, I found her car where it was when I left. Dew still wetting the windshield, except where someone had sliced his finger across the driver's side, neck high."

Calvin shook his head. "I didn't know what to think. I thought maybe she'd just forgotten to set her alarm the night before or maybe she was sick or had fallen in the bathtub and couldn't make it to the phone. The front door was open, which seemed odd because I was certain I'd double locked it so her cats couldn't escape. I went in and walked around downstairs, calling for her. When there was no answer, I went upstairs."

Calvin walked back and sat next to Thompson. "It was Alexander," he said in a whispery voice, like that of a ghost from another time. "I know it was him. It was Alexander who killed her."

Thompson looked into the eyes of his friend, words harboring in his throat, but he could say nothing.

"I've been searching for him. For the last five months. That's why I'm here. I need your help to find him."

Thompson turned away and looked into the remains of the fire, its coals burning yellow. Like the incandescent eyes of something disturbed in the night it would be better to leave alone.

"Ben?"

CHAPTER 2

AFTER HE LEFT Thompson's office, Calvin walked out the front courthouse doors and down the steps to Main Street, the wind-driven sleet beak-pecking at his face. He turned left at the corner and made his way up Court Street, bent forward against the wind like a hunchback, his hands buried into his armpits, walking fast, his gray breath rifling in and out. He kept his face turned away from what little traffic passed, but he needn't bother. The few who took note no longer remembered him. They saw only another of the homeless who sometimes strayed through Hanna, and being Christians they wished him Godspeed. But they also wished him gone.

When he reached Cemetery Hill, it took him some minutes in the near whiteout to find the markers for his grandfather and John Rogers, and after brushing the snow from theirs and the surrounding markers, he found where his wife was buried.

"Odd that you'd be buried right behind Granddad." Calvin looked at the next grave over. "Odder still that you'd be buried right next to John."

He swept her marker clean with the palms of his hands and stooped and traced a numbed finger over each letter of her name, her birth date, which was different from the one she'd given him. When he came to the date she died, his hand fell into the snow, and he could only stare at the month and day and year.

Near dusk the snow let up, and the sky in the west grew gray as the sun sank to ash. Calvin kicked clear of snow a patch of ground behind the marker for his grandfather. He sat on the ground and crossed his legs tailor-style, and stared at the markers before him, at the fingerlings of fog seeping through the tree branches. A crow landed on his wife's marker, and it paced stiff-legged back and across the granite top.

"So what was it that brought the four of us together?" Calvin asked. "Here. In this place. This place, of all places."

The crow twisted its head around, regarding him.

"Well?"

The crow shrilled back at him, raised its wings, and cawed at him again. Calvin ducked his head to between his knees, covering his ears in the cups of his hands, and waited. He sat there waiting a long time.

CHAPTER 3

1980

CALVIN TOOK THE courthouse stairs two at a time, the echo of his steps falling far down into the stairwell before they were lost below. When he reached the top of the stairs, he shoved open an age-yellowed door with PUBLIC DEFENDER stenciled in an arc across the pebbled glass.

The bottom right corner of the door glass was missing, knocked out over a year before after a client had told him that he would just as soon spend Christmas in the Lucasville Penitentiary as cut his hair and shave his beard, and he would be triple damned in Hell if he was *ever* going to work again so long as his old lady was fit and able and making good tip money serving drinks down at Ernest's. Then to be certain his point hadn't been missed, he slammed the door shut on his way out. Every few months since his sentencing, he

had sent Calvin a letter on the blue stationary the penitentiary provided asking if there wasn't some way he couldn't
get him out.

Just inside the door, Calvin found a handcuffed prisoner
wearing a county-issued orange jumpsuit slouching in a
World War I surplus chair. Although he was no taller than
Calvin, his un-socked feet shod in ratty, lace-free sneakers
two sizes too large stretched halfway across the narrow anteroom floor. With the arrogance particular to frightened
young men, he didn't turn to see who had come in, but continued to grimace straight ahead at the false-walnut-paneled
wall Calvin had papered with FBI Most Wanted posters he
had taken from the post office.

He looked from the boy to Denise, the paralegal-secre-
tary, who was sitting behind her desk before the door. She
cradled the telephone receiver against her ear with her shoulder and held up an index finger and shook her head while she
looked up at the flaking ceiling in supplication for her deliverance from all bureaucratic imbeciles. "Okay. I'll let you
know after I talk to him. Bye-bye." She rolled her eyes as
she hung up; but then smiled and said good afternoon.

Calvin brushed the snow from the shoulders of his gray
greatcoat. "Afternoon, Denise. New customer?" he said,
cocking his head toward the boy.

"This is John Rogers." The boy still slouched in the
chair, still refusing to acknowledge them. "He was just
arraigned this afternoon for felony theft. Judge Biltmore

entered a plea of not guilty and ordered him released on his own recognizance. It's his second felony theft."

"When was his first?"

"Last July."

Calvin raised his eyebrows. "That's not like Judge Biltmore. To let a potential two-time loser out on his own recognizance."

"Jail's full," Denise said with a shrug.

"Lucky for him it is."

"The deputy had to go back downstairs for another arraignment. He said, though, that he'd be back in half an hour to take John back up to the jail for his clothes before they process him out. You want to talk to him now while you have the chance?"

Rogers continued to stare straight ahead.

"I guess I'd better, seeing how so many of our clients feel a general reluctance to come back to see me once they get out of jail."

"That's sad, but all too true."

Calvin studied Rogers a moment. "That Hargrove trial I had last week. How many appointments did he miss? Six?"

Denise looked down and flipped through the pages of her desk calendar. "Only six? No, it was seven. No eight. He missed his appointment on the Friday right before his trial too. All together he missed eight consecutive appointments."

"Eight? That many? Really? Are you sure?"

She nodded her head. "Yep. Eight."

"And I didn't even meet him until eight-fifty on the morning of his trial. Didn't even know what he looked like."

"You didn't?"

"Nope, but he wasn't a hard one to spot."

"Why's that?" Denise said.

"He was the only one on the second floor wearing jeans and a lumberjack shirt. Just sitting there on the steps. Before we went into the courtroom, I had to tell him to tuck his shirt in. Twice."

"Decided to dress for the occasion, did he?"

"And the dumb jerk asked me for change for the parking meter. Can you believe that? Change for the parking meter."

"Some nerve."

"Said he didn't want to see his mom's car towed twice in as many days."

"Did you give it to him?"

"Are you kidding? No, and hell, no, I didn't give it to him. I told him his losing his mom's car was the least of his troubles that morning."

"No kidding."

"Short trial, though."

"Yeah?" Denise said.

"Oh, yeah. Old Ben put the car owner on the stand and then the cop. That's all he had to do. Hargrove did the rest of his job for him. Convicted himself."

"How'd he manage that?"

"As he was our only witness, I had to put him on the

21

stand or we'd have presented no evidence at all. Then Thompson caught him in so many lies that by the time he stepped down he couldn't have told you his name was 'Hargrove' and been believed."

"That's a shame."

"And of course since he didn't come in to see me before trial, he didn't understand he had to have his witnesses in the courtroom that morning and that Judge Biltmore was in no mood to grant him a continuance."

"A disaster?"

"Completely," Calvin said. "The jury was out for thirty minutes. Maybe. Convicted by two o'clock. On his way to Lucasville by three. Probably butt-fucked for the first time by eight. Had to be a bad day for Hargrove all the way around."

Denise winced and raised her shoulders. Rogers still stared straight ahead, but he was now sitting up, tapping his feet like a man with places to go.

"Keep your voice down," she whispered in a voice loud enough for Rogers to hear. "Or this one won't even bother coming in for trial."

"Not with my luck, Denise. Not with my luck."

Calvin took the file she handed him and walked to the door to his inner office. "John. Come on in. Coffee?"

The boy stopped tapping his feet and for the first time looked at Calvin. He rose and shuffled to the door Calvin held open for him, the manacles hanging from his legs jingling. "No. No, thank you, sir."

The boy walked into the office, and Denise winked at Calvin as he shut the door behind them.

The Public Defender's Office was on the third floor of a three-story, nineteenth-century courthouse built out of sandstone quarried out of south county. Until the 1940s, it had been only two stories with a storage attic, but as the county grew after the war and needed more offices, the second-story ceiling was lowered and the courthouse attic converted into the third floor. The county commissioners, however, who never got hold of a penny they didn't feel obligated to keep for a rainier day, refused to pay to convert the attic windows to rectangular office windows, so the third-floor occupants continued to look out attic-eye windows that had been popular when the county first built its courthouse.

Calvin's windows looked down on the Court Street storefronts built of wood and brick; while two or three had been constructed within the last decade, after some fire had destroyed their predecessor, most dated from the early years of the century. Some even encased the original log structures of the first Hanna settlers, using the older buildings as cheap insulation.

The office of the public defender was just three rooms: the outer secretarial-anteroom, the inner attorney office, and a storage room where Calvin maintained the office dead files. In addition to Denise, the county employed him as a part-time public defender. When he was not representing indigents, he struggled to grow his private practice out of his office just across the street over the Hanna Bank & Trust building.

Rogers hobbled to the middle of the office, and Calvin waved for him to sit on the folding card table chair, its seat split open and padding spilling out and all but gone. After he hung up his coat and scarf, Calvin sat behind a gray metal desk and opened the file. While he read, the ancient coal steam radiator provided mostly noise and little heat as it bumped and clanged.

Calvin looked up after several minutes. He opened a desk drawer and found a pack of cigarettes and offered one to Rogers. He lit them both, and the boy drew the smoke in deep and held it.

"John," he said. "Why don't you just tell me your side of what happened?"

The boy drew on his cigarette once more before he began. "Well, sir, me and her . . ."

"Who's her?"

"My girl. Sissy."

"Go on."

"Well, sir, me and her, my girl, Sissy, we was down at the swap meet just outside of town. Just outside of Goshen. And there was this jewelry stall she wanted to go into, so we went on in. And she was there looking around and trying on all different sorts of stuff—you know how girls like to do—and I was just looking around minding my own business when this lady's husband . . ."

24

"What lady?"

"The one that runs the jewelry stall we was at."

Calvin nodded for him to go on.

"And he comes up and puts this hand on my shoulder. It was about the size of a gorilla's and twice as hairy. And he says to me, 'Let's have it, son.' And I told him I didn't know nothing about what he was talking about and he says yes I did so and then he called the cops on us. Had a couple of his buddies watching me until the Goshen police shows up."

"So did you take anything?"

"No, sir, I sure didn't."

He looked at the boy. "Are you lying to me?"

"No, sir." He leaned forward and tipped the ash from his cigarette into the wastebasket. "I wouldn't do nothing stupid like that, like lying to my lawyer."

"You're sure you wouldn't do something stupid like that?"

The two regarded one another for a moment. "Honest," the boy finally said.

"Well, that's good that you wouldn't. But why'd the lady's husband say you did when you didn't?"

"I don't know."

"Did he have it in for you?"

"No, sir. Not that I knowed of."

"Just didn't like you?"

"Must not of."

"You weren't making eyes at his wife, were you, John?"

"Making eyes?"

"Yeah. Making eyes at her."

The boy's face puckered as though he'd smelled something foul. "She must weigh all of three hundred pounds. Maybe even three-fifty. I don't even think they make underwear large enough for her to fit into, Mr. Samuels."

Calvin raised his hand to his mouth and pretended to cough. "No, they probably don't," he said. "But tell me. Why would a man for no good reason just decide he doesn't like you and accuse you of stealing?"

"I don't know."

"Man you'd never seen before in your whole entire life."

"Yes, sir."

"Man who had absolutely no reason to lie."

Rogers didn't answer.

"You can see how a jury might have a difficult time believing you."

The boy sat with his hands folded before him. He could have been sitting in a confessional were it not for the cigarette in his hand. He looked at the bottom of the wastebasket and nodded into it. "Yes, sir. I can see that all right."

Calvin read several more pages in the file. After a minute he said, "Says here the arresting officer found some jewelry on you that the lady owner identified as hers."

"That's a lie. They was mine," the boy said, but he didn't look up from the bottom of the wastebasket.

"I'm not saying they're not, but do you always carry jewelry around in your pockets? Women's jewelry, at that?"

"No, sir. Not always."

"Not usually?"

The boy shrugged.

Calvin watched him, the ash of the boy's cigarette now burned down almost to his fingers. "Again, John, you can appreciate how a jury might experience some hesitation in reaching a favorable verdict for you."

"Yes, sir. I can see that."

Calvin flipped through the remaining pages of the report before he tossed it onto his desk. "And finally, it says in here you confessed to the arresting officer that you stole the jewelry."

The boy didn't answer.

"Is that true?"

"Yes, sir. It's true."

"And before the police officer asked you any questions, did he tell you that you had the right to remain silent?"

"Yes, sir."

"And that you had the right to speak to a lawyer before answering any questions?"

"Yes, sir, he did."

"Is your statement in this report true?"

"Yes, sir."

"So you did take the jewelry?"

Rogers didn't answer, and he wouldn't look up.

"John. Look at me," Calvin said, not unkindly.

The boy rubbed out his cigarette on the side of the

wastebasket and dropped it in. He did not look up.

"Did you hear me and Denise talking outside? When we were talking about another wiseguy. A wiseguy who thought he knew it all and ended up getting butt-fucked by his whole cellblock because he was too stupid to show up for appointments. Did you hear us?"

"Yes, sir. I heard you."

"Well, the same thing happens to wiseguys who are too stupid to tell me the truth. And then their rectums could just as well be a train tunnel along the Baltimore and Ohio. You hear what I'm telling you?"

The boy nodded. Calvin picked up the file once more and read through it again. When he finished reading, he looked out his window to the storefronts below. One abandoned store had been a Jehovah's Witness bookstore some years before. Over its door hung a painting of Jesus in prayer in the garden at Gethsemane on the night before his crucifixion. In the background Judas Iscariot was leading the temple guards through the garden gate in search of him while all about his disciples were asleep and useless. Jesus was kneeling in the garden, asking if the cup might not pass to another, but one of the wires holding the painting to the wall had snapped and now it hung crooked and askew and Jesus, instead of looking heavenward, could beseech only Calvin Samuels. He nodded and turned back to Rogers.

"You got a ride home?" Calvin said.

"No, sir."

"How you going to get home after you're released from jail? The sheriff doesn't run a taxi service."

"Hitch, I guess. Or walk. It ain't all that far."

Calvin leaned forward in his chair and folded his hands before him; and he spoke to the boy with the same tone he would use to a stray dog he might find injured alongside the road. "This would be your second felony conviction, wouldn't it?"

"Yes, sir."

"Any other offenses as an adult?"

"No, sir."

"Traffic?"

"Don't have no car."

"Juvenile?"

The boy hesitated, but finally said that he did not.

"You're certain?"

"Yes, sir."

"Do you have a job?"

He shook his head. "No car to get to one."

"Do you live with your folks?"

"No, sir. With Grams. My grandma. About a mile south of here."

"Where're your folks? Your mom and dad."

"Don't know."

"Any character references who can speak up for you? Minister? Teacher?"

The boy hesitated again before he answered, but finally

he said there was no one he could think of.

Calvin bounced his pen up and down on his desk. He looked at the boy and he looked at his file that lay open before him. He looked out the window at Jesus looking up at him.

"Okay, John. Listen up. I'm going to be real straight with you about this."

"Yes, sir."

"If you're convicted, this is going to be your second felony offense is as many years."

"Yes, sir."

"You received probation the last go-around. The way Judge Biltmore is going to see it is he went out on a limb for you once before. Gave you a break. And you went and sawed it off from under him."

"I know I did."

"And he's got an election coming up later this year. At your last probation hearing, Thompson recommended prison time, but Judge Biltmore gave you a chance anyway. Believe me when I tell you he doesn't need any help from you in looking stupid."

"No, sir."

"You go to trial, you've got almost no chance of winning. Thompson will have a couple of witnesses and your confession; he'll place the stolen jewelry they found in your pocket into evidence. You could get lucky. Witnesses might not show up, the jewelry might get misplaced, but it's not likely. Doesn't happen often."

The boy said nothing.

"If you testify, Thompson will bring up your first theft conviction to the jury. If you're convicted, you'll be in Lucasville that night. I've never yet seen a defendant in this county go to trial and lose and not go to prison. Immediately. Judge Biltmore won't even order a probation report if you go to trial and lose. You'll just go. Same day. You understand what I'm saying, John?"

"Yes, sir."

"Your best chance for staying out of prison is to enter a guilty plea. Since you're out now, if you enter a plea, chances are Judge Biltmore will let you stay out while the Probation Department works up its report, which will take it a couple of months. During that time you get a job. You work your butt off so your boss comes in and talks to Judge Biltmore. Tells him you're so good he wants you to run the business for him and marry his daughter if he has a daughter or adopt you as a son if he doesn't. You stay out of trouble. You keep your nose clean. You do that, you've got a chance, you've got a shot."

"Yes, sir."

"You don't, you're going to be the girlfriend of some uncircumcised, three-hundred-pound black son of a bitch from Cleveland who doesn't smell so good because he hasn't bothered to wash his pecker for the last seven years since he's been in there."

This was where his clients swore up and down they

would do whatever Calvin told them. He waited for the boy to say something. After a minute, he said, "Can you do that, John?"

"Yes, sir. I can." Then he added, "I trust you, Mr. Samuels."

Denise knocked at the door. The deputy was back to take his prisoner up to County and could Calvin please hurry the hell up. "He did say please," she said.

Calvin told her they were done and then the two stood and shook hands. "I'll be in touch," Calvin said. "And when Denise sets up an appointment, you be here."

"Yes, sir."

The boy walked toward the door, shuffling his manacled feet like an old man, like an old man whose time was running out. When he reached the door, though, he turned and smiled and raised his hand and thanked Calvin, and then he shut the door behind him.

Calvin smiled and shook his head. He looked at the file on his desk, and then out at the snowfall and toward Cemetery Hill and the winter barren trees beyond.

CHAPTER 4

AFTER THE DEPUTY took Rogers back up to the jail, Calvin walked down the one flight of stairs to Judge Biltmore's courtroom where, until well past six o'clock, he handled the arraignments for the remaining dozen prisoners. While he should have been there as well for the earlier arraignments, Judge Biltmore considered his presence to be at most a courtesy. On those days when he was feeling less than courteous, he simply failed to have his bailiff call Calvin in. While due process might suffer in some vague theoretical sense, Judge Biltmore's procedure increased the number of those pleading guilty, whether they were or not, and decreased the number of jury trials and the consequent cost to the county. Few complained. In fact, Judge Biltmore was something of a hero to the voters who saw him as their great bulwark of law and order. When he ran for reelection, no lawyer dare run against him even after a rookie state trooper made the mistake of stopping him for driving while under the influence, and his arrest made it into the papers, albeit only those circulated outside the county.

By the time Calvin left the courtroom, most of the county workers had gone home for the day, and the second-floor hallway was quiet and dark except for a single yellow nightlight hanging from the ceiling. He walked back upstairs carrying the bundle of legal files under his arm. Each one held only a single-page indictment, a few notes he might have scribbled, and, if he were lucky, a detailed police or constable's report. On the tab of each file Calvin had penciled in the name of his new client. Tomorrow, Denise would cover the penciled name with a proper typed label.

He unlocked the office door with his free hand and stacked his bundle of files on Denise's desk. He removed a legal tablet from a drawer and wrote his notes to her for the necessary follow up: scheduling client appointments, telephoning potential witnesses, contacting a family member for any client not released on bail.

When he finished, Calvin walked into his office and put on his coat and wrapped his scarf around his neck. He turned off the lights and made certain the office door was locked. Since the public courthouse doors were locked by now, he walked down the inside fire escape where the janitor and his wife were stacking bags of garbage just inside the door.

"Goodnight, Mr. Samuels."

"Goodnight, Clarence. Haven't seen Clarence Junior

around for a while. How's he been doing?"

"Oh, he doing real good, Mr. Samuels. Got hisself a job just like you told him to. And he be keeping out of trouble. Attending Sunday services again. Staying on that straight and narrow."

His wife smiled and nodded. "I says a prayer for you every night, Mr. Samuels, thanking the good lord Jesus you come our way."

Calvin nodded and went out.

When he stepped out into the night, the cold, dead air of February snatched his breath away. He reached into his pocket for his cigarettes and struck a match. The courthouse clock chimed eight o'clock. He stood there a moment smoking and looked up and down a deserted Court Street, still unplowed from the day's snowstorm because of a deficit in village funds. The night sky was clear, and a cocked moon hung overhead like a one-eyed divine jester. He smiled back and walked down the courthouse steps.

During the Depression, when his grandfather had auctioned a tenth or more of the Creek County farms from these same courthouse steps, some of the farmers from the local Grange still hanging on had pulled together and placed a price on his head. The way the old-timers told it, because the county bootleggers were not only happy with the ownership of the farms out of which they ran their stills, but with the sheriff as well, they suggested to the Grange members that they consider retracting their reward. Then they

35

made a sizeable contribution to the sheriff's reelection campaign, still over three years off, and suggested he be just a little less hasty with his foreclosures if only to be certain that the lawyer for the goddamned Hanna Bank & Trust had paid sufficient attention to all of the legal niceties. They also said they would see what they could do to discourage any opposition from running against him in the next election. The sheriff could see the benefit of a contented electorate in those troubled times, and the number of foreclosures precipitously dropped.

At the bottom of the steps, Calvin turned left from the courthouse for the half-mile home, and he swung his briefcase beside him as he walked. He said hello to a villager, familiar by sight if not by name, who was shoveling his sidewalk. He had walked only a few blocks when a squad car pulled up alongside, and the officer rolled down his window. "Can I trouble to give you a ride home there, counselor? This night's got a real bite to it."

Big Jim Walker and Calvin had been classmates at Hanna High School, and they had played baseball together on the American Legion team. After graduation, Walker had enlisted in the Army. Following his discharge he married a girl from Goshen and joined the police force there.

"You're a long way from home on such a miserable night," Calvin said.

"Yeah, I am. Had to drop off a prisoner at County. Can I offer you that ride?"

"I'm about home, but thanks for the offer."

Walker nodded and rolled up his window and drove on.

After five minutes of walking and almost falling a half-dozen times on the ice, Calvin reached the two-bedroom cottage his father had purchased not long before his enlisting in the Army. The house sat on a large Main Street lot enclosed by a wooden fence. Calvin rested his hand a moment on the front trellised gate and looked down the brick walk leading to his front door that must have been freshly swept by his neighbor's maintenance man. His house was dark, and he stood there a moment swinging the gate back and forth in his hand.

"Calvin!" shouted a voice out of the dark. "Calvin Samuels. Is that you?"

He turned toward his neighbor's house. "Yes, Mrs. Ferguson. It's me. How are you this evening?"

His neighbor was standing beneath the front porch light, her winter shawl wrapped over her shoulders. "I'm out here in the cold freezing off my one last good tit I got left, talking to a good for nothing lying lawyer who won't keep his promise to an old lady to come to tea is what I'm doing."

Her voice carried a long way in the cold night air. A neighbor two houses down switched on a porch light.

"I've already lost one tit to cancer," she said. "If I lose the other one to frostbite on account of you I'm going to preserve it in a jar and set it in my parlor and *then* I'm going to tell the whole Ladies' Aid Society what you did to me." She pulled her shawl closer around her. "Robbed an old lady of her last good tit."

Calvin's cottage had once been the caretaker's house for the Hanna mansion. It had been in back then, but during World War II Maude Ferguson moved it to her side lot when she decided she needed a larger victory garden between her rear sun porch and the carriage house that had become her garage.

She had been a Hanna before she married Judge Ferguson, and she was the sole remaining descendant still residing in the village of the great robber baron , the rest of his progeny long ago having fled to Cleveland and Akron to better enjoy his ill-gotten gains. Her husband, Thucydides Ferguson, had been the common pleas court judge before Judge Biltmore. Even in a village as small as Hanna, no one knew for certain the extent of their wealth; but the rumor inside the courthouse had been that Thucydides had instructed the county treasurer to simply mail his entire judicial paycheck to Washington as restitution for the income-tax liability that had accrued from their considerable holdings. This, during the Depression.

Mrs. Ferguson had been Calvin's high-school English teacher and before that she had taught his Sunday-school class. She had also taught his father when he attended Hanna High School, and it was from her Calvin learned almost every scrap about him that he was ever to know. Who his father was and who he had been. She told him how his father had lived, but like most war dead, the details of his dying were a secret, as though sparing him the details of his death made his dying less of a death, as though he were only a sojourner far away in a strange land. Perhaps, in any case, no one knew the details of how he died. Perhaps Henry Samuels was just one of many men in a foxhole along the Chosin Reservoir bayoneted while he slept.

A few years before, while Calvin was away at college, Mrs. Ferguson underwent radiation and chemotherapy, and it was after she came home that she developed her propensity for profanity. While she did not do so often, when she did it was always at the most indelicate of times. Such as when she was leaving Easter services at the Hanna Lutheran church and she told Reverend Barker it was the best goddamn sermon he'd given all year.

Some of the local wags, several no doubt her former students, soon took to ensuring that she was invited to the more important village ceremonies as a guest speaker in the hope she would cut loose at a particularly inappropriate moment. Usually Mrs. Ferguson did not oblige them, but on occasion she did, and it was not uncommon for members of the American Legion to have, for example, a Fourth of July pool as to whether she would or would not.

Profanity, coming from someone who for decades had been the very model of decorum for the village, was attributed by her supporters, and she had many, to the shock of surgery and to the rigors of her treatment. Calvin, however, on his visits when he stopped by to say hello when he was home on break from college and later from law school, had smelled in the mansion the sweetish odor of marijuana. More than once following her surgery, he watched Mrs. Ferguson tend the marijuana plants she now grew on her sun porch as tenderly as she pruned her prize roses, usually with a cigarette that appeared to him to be of dubious legality dangling from her lips.

The Hanna mansion—no one dare refer to it as the Ferguson house—was a Queen Anne Victorian with a wrap-around porch, stained- and leaded-glass windows, polished hardwood floors, and a carriage house converted to a garage in the 1920s. Inside her mansion, Mrs. Ferguson tooted up and waited to die and tried to be of some counsel to Calvin before she did.

"I'm real sorry about that, Mrs. Ferguson," Calvin said. "But you never gave me a day and time."

Mrs. Ferguson did not answer at once, but stood under her porch light, wrinkling her nose at him much as she did when he had stood in her classroom telling her he had indeed read the required chapters in *Silas Marner* the night before, but he must have forgotten the plot in his sleep. "That sounds to me like just another one of your weenie lawyer arguments expressly designed to trick a jury," she said. "What's wrong with right now?"

Calvin looked at his cottage, at the windows dark. "Now is good," he said after a moment. "Now is perfect, in fact."

"Well, come on then," she said, and waved for him to come over. Ferguson opened the door, turned back, and waited while he walked up the rotten slate sidewalk and onto the steps. She was adamant about not repaving the walkway with concrete, which she considered ugly.

"So how are you, Mrs. Ferguson?"

"I've been better," she said as she went inside. "But I've been worse, too, so I won't complain. How about you?"

"I've no complaints either." Calvin entered the hallway and handed her his coat. "And if I did, you wouldn't want to hear them anyway."

"Lord, that's a fact." She took the coat he held out and hung it on a cloak rack. "But what's a handsome young lawyer like you got to complain about?"

"I'm sure I could think of something if I tried."

"Well, don't. And why aren't you married yet? I was in the Hanna Bank & Trust when you walked through the lobby last week, and every teller's head turned to watch you. Even Sadie Armstrong—and she's nearly as old as I am with at least two husbands planted up in Cemetery Hill. Maybe more. If she were much younger, or you much older, I'd be warning you to take care not to be the third."

"Still looking for a girl like you, I guess," Calvin said.

Mrs. Ferguson regarded him over the glasses perched on the edge of her nose.

"I was engaged last fall. To Sally Anne Rutherford.

Don't you remember?"

"Yes, but you let her go."

"I didn't let her go," Calvin said. "She went back to her old boyfriend."

Mrs. Ferguson rolled her eyes. "She was expecting you to go after her, Calvin."

"She was?"

"What good is a man to a woman if he doesn't love her enough to go after her?"

"Really?" Calvin frowned. "Sally Anne was expecting me to go after her?"

Mrs. Ferguson shook her head. "Give me your scarf and take a seat by the fire. I hope you like Dvorak because that's what I'm playing, and I don't feel like changing him."

"Dvorak's fine."

Calvin watched her go and waited until she was almost to the kitchen before he spoke. "May I give you some help with the tea?"

Mrs. Ferguson turned and looked at him as she would had he offered to scythe her marijuana crop. "You may not help me with the tea! If I needed any help with the tea, Calvin Samuels, I would have asked for it."

"Sorry."

"I never saw a man yet who knew the first thing about brewing tea, at least about brewing tea that was halfway drinkable."

Calvin grinned.

"I've been serving tea since I was three years old. First to my dolls and then to the other neighborhood children out on that porch right there," she said and pointed into the night. "When I need a man's help to serve tea you'll know it's time for you to load me into Otis's Hearst and haul me on out of here. And it's not."

"Yes, ma'am," he said.

Mrs. Ferguson walked into the kitchen through the double swinging doors. "And don't you go sneaking off on me while my back's turned. You hear?"

Calvin sat down and leaned back in his chair. He thought of it as his because it was the same cherry-wood rocker in which he had always sat, ever since he was a child and Mrs. Ferguson would baby-sit for his mother. As he rocked he watched the reflection in the window of the fire in the fireplace. The window of leaded glass ringed by stained glass had been manufactured by the Hanna Glass and Mirror Company. The glassmaker was a German immigrant who had moved to Hanna in the 1890s and was an artist of remarkable skill. His work was in demand as far away as San Francisco and Seattle, but then his artistry along with his factory died when he did. The window in Mrs. Ferguson's parlor was one of his few works known to still exist outside of art museums. Almost once each year some antique dealer would arrive unannounced and attempt to purchase the window for a pittance of its worth, but all they ever received was a door in the face.

Calvin reached up and switched off the floor lamp. It was an old phonograph album, now badly scratched, that Mrs. Ferguson had played ever since he could remember. Calvin closed his eyes and listened to the cello concerto.

When she had taken care of him, Mrs. Ferguson often entertained Calvin with stories about Judge Ferguson before he became a judge, when he was only a young lawyer in Hanna struggling to build his practice. But the story Calvin asked her to tell over and over again was how he had saved from the electric chair a young man charged with murder. Some months after his acquittal, the real killer had confessed. Every year after, Judge Ferguson received a Christmas card from his client. Mrs. Ferguson still received a Christmas card from him. "I guess Thucydides must have been something of a hero to that young man," Mrs. Ferguson had said, and it was then Calvin knew what he wanted to be when he grew up.

As the concerto ended, the double kitchen doors creaked. Mrs. Ferguson came in with a serving tray she set on a small table.

"So," she said after she had poured their tea. "Are you still at the Public Defender's Office? Setting those criminals free so they can go out to pillage and rape old widow women."

"Only if they pillage and rape old Methodist widow women. If they bothered any Lutheran women, I'd let them rot."

"From the way I hear them talk down at Martha's, some of those Methodist women wouldn't mind a little bothering."

Calvin looked at her. She was stirring her tea as though she had said nothing at all. He sniffed at the air. "You all through with your chemotherapy, Mrs. Ferguson?"

"For now," she said. She propped her feet up on a footstool and sat back. She looked into her teacup as she stirred. "Doctor says it's in remission, which means to me it's in hibernation. But it'll wake up one of these days and be as hungry as one of those old woodchucks in springtime we had out back I used to pay you a dollar a piece to shoot."

"Is that why you grow the marijuana? In case it comes back?"

She looked up. Mrs. Ferguson did not quite smile, but the devil danced in her eyes. "No," she said. "Not really." She blew on the tea. "You know, I kind of hate to admit it, but I've grown to like the stuff."

"That doesn't sound like you."

"Never thought I'd go in for it, but I got so sick during the radiation therapy and the chemo. And the drugs the doctors prescribed for the side effects only made it worse. Dr. David said it was too bad he couldn't prescribe some reefer for me."

"Reefer?"

"That's what we called it in the twenties. He said there'd been some studies written up about it in medical journals. Well, my grandson Gregg. Do you know Gregg?"

"Yes, ma'am."

"I thought you did. Well, Gregg was home from college

a few years ago. My son-in-law didn't take to the idea of him sitting at home all day and just sleeping in and watching the soaps and the game shows for three months until he went back to college. So he put him to work painting my house."

"I remember his ladder tipped over on him and he landed in your roses. Broke his leg, didn't he?"

"Yes. Yes, he did," she said. "Broke some of my bushes, too. But some days before that, I'd just come back from the Cleveland Clinic after a chemo session, and Gregg was here painting. And it was a hot one that day so I made up a pitcher of lemonade for us. I took it out and set it on the picnic table under the big elm and walked over to where Gregg was up on the ladder painting the eaves. One second I was just standing there looking up and telling him how I wanted it done and the next second I was flat on my back, dead to the world. Out like a light."

"Must've scared Gregg half to death."

"Probably," Mrs. Ferguson said. "Because when I came to, there Gregg was standing over me, fanning me with his paint cap. After a minute he got me to my feet and brought me in here. Laid me on the couch and sat beside me to make certain I was all right. I think he was more shaken up than I was. He wanted to telephone my doctor, but I told him I'd my fill of doctors for that week and what good were they anyway when they wouldn't even get me the medicine that would really help. When Gregg asked me what I meant, I told him Dr. David had said the best thing in the world for me was marijuana but that it was illegal for him to prescribe it."

Mrs. Ferguson set down her teacup and leaned toward Calvin. "Well, Gregg reached into his shirt pocket, and he pulls out a little bitty butt of marijuana, a beetle I think he called it."

"Do you mean a roach?"

"That's it. He called it a roach. Then he put it between my lips and lit me up." She sighed. "My life just hasn't been the same since."

"I didn't know Gregg indulged."

"Oh, he doesn't," Mrs. Ferguson said. "He found it in Hanna Park on his way over that morning and was going to turn it in to the police on his way home."

Calvin started to pose a question, but stopped. Then he said, "So you finally succumbed to reefer madness."

"Oh, heavens no," she said, and she sat back and laughed. "But you know it got so I started looking forward to my chemo session just so I'd have an excuse to light up. Lizzy Fender said she never saw anyone so excited about coming in for chemotherapy. But when I smoked, I didn't feel so old any more. Or at least I didn't feel so bad about being old. The whole world had a more pleasant glow to it."

"Yes, ma'am."

"Oh, what do you know, Calvin Samuels, about growing old?" She looked at him as though he were the culprit responsible for her infirmity. "And don't go changing the subject on me by asking me about my chemo. What's a good looking lawyer like you doing defending desperados?"

"Desperados?"

"You know what I mean. Those gangsters."

"Gangsters? Do we still have gangsters?"

"Yes, gangsters," Mrs. Ferguson said. "That no good scum and riffraff too cheap to hire a proper crooked lawyer out of Youngstown to buy their way out. Then you could spend full time developing a practice for decent folks."

"You mean like pot-smoking, fallen Sunday-school teachers?"

She did not let him off the hook by smiling.

"Because," he said, "I see them, and I think there but for a few breaks, there but for the grace of God, go I."

"You can't see yourself in them."

"But I do. They're our outcasts, you know. And it's easy to become one. You just have to live on the wrong side of the street. Be a little bit different. Not quite fit in. Be the kid everyone picks on the first day of school, and they never stop. All you need have is a drunken father."

"Or a mother not quite right in the head?"

"Or that. That's all it takes. Then you're an outcast."

Mrs. Ferguson studied him a moment and shook her head. "You've always been a strange one."

"Yes, ma'am. But isn't that putting into practice your Sunday-school lessons?"

"Maybe, but even if it were that's not why you do it."

"Oh?"

She rose and poked at a log in the fireplace. "Did I ever tell you how that came out? About your mother."

"No, ma'am. You never did."

Mrs. Ferguson nodded. "It was a couple of years after Henry died. Esther took his death real hard. She never showed it all that much, and if you didn't know her well, she didn't show it at all. But I saw. They hadn't been married all that long, but they were so much in love. Or perhaps they were so much in love because they hadn't been married all that long. I don't know which. But after his death, Esther stopped coming out of the house much. In the summer, I might see her trimming the roses I'd given her to keep her occupied, but that was about it. Stopped attending services. Just lived off the pension the Army paid her."

"With just her and me, we didn't have many needs," Calvin said. "House was paid for."

"But then one day Esther invited me over for tea. We both love our tea. I walked over, and she took my hat and coat, and she took me into your living room where she introduced me to Mrs. Hancock."

"I don't know that I recall any Mrs. Hancock."

"That's because there was no Mrs. Hancock there. We were the only ones in the house. At first I thought she was teasing me, but then I saw she was serious. She was holding an imaginary tea party as though she were a little girl again. Only she thought Mrs. Hancock was real."

"You two weren't imbibing in the evil weed, were you?"

"Calvin Samuels, don't you go getting smart-alecky. And don't you even joke about your mother doing anything like that. She was—and is—a saint, except that . . ."

"She's mad as a hatter."

"Well, I left as soon as I could get away, and I went immediately to see Dr. David. We talked, and he stopped by a few days later to talk to Esther. After he left he telephoned me."

"What did he say?" Calvin said.

"He said he was in agreement with my diagnosis. That's what he called it. My diagnosis. But seeing how your mom was only having conversations with imaginary people and wasn't a threat to you or herself, or anyone else for that matter, there was no sense in putting her away in a hospital. He said you would've just been placed in foster care and then put up for adoption if Esther didn't get better after a time and what would be the sense in that?"

"I've seen what comes of children who go into foster care."

"I have, too."

"Too many of my clients have spent time there," Calvin said. "What else did Dr. David say?"

"He said that if I could keep an eye out, he would speak to Police Chief McGukin, and then we all agreed. That's how we took care of our neighbors in those days. None of this courtroom stuff. Just neighbors helping neighbors."

"Yes, ma'am."

"And it would have worked, too, if nobody else would have found out. But we were naïve. Stupid, really. You can't keep something like that a secret. Not in a town as small as Hanna."

"No. I expect not."

"That was the one flaw in our plan," she said.

"Yes, ma'am."

"And once the other children found out, well, you were a goner for sure."

"Well, I solved our problem for us, didn't I?" Calvin said.

"I wouldn't say that. And you mustn't think it either. It was time for Esther to leave Hanna."

"But I didn't need to shove her along on her way."

"You didn't shove her."

"You know as well as I that I did, Mrs. Ferguson. That time we built our snow fort in the A&P parking lot, and we were having snowball fights, and Nick Gatz said, 'Hey, here comes Calvin's crazy mother.' And all the kids pelted her with snowballs."

"But you didn't. You didn't throw snowballs at her."

"No. I didn't throw any. But I didn't stand up for her either. I just watched. And she saw me watching. She looked to me for help, and she saw that I wouldn't. She saw that I just wanted her gone, that I only wanted her out of my life and be gone and that I didn't care how much she was harmed or hurt. She saw that. It was then she decided to leave Hanna, had to leave me because she would only be a torment to an ungrateful child."

"You torture yourself, son."

"You know what I should have done?"

"No," Mrs. Ferguson said. "What?"

"I should have walked out of that parking lot and taken her home. I should have walked her home and put her to bed and made her some tea. I should have read to her whatever it was I'd been reading in school that day."

Calvin looked into the fireplace.

"And you think by saving someone else, you can make that right?"

They were both silent for several minutes. Finally, Calvin smiled at his old teacher. "It's getting late," he said. "I thank you for the tea. I'm sorry we didn't get together earlier. We should do it again. Soon."

He rose and walked to the cloak rack in the breezeway. Mrs. Ferguson walked with him to the steps of her front porch and watched as Calvin went down her walk that was again dusted with snow. When he had reached his own front gate, she called to him to be careful, but with his back to her when he answered, she couldn't hear his reply. She could only see his answer rise in a bluish wisp over his head as if his words might have been of some substance and not mere ghosts of words, some phantom of meaning, which soon dissipated into the winter night.

CHAPTER 5

EARLY THE NEXT morning Calvin walked to the courthouse from his house down the back alley that ran in between and parallel to Main Street. Mrs. Ferguson often scolded him for taking the alley and not Main Street like normal folks, but he preferred it. While the villagers had modernized the facades of their homes, those which backed onto the alley they had left alone, and he saw how Hanna must of looked a half-century before. As he passed their garbage cans and small refuse piles, he saw also a side of his neighbors they would have preferred no one witness.

He entered by the back courthouse door and kicked the snow off his galoshes and walked up the half-flight of stairs to the first floor. The long corridor was dark and empty and only an occasional murmur drifted out from one or another of the adjoining offices.

He started to climb the flight of steps that led to the second floor, but midway he stopped and looked back. Calvin rapped his gloved knuckles on the stair banister. After a moment, he walked back down the steps and then down the hall to the office of Renate Thompson, Assistant to the Director of Child Services for Creek County.

The office receptionist was out on another of her gossip breaks, but he could hear Renate's voice. Calvin walked around the corner of the counter that separated the county employees from the public and back to her office where he could see she was behind her desk and speaking into the telephone. When he knocked, she looked up and waved him in. Calvin came in and sat in one of the chairs before her desk, and she swiveled around so her back was to him and dropped her voice.

While Renate's gray metal desk was neat and organized, a dozen or more stacks of files surrounded it awaiting the county commissioners' approval to purchase more cabinets. Some of the stacks nearest her desk were laced together with intricate spiders' webs. On the wall opposite the door hung a faded portrait of William McKinley that may have hung there since before his election. After a minute Renate twirled her chair back around, and when she hung up the telephone she added some necessary emphasis. She looked at him squarely. "Why are you lawyers such jerks anyway?"

"You mean husband Ben or just lawyers in general?"

"Both," she said. She still had not yet smiled.

"Genetics, I guess. A chromosome thing. Or is it a hormone thing? I forget which."

They looked stone-faced at one another for a moment until Renate broke and smiled. It was a game they often played, who would smile first; and her grin lit up a dreary county office on a pale morning in late winter.

"Calvin, you need to visit us more often. We miss you."

"Wouldn't think you'd want to see me anymore. Not since I stopped working for Ben and started working for the good guys."

She shook her head. "Nonsense. I keep hoping you'll come back to us for good. Since I've been with Child Services you've been the only assistant prosecutor who took us seriously. The only prosecutor—period—who took us seriously, including my husband."

"Really?"

"I've told Ben that if his attitude doesn't soon improve he can forget about even my vote in two years."

"Yeah, but wouldn't it be embarrassing if he only received one vote, and it was obvious even his own wife wouldn't vote for him?"

"Serve the bastard right." She leaned back in her chair and folded her hands beneath her chin. "So I can't lure you back to juvenile?"

"Not a chance."

"Pretty please, Calvin."

"Nope."

Renate sighed. "Okay. Why not?"

"Because the only thing I ever did for your kids was to not make their lives any worse is why not. Because I could never make their lives any better."

"Oh, Calvin. You're a romantic. Not making their lives any worse can be an art form in and of itself. An art form your predecessor should have learned and your successor should learn."

"Flattery will get you everywhere. Everywhere except getting me back into juvie," Calvin said. "The only good I ever did was to not make them live it over again by putting them on the witness stand. But I couldn't do anything to make it better. I couldn't heal them. I couldn't make them better again. I couldn't make them the children they once were or that they should've been and would never be." He looked out the window, searching for an answer that was out there, just beyond his grasp. "I couldn't even hope for the satisfaction of retribution by sending their parents off to prison, which had always been how we'd settled. Now they give up their kids in exchange for no prison time."

"You're worse than Ben."

Calvin raised his eyebrows.

"Don't look at me like that. You are. You both want to save the world. You both want to be heroes, for Christ's sake, and you want to be loved for it. But the children you protected are some place better. Some place where they might recover."

"Might? Snowball's chance," Calvin said. "The damage is done. They're never the same. Never the same as you and me. And now your kids are starting to show up at the PD office. And in another few years you'll be seeing their kids."

"I know."

Renate stood and lifted the file that had been lying on her desk and tossed it on the stack of files most near her office door.

"Let me ask you about John Rogers," Calvin said.

Renate frowned. "I heard he was arrested again. But you know his records are confidential. My husband could put me in jail if he heard I discussed John's file with you. He would put me in jail too, the bastard."

"And lose the best shot he has at getting more than one vote in the next election? Never. Besides, you know Rogers's juvie record will be in his probation report anyway. I'd just like to know now rather than the day before his sentencing, which is when the Probation Department usually gets it to me. Give me a chance to develop a strategy. Some alternative to prison."

She shook her head.

"Think of it as revenge. Think of it as revenge on your asshole husband for sending his asshole problems to you."

Renate leaned back in her chair and laughed. "I give up," she said. "You've won me over." Then her smile fell away. "I can tell you that John has no criminal record as a juvenile."

"But?"

57

"But he's known to the department."

"Come on, Renate, you can tell me more than that. Think of it as an extension of your social services. He's only twenty."

"Nineteen."

"All the more reason to help the kid out. So how's he known to the department?"

She looked at her door and lowered her voice. "When he was twelve we received a call from the emergency room. His mother had beaten him with a straightened coat hanger. Straightened except for the hook on the end."

"Was it bad?"

"As bad as I've ever seen."

"How bad?"

"With the hook of the coat hanger she flayed nearly every stitch of skin from his back, Calvin. Then I did the follow up. Spoke to the neighbors."

"What did they tell you?"

"That when his mother wanted to go out for the night she would just chain John to a tree like a dog so he wouldn't make a mess inside her trailer and leave him with a can of water."

"Nice of them to call the police."

"Most of them couldn't."

"How come? No telephone?"

"Outstanding warrants. Some of them said they would take him food, give him a blanket. But John told me he only remembered a neighbor kicking or hitting him with a stick of firewood if he cried in the night. Sometimes the neighborhood kids would torment him since he was chained. Once they threw a beehive at him. Fortunately, he knew to stay still and he received only half a dozen or so stings."

"So what happened?"

"His mother skipped before the emergency room even called us. Father already had been long gone. A grandmother who seemed interested, but I wasn't certain as to how much she knew about what was going on."

"What'd you do?"

"We had John in foster homes until he was eighteen and then set loose on society."

"With nowhere to go."

"County jail."

"Anything else you can tell me that might help?"

"Afraid not, Calvin. Wish I did."

The two talked a while longer about their other cases until Calvin said he had to leave for an appointment upstairs with one of his newly indicted clients from the day before. He stood and walked to the door. "You want some good news?"

"Please."

"Spring's coming. There's a robin on your window ledge."

Renate turned and saw a robin huddling under its wings. She shook her head. "It won't live."

"Why won't it?"

"Too early. It's too cold and there's too much snow for it to find food. Poor thing."

"Maybe we'll have an early spring. Aren't animals

supposed to have a sixth sense about these things?"

"It's February, Calvin, and you don't have an early spring in February. In Florida maybe, but not around here you don't."

"Then why the robin?"

She watched it on the stone window ledge, the snow-flakes on its wings melting and then freezing. Its eyes already encrusted in ice. "I suppose there are animals just like there are people who are just not meant to be among us as long as we would like. No matter how much we wish it weren't so."

Renate was still watching the robin outside her window when Calvin left her office and walked back down the court-house corridor.

CHAPTER 6

WHEN HE HAD seen enough abused children who did little more than scrutinize him with broken eyes, Calvin tendered his resignation as assistant prosecutor. He shook hands with Thompson and walked across the hall to the Public Defender's Office.

On the following Thursday, Judge Biltmore assigned him his first shock probation hearing, scheduled for the next afternoon. The defendant's attorney of record had called Judge Biltmore late Thursday morning and asked that he find him a substitute because he had a hearing up in Youngstown he said he had forgotten to note in his calendar. It was to be Calvin's rite of passage into the vagaries of criminal defense.

After conviction, Judge Biltmore usually just sentenced the defendant to Lucasville Penitentiary, especially if he had the temerity to waste the judge's time and the county's money by exercising his constitutional rights and actually go to trial.

On occasion, however, Judge Biltmore granted the defendant probation on the belief he would not commit another crime, or would at least exercise sufficient judgment so as not to be caught doing so—at least not in Creek County.

Even if sentenced to the penitentiary, all was not lost. Thirty days later the defendant's lawyer could request Judge Biltmore to consider shock probation, so called because a month of sodomy supposedly shocked the defendant into a fit of good citizenry. While the Ohio Legislature must have seen it as the moral equivalent to an enema, Calvin failed to see the logic of further brutalizing someone who most often had already suffered a lifetime of abuse.

Calvin studied the file. It took only a couple of minutes reading for him to see that his first shock probation hearing was going to be a good case from which he could learn. At least there would be no innocent victims. And sometimes, Calvin knew, you got lucky. Judge Biltmore saw when a lawyer made a real effort and when he was just going through the motions. So he prepared for it all Friday morning.

His client, Wayne "Buster" Healy, had been convicted after a non-jury court trial for the attempted murder of a deputy sheriff—which in Creek County was about as certain a means of finding yourself at the gates of Lucasville Penitentiary as purchasing a Greyhound bus ticket and asking the driver to drop you off out front.

Buster was one of the Creek County citizens adding to its color. He saw himself as something like Daniel Boone.

He worked some, on and off. Mostly off. He hunted and trapped in the hills of south county, almost always out of season. What he did best, though, was to father children with a breathtaking profligacy. Buster would then marry the woman, or not, depending upon whether she was willing to support him, his hobbies, his past and present and future harems, his carousing, and his general good-natured debauchery. If not, he would leave her and his children and move on to greener pastures.

After Buster had moved on from his most recent wife, she applied for welfare to support herself and her brood, all of whom, she claimed, to have been fathered by Buster. The County Bureau of Support sought reimbursement from Buster, which to Buster seemed all backward and contrary to his normal living arrangements with women to say nothing of the laws of nature. Not surprisingly, he failed to respond to the county's written demand for reimbursement. In due course, Judge Biltmore issued a warrant for his arrest.

When Buster received the Bureau's letter, he knew—either from past experience, tavern lawyers, or just intuition—that he was about to be lawed. So as Deputy Pete Clemson made his way up the dirt lane to Buster's shack, Buster was not caught off-guard. With his .30-06 he put a hole in the cruiser windshield four inches to the left of Pete's head.

As Buster was a crack shot, sober or drunk, Mike Folker, Buster's trial attorney, argued that if Buster had really been serious about hitting Pete, and not just funning him some, he wouldn't have missed him by a solid four inches. Buster, Mike said, was only guilty of assault by trying to shake up an officer of the law a little, which was a much lesser offense. Only a first-degree misdemeanor, at most.

Calvin thought it not a bad defense considering the hopelessness of Buster's case, but Judge Biltmore, whose hemorrhoids had been surgically removed the week before, failed to see the humor of the argument, let alone its logic, and sentenced Buster to the maximum sentence of seven to twenty-five years and for good measure ordered him to reimburse the county for his legal fees on account of his wasting the court's time.

Calvin decided his best strategy was to emphasize one strong point and sit down. Truth be told, though, he had to struggle all morning to find even one middling point, let alone a strong one.

Judge Biltmore's bailiff called Buster's case late on a hot and sultry Friday afternoon deep in the depths of August. Fridays were the court days for motions and marital dissolutions. Mondays through Thursdays were the heavy trial days, but Fridays were the judicial equivalent of taking the garbage out to the curb.

Calvin arrived an hour early and sat in the back of the courtroom to better ascertain Judge Biltmore's mood, but he seemed to be in no particular mood, or rather he seemed to be in every mood imaginable. He swung between laughing in one case to screaming himself aneurysm red in the next.

Judge Biltmore always held the public-defender cases until the end of the day, and it was a few minutes past four o'clock when he called Buster's. The gallery benches filled with lawyers waiting for their matters to be heard when Calvin entered the courtroom had thinned to only him, and the hallway outside the courtroom door had crowded with county employees on their way home for the weekend.

Judge Biltmore looked up at the courtroom clock and frowned. "The next matter is the State of Ohio versus Wayne Healy," Judge Biltmore said, not quite running all of his words into one. "Defendant's motion for shock probation. Mr. Samuels."

Calvin stood and walked past the bar. He set down his briefcase on second counsel's table and went behind the podium. "Your Honor," he began, "I'm not going to repeat for you the same considerations Mr. Folker made at the original sentencing hearing."

Judge Biltmore was bouncing his pencil up and down on its eraser.

"I would only remind the court that this was Mr. Healy's first felony conviction, and while he has served county jail time before, this is his first sentence to the penitentiary. I think it likely Mr. Healy has learned his lesson, Your Honor. Perhaps the court could give him one last chance. Perhaps you could consider granting Mr. Healy shock probation upon condition of his delivering to the sheriff all of his firearms in which case he would be less likely to find himself on the wrong end of the law."

Judge Biltmore stopped bouncing his pencil and opened a notebook he kept on the bench beside his gavel, flipping back and forth through the pages.

"Thank you, Your Honor," Calvin said, and he sat down at second counsel's table.

While he waited for Judge Biltmore's ruling, muffled laughter came from a group of women as they walked past the courtroom door. After a minute Judge Biltmore closed the notebook and leaned forward in his chair and looked down. "Mr. Thompson," he said.

Thompson looked up from his legal pad.

"I can't seem to find it here in my notes. But when I sentenced him a few months back, is this the same sonnuvabitch who called me a motherfucker?"

Thompson said he did seem to recall the use of that particular epithet at the time His Honor had sentenced the defendant. He also seemed to recall that Mrs. Miller's second-grade class had been in the gallery that afternoon as part of their fieldtrip to the courthouse.

"Motion denied. Court's adjourned. Let's go home."

Calvin looked from the door behind which Judge Biltmore had disappeared to Thompson. Thompson was packing up his briefcase and shaking his head, choking down his own laughter.

CHAPTER 7

CALVIN WALKED DOWN the steps from the second-story landing at the rear of the Hanna Bank & Trust Company building from where he leased his private office. The bank stood down a block and across Main Street from the courthouse, and its rear parking lot backed onto the same alley as did the town library and high school. It was when he had attended Hanna High School that Calvin first began taking the alley home rather than Main Street.

After Judge Ferguson convinced her to sell her car, Esther Samuels often walked along Main Street in the late afternoons just about the same time school was letting out. She had been home alone all day, and she missed her son. She wanted to talk to him, and if she couldn't find him, then someone else.

That few in the village were willing to talk to her any

more was no obstacle to Mrs. Samuels holding a conversation. On her walks around town, she would look off to her side and talk and gesture just as though someone was there to listen. Sometimes she stopped before Martha's Dress Shop and looked in the window and pointed and discussed the various fashions of the day with her phantom companion.

When they saw her approaching, most villagers trotted to the other side of the street or darted into whatever store might be handy. If she actually cornered one of them into conversation, the store windows would fill, and those inside would point and guffaw. Only Mrs. Ferguson, if the two met on her way home from the high school, never crossed to the other side, and as she walked Mrs. Samuels back home they would hold a three-way conversation, ignoring the remarks of the children, the stares of their parents.

Yet even after all these years, Calvin still almost always took the alley home.

He crossed the parking lot to the alley and dropped a garbage bag full of papers into a trashcan. He was about to turn for home when he saw someone coming toward him. Calvin held his hand to his forehead to shield his eyes from the glare of the sun. He squinted to recognize whoever it might be, but he did not know who it was until he was spoken to.

"Howdy, Mr. Samuels."

Calvin lowered his hand from his forehead and studied the boy approaching him. A gaunt boy walking out of the sun carrying a stack of books under his arm. "That you, John Rogers?"

"Yes, sir, Mr. Samuels," the boy said, and he smiled, showing a gap between his front teeth. "It's me all right."

Calvin looked down at the armload of well-worn books the boy carried, the lettering of their covers faded and all but illegible in the dingy March light. The spines of some of the books were broken from use and overuse and misuse, and their pages seemed ready to spill out into the alleyway at the slightest breeze and be blown away like so much refuse.

"What you got there, John?"

"Books."

"From where?"

"I just checked them out. From the library."

Calvin raised his eyebrows.

"Honest."

Calvin shook his head and laughed. "Excuse my cynicism. But my other PD clients wouldn't have the faintest idea of where the public library is even at. So I know if you're carrying around an armload of books you must've checked them out."

"Yes, sir. I did."

"So what're you reading?"

The boy studied the tops of his dirty red Keds. "Do you know Mrs. Ferguson? Used to teach English at the high school."

"Oh, yes. I recall Mrs. Ferguson. Among other things, we got to be fairly well acquainted one winter when she was keeping me in on a regular basis."

"You?"

"You find that hard to believe?"

"No, sir."

"So you're one of those who believe all lawyers to be ir-redeemable reprobates?"

The boy only shook his head, openmouthed.

"Well, you should. So what are you reading?"

The boy looked at his load of books. "Well, the first day we met, after I was released from jail, I was walking home and I was thinking about what you asked me. About having someone to speak up for me like a minister or a teacher, and I said I didn't know of no one."

"Yes, I remember," Calvin said. "What we call a charac-ter witness. Someone who can say there's something more to you than just badness."

"Right. A character witness. Well, when I was walk-ing home after I'd been let out of jail, I remembered Mrs. Ferguson and . . . well . . ." The boy grinned. "You know, she kept me in, too."

Calvin placed his hand on the boy's shoulder. "Don't give it a second thought. It's happened to the best of us."

"I didn't like it much at first. Especially the reading out loud she made me do."

"Nor did I."

"Especially the poetry." The boy looked back down the alley toward the high school. "But you know, the funny

70

thing was, after a while I began to like it. After a while."

"You going this way?" Calvin said, pointing down the alley toward his own home.

"No, sir. Other way. I thought I'd seen you when you come out the back of the bank so I walked down this way."

"Mind then if I walk with you a while?"

The two headed up the alley running behind Hanna's business district and then out of town. Calvin asked the boy to continue with what he had started to say about Mrs. Ferguson.

"Well, day after I got out of jail, I walked back into town and asked her if she would speak up for me or maybe just write a letter to the judge."

"And what did she say?"

"At first she was mad."

"I bet."

"Told me I was wasting my life away. I didn't think she was going to do it."

"No?"

"No, sir. And she kept going on about how I must be stupid if I was just going to waste my life away like I was."

"She has her persnickety days, doesn't she?"

"Then she was quiet a long time. Just kept rocking and looking at me like she used to back when she was my teacher. And then she finally said she would testify for me if between now and then I made an honest effort to make something of myself because she was getting to be too old to be wasting her time on no jail birds."

"She did?" Calvin said. "Mrs. Ferguson said that?"

"Yes, sir, she did. And I asked her what it was I could possibly do, and she give me a look that could have knocked me over stone cold dead."

"I know the look you're talking about."

"Then she told me if I didn't stop talking like an idiot she was going to call the sheriff herself to come over right then and there and pick me up and take me off to Lucasville. She said the only thing standing between me and my making something of myself was a good break, and she was going to see to it that I got one."

"She was?"

"Yes, sir."

"What kind of a break?"

The boy didn't answer.

"It's okay, John. You can tell me. What kind of a break is Mrs. Ferguson going to help you get?"

"She said she was going to help me get into the Kent State Extension so I could maybe begin working on an associate degree and maybe that would help me out at my sentencing. She said old Judge Ferguson, before he died, always looked for something like that. Some kind of change of heart."

The two walked on for a minute, neither speaking.

"So what do you think, Mr. Samuels?"

"I think Mrs. Ferguson might be on to something. She's

72

been around a long time. She's taught about half the folks in Hanna. And she's just as right now as she was when she kept you and me in after school."

"She is?"

"She is. If you're holding down a job and taking classes at the Extension, there's not much more you can do to keep out of Lucasville except not getting caught to begin with."

"Yes, sir."

"It's not a sure thing, mind you. Not by a long shot. It's sure as hell's not a slam-dunk. But it's the best chance you got."

"Yes, sir. That's what I thought. It's probably the best chance I got. The only one I got."

"What're you considering studying at the Extension?"

"Well, you know, I always liked reading."

"Yeah?" Calvin said.

"Yeah. You know, I was raised in about six foster homes after they took me away from my mom. Maybe seven. Stay in one for a year, sometimes less, and then move on to the next. And then the next."

"You've had a good variety of living with different sorts of people, I guess. That could be useful to you someday."

"Foster homes were okay. But usually they had their own kids in addition to one or two of us rent-a-kids, and so with their working and all, there wasn't all that much attention for them to give out."

"No, I expect not."

"But the year after Mrs. Ferguson taught me, the foster dad I had liked to read. Sometimes he'd read to me."

"What'd he read to you?"

"Different stuff. I liked Mark Twain the best though. Couldn't hardly understand him, but I liked the way he sounded when my foster dad read him to me. He was from the South. He knew how to read Southern real good."

"What would you do with an associate degree once you got it?"

The boy didn't answer at first. In a yard that backed onto the alleyway, two robins stood footed to their shadows lengthening in the evening sunset and pecked at the still frozen earth. "Maybe, if I do okay, I'd transfer to the main campus. Get my teacher's certificate. Maybe."

The two walked on, past Shorty Stevens's pool hall and across the Penn Central train tracks. "What about finding a job? Any success yet? Any leads, even?"

"No, sir. I've been trying to be straight with them, telling them it might only be temporary."

"And then they want to know why."

"And when I tell them why . . . well . . . you know." He shook his head and looked down. "I sure wish I'd gone to see Mrs. Ferguson before all of this happened. Or even listened to her when I had the chance to a couple of years ago."

"You keep right on being straight with them, John. Having a job and losing it because your boss discovers you lied to him is a whole lot worse than never having had one at all."

"I know it."

"Meantime, let me ask around. I might come across something. Might."

"Thanks, Mr. Samuels."

"No promises. You keep looking, too. Hear? But I just might hear of something. Pull some strings if I do."

"Yes, sir. I will."

The two were now walking through a section of south Hanna where the homes were falling into disrepair and had been for the better part of a decade. A low growl came out of a backyard cluttered with refuse and junk cars and a collapsed shed, and when they stopped and looked into the yard, a German Shepherd lunged toward them.

"Good God almighty," Rogers said.

Just as Calvin stepped in front of Rogers, the dog cartwheeled over backward as it hit the end of its chain. It gave out a little yelp when it landed on its head and then ran back behind the tree to which it was chained and barked at them. The two looked at each other and grinned and walked on.

"Where you staying at now, John?"

"Same as last time you asked me. My grams'," the boy said and pointed south with his free hand. "She lives a ways out of town."

"You told me your folks weren't around any more, but what about a brother or sister?"

"No, sir."

"Too bad," Calvin said.

"Yeah, don't I know it. Without my mom or dad, I sure could've used an older brother. Even an older sister. Even a younger brother or sister might've kept me out of trouble."

"How soon do you intend on applying to the Extension?"

"Just got the application in the mail today. Me and Mrs. Ferguson are going to fill it out tomorrow and mail it back in."

The two crossed the intersection with Grant Street.

"I've got to ask you something," Calvin said. "You might not be able to answer it now. But by the time of your sentencing, you better have a good one."

"What is it?"

"Why'd you do it? The stealing. You're better than that."

"I know it. I know it now anyways. Didn't then. But I wanted to impress Sissy, my girl. The two guys we was there with. Wanted some attention. Wanted to be looked up to."

"Where's she at now? Sissy."

"I heard her daddy sent her to go live with an aunt over in Wayne County for a while. She's just seventeen, anyways. Can't say I blame him much. Wanting to keep her away from the likes of me."

"You know, John. I have to tell you. Even if you're taking classes and get a job and Mrs. Ferguson testifies for you and even if she did teach Judge Biltmore, at the end of the day you might still be riding in the back of a sheriff's cruiser to Lucasville."

"I know it."

"Then what?"

"I thought about that. The Extension will still be there, I expect, when I get out. I just hope Mrs. Ferguson still is."

At the last intersection at the edge of Hanna, the two stopped. "I guess I should be turning back," Calvin said. He looked down the alley from where they'd come. "You get accepted to the Extension, you come see me about your class selection."

"Yes, sir. I will. I sure will. Thank you."

"Goodnight. And good luck."

"Thank you. Goodnight, sir."

Calvin watched until the boy disappeared into the gathering twilight. The elder male walked up a side alley to Main Street and turned back toward downtown. He headed home, slowly, his hands in his jacket pockets against the last of the winter chill.

CHAPTER 8

CALVIN LEANED BACK on his haunches and wrung out his bandana before wiping the sweat from his eyes with it. A mile to the West he could see the late Sunday-morning haze still rising from the fresh-plowed cornfields. He reached behind for his now half-empty two-gallon thermos jug he had filled with lemon Kool-Aid four hours before. He twisted off the cap and drank in long, greedy swallows, the Kool-Aid dripping onto his chin and then evaporating as it trickled down the asphalt shingles. As he drank, a crow cawed, her cry as shrill as a banshee, and Calvin lowered his thermos and looked off into the haze, but he saw nothing.

He recapped his thermos, and as he turned to set it back behind him he look down from his roof. Below, Mrs. Ferguson was inspecting the discarded shingles scattered over their respective yards and shaking her head.

At the south corner of his cottage next to his ladder, Calvin had stacked four columns of new, shiny black-asphalt shingles. On the other side of his ladder, he had parked a John Deere tractor with a wood-plank-hauling wagon hitched behind it. He had borrowed the tractor and wagon from Anse Yoder in exchange for his preparing a deed for the Mennonite farmer the prior winter.

Like most farmers with less than one hundred-fifty acres under till, Anse found it difficult to make financial ends meet for his family of eight solely from farming, much as he would have liked to limit his contact with outsiders. So Anse also worked a crew of Mennonite boys from his church during the summer. They roofed houses and garages and barns, and Anse had hired on Calvin during the summers when he was home on break from college and law school.

In time, Calvin came to enjoy the work and he looked forward to it each summer. His first month at it, though, had been brutal. They were on the roofs five and sometimes six mornings a week by six o'clock so the Mennonites could be home for the afternoon milking at five. Calvin had nearly passed out from the heat his first day on the job. All day he carried stack after fifty-pound stack of asphalt shingles up the ladder for the nailers. The course-grained shingles bit into his shoulders, and before noon his skin had been rubbed raw, and his shirt was dark and sticky with blood.

When not carrying stacks up the ladder, Calvin picked up discarded shingles from the ground where the nailers had thrown them and more than once a tossed shingle knocked him face-first into the dirt. But he got up, and when he went home at the end of his first day he collapsed into bed with more than an hour of daylight remaining. The next morning Calvin had gotten up at four. He found his heaviest denim shirt and sewed patches over its shoulders and was back at the work site before Anse pulled in, picking up the discarded shingles left from the day before.

He made it through his first week and then the month, and then he was all right. Then he enjoyed the work and the people with whom he worked. Calvin enjoyed their lunch-time debates where the Mennonites liked to pick arguments with the Anglisher studying law, and he obligingly defended even the reprobate Darwin, the devil incarnate to them.

They respected his work, though, and they grew to like him even though he was an Anglisher and even though he defended the reprobate Darwin. Once they had accepted him, they worried over his soul as they might over one of their prematurely born calves, and they often invited him to their services.

Calvin's first month had been a test. A test to see if he could take it, and when he had he was almost accepted as one of the Dutch. By the end of the first summer, Anse allowed him up on the roofs to rip off the old shingles. By the end of his second, Calvin had nailed in his first new shingle, and in time he could keep up with the best of the experienced nailers.

On some Saturdays Anse invited him to one of their barn raisings, some in other congregations as far away as Holms County, where he worked the day for free. There he flirted with the braver of the Mennonite girls, who would bring him water or iced tea made from sassafras, and then lunch usually of pork, sauerkraut, and German potato salad. He knew some of the girls at the local raisings because they had attended the public school in Hanna until the eighth grade before they vanished back into a different world entirely. As the girls flirted back, some of the boys glared at the Anglisher, and then the girls giggled into their hands at their having succeeded in making them jealous. Girls wearing ghost-gray prayer bonnets up into which they tied their hair so only their husbands would know their beauty. Their summer dresses, never bright, but plain blue or calico or some pattern of flowers, dark on dark, reaching down to their ankles where dark stockings covered unshaved legs.

"Calvin Samuels! What in Heaven's sake are you doing up there?" Calvin peered back over his roof. "You break a leg, don't expect me to call you an ambulance. My phone bill's high enough as it is."

Mrs. Ferguson had ceased her inspection of their yards and of his roofing materials. She stood beneath his ladder, hands on her hips. She wore a black dress of a long-forgotten style, one only women of a certain age still exhibited on Sunday mornings; above her missing breast she had pinned a wilting pink carnation. She was looking up at him with much sternness.

"Good morning, Mrs. Ferguson," he said as he retied the bandana around his forehead. "And how was the Reverend Barker this morning?"

"The Reverend Barker was fine, Calvin. It's his sermon that wasn't for shit."

Calvin looked over to Mrs. Ferguson's sun porch where the layers of potted ferns concealed her marijuana plants.

"I've been trying to keep my mess off your yard," he said. "Sorry for the shingles. I'll get them when I clean up."

"Well, you wouldn't have to keep your mess off my yard if you'd only get a regular roofer. Why don't you hire an expert?"

"What do you mean hire an expert? I am an expert. During seven summers I re-roofed more houses and garages and barns than I care to remember. Don't you recall when we re-roofed your house and garage some years back?"

"Yes, but you're a lawyer now, and a lawyer shouldn't be seen fixing roofs," Mrs. Ferguson said. "It looks bad to the townsfolk."

"Well, if the townsfolk would pay me what they owe me, I could hire an expert. Besides, working with my hands is therapeutic."

Mrs. Ferguson frowned up at him. "Why don't you at least put that John Rogers to work? He's to come over for his tutoring after dinner."

"Because I couldn't afford to pay him. And if I did pay him he'd no longer be indigent and I couldn't represent him any more." Calvin climbed down the ladder. "So how's he doing anyway?"

"Oh, about like you'd expect. It's hard for him. Hard to develop good study habits this late in life. But he's making an effort. I'll give him that. He's making a real effort."

"Well, hopefully, he'll make it to his sentencing. Hopefully, he'll make it past his sentencing. But I hope he at least makes it to then. And maybe go from there and make something with his life."

"Hopefully," Mrs. Ferguson said. "Yes, of course. Hopefully. But I wouldn't put too much of your own hope into it."

"Why not?"

Mrs. Ferguson didn't answer at first. She turned and looked back at her still barren flowerbed. She looked at it for a long time. After a while, though, she turned back. "You know, Calvin, the Judge, before he was a judge, used to take a criminal case now and again when he was younger."

"Yes. I remember you telling me some of his war stories when you used to watch me. You told some good ones."

Mrs. Ferguson nodded. "As he got older, he stopped taking them, and I asked him why. I asked him if it was the money because usually they couldn't pay him much if anything. Even when they could afford to, he'd usually refuse payment. Said he didn't want money that'd been stolen so, so recently. You know what he told me?"

"No, ma'am."

"The practice of criminal law will break your heart.

Your clients. If you let them. Like an errant child."

"How's that?" asked Calvin.

"I think for the Judge they were like his children. He sometimes, if he could, snatched them from just outside the gates of Hell. But he hated it when he failed."

"Yes. I hate that too about the practice. What I hate more is that I'll be representing some kid, some kid who's acting pretty tough, but he's only acting. Underneath he's scared to death. And I'll badger him into entering a guilty plea because there's no way on God's green earth he's going to be acquitted, and if he goes to trial he's just going to be in prison three times longer than if he'd entered a guilty plea. But if he knew what was waiting for him when he got to prison, he would never, ever, enter a guilty plea. Never."

"Someone," Mrs. Ferguson said, "someone maybe a little like John, a child who never had a break in his whole miserable life. And the Judge would give him one break that could make a difference to him. But since he'd never had one, when a break finally, finally, came his way, he wouldn't know what to do with it. So he'd miss it. He'd let it pass him by like a funeral procession without realizing it was his own."

Calvin waited for his old Sunday-school teacher to say something more, but she did not. "So what're you telling me?"

"Do your best for him. Do your best. But don't break your heart doing it, Calvin. Don't expect John to be a different person for your efforts. After you've done your best. Expect him to squander the gift you've given him. But don't give him the power to break your heart. Because he will. He has no choice." She smiled. "Do you understand?"

But Calvin seemed not to be listening. He had shouldered a fifty-pound pack of shingles and was climbing back up the ladder. Mrs. Ferguson watched him a moment. After a minute she shook her head, turned, walked to her flower-bed, and inspected it again for signs of germination from the seeds she had planted the Monday before and had sprinkled every day since. She would disseminate them again in the cool of the evening.

Calvin returned to his roofing, but as he was nailing in a shingle, a crow cawed again. He looked once more for it in the haze, but still he saw nothing.

He holstered his hammer. He stood and picked up his shovel and began to scoop off the last of his shingles. Shingles covering the roof of a little cottage house in an Ohio village on a hot Sunday morning in May. A house that his father had purchased just before he had shipped out for Korea to die.

CHAPTER 9

THE MORNING FOLLOWING, Calvin worked in his private office on a personal injury case one of the other lawyers in Hanna had thrown his way. The case was worth a fair number of dollars, but it demanded more work than the older attorney cared for now that he could sit in his office and grow fat probating the estates of the husbands of the town's widows who liked him for his boyish smile and courtly manners. In the afternoon, he was working on what he referred to as his office administrative duties when Denise called from the courthouse.

"The sentencing report for Warren Bowman is done."

"Huh, huh," Calvin said. "I'll look at it next time I'm in. Thanks, Denise."

"You don't have that kind of luxury."

"How come?" Calvin was only half listening as he compared the balance in his checkbook to a stack of bills, marking off which he would pay in May and which he could defer until June or beyond.

"Because he's being sentenced today. At three o'clock."

Calvin straightened in his chair. "Three o'clock. Today?"

"Yep. Three o'clock. Today."

"Why today?"

"Judge Biltmore's civil case settled just before noon, and he wants to clear out some of his criminal docket. Judicial review by the Ohio Supreme Court and all coming up later this year. So Warren's being sentenced along with some of the others who've been sitting up at County for too long."

Calvin laid down his pen. "Damn."

"If you want to meet with him before he's sentenced, the Sheriff's Office wants to know if you can do it at counsel's room downstairs. It's visiting day, and they said they've got a full house up at the jail."

Calvin rubbed his forehead. "Sure. But ask Smitty if he'll drive Warren down from the jail as soon as possible. Within the next thirty minutes if he can."

"Will do. That all?"

"Yeah. That's all. Thanks, Denise."

Calvin dropped the receiver. "Damn," he said. "Damn, damn, damn, and double damn."

He found Warren's file and studied it for half an hour. He still could not afford a secretary, so when he left for the hearing he hung a sign on the door stating that he would return, but not specifying when.

The afternoon was hazy and sultry, like the day before, like the summer to come. Calvin's forehead was damp even before he walked up the first flight of the courthouse steps. Most days on the second floor he would stop a minute and flirt with the court clerks at their window, but today he did not. Several of them waved and then looked at one another when he only nodded and didn't smile back.

Deputy Smith was sitting outside the door to counsel's room, leaning his chair back on two legs and reading the *Weirton Racing News* with a pencil in hand. He handed Calvin a copy of the sentencing report Denise had walked down for him without looking up and told him to go on in.

No one had turned the lights on inside counsel's room. He set his briefcase down on the plain yellow oak table that filled the room. "How you doing, Warren?"

The reply came after a long while. "Okay."

The mesh-wired window to counsel's room looked out across a ten-foot alley. On the other side stood a three-story brick boardinghouse, so that even on the brightest of summer days, counsel's room seemed to be no more than in twilight. Yet even in this noon twilight, Warren did not look okay.

He had been arraigned on the same day as John Rogers before Calvin had come down, but on a charge of burglary of a residence. Thompson had not even needed to request a cash bond impossibly high for Warren to meet; for three months he sat up in the county jail, until the Probation

Department completed its sentencing report.

Out in the exercise yard, he talked to the other prisoners. Most were first-timers like him, but some had been to Lucasville. Some more than once. They told Warren what awaited him. "And there ain't nothing you can do about it but die, kid," one prisoner told him, laughing and rubbing his backside as he walked off.

Calvin sat in the chair across the table. "Your big day," he said. "Sentencing at three."

"Yes, sir," he said, his voice cracking. "I know it, Mr. Samuels." He would not look at Calvin, but only stared down at his hands folded on the table before him. He could have been mistaken for a boy interrupted in prayer was it not for the fresh blood on his left hand where his fingernails dug deep into his knuckles. His cheeks were flushed and his face wet. Blue, perpetually bloodshot eyes, and blond hair.

Warren barely stood five feet tall and, maybe, weighed one hundred pounds. The county had given him the smallest size robin's-egg-blue jumpsuit it ordinarily issued only to women—not orange like it issued to men—and still he was all but lost in his clothes. He seemed altogether insufficient for what he would have to endure at Lucasville. Warren would be no match for the two-hundred-fifty-pound monsters the State of Ohio kept caged there. Monsters who bench pressed their own weight for twenty, thirty, and more repetitions, day in and day out. They would trade him back and forth between themselves as they might have once traded baseball cards until they either grew tired of him or until his rectum protruded and he was no longer any fun for them. Or until he was dead. The best Calvin could do for him was not to make it any worse than it was going to be.

Warren had been found by the police inside a home occupied by a recently widowed father and his three young daughters. He confessed that he was only looking for something to steal. Something he could fence to buy some beer or marijuana. Something small the family would never notice. The father nonetheless had screamed bloody murder that Warren be locked away to protect his daughters, though his daughters had not even seen him that night, and it was doubtful Warren even knew into whose house he had stumbled or who lived there.

Absent divine intervention, Judge Biltmore would never grant Warren probation. The father would be badmouthing him in every election so long as he continued to run. The best chance for Warren of surviving with his sanity, or even just surviving, was to plead guilty and, maybe, be paroled five years earlier than if he had stood trial, assuming he managed to stay alive until his parole. But if Calvin had told Warren what awaited him, he would never have pled guilty.

So Calvin never told him. Never told the person who trusted him most, trusted him more than he had trusted any other in his nineteen years. Calvin didn't tell him for it would have been Warren's fate irrespective of whether he pled guilty. The question was not whether, but for how long. Perhaps that was not important either, for Warren would have to live with the shame forever. Live with the betrayal forever.

"Let's go through the report. You let me know if there's anything in here that's not right or that you don't agree with," Calvin said.

"Okay."

After Calvin read the report, he read it again out loud, stopping often and questioning Warren.

"You never completed high school?"

"No."

"If Judge Biltmore speaks to you, say 'no, sir'."

"No, sir."

"How far did you go?"

"Seventh. Seventh grade, I think." He continued to look down at his hands, one still gripping the other to somehow hold onto himself.

"But you're not sure?"

He didn't answer.

"Warren," Calvin said, "are you certain you completed the seventh grade?"

"No. No, sir. I ain't certain. I ain't certain about nothing."

Calvin scribbled a note on the sentencing report. "Any witnesses you could ask to come in to testify in your behalf?"

Warren didn't answer.

"I know we discussed this before. When I visited you up at the jail last time. You said you'd think about it. Someone who could come in and say something good about you.

Minister, schoolteacher, employer. Even a friend or relative is better than no one at all. If you did, I could ask for a continuance so we could get them in."

Warren shook his head.

"Do you want to testify?"

"As to what?"

"What you did. Why. Say you're sorry. It might help."

Warren continued to look down at his hands. He shut his eyes and shook his head.

"It's probably your only hope for probation. For not going to prison. To Lucasville."

Again he shook his head and started to cry.

Calvin watched the boy and then reached over and placed his hand on his shoulder. "It's okay, Warren. Try to relax. It'll be okay."

He looked up at Calvin, his eyes swimming, and shook his head no.

Calvin read through the sentencing report once more. A few minutes past three o'clock, Smitty knocked at the door and said Judge Biltmore was ready for them.

Calvin looked at Smitty and tilted his head at Warren. Smitty walked behind Warren and scooted back his chair and told him again that Judge Biltmore was waiting. Warren rose on wobbling legs. For a moment Calvin thought Smitty would need to assist him into the courtroom, but Warren placed his hand on the table and steadied himself. He looked up at Calvin and tried to smile. He tried not to cry again.

The three of them entered the near-empty courtroom through the front courtroom door beside Judge Biltmore's bench. Thompson was standing before the bench speaking with Judge Biltmore who was laughing at something. When he saw Calvin, he ceased laughing, and he leaned over and said something to Thompson. Thompson straightened and turned and nodded to Calvin and then walked to first counsel's table. Calvin and Warren sat at second counsel's table, and the deputy sat a few feet behind.

Calvin looked at Warren. "Ready?"

"I'll be okay, Mr. Samuels."

Calvin looked at the boy. He started to raise his arm as though to give the boy some comfort, but lowered it again.

"State of Ohio versus Warren Bowman," Judge Biltmore said, "82-CR-26. Defendant's motion for probation, having entered a plea of guilty on February twenty-third to a charge of aggravated burglary." Judge Biltmore looked up. "Mr. Samuels."

Calvin rose and walked to the podium a few feet to his left and before the empty jury box. "Thank you, Your Honor. Mr. Bowman has no witnesses to call and waives his right to testify. I do, however, request to be heard before this court passes sentence."

"Very well," Judge Biltmore said. "Proceed."

The afternoon sunlight fell through the windows behind the jury box and across the floor between Judge Biltmore and Calvin. The overhead fan clicked like a clock, but it was measuring something more than the mere passage of time.

"Your Honor," Calvin said. "In passing sentence I would ask you to consider that this is Warren's first offense as an adult. I would also ask you to consider that he never finished high school—he went only as far as the seventh grade—and as is stated in the sentencing report, he is borderline mentally retarded. The sentencing report clearly shows Lucasville is not the best answer, and we respectfully request the court grant our motion for probation and give Warren one more chance. Thank you, Your Honor."

Calvin sat down. Warren would not look at him. He looked at his hands he kept folded in his lap.

The back courtroom door opened. Judge Biltmore looked up. He nodded and looked toward first counsel's table. Calvin turned around. The father of the three little girls was standing just inside the door.

"Mr. Thompson," Judge Biltmore said.

Thompson walked to the podium. He looked at Calvin, but, for the benefit of the reporter from the *Hanna Daily Journal* sitting in the gallery, he did not smile. "Thank you, Your Honor. While Mr. Samuels is correct that this is the defendant's first adult offense, that offense was burglary of a residence. A very serious crime indeed. A residence of a single father and his three children. Three little girls who had recently lost their mother."

Judge Biltmore nodded.

"Also, as a juvenile, the defendant was found guilty of

trespassing; petty theft; theft of an automobile; assault upon a twelve-year-old boy when he himself, the defendant, was seventeen years old; and telephone harassment of a family where the father had filed a complaint against the defendant with the police. In addition, the defendant has no job. The defendant has never had a job."

"Never?"

"No, Your Honor."

Judge Biltmore frowned.

"And if you give Warren Bowman probation, we don't know he's not going to return to that same residence. To where those three young girls, who so recently lost their mother, live."

Thompson turned and pointed to Warren. "I disagree strongly, Your Honor—quite strongly—with Mr. Samuels. Lucasville is exactly the place for someone like this, and the state respectfully requests the court to sentence the defendant to the penitentiary for the maximum time permitted by law."

Thompson returned to first counsel's table, but he had not crossed even half the distance before Judge Biltmore ordered Warren to rise. Calvin and Warren rose and stood together, side by side.

"Does the defendant have any reason as to why the judgment of this court should not now be passed?"

Calvin waited for Warren to answer, but he saw that he was trembling. The courtroom was silent save for the clicking overhead.

"No, Your Honor," Calvin said.

"Very well," Judge Biltmore said. "Then it is the judgment of this court that the defendant serve not less than three nor more than ten years in the Lucasville Penitentiary for Men."

Three years. Maybe out in eighteen months. He might make it. *Might*.

Calvin turned to speak to Warren, but Smitty had already risen and placed his hand on Warren's shoulder, guiding him toward the courtroom door as though he were offering counsel to the boy. The father of the three little girls was nowhere to be seen, but from somewhere down the hall outside came a cry like a war whoop, as though the hometown team had just scored the winning goal.

When Smitty and Warren reached the courtroom door, the deputy went ahead and opened the door, and as he did so, Warren turned and looked back at Calvin and tried to smile, but he just started to cry all over again. Calvin watched as the deputy took the boy by the elbow and led him away. He closed his briefcase and left the courtroom.

Outside, Calvin stood on the courthouse steps, and watched as the deputy loaded Warren into the back of the cruiser. He waited for Warren to turn toward him so he could give him some sign of encouragement, some sign of hope, but he did not. He was looking across the street where the father stood, smiling and pretending to wave goodbye.

The cruiser made an illegal U-turn on Main Street, and Smitty drove back up the hill to the jail where he would transfer Warren to another cruiser carrying two other prisoners Judge Biltmore had sentenced earlier in the afternoon. When the cruiser was no longer in sight, Calvin walked down the courthouse steps, and then in the direction opposite and returned to the Hanna Bank & Trust building. He worked until ten o'clock that night, worked until he thought he could sleep, and then he walked home on a quiet spring night.

It was on just such a spring night as a child that he had walked these same streets and believed anything was possible, anything could happen, anything at all. Tonight he knew it to be so. Tonight he knew that indeed anything could happen. Anything at all.

When Calvin reached home, he was not hungry, and he did not turn on the lights. He lay in bed a long time before he fell asleep.

CHAPTER 10

SOMETIME DURING THE night, Calvin woke. He had been dreaming he was again in Judge Biltmore's courtroom after Warren Bowman had been taken away, the gray courtroom curtains dancing in the breeze. What woke him was the danseuse of his own curtains. Outside his window an almost burned-out streetlight flickered. The A&P delivery truck rattled down Main Street past his house, but then the night was again quiet.

Calvin watched his curtains a moment. Then he looked to the bedroom door, but the brass bars at the foot of his bed obstructed his line of vision. It was the same brass bed where his father and mother had slept during the one night of their short marriage when they had both slept in their cottage house. It was the bed where he had been conceived. He propped himself up on his elbows. "Who's there?"

No one answered. Calvin waited for his pupils to dilate.

"Do I know you?"

The voice that answered, if indeed it was a voice that answered, was neither loud nor soft. What Calvin would always recall was its great clarity, its singular earnestness. "Not yet," it said. There was a passage of time. Perhaps a minute, perhaps ten. "But you will," the voice said. "In time, you will."

"What is it you want?"

"I guess what I want to know is if what happened today is also to be the fate of John Rogers?"

Then Calvin woke. He did not sleep again that night.

CHAPTER 11

CALVIN LAY AWAKE a long time. Finally, before dawn, he got out of bed. He found the tee shirt he had worn the day before and walked into his small kitchen. He lit the stove burner and heated the coffee remaining from the morning before.

After the coffee had boiled, Calvin carried his cup out into the garden behind his cottage, still wearing only boxer shorts and a tee shirt. He turned his chair to face east. He blew on his coffee and watched the sun come up. When the papergirl came up to deliver his paper, she handed it out to him at full arm's length, holding it with just the tips of her fingers. She looked like she was trying hard not to stare at his underwear, but her eyes flicked down when she handed him his paper. She backed away from him until she disappeared around the corner of his house; then from back across the lawn came the thump of her paper bag bumping on her hip as she ran to the next house. Calvin shook his head. "Not even thirty yet, and I'll be branded the village pedophile before this day is out."

After an hour, Calvin stood and went back inside where he showered and shaved and dressed. When he left for the courthouse, Mrs. Ferguson's maintenance man was in the driveway washing her 1955 Cadillac. Each raised his hand in greeting to the other. Calvin walked on down the sidewalk, but when he reached his front gate, he turned and looked back. He stood there a moment, watching the maintenance man as he hosed off the last of the soapsuds. Then he smiled.

After he closed the gate behind him, instead of turning right for downtown, he walked the other way. Calvin crossed Salem Street and turned left at the parking lot to an Isley convenience store. An Isley convenience store owned by a client. A client who owed him money. A client who owed him money and had just opened Hanna's first carwash. Ten minutes later, Calvin came out the back of the store. The next day John Rogers started washing cars next door.

For the rest of the summer up until Rogers's sentencing, two or three times a week, Calvin walked to the Isley store at lunchtime. He would purchase a sandwich of ham or chicken and a carton of milk, and maybe an apple. With his purchases he would walk behind the store to a picnic table under a maple shade tree the owner kept for his employees.

At lunchtime John wore the rubber boots he never

bothered to take off, and he was so wet he looked like he never changed his clothes before bathing. Under the tree they would eat their sandwiches, and afterward John would pull his assignments from his backpack, Calvin tutoring him wherever he was stuck, which at first was everywhere.

At one o'clock, the owner would come to the back delivery door and whistle. John would then pack up his books and thank Calvin. Calvin would nod and either walk back to his office over at the Hanna Bank & Trust or to the courthouse if he had a hearing that afternoon.

A few days before John's sentencing, Calvin had just left the carwash and was walking down the sidewalk back to the courthouse when he turned and looked back. He watched John for a moment as he was wiping down a car leaving the wash.

John was not the right person. He was not the right person, and he definitely was not in the right place. He was like one of the ghetto kids the churches in Hanna imported each summer from Cleveland. Kids who seemed happy enough while they were visiting, but whose presences in Hanna were only temporary and who had another life somewhere else.

John looked up from the car he was wiping down, and he saw Calvin standing on the sidewalk watching. He smiled and raised his hand holding his drying cloth. Calvin raised his hand back, not quite in a farewell. Then he walked back to his office, hands in his pockets and looking down at the sidewalk.

CHAPTER 12

ON A SEPTEMBER Sunday morning, Calvin walked into the Country Kitchen. The restaurant stood across and down Main Street from the courthouse and next to the Hanna Bank & Trust. As he walked back between the rows of booths along each side, a few men looked up from their coffees and late breakfasts and nodded. A farmer Calvin had known all his life and had attended Hanna High School with his father looked up from his paper and said good morning. Calvin stopped a moment to ask after his wife and about how the corn seeding had gone that spring. "What's the harvest looking like?" he asked. The farmer later said it was just such a courtesy as Calvin's father would have shown.

Calvin took a booth in the back where he could catch the breeze from the open rear door, and he laid the Yankees baseball cap he liked to wear on weekends upon the tabletop next to the wall.

"Coffee, honey?" said a stout woman with peroxide scalded hair. She would have called him honey even if she had not known him all his life. She filled his cup not waiting for his answer, knowing it before had she even posed the question. Posing it only to initiate her flirtation.

"Only coffee for now, Margaret." He looked up at her and winked. "I'm waiting for a friend."

Margaret stopped pouring the coffee and laid her free hand on her more than ample hip. She looked down at him with one eye closed so as to better scrutinize his veracity. "Just what kind of friend we talking about here, Mr. Calvin Samuels?" She waited, but received in reply only a still wider grin. "You got some sure enough filly lassoed and on the end of a rope that you're stringing in here so I can give her a good looking over? Is that it?"

Calvin stirred his coffee, shaking his head. "Now Margaret, you know, I mean you know," he said drawing out the "o," "that there could never, ever, be anyone else in my heart but you."

Margaret's daughter and Calvin had graduated the same year from Hanna High School, classmates since kindergarten.

"You must be a sure enough lawyer, Calvin Samuels," she said as she took her hand from her hip and placed it on his shoulder and laughed. "Because you lie worse than that ratty bear rug my old man's got up in our attic."

Calvin blew on his coffee and sipped at the rim. "And

how's the other beauty in the family, the lovely Miss Michele?"

"Oh, the lovely Miss Michele is about like you'd expect only worse," she said, sounding like she had risen even earlier than her actual four o'clock awakening. "Especially after that divorce you got for her with three kids and less than half the support you promised her she'd be getting."

"That I promised her she'd be getting?"

"Well, that you got old Bitty to award to her anyway." She again cocked one eye at him. "But ain't that the way it works? Ex-husband don't pay over the child support, wife's lawyer got to make up the difference? Ain't that the way it works, Mr. Calvin Samuels? 'Cause if it ain't, it ought to be. There ought to be a law to that effect somewheres."

Calvin shook his head doubtfully. "If that's the way it works, I might have to marry Miss Michele myself. You just might have a lawyer for a son-in-law."

"Oh, no, you don't, Mr. Calvin Samuels. Nope. Can't have none of that." She fussed with her hair. "I want you all to myself."

"But what about Miss Michele and her three young ones?"

"Well," Margaret said, "Miss Michele can just fend for herself for a while longer until I'm through, if I haven't worn you all out by then."

Margaret turned to the other waitress who was nearby filling the water reservoir for the coffeemaker. "Hey, Naomi. Looky here at my new beau. Don't we just make the handsome couple?"

Naomi frowned at the water pitcher from which she was pouring. "Not in your dreams, Margaret. Not in your wildest dreams."

Margaret turned full around to face her. "Who says?"

"Well, probably Mr. Charles for one."

"Who?"

"You know. Mr. Charles. Your husband."

"Oh, him."

"And besides, Margaret," Calvin said. "If you were to marry me, I'd make you get a second job."

"A second job?"

"Yeah," Calvin said. "You finish up here at what? Noon?"

"Eleven-thirty."

"All the better. You can work a second job until, say, eight at night, and you'd still have enough time to get home to cook a late dinner for us."

"Honey, you keep on talking like that and you'll never get a wife. Not even Miss Michelle would marry you as bad off as she is."

Calvin lifted his coffee cup. "I've considered that as a possible consequence."

Margaret just frowned at him with too much severity.

"That's too bad about Michele," he said. "But I told her not to expect it. Told her she'd be lucky to see half of that support. And she won't be seeing it for much longer. Dale will be walking soon. I'm surprised he hasn't already."

"Well, aren't you the cheery one on a Sunday morning?

Who needs Reverend Barker's hellfire and brimstone with you nearby?"

A patron up front raised his coffee cup.

"I'll check back about your breakfast later, honey-buns," she said, and as she walked toward the front of the restaurant, she exaggerated the swing of her hips and then she turned and clucked her tongue back at him.

By eleven o'clock most of the breakfast crowd had come and gone, but the Sunday dinner crowd would not start arriving until the churches let out. After Margaret left, Calvin looked out the window and watched the heat mirages already rising around the Hanna town square obscure the day. After a few minutes he sat up and opened the *Cleveland Plain Dealer* to the editorial section. *A retired B-movie actor might be the next president of the United States*, one commentator wrote. Calvin shook his head. He had moved on to the book-review section when John Rogers slid into the booth. Calvin peered over the top of his paper at a boy with bright eyes. A boy with very bright eyes.

"How you doing, Mr. Samuels?"

"No complaints," Calvin said as he laid the paper across the table. "And yourself?"

"Me? Oh well, me," he said, and hung his thumbs under his armpits, as might a small town tycoon. "I'm doing outstanding, if I do say so myself. Simply outstanding."

John held his hand up high and swung it slowly back and forth like a pendulum until Margaret saw him. She waved back at him, not quite in a dismissal.

"Got my day off. Got to sleep in, and I wake up on a beautiful summer Sunday morning. The last Sunday of the summer. Did you know that, Mr. Samuels?" he said, tapping the table with his index finger. "This is the last Sunday of the summer. And there won't be another. Ever."

"That's true enough."

"Get to go out for breakfast. And after breakfast I get to study subjects that really matter something to me. Now I ask you, what could be better than that?"

"God's in His Heaven and all's right with the world. Is that it?"

"That's where I see things from where I sit. I'm in the catbird's seat as Grams would say."

"Glad to hear it," Calvin said. "But what about the job? Everything okay there? You showing up on time? Keeping Mr. Baldwin real happy? You lose your job, you lose your probation."

"Don't I know it. You don't have to remind me. Don't I know it."

"Yes. I expect you do by now. I've nagged at you about it often enough."

"Well, I imagine I'll like washing cars a whole lot less when winter comes than in the summer. But it's keeping me out of Lucasville. Pays my tuition, and I can help Grams make her rent, so like you I can't complain. Or won't. Not on a day like this," and he threw his arms up and slunk back in the booth.

Calvin laughed. "You got some lithesome lassie on your mind, too?"

John sat up. "Oh, no, Mr. Samuels. The landlady at my rooming house won't allow me to have no dog. I already asked her about it."

"I meant a girl."

John raised his eyebrows up and down and grinned, but admitted to nothing.

In a few minutes Margaret took their orders. John read the sports page. After a while, Margaret returned with thick crockery plates filled with eggs and fried potatoes and toast made from homemade bread. After they ate, they sat drinking their coffees.

"I gotta thank you one more time for lining up that job for me the way you did. That was a lifesaver if ever there was one."

"That's okay. Bob Baldwin owed me for some work I did for him that he's been more than a little slow in paying. His new housing tract outside of Hanna is drawing him down kind of tight I guess."

"Yeah?"

Calvin nodded. "He was hesitant about giving you a job at first, but then I told him that whatever he might lose on you would come off his bill."

"Really?"

"Yes, really. But I knew I wasn't at risk. Not really.

And Bob did a good job of testifying for you at your sentencing, didn't he?"

"Boy, did he ever!" John said. "I about fell off my chair when he told Judge Biltmore he was going to make me the manager of his new carwash down in Goshen."

"Yes, that was the clincher all right. But I knew you had it bagged after Mrs. Ferguson's testimony."

John looked out the window, his lips pursed.

"What is it?" asked Calvin.

"I'm not sure if I should ask it."

"Go ahead."

"Remember after my hearing, when we was all standing outside the courtroom in the hallway with my probation officer working out my reporting times?"

"Yes. What of it?"

"Did you ever hear what all that commotion was about inside the courtroom after we left?"

Calvin nodded. "Right before your hearing there was a suppression hearing in a marijuana case, and Thompson left a baggy near the witness stand that turned up missing."

"Glad it wasn't anywhere near me."

"Yeah, you got that right," Calvin said.

"You know," John said in a whisper, "Mrs. Ferguson grows some marijuana in her back sun porch. I seen it once when I was over there during my tutoring."

"Yes, I know. But keep that to yourself."

"I will, Mr. Samuels, but you don't think she . . . ?"

Calvin rolled his eyes. "Lord knows. She was complaining to me that morning about her aphid problem, but I thought she was talking about her roses." Calvin shrugged. "Maybe she was getting desperate."

"Maybe then I should introduce her to Walter."

"Who's Walter?"

"He's the one who deals to all the high-school kids."

"Maybe you shouldn't, John."

Margaret walked by their table at the end of her shift and waved, and the two waved back and told her thank you. After she went out by the back door, John turned to Calvin. "I didn't know Mrs. Ferguson taught Judge Biltmore."

"She didn't want you getting cocky."

"No need for her to have worried about that."

"She's probably taught everyone who's attended school in Hanna over the past forty years."

"I'd of thought she and Judge Biltmore to be about the same age," John said.

"I'm glad you didn't say that to Judge Biltmore."

"Yeah. Guess I'm learning to keep my mouth shut."

"What else you learning? How's school?"

"School's good," John said.

"What subjects you taking this quarter?"

"Introduction to Fiction. Remedial Reading. Remedial Writing. Got to catch up before I can go much further ahead."

"Yes," Calvin said. "I expect you do. You need any more tutoring, you let me know. You might want to spell

Mrs. Ferguson for a while."

"Thanks. But since my sentencing I've been trying to do as much as I can on my own. But I'll sure come see you if I need some help."

"See that you do."

After they finished their coffees, the two walked out of the restaurant together. They told each other to take care, and John left for his grandmother's to see how she was before he returned to study at his rooming house in Goshen. Calvin watched after him until he turned the corner, and then he walked the few blocks to the Hanna park where he intended to find an empty bench by the pond and feed the ducks with a piece of bread he had wrapped in a napkin and finish reading the paper.

Before crossing Main Street to enter the park, Calvin stood outside the gate to the cemetery, pausing to let the church traffic pass, and he looked back to where he and John had parted company. A crow cawed from somewhere up Cemetery Hill, and Calvin shuddered, the heat notwithstanding, and he hurried to cross the street. He did not look back.

CHAPTER 13

SEPTEMBER SUMMER FADED into autumn. Calvin kept busy at the Public Defender's Office representing the county's indigents with their hopeless cases that now seemed a little less hopeless and at growing his private practice that seemed to be doing a little better. He passed from one pretty local girl to another until one afternoon he saw Sally Anne Rutherford downstairs at the Hanna Bank & Trust. He asked her how she had been, and Sally Anne told him that she had recently broken up with the boyfriend for whom she had left Calvin, and Calvin told her that was too bad. They got to talking and, as the afternoon was late, Calvin walked her home. Sally Anne's aunt, with whom she lived, asked him to stay for dinner, and it was almost midnight when he kissed Sally Anne goodnight on the front porch. The next morning she told her aunt she couldn't believe the change in Calvin in just a few months.

He seemed so happy now. In a week, Calvin and Sally Anne were an item again in Hanna.

On the weekends, usually on Sunday, Calvin and Sally Anne drove to Goshen where they would meet up with John at Ernest's Bar & Grill. They would watch the game and drink pitchers of Rolling Rock beer. Afterward they might go to Solly's for dinner and drink more Rolling Rock beer. Sometime after midnight, they would drop John off who, once he managed to struggle out of the backseat of Calvin's Volkswagen Bug, would weave his way down the sidewalk and up the steps to his rooming house.

John managed the carwash in Goshen during the day and attended classes three nights a week at the Kent State Extension. He had saved some money and managed to purchase a fourth- or fifth-hand 1964 powder-blue Dodge Valiant that, so far, always delivered him to his classes on time. As autumn deepened, John gained sufficient confidence in his studies so that he seldom asked Calvin for help with his class work. He never discussed his past, but only talked about his future, which seemed to Calvin to be bright and not too far away.

The winter of 1980 was particularly brutal. Three-foot snowfalls that, on some nights, were whipped into ten-foot drifts by gale-force winds. Icy, treacherous roads. On the few days he ventured outside of Hanna, it was common for Calvin to find cars abandoned along the road where a driver had missed his turn because there was no turn for him to see. Twice that winter the *Hanna Daily Journal* reported the Sheriff's Office finding some driver who had careened off the road in a whiteout and frozen to death behind the wheel. At country intersections where snowplows somehow managed to open up the roads, giant snow mountains rose fifteen feet high and beyond. Come summer, it would be almost the Fourth of July before the Hanna School District made up for all of its snow days.

Calvin stopped driving to Goshen on Sundays after December, and John had no telephone. *In the spring*, he told himself. In the spring, they would drive to Pittsburgh and watch the Pirates and drink beer. In the spring.

The winter dragged on, though. One dark, brutal day after another without cessation. The United Coal Miners Union had been out on strike for six months, and the truck drivers of nonunion coal refused to pull onto the road after two truckers lost their windshields to gunshots, the Highway Patrol convoys notwithstanding. Ohio Edison had ordered the village to cease using its streetlights. It said in another month it would be ordering rolling blackouts. Villagers turned down their thermostats to sixty degrees and looked ten pounds heavier for all the sweaters they wore underneath.

"You know," Calvin said to Denise toward the end of February. "Sometimes I think my clients just use me. They use me like a businessman might use an accountant to cut his taxes. Jail time is just a cost of doing business to these guys. A cost they expect me to minimize if not eliminate. It's like the government providing them with a free accountant. But they're not going to grab any life preserver I throw them."

Denise nodded, but didn't say whether she agreed or, if she did say, he didn't hear.

Calvin puttered about his cottage in March as he waited for winter to break. He installed a new sink in the kitchen and redid the bathroom plumbing. He looked through seed catalogs and considered planting roses and tomatoes in his garden in the spring, painting his cottage a violent shock of pink in the summer.

It was not until late April when Bob Baldwin walked up the back stairs of the Hanna Bank & Trust and told him he thought he would have to file for bankruptcy if he wanted to save anything at all. He knew John was in trouble. Baldwin had collateralized his small housing development outside of Hanna with both of his carwashes, but the eighteen-per-cent interest rates, the brutal winter, and the late spring had killed his last hopes for making a go of his development, which had been struggling even when he had hired John on. Baldwin lost both carwashes, and the week before he had laid off John who had worked that winter nailing in sheet-rock for him instead of washing cars.

"God damn it," Calvin said after Baldwin left his office. "Just God damn it to hell anyway."

The next Sunday, without Sally Anne, he drove to John's rooming house in Goshen, but John's landlady said he had moved on and left without any forwarding address.

Calvin walked all over Goshen that afternoon, up one street and down the next. He inquired of everyone he met, pedestrians, the attendant at the village's one gas station, even the barkeeper at Ernest's, but to no avail. He stopped at the Goshen Police Department. Big Jim Walker said that come to think of it, he hadn't seen John either. He told Calvin he would ask around and let him know if he learned anything.

That Sunday was the first warm day of spring. When Calvin finished walking, he sat on the unpainted bench outside of Wally's Drugstore. To be better seen, he sat on the back of the bench with his feet propped on the seat, and he smoked cigarette after cigarette, lighting one with the butt of the other and watched the Sunday traffic. Perhaps John would drive by in his fourth- or fifth-hand Dodge Valiant and see him and stop. Perhaps he had run out of toothpaste and would walk to the drugstore and see Calvin and ask what he was doing in Goshen. The two of them would then walk to Ernest's and drink beer and watch the Pirates; or if the Pirates weren't playing, they would watch the Indians; and if the Indians weren't playing, they would watch the Reds. They would get drunk on pitchers of Rolling Rock beer, and the next day he would help his friend find a new job.

John did not drive by that Sunday afternoon and he did not walk to Wally's Drugstore in need of anything, least of all toothpaste. Calvin sat on the bench and watched the sun set. He shivered as the evening grew cold, but still he sat and watched the cars in their dwindling numbers pass. When he had finished the last of his cigarettes, he stood up to purchase another pack, but the drugstore was now dark inside. "God damn it," he said. "Just God damn it all to hell anyway."

A month passed and then two. Terry Dominic, John's probation officer, called. He asked Calvin if he knew of John's whereabouts. John had missed both of his prior appointment dates and, much as he didn't want to, he was afraid he was going to have to violate him if he didn't show up soon. Calvin told him John's grandmother had taken ill and had moved in with a sister in Pennsylvania, and he thought John was taking care of her back there, somewhere in Pennsylvania. John had once told him that his grandmother was the youngest and last survivor of her siblings.

Another summer passed, and still Calvin heard nothing. He asked his public-defender clients, both old and new, if any had heard something. None had or at least none would admit to having heard something. Calvin took to sitting in his garden until the early morning, drinking too much Irish whiskey. He stopped calling Sally Anne. She soon moved to Columbus, and it wasn't long before Mrs. Ferguson overheard Sally Anne's aunt in Martha's Dress Shop telling the clerk that Sally Anne had gotten engaged the weekend before.

CHAPTER 14

SUMMER ROLLED AGAIN into August. On a hot
Saturday evening, Calvin sat at his desk in the Public
Defender's Office preparing for an armed-robbery trial
the following Monday while he only half-listened to the Pirates game on KDKA. It was the bottom of the ninth with the
Pirates behind by one run. They were at bat with two outs
and one player on third. Calvin put down his pen and leaned
back in his chair. The telephone rang, and he let it ring without answer. If it were important, they would call back.

The batter struck out. Calvin shook his head, but when
he reached down to pick up his pen a whisper of wind blew
through the opened window and scattered his papers across
the office. Whomever it was never called back.

CHAPTER 15

THE FOLLOWING THURSDAY, Calvin received a brown-stained envelope from John, postmarked Goshen, and dated Monday AM. No return address. Inside the envelope was a letter and another envelope.

John said he hoped Calvin was well, and he hoped they would get together soon. Maybe they could even get together for breakfast one more time before he turned himself in for probation violation. He apologized for the bad spelling in the letter, but as Calvin knew, he had kind of let down on his studies.

John said he knew he was in trouble with the law again. Big trouble. He did not expect any help this time from Calvin. He did not deserve any. It was time for him to pay the piper and do his time.

He said he would be contacting Terry Dominic either next week or the week following. He had something he had to do just now, though. Something important. Something important for someone else. Like what Calvin did for him last summer. Yes, it involved a girl. Someone special. John said he thought Calvin would like her. He hoped the two of them would meet someday. Just now, though, her life was in danger and so was his. Once she was safe, he would try calling again. He had tried calling Calvin on Saturday, but couldn't reach him.

Calvin looked at his phone and swore softly to himself.

The other envelope, John said, held his handwritten will. He did not know if it was legal, but he knew Calvin would find a way if there was a way to be found. Calvin was, however, only to open the envelope upon his death.

Near the end of the letter, Calvin had to sit down. John said that if his life were to end under mysterious circumstances, Calvin was not to investigate. His and the girl's lives were at risk, he said, and if the killer got to Calvin, he might, without intending to, lead the killer to her.

That was all there was to the letter. No signature. The calligraphic handwriting was shaky, entirely illegible where it had been moisture-smeared.

Calvin folded the letter and placed it and the holographic will in John's file.

That night he walked the streets of Hanna until dawn. Sometimes just staring, sometimes his head down. After the third time the police cruiser passed him that night, the rookie patrolman pulled along side and asked him if he were all right. He thanked the officer for his concern, but said he just needed to think something through. The policeman nodded and drove on.

Calvin walked the streets of Hanna until he walked the sun up on a gray dawn.

CHAPTER 16

NEAR MIDNIGHT ON the same Saturday that Calvin was working in his office and only half-listening to the Pirates game, the driver of a white Chevy pickup and her passenger were making their run from Goshen, the truck headlights burning through the darkness. They were southbound on CR-141, now nearly abandoned by the county. The road followed Bear Cross Creek as it dropped toward the Ohio River, and what more John Rogers could not have said. No oncoming traffic passed them. Neither could he see headlights behind nor taillights up ahead.

The boy sat regarding the night as it rushed past his window until a flash of thunderless lightning silhouetted the hills that rose up beyond the creek. He turned toward the driver, she only a little older than himself. The wind from her open window blew back her deep, ink-black hair and she studied the road before her with dark possessing eyes, or perhaps they were the eyes of one possessed. He still could not say.

After the lightning waned back into the darkness, the only illumination inside the truck cab glowed from the radio dial. He reached down to better tune in some country-western song of a love lost; it faded in and out before finally disappearing altogether, replaced by a loud burst of storm static.

"John!" The driver made no effort to disguise the irritation in her voice.

The boy twisted the knob for the radio dial. "Yeah, Allison."

"Can't you find anything else on the goddamn radio except country-western? Anything at all?" She lifted her hands from the steering wheel, askance. "What kind of place is this anyway? Nothing but a single station and that's got to be a hillbilly one."

He looked for a moment at the driver, her face too in silhouette, her features inscrutable. He turned back to the radio and once more turned the dial up and down the width of the band. "No," he finally said. "Afraid not. Not after midnight. Not in these hills. Maybe once we get to the Ohio." He tuned in the country-western station once again as best he could and sat back. "Besides, I kind of like it."

"You would."

John smiled. "When I was little, I remember Mama would play it on the radio after I'd gone to bed. Used to just lie there at night before I fell asleep, listening to it. And she'd sing right along. Had a real pretty voice. Could've

124

been on the radio herself." He again looked over at Allison. "Like you. You have a real pretty voice when you care to use it."

"So where's she at now?" she said, still looking straight ahead. "Your mom."

John shrugged. "Haven't seen her much since the county dumped me in foster care."

"Did you ever see her?"

He turned the question over for a minute. "One Christmas I did. One Christmas I remember Mrs. Thompson from County let me stay with Grams, and Mom showed up for dinner. Bought me a watch. Or at least she gave me a watch." John held up his arm and looked over at Allison, but she didn't turn to look. "Guess you can't see it so good in the dark anyway." He lowered his arm and looked down at his wrist a moment. "It wasn't gift wrapped or nothing. Probably shoplifted it."

"Well," Allison said. "It's the thought that counts."

"Yeah, I guess. It's the thought that counts. But I haven't seen her since. She'll call Grams every once in a while. Maybe twice a year. Usually around Christmas and Easter. Asks about me. About how I'm doing and stuff. At least Grams tells me she does."

"You don't think she really asks? That your mom doesn't really care about what happens to you?"

"Seems to me if she cared all that much, I never would have landed in foster care."

"Sometimes, John. Sometimes even with the best of intentions we can't help what happens to others. What we do to others. To those around us. To those we love. Don't you think?"

John looked at the radio dial. "I suppose. I suppose that's so."

"No, you don't."

John didn't answer.

"You don't believe me, do you?"

"No," he said. "No, I guess I really don't."

Allison nodded and peered out the dusty windshield at the darkness just beyond the headlights. After a while, she asked, "So where you going to now?"

John drummed the door armrest with his fingers and looked out.

"Any idea? Any idea at all?"

"Yeah, though at first I considered just turning myself in to the law and be done with it."

Allison snapped her face around toward him, all but ignoring the twisting road before them.

"But you know he could get to me in jail just as easy as somewheres else if he wanted to. I don't know. Maybe just somewheres he can't find me."

After a minute, Allison said, "Such as where?"

"I don't know. Maybe California."

"California?"

"Yeah. Maybe. Or maybe Texas. Grams says I got a

126

cousin in East Texas working in the oilfields. Maybe I could get hired on as a roughneck there. I hear it pays good. Real good, as a matter of fact. More than enough to support me."

The two rode on in silence for almost a mile. A moth splattered on the windshield between them, its entrails green and yellow.

"What about you?" John said. "Where you headed?"

"Oh, go back to my folks. Or try to. If they'll take me back."

"Ah. They'll take you back. They got to. They're your folks, after all."

"I don't know. Maybe not. They were real upset when I started working down at the track to begin with. Told me no good would ever come of it. And then when me and Mark moved in together." She shook her head. "Lord, you'd of thought we murdered someone the way those two carried on."

Allison was quiet for a moment. Then she smiled, but it was a smile only for herself. "But then I guess maybe him and me did anyways in the end, didn't we?"

She pushed in the cigarette lighter, her fingers lingering on its knob. Again lightning illuminated the cab, the storm still too distant for them to hear the thunder. Just a telarian flash of light somewhere beyond the Ohio, intricate as a spider's web.

"If you do go home, if you do go to your parents', he'll find you if he wants to," John said. "And he'll want to. So long as you was back at the farm, he had you, and he didn't need to worry about you talking to no one he didn't want you to. But you know him. By next weekend he'll have someone else out there."

"We won't have to wait 'til next weekend. He's already got himself a new girl."

"Then you're nothing to him anymore. You're nothing but a problem waiting to happen."

"Maybe," she said.

"Listen to me, will you. When you get home, you don't go nowheres by yourself. You hear me. Nowheres. Not for the next year. Maybe longer. Not shopping. Not to church. Nowheres. Just sit at home."

She dragged on her cigarette and held it out for him. "You want the rest of this?"

John reached for her outstretched hand and when their fingertips touched he looked at her face by the light from the cigarette, but she only concentrated ahead of them. He sat back and looked out his window and smoked. They drove on. Another country-western song played, but the words were carried away by the rush of wind through their open windows.

"Doesn't it bother you?" John said. "Driving their truck. Riding in their truck." He turned and looked back into the truck bed. "Still has some of their stuff in here. We've been smoking their cigarettes. Hell, some of these ashes in the goddamn ashtray are from their goddamn cigarettes they smoked. And you and I are sitting right where the two of them did."

Allison looked into the rearview mirror.

"We're using their truck to get away in," John said. "And yet we haven't done right by them. They're still dumped back there. Dumped back there without even a proper burial."

"They were drug-runners. For Christ's sake," Allison said. "Don't go crying over them. A lot of people, a lot of kids, are dead because of them. And they messed up the lives of a lot more people." She turned and faced him. "And they sure as hell didn't do you and me any good."

John dragged on his cigarette one last time and then flicked it out the window. He watched it circle out into the darkness. Circles within circles.

"They had some help from us along the way, you know," he said. "They didn't force us to do their drugs. It's not like they sat on us and poured them down our throats or something. We had something to say in the matter. And we didn't say nothing except 'give us more'."

"If a person's dying of thirst, John, you don't need to hold a gun to their head to get them to drink your water."

"Yeah. I suppose. Meaning what?"

"Meaning that if you got enough hurt in your life, drugs are just like water to a man in the desert dying of thirst."

John waited for her to say something more, but she did not. "Everybody's got hurt," he said after a minute. "You. Me. The whole world. Everybody. There ain't no exceptions out there that I knowed of."

Allison drove on without answering.

"But what I started to say is that it ain't right for us to be using their truck unless we do right by them," he said. "And until we do, I think no good can come of it."

"Come on, John."

"And what about their folks? I don't care what they done. They still had moms and dads and sisses. You know Heath used to go to Ernest's every day just to call his mom up in Flint?"

"Yes, I knew that," Allison said. "But how could we have told—who could we have told—without ending up dead too? Or maybe, if we're not dead, we're charged as accomplices and he just has us done in jail. And you know he could. Easy."

John leaned his head on his fist, his elbow propped against the door, and he squinted his eyes against the rush of wind from the open window. His eyes teared—but not only from the gale.

"Who was that you were talking to on the phone back at Ernest's?"

John brought his face back into the cab. "My lawyer."

"What'd you tell him?"

"Nothing. He wasn't in."

"Goddamn lawyers," she said. "They'll stick it to you six ways to Sunday every time."

"No, he won't. Not Mr. Samuels."

"Never heard of him. And if I haven't heard of him, he can't be worth knowing."

"He's okay," John said. "He did all right by me. I'll say that for him straight out. Kept me out of Lucasville. Got me a job. Helped me with my classes. That's who I mailed my letter to back at the post office on our way out of Goshen."

"What'd you say in it?"

"Not much, really. Told him not to worry. Said I had some things to clear up first, but then I'd be turning myself in soon."

Allison looked again in the mirror. "And are you?" she said. "Are you turning yourself in?"

"I don't know. I meant it when I wrote it. But I keep going back and forth. I can't decide. Can't decide."

"I sure wouldn't relish going to Lucasville if I were you."

"Yeah. Me either."

"Did you say anything about me?"

"No. Not really."

"What else did you write?"

"Before you got to Ernest's, I was getting a little scared. So I made out a will."

"A will?" Allison said and laughed at him. "Since when did you become a man of property?"

"I'm not. Not much leastways. But even if I don't have much, it's still a way of saying thanks to those who helped you along the way."

"So what else did you write?"

"I didn't mention you by name if that's what's bugging you."

"Good," she said. "It's a good goddamn thing you didn't."

"I did ask Mr. Samuels that if something happened to me to see to it I was properly buried."

"Oh, now I can relax. That won't raise any suspicions."

"I also asked him that if something happened to me if he couldn't visit my grave on the anniversary of my death."

Allison laughed at him again. "Don't you think that's kind of hokey? On the anniversary of your death. Come on."

"If I have to die alone, it'll make it easier. Knowing that my friend will be thinking of me within a year's time. And he's the best friend I got in the world. And I'll tell you something else."

"Okay. Tell me," Allison said.

"You got a problem, you go see him."

"Okay. Maybe I will. What's his name again?"

"Mr. Samuels. Calvin Samuels. Tell him we're friends."

"Friends?"

"Well, we are, I hope."

"John," she said. "After what we've been through this summer, I'd like to think that we're a lot more than friends to each other."

He didn't answer, but only looked out his window, the hills across Bear Cross Creek quickly falling away as the pickup dropped toward the Ohio.

"Let's keep going," John said. "To Texas. Or California. Somewheres far off and not tell anyone where we're at. Then we could call them up and just tell them what's buried back at the farm."

The lights scattered before them along the river. Allison looked once more into the rearview mirror, and nodded.

"Maybe if I was to go somewheres else," John said. "Maybe then I could sleep at night without seeing them."

"Nightmares?"

"Yeah. Sometimes. Sometimes I wake up and they're both just standing there, looking at me. As if they're asking me why." John closed his eyes and leaned his head back against the window. "I just want to be able to sleep again. To just be able to forget."

A flash illuminated the truck cab. "You feel that?" Allison said after a minute.

John opened his eyes. "No. What was it?"

"Feels like it might be a flat. I better pull over so we can check it out."

"I don't feel nothing." John turned around and saw headlights behind them. "Maybe we should just keep on going 'til we get to a filling station."

"Wouldn't want to chance it. Could ruin the tire running on the rim like that. Then we'd have no spare."

She braked the truck and pulled over. Lightning flashed again, and now they heard thunder echoing from across the Ohio. As the two walked behind the pickup to inspect the tires, a van pulled in behind them and cut its lights.

CHAPTER 17

TWO DAYS AFTER receiving John's letter, Calvin read the *Hanna Morning Journal* story reporting that John's body had washed up on the banks of the Ohio River twenty miles downstream from Creek County. Accompanying the story was a photograph of two boys, both about twelve years old, smiling for the camera, fishing poles in hand, and pointing back toward the bushes where they had discovered John's bloated body.

Calvin tried all day to somehow reach John's grandmother. The sheriff from Erie, Pennsylvania, finally telephoned him back a little after nine o'clock that night to tell him John's grandmother had passed away two months before.

The day following, Calvin drove to the Donaldson Funeral Home to claim John's body. Brad McLain, the reporter who worked the courthouse beat for the *Hanna Morning Journal*, was standing outside the funeral home when Calvin pulled into the parking lot. McLain had told his editor earlier that morning he remembered John's sentencing hearing. Remembered it because it was rare for Judge Biltmore to grant probation following a second felony conviction. Remembered it because it was rarer still for a felon to be known by his first name by the village librarian, and for her to testify in his behalf. It made for a great human-interest story in the Sunday edition.

McLain had already spoken to the funeral director. He told Calvin that John had died from two gunshots to the back of the head. Whoever killed him had first tied his hands behind his back with a thick, rusty wire. It may have been a piece of some old clothes hanger. The police speculated that, most likely, John's death was due to a drug deal gone bad. For some reason south county was overflowing with drugs and drug-dealers that summer, but the police didn't really know why someone would want John dead. Said they would probably never know.

After he told Calvin most of what he knew of John's death, McLain started walking toward his car, but stopped and walked back to where Calvin still stood looking at the door to the funeral home. McLain hesitated a moment. "There was something else," he said.

"Something else?"

"Yes," McLain said. "The coroner said that before John died, someone burned his eyeballs out of their sockets. Looked like they might have used a cigarette lighter from a car or something."

Calvin leaned against the door of the funeral home. "The coroner could tell someone did that to him before he died?"

"He could tell that."

It was a minute before Calvin spoke. "Why?" he said. "Why burn out his eyes if he was going to kill him anyways?"

McLain shrugged. "I don't know. Maybe it was just gratuitous. For kicks. Maybe for information. I just don't know."

And for two years, that was all he was to know about the death of his friend.

Calvin drove back to his office. After a while, his hands were steady enough to remove John's will from the file and hold it still enough to read it. The will was more of a letter than a testament, the script uncommonly fine, almost like that of a calligrapher. John asked him to see to his burial, and he asked him to visit him on each anniversary of his death. Calvin looked down at the calendar on his desk.

The envelope also contained a passbook for a payable-on-death account from the Hanna Bank & Trust. In the passbook, John had named him as his beneficiary. The last entry was almost a year old and showed a balance of two hundred fifty-three dollars. John hoped it would be enough to cover his funeral expenses. Finally, John thanked him for all he had done, and for all that he would do. He reminded Calvin he was not to seek vengeance or justice or to even investigate. There was a danger to another. Someone who was in need of protection. There would be a danger to him, too, if he did investigate. The letter/will ended with John wishing him well and for a good and long and happy life and closed with GOODBYE. YOUR FRIEND, JOHN ROGERS—and that was all. That was all there would ever be.

Calvin folded the will, and after a while he returned it to its file and closed the drawer.

CHAPTER 18

A T ABOUT THE same time on the morning that Calvin was reading about John Rogers's death, the bartender at Ernest's was taking a break from his cleaning up of the mess from the bar fight the night before. He got the *Hanna Morning Journal* from the tavern door and poured himself a cup of coffee.

The bartender took a chair at a table near the jukebox and read until he came to the article reporting the death. He read the article over again, slowly, and then he read it a third time. When he finished he stood and took out his wallet and walked to the bar.

"Miza," he said to the woman cleaning behind the bar. "Give me some quarters for the phone will you, honey."

"Sure, John," the woman said. "How many you going to be needing?"

"Just enough to call Detroit from our payphone."

CHAPTER 19

C ALVIN BURIED HIS friend a week later on Cemetery Hill, across the street from the park. He buried him just south of the summit, near where the memorial stone for Calvin's father stood and behind where his maternal grandfather was buried.

Except for Calvin, Mrs. Ferguson, and Reverend Barker, no one attended the services. The minister read from the Book of Ecclesiastes. Mrs. Ferguson read from "A Song of Myself," which she and John had enjoyed reading together during their late tutorials. Calvin nodded goodbye as the three turned to leave, and that was all.

CHAPTER 20

NEARLY TWO YEARS passed. After John Rogers's death, Calvin worked at building his private practice, but the Reagan Recession had hit hard rustbelt towns like Hanna. Many needed his help, but few could pay. Calvin helped them all notwithstanding. Sometimes they could pay him something in cash. Sometimes, if they were craftsmen, they helped him with his house. Sometimes they paid only with their gratitude and a promise. Sometimes it cost Calvin out of his own pocket to help.

His salary as a public defender kept his private practice open, but just barely, and he told himself it would pay off for him when business picked up again. He told himself too that it must have been something like this for his father during the Depression, only more so, and his father had survived it somehow. Still, he wished he could talk to him about it.

Yet if his private practice discouraged Calvin, his

public-defender clients were, as always, more than hopeless. He looked for a John Rogers in each of them, but saw not even a shadow.

In February, 1982, when the recession and the winter were their most bitter, Calvin knocked at Judge Biltmore's door late one afternoon. The next time a murder case needed assignment, he told Judge Biltmore, he would appreciate it if he would consider assigning the case to the Public Defender's Office instead of to one of the older lawyers.

He made the request partly for something to do, partly hoping the notoriety would spill over to his private practice. Judge Biltmore looked up from the motion papers he held as he stood reading by his window. He nodded, but did not say whether he would or would not. In later years, Judge Biltmore never remarked upon Calvin's request.

CHAPTER 21

AT THREE O'CLOCK on Good Friday afternoon, Calvin took a seat in the last row of the spectators' gallery. The courtroom was empty save for Calvin and a crow perched on the sill of an opened window, silent, watching.

He opened the briefcase Mrs. Ferguson had given him the day he left for law school, and took out his checkbook. Fridays were county paydays, and Calvin used the briefcase for his desk as he paid his bills.

He was still paying off his student loans. Then there was the rent for his private office. The premium for his malpractice insurance always made him wince. Office supplies. And the curmudgeons at the Hanna Bank & Trust each month insisted he make a payment on the loan he had taken out to purchase his office equipment and furniture.

As he sat writing, the courtroom door creaked open.

Calvin looked up. Brad McLain's head popped through the door crack, and Calvin raised his hand.

Following a hard-fought trial, the tradition between the prosecutor and the public defender required the loser to purchase the first round at the Oak Tree Inn, a roadhouse just outside the Hanna village limits. McLain often tagged along to purchase the second and sometimes the third and fourth rounds. One night he purchased rounds long past the reservation his former wife had made for their anniversary dinner at a fancy Pittsburgh restaurant.

McLain sat in the row in front of Calvin. "You here for the show?"

"Show?"

Thompson had just telephoned him at the paper. He had finally gotten a break in the case of the two bodies the Goshen police had dug up two years before. Thompson told him that one of those present at the murders was to plead guilty that afternoon to a charge of conspiracy in exchange for his testimony against the killer. As he was concerned about the safety of the prisoner, Judge Biltmore had agreed to accept the plea with little fanfare, but Thompson still wanted McLain there. "Guess it's never too early to be thinking about November."

The two sat talking over the murders until the courtroom bailiff came in, knocked, and opened the door to Judge Biltmore's chambers. The bailiff said something and stood listening for a moment. Then he closed the door and walked to his own small desk before Judge Biltmore's bench. He picked up the telephone receiver and spoke a few words and hung up. Some minutes later Thompson came down from his office. He nodded at Calvin and McLain without smiling and took his chair before the bench at first counsel's table. The bailiff lifted the telephone receiver again. Thirty seconds later two deputies half-carried a prisoner through the back courtroom door followed by Mike Folker, who had been the Creek County Public Defender before Calvin but was now in private practice.

The prisoner was unshaved and wild-eyed, like an addict in cold turkey who had not slept in days, and the deputies looked like they were trying not to breathe through their noses. He wore a county-issued jumpsuit, and his arms and legs were manacled, and a chain ran from his wrist manacles to those cuffing his ankles, and when he walked he had to stoop forward.

The prisoner and Folker sat at second counsel's table behind Thompson. As Folker unpacked his briefcase, the prisoner leaned over and said something. Folker shook his head and the prisoner sat back in his chair, resigned and saying nothing more. The two deputies stood three feet behind the prisoner, one on each side. They did not remove the manacles. The prisoner turned around, his face showing the same comprehension as an impounded stray dog, but still seemed disappointed that he had only two spectators and those two strangers to him.

Judge Biltmore entered the courtroom from his chamber's door, his black robes parading in a rustle behind him, a bulge at his waist where he wore his .38 revolver. He opened the file he had carried from his chambers. After a minute he looked down at the court reporter who nodded at him. "The next matter before the court is the State of Ohio versus James Walters." He looked down at first counsel's table. "Mr. Thompson."

As Thompson stood and walked to the podium next to the empty jury box, the back courtroom door opened. A young woman with long, crow-black hair and dark eyes entered. She looked about the courtroom a moment and took a seat in the rear of the gallery, but on the opposite side from Calvin and McLain. As she crossed the floor, even Judge Biltmore looked up from his file and followed her. Walters turned to look also, but the two deputies blocked his view, and he took no further notice of her. Calvin and McLain looked at one another, and McLain raised his eyebrows. "Wow," he whispered to Calvin. "Have you ever in your life?"

"If it please the court," Thompson said. "The state and legal counsel for Mr. Walters have entered into plea negotiations. It is my understanding that at this time Mr. Walters is willing to enter a plea of guilty to a charge of conspiracy to conceal the commission of a felony after the fact. Through his counsel, the state has advised the defendant that were he to enter a plea of guilty to such a charge, the state would recommend the minimum sentence. As part of our agreement, Mr.

Walters is to testify at any future trial of his co-conspirator."

Thompson sat down and Judge Biltmore nodded toward second counsel's table. "Mr. Folker."

Folker walked to the podium without notes or file. "Your Honor, Mr. Thompson has correctly stated the agreement between the State of Ohio and Mr. Walters, and at this time Mr. Walters respectfully moves the court to accept his plea of guilty to the charge of conspiracy."

Folker crooked his finger at Walters. The deputies who stood behind Walters stepped forward, and after they half-lifted him to his feet, Walters shuffled to the podium, bent forward, chains clanking.

"Mr. Walters," Judge Biltmore said. "You have heard what Mr. Thompson and your own counsel have said."

"Yeah," Walters said. "I heard him."

Judge Biltmore frowned at Folker. Folker whispered to Walters. Walters tried to stand straight. "Yes, Your Honor. I heard."

Judge Biltmore nodded and looked at the file. "The amended indictment reads that on or about July twenty-seventh to July thirty-first, nineteen eighty-four, while in Creek County, you knowingly conspired to conceal the commission of a felony after the fact, to wit, the murders of Peter Bonner and Taylor Heath, a felony in the first degree." Judge Biltmore looked up. "Do you understand the charge, Mr. Walters?"

"Yes, Your Honor."

"Do you understand that if your plea of guilty is accepted

by this court you will not be eligible for probation?"

"Yes, Your Honor."

"Do you understand that you will not be eligible for parole until after serving four-and-one-half years in the Ohio State Penitentiary at Lucasville?"

"Yes, Your Honor."

Judge Biltmore questioned Walters for another ten minutes. He asked Walters if he was entering his plea of guilty voluntarily and if he was satisfied with the representation of his counsel. To each question, Walters would look to Folker who would either nod or shake his head, and Walters would answer accordingly.

"How far did you go in school, Mr. Walters?"

"Tenth. Tenth grade, Your Honor."

"Do you have a local address, Mr. Walters?"

Walters shook his head. Folker whispered to him. Then Walters said, "But sometimes I stay with my uncle. My granduncle, really."

"Where's your granduncle live?"

"Outside of Goshen. On the Old Church Road. I don't know his exact address."

"What's your uncle's name?"

"Katz, Your Honor," Walters said. "Harry Katz."

Judge Biltmore nodded. "Very well. How do you plead, Mr. Walters?"

Walters looked down. He did not look at his lawyer. "Guilty," he said, his plea barely audible in the courtroom gallery. "Guilty, Your Honor."

"Very well then," Judge Biltmore said. "Plea of guilty is accepted by the court. Sentencing upon this matter will be on a date to be set."

Judge Biltmore rose and returned to his chambers. The deputies who had stood behind Walters while he was at the podium immediately took him by each elbow and walked him out of the courtroom. Thompson stood and nodded at the woman sitting in the back, and the two left by the front courtroom door. McLain stood to follow them. "I'll let you know if I get her phone number, old buddy," he said.

The crow, still perched on the windowsill, watched as Thompson, the woman, and McLain left. After the courtroom door closed upon them, it turned toward Calvin, regarding him, and as Calvin looked back at it, the crow raised its wings and shrieked at him—not once, but twice and then three times. Calvin felt goose bumps race up and down his arms. He waited for the crow to fly away, but it did not. Finally, it was he who stood and left the courtroom.

CHAPTER 22

THE FOLLOWING FRIDAY afternoon, Calvin stood bent over a stack of boxes in the county storage room filing his recently closed cases. The day was hot and sweat dripped off his forehead and nose, staining the files with off-colored drops. The room had no ventilation, not even a window. The whole week, in fact, had been preternaturally warm for so early in the spring.

He was filing the folder for Neal Rollins, whom Judge Biltmore had released from probation two years early a few weeks prior. As Calvin thumbed through the "R" folders, he came to that of John Rogers. His fingers paused, like a pianist who has lost his way among the notes of a piece long unplayed, and he looked down at the file for a moment. He ran his thumb over the name label, already beginning to fade, and wiped away the dust that had gathered over it. He wiped his thumb on his trousers and continued on through the files.

He found where the Rollins folder should go, and he closed and tied shut the bankers' box and slid it back and out of the way. He switched off the storage-room light and closed the door behind him, but he couldn't let go of the doorknob, and he stood there turning it back and forth, first one way then the other, until the courthouse clock tolled the quarter-hour.

Calvin went back into the storage room and pulled out the file. He unfolded a chair and sat and read over his yellowing notes until he came to a name he had heard just the week before at Walters's hearing. A name he had forgotten since John had given it to him.

He carried the file back to his office and copied down the name and address on a note pad. A granduncle John had asked him not to speak to. The old man, John had told him, was senile, or worse, and would be less than useless to them. He could only make a mess of matters or make more of a mess than things already were. Stay away from the old man, John had warned him. Leave him alone. Just stay away.

Calvin returned the file to the storage room. When he had re-filed it, he again switched off the light, but as he turned to leave he walked into a spider's web that covered his face, and he stepped back and shuddered, for it was as though someone unseen had laid a hand over his mouth. A telarian hand with a hundred capillary fingers, each one cautioning him to silence.

In the evening he drove south out of Hanna. On the other side of Goshen, he turned left at the Old Church Road, and after a mile he pulled into the lane for Harry Katz's farm. Next to the house stooped a man, tall and spare of build, hoeing at the dirt. He wore no shirt, but only the faded and patched blue-denim overalls common to the Depression-era farmers in that part of the county. Calvin got out and walked over and introduced himself.

"You don't mind if I keeps on a-hoeing while we's talking, do you, Mr. Samuels?" He rested a moment on the end of his hoe and looked up at the sky. "Most likely we're going to be having us an early summer, so I best be getting my tomater plants in. Otherwise they'll be a-wilting on me."

Calvin said he didn't mind at all. He walked over to the wheelbarrow and took the rake leaning against it and began to rake out the stones from where the old man had broken up the ground. The old man watched, and after a minute he shook his head and began to hoe again. He asked Calvin if he was the lawyer representing his grandnephew. Calvin said he was, but didn't add that his representation had died with his grandnephew.

"I allowed that you was," he said. "I allowed that you was his lawyer. I suppose then it was the sheriff who told you about all them shenanigans going on out here a couple of summers back."

Calvin continued to rake and pretended he'd not heard the question.

The old man raised his voice. "And I suppose you're wondering just how it was I come to see what I did?"

Calvin looked up. "Yes. Yes, I am, Mr. Katz. That's why I drove down here this evening."

"Do you like baseball?"

"Baseball, sir?"

The old man nodded. "Well, I'll tell you, Mr. Samuels. On many a summer evening I likes to sit in my porch rocker out front with my winder open, listening to the baseball games on the radio."

"No television?" Calvin said.

"Nope. Sitting down here in the holler, as I do, the reception would be just terrible anyways. So I listens to the games on the radio."

He straightened from hoeing, studied his work, and waved for Calvin to follow. The two went behind the house to the opposite side where the old man walked along the south wall studying where he'd planted tomatoes the week before. He stopped and stooped on his haunches and picked a weedy clump of dirt out of the ground and examined it. The old man grimaced, swore, and threw the clump over his shoulder into the adjoining field without looking, almost catching Calvin in the face.

"Oh," he said, and waved his arm behind him toward the hills. "I suppose I could put up an antenner on one of them hills behind here, but I'm not much interested." He looked at Calvin. "I've heard talk of them bringing in cable in a few years, but even when it comes I don't think I'll be much interested in taking it. What little I've seen of it looks like junk. Just junk."

"Yes, sir."

"Once when I was in Goshen a few years back I went into Ernest's for a beer. It was a hot Saturday afternoon in July. Temperature must have been a hundred or better and the humidity worse. There was a game playing on the TV hanging up over the bar. I watched part of it while I nursed my beer. But I didn't like much what I seen."

"No?" Calvin asked.

"No, sir. Didn't like what I seen much. What I like is listening to a game while sitting on my porch in the evening. Mosquiteers and all."

"Yes, sir."

"I suppose that seems kind of backward and ignorant to city-folk. But I can sit on my porch and rock. I can sit and rock and listen to the game and look across to where it was I growed up."

He had grown up on the farm just across the road, but it hadn't been all that much of a farm—the ground was too hilly and too rocky and not much good for anything except as pasture for their small herd of milk cows. Even then, the cows were always pulling up lame after stumbling over rocks and picking up stones in their hoofs. "Cows is dumb, in case you didn't know it," the old man said.

"No, sir. I'd never heard that."

He pointed to the side of the house across the road where the ground had only a marginal slope to it. It was there he and his three brothers and two sisters and the two Rogers boys from the next farm up the road had carved out their baseball diamond. Or at least what they all agreed a baseball diamond must look like, since none of them had ever actually seen a real one other than in the pictures posted in Mr. Lufkin's Goshen barbershop from the newspaper's sports page.

"And as I said, in the evening I like to sit on my front porch and listen to the baseball game. I like to look across the road and remember the games I played as a young'un." He looked down at the dirt, drawing lines in it with the toe of his boot. "We'd play all day following Sunday dinner and in the evening during the week after supper whenever we'd get enough players together."

With no money, baseball was their summer fun. They were too far out in the country, and KDKA was fifty miles east, too distant for reception until the late 1930s. They were isolated and isolated by more than just living in the country. "Depression come to Goshen ten year before the rest of the country. Did you know that?"

"No, sir. I didn't."

"Goddamn right you didn't know that. City-folk don't know nothing about farming. Never did and never will." The old man leaned and spat. "During the Great War, the steel mills needed our coal from the mines back behind here.

Life was good then. Life was good then, for a while. My daddy quit farming and just did mining. He was able to build this house here and buy us a used tin lizzie." He shook his head. "Didn't last, though. Good times never do. Never do. Why do you suppose that is, Mr. Samuels?"

"Why's what?"

"Good times never last, but the hard times, hard times are like the River Jordan. They just seem to go rolling along forever."

When the Great War ended, the steel mills only wanted the hard anthracite coal mined in eastern Pennsylvania. "All the mines around here closed up just about as fast as they'd opened. My daddy had to go back to farming." The old man kicked at a stone. "Goddamn mine owners."

He walked around to the front of his house, and Calvin followed without being bidden. "I can sit right there and rock and shut my eyes and see them all over again. My brothers and sisters. The Rogers boys. Their sister Jessie." He stood with his hands in his overhaul pockets and looked back across the road.

"I later married Jessie. Bet you didn't know that neither."

"No, sir," Calvin said and smiled. "No, I didn't."

"Goddamn right you didn't know that."

"What position'd she play?"

"Jessie? Oh, she never played no position. She was never much interested in playing. Too small and too skinny. And too shy. And besides, she was a girl, after all."

"Yes, sir," Calvin said. "That can be a handicap all right."

"At first I hardly paid attention to her except to send her down the hill to the house with the bucket to pump some water for us. That went on for a summer or two. Us boys playing ball and sending Jessie down the hill to pump us some water. Continued until one summer." The old man offered a smile still shy after fifty years. "Until one summer I did notice her."

A Chevy half-ton flatbed drove by. A young woman seated on the passenger side in the half-shadow looked out. She did not smile, but the old man seemed not to have noticed. He turned back to Calvin. "Sometimes in the summer I'll fall asleep in my porch rocker, and when I wake up the sun'll be coming up over Peckham's Hill."

"Yes, sir."

"That's what happened on the morning I told the sheriff about. Woke up in my rocker, and I was already sweating. By God, I said to myself, it was going to be a hot one. As I was working up the ambition to get up and go inside, I saw a white pickup turn out from the lane and into the road yonder."

"Coming from your old homestead?" Calvin said.

"My eyes ain't so good no more to see who was in it. Might've been one of my grandnephews who was staying over there that summer. I told the sheriff it was later that same morning I heard gunshots coming from down by Bear Cross Creek."

"Gunshots?"

"It wasn't long after that the outhouse caught on fire."

Calvin waited for him to explain the significance of the white pickup and the gunshots and the burning outhouse, but the old man only walked to the end of his lane and looked off to where the farmhouse stood abandoned, hidden by the onset of dusk. "Should've been me rather than her that died, you know."

"Sir?"

They had moved from across the road to where he now lived after his parents had died. By then his brothers and sisters had all moved away. He still, however, kept his tomato patch where it had always been back across the road. "For some reason, the tomaters just did better over there. I don't know why that was. Even my mother grew her tomaters over there after she and my daddy moved over here." The old man looked at him. "You grow any tomaters?"

Calvin said he had done so as a youngster one year for his 4-H project.

"Nothing like homegrown tomaters. Beats the hell out of them store-bought ones."

"That's a fact," Calvin said. He looked to where the old man had been hoeing. "But isn't it a little too early for you to be planting tomatoes? I recall waiting until later before planting mine. Because of the danger of a late frost."

The old man shook his head. "Ain't gonna see no more frost this spring. Summer's coming early, young fellow. And I'll tell you something else. It's going to be a strange one."

"Strange one, how?"

"We're having us an early summer for now. But it's going to get as cold as October, but it'll only be the middle of July. Then it'll get hotter than blazes for the rest of the summer and on into November even."

"How do you know that?" asked Calvin. *"Farmers' Almanac?"*

"No," the old man said, spitting into the dust. "Not the goddamn *Farmers' Almanac.*"

"How, then?"

"Because that's the way it was the summer before my folks bought the farm across the way."

"The Old Church Road farm?"

"Yep. And I'll tell you something else."

"All right."

"That summer before my folks bought it was the same summer them Mennonites that broke off of their church north of Hanna all started hanging themselves in the barn yonder. That's the only way my folks could afford it. So cheap nobody else would take it, at least not if they had to pay anything for it."

Calvin studied the old man. "Mr. Katz. Forgive me for asking, but just how did Mrs. Katz die?"

The hand pump over at the Old Church Road farm had stopped working. "After we had moved back over here, to water our tomater plants I had to move the stone from the cistern opening and throw in a pail with a rope tied onto it.

Worked fine until the summer when I got taken down by the influenza epidemic. Since it passed Jessie by, she took it upon herself to keep the tomaters watered until I was back up and about. Somehow, nobody knows how exactly, she fell into the cistern. Drowned."

"I'm sorry," Calvin said.

It was two days before his fever broke. "When I woke up, I panicked with Jessie not about. I got out of bed and looked for her, but I was so weak it was difficult for me to even stand up. I could only walk a few steps at a time before I had to stop and rest, right down on my hands and knees. I looked everywhere, but I finally found her floating in the cistern. She'd managed to roll away the stone cover. When I looked down I saw her hair'd come all undone from where she'd tied it up in a bun. There was just her hair floating atop the water. That's all I seen."

"How old was Mrs. Katz?"

"Twenty. She'd just turned twenty," the old man said. "Still, I loved her. Her laugh. The twinkling of her eyes that give away her mischief. Though we was poor and likely to remain so we was so young and ignorant it didn't bother us none."

He pointed to where he had buried his wife, behind the old kitchen, not more than a hundred feet from where she had died. An old Mennonite cemetery behind the house where his parents were buried.

"Jessie must have been in the cistern for near two days before I found her. I managed to drive down to the Rogers's farm for help. One of the boys was lowered into the cistern with a rope by his brothers, and he untied it and knotted it under her arms. They lifted her out and took her inside where they laid her out on the kitchen table and covered her up until Doc Pearson made it out that evening."

He remembered the sheet covering her was too short, and her legs below her knees and the soles of her feet were just a mass of wrinkles. "She'd probably swum about," the old man said. "Tried to climb the walls, but just couldn't make it up on account of the moss on the side made it too slick. She would of called for me, too, but her voice wouldn't have carried more than a few feet beyond the hole."

"What did the doctor say when he got out here?" Calvin said.

"Said she hadn't died right away. He thought she'd treaded water until she exhausted herself and hypothermia set in. The cistern's ten feet deep, and the water level's four feet beneath that, but no way for her to reach it."

The old man looked at Calvin. "You know what was strange?"

"What?"

"Doc Pearson told me that when he examined her, he seen there were these hand marks on Jessie's neck. Finger and thumb bruises he said. Like someone'd wrapped their hands around her neck."

"Someone strangled her from behind and threw her in, you think?"

160

"That's what I asked Doc Pearson, but he said no. He didn't think so. The finger- and thumb-marks on Jessie's neck was all at the wrong angle. Said he couldn't explain them. It was as though when she rolled away the cistern stone, there was someone waiting for her in there. Someone who reached up and grabbed her and pulled her in. Doc Pearson couldn't explain it." The old man shook his head. "That's always bothered me. Why them finger-marks on the front of her neck. I even asked that psychic the sheriff had out here two winters back, but he was no help. Just mumbled something about the evilness of the place."

"What psychic?" Calvin said.

But the old man wouldn't say anything more about the psychic, and he walked up to the rocker on his porch. John Rogers must have been right. The old man was senile. Or worse. "Sometimes I'll have nightmares of Jessie drowning and I'll wake up crying and I'll walk outside and sit here and look across the road to where she died and where she was buried, and I'll ask for her forgiveness. Sometimes I'll just sit here and rock until I drift off to sleep near morning."

There never was any forgiveness, though, the old man said. Never.

He looked up at Calvin and asked if there was anything else he wanted to know. Calvin said there was not, and he thanked him for his time. The old man nodded, but said nothing more.

Calvin walked out to his car. He backed down the lane

and onto the road. He rolled down his passenger window to wave, but he didn't because the old man would not have seen him. He was rocking in his chair and looking across the field behind the abandoned house. He sat and rocked and waited for an absolution that would never come. Calvin watched him. After a minute he said out loud, "I hope I never get as crazy as that." Then he rolled up his window and drove off into the gathering darkness that awaited him.

CHAPTER 23

CALVIN CROSSED THE corridor dividing the Public Defender's Office from that of the County Prosecutor. Up and down the hall county workers were coming back from lunch. Most were young women working until they married or until they remarried, or if already married, working until they bore children. Some were already wearing their summer cotton dresses of prints and flower pastels, their bare arms and legs still cadaver pale from winter.

Two of the women going up the hall spoke to Calvin, and he smiled and asked after them, not paying much attention to their answers. They watched as he walked on, and the two turned to each other and whispered between themselves, and then they laughed with a lustiness not encumbered by embarrassment.

The ancient wood door to the Prosecutor's Office had

long ago warped, and Calvin had to push against it hard with the heel of his hand before it shrieked open. The secretary behind the counter looked up and scowled at him from her desk when he entered, but did not otherwise allow Calvin to interrupt her telephone conversation. So he stood at the counter for a minute, studying the many fine attributes of the John Deere tractor from a calendar one of Thompson's campaign contributors who ran a dealership had forced upon him until the secretary tired of his listening in on her personal telephone conversation and looked up at him again.

"Ben's expecting me," he said.

"Hang on a minute, Verdi. Someone's here." She pushed a button beneath the telephone keypad and then another. "Ben. That Calvin Samuels is here. Claims you're expecting him, but it's not on my calendar." As she spoke she scrutinized Calvin for any telltale signs of prevarication. He could see no calendar on her desk, but he smiled at her all the same, just as he had smiled at the two women in the hallway.

"Oh," she said and hung up. "Have a seat. It'll be just a minute he says." She pushed another button and turned away, holding her hand around the telephone mouthpiece and lowering her voice.

Calvin sat in one of four chairs lined along the wall opposite the reception counter. He leaned the chair back on two legs against the wall and closed his eyes and soon fell asleep. In his dream he seemed to be walking along a road somewhere far out in the country, but as he had no sight in the dream he couldn't be certain. He believed he was in the country because there were no town sounds, but only the insistent cawing of a solitary crow. He had slept for only a minute when he was awakened by the shriek of the door, but in his dream what he heard was the death cry of the crow.

He looked up and saw Deputy Smith holding on to the doorknob. Calvin's fright must have shown on his face because when he woke the deputy was laughing, but he closed the door behind him as he left the office without saying anything.

"You can go on in now," the secretary said over her shoulder.

Calvin righted his chair and picked up his legal pad from the chair next to him and walked through the swinging door that separated the counter from the wall.

"Remember where it is?" she said.

"Sure. Couldn't forget."

He walked down the hall to the end and knocked on the door to his left. He heard a muffled voice that he took for permission to enter.

Thompson's office was similarly furnished with the same tasteless stinginess as was the Public Defender's Office, the county commissioners forever fearful of an election-year accusation of excessiveness with the public weal. Similar wood paneling and twenty-year-old linoleum. Real wood furniture and bookcases, though, instead of rusting war-surplus metal. On the wall hung autographed photographs of state and federal officials, some of whom in later years would find themselves in prison for tax evasion or embezzlement of public funds. Thompson half-rose from his chair and removed a cheap cigar he held between his teeth.

"Calvin. How the hell are you?" Thompson said, offering his hand.

"I'm doing well," said Calvin as they shook hands. "And yourself?"

"No complaints."

"That's because no one ever wants to hear them anyway."

"Never a truer word spoken, my boy. Never a truer word spoken."

Thompson motioned toward a chair and sat himself, placing his unlit cigar in an ashtray on which the hindquarters of a donkey emerged out of the ash.

"So what can you tell me about . . . ?" Calvin said.

"Mark Alexander?"

"Thank you. So what can you . . . ?"

"Tell you about your client?" Thompson lifted the cigar butt and relit it. He leaned back and puffed. "I can tell you he's one mean sonnuvabitch."

"And your reason for holding such an opinion is?"

Thompson pulled on his cigar. He reflected on its ash before returning it to the receptacle. "He offed two drug-dealers, for starters."

"So your reason for holding such a low opinion of my client, of someone who might otherwise be an upstanding citizen and a Democrat to boot, is that he's been doing the job you were elected to do, and if he should happen to be a Republican he could offer you some serious competition come November?"

"Speaking of November, thanks for the campaign contribution."

"You may be a sonnuvabitch, but at least you're not a stupid sonnuvabitch like Folker."

"Thanks. Maybe I'll use that as my campaign slogan."

"I read in the paper about the drug-dealers," Calvin said. "But can't you give me some details I could present to my client and maybe convince him to just plead guilty?"

Thompson shook his head.

"Save me the trouble of having to file a lot of motions, save you the trouble of having to answer them so you'd have more time for campaigning, and save Judge Biltmore a lot of aggravation from having to listen to them and making a ruling. You know how aggravated he gets in the summer since he's had his hemorrhoids removed."

Thompson smiled and rolled his eyes and leaned back in his chair. "You know, you kill me, Calvin," he said. "You really do."

"How so?"

"Ever since you quit working for me—ever since you quit working for right, truth, and justice . . ."

"Don't forget and the American way."

"And the American way," Thompson said. "Ever since you started working as the Creek County Public Defender, you come in here with your song and dance and your shit-face grin like you're still working here and you're going to convince your client to plead guilty. I give you my case on a silver platter—no make that on a platinum platter—and then you take my 'can't lose case' and you turn around and kick me in the balls."

"Ben. I'm shocked. Shocked you would accuse me of some impropriety. Can I help it if your cases are sometimes weaker than you'd have me believe?"

"And even when your client doesn't win, you still manage to kick me in the balls because I'm sweating right down until the jury comes back with a conviction."

"Oh, Ben. It's not as bad as all that. Some of my clients do plead guilty. Sometimes."

"I'm not telling you a thing anymore. You want to know what happened, you talk to your client."

"I was hoping you'd give me a fair approximation of the truth before I did."

Thompson smiled and shook his head. "You've gotten even lazier since you've left here. It's one thing for me to have done all your heavy lifting while you were working for me. But it's another thing, another thing entirely, for you to expect me to do all of it now that you're working the other side of the street. And don't sit there and give me that ah-shucks-you-mean-me grin."

Calvin grinned. "Ah, shucks, Ben. Maybe it really will be different this time. I mean, you never know. Right?"

"This time will be different, my friend," Thompson said. His voice dropped, and his smile disappeared. "I have a witness. I have a witness who will testify that your guy, Alexander, told her just two days before the murders that he was going to kill Peter Bonner and Taylor Heath."

"That's not much of a case."

"Well, how's this? I've another witness who'll testify he watched Alexander murder the two aforementioned individuals."

Calvin wrote and waited for Thompson to continue. When he did not, Calvin looked up from his legal pad. "Anything else you can tell me?"

"There is, but I won't."

"How'd he kill them?"

"Ask your client."

"You must be pretty sure of your case."

"I am."

"Sure enough you want to try it?"

"I am."

"When will Judge Biltmore be calendaring this?" Calvin asked.

"Late August, early September."

"And an election coming up in November. A lot of publicity about the murders already. During the trial, you'd be front page for a week."

"Maybe more."

"Maybe more," Calvin said. "So you offering anything?"

"Alexander can plead to two counts of voluntary man-slaughter. I'll recommend he serve them concurrently."

"He wouldn't be out for four years."

"More or less," Thompson said. "But if he's convicted of aggravated murder, he'll do ten. Minimum."

"More or less, but if he's acquitted he'll walk in sixty days. And he and his attorney may even file suit against the county for malicious prosecution. A multimillion-dollar lawsuit wouldn't look good come November."

"Alexander isn't going to walk in sixty days."

Calvin studied his friend. "There's something you're not telling me, isn't there? Something you want me to walk into. Preferably in front of a jury. Something you want me to walk into in front of a jury so it'll make the *Hanna Morning Journal* two months before the election."

Thompson rocked his head sideways. "Maybe," he said. "Maybe."

"You'll make your witnesses available for me to talk to before trial?"

"If they feel like talking to you."

Calvin smiled and shook his head. "Why are you being so helpful?"

"It's springtime. And today, well, today I'm in a good mood."

"With visions of a landslide election dancing in your head."

Calvin closed his pen and rose and started for the door. "Well, I thank you for your time." Calvin sighed. "Too bad it's too late to stop payment on that check."

"Before you go, Calvin," Thompson said, his voice again serious. "Just one more thing."

"Sure."

"Just a bit of advice. I don't usually give advice to defense counsel. Especially to turncoats who cross the hall. But the reason I'm so taciturn on this one is that this guy isn't just bad. He's evil."

"Oh, come on."

"Listen to me on this one, will you. I've been working this for two years now. Ever since we dug up those bodies where Alexander dumped them. He scares me. And he should scare you, too."

"Me?"

"While you were working for me, and even more so since you've crossed the hall, you . . . well, sometimes you get too involved in your cases. You care too much. You believe in your client too much. It's never clouded your judgment. And it's something we admire. All of us. Lawyers and judges alike. When you come on like gangbusters, we know you really believe in your guy. Alexander isn't that kind of guy. He'll exploit your passion and turn it against you. If you let him. If you're not on your guard. You be careful. Be careful not to allow yourself to be sucked in."

Calvin studied Thompson a moment before he answered. "Thanks. I'll do that." He walked to the door and started to open it.

"And you've another reason to be careful."

Calvin turned back. "Why's that?"

"I've got some unwanted help."

"What kind of unwanted help?"

"Bonner and Heath were running drugs for the mob up in Detroit."

"Yeah?"

"Yeah. And the mobsters want Alexander convicted or dead. Or both."

Calvin smiled. "I guess you could say it's going to be an interesting summer for both of us. Thanks, Ben."

Calvin closed the door and walked back to the reception room, but there was no receptionist in sight. Just the telephone off the hook, the buzzing of the person on the other end still talking and not knowing there was no one there to listen.

CHAPTER 24

AFTER HE LEFT Thompson's office, Calvin stood a moment looking at the cracked glass in his own door just across the hall. He smiled to himself and walked down the back courthouse steps and out the rear door to the alley. At Masterson's Drugstore on the corner, Calvin stopped to purchase a pack of Marlboros. He walked the quarter-mile up Court Street to the county jail.

From the first day of its construction, the Creek County Jail had been infamous. Following their victories at Gettysburg and Vicksburg, the Union Army built the jail as a garrison to hold its prisoners-of-war as Confederate soldiers recognized—via the ever-increasing number of inmates—that the Lost Cause truly was to be a lost cause. Prisoners collected along the Mississippi or the Ohio or the Tennessee Rivers were crowded onto open barges and shipped, often in inclement weather, and finally offloaded for a twenty-mile march from the Ohio and through what is now Goshen and then on into Hanna. Weakened by the war and their river journey, many died along the march, and when the county paved its roads sixty years later, construction crews excavated the remains of more than a few who were buried by their comrades not twenty feet from where they dropped.

After the war, the Army turned the garrison over to the county, and the county had used it for its jail ever since. In time, as is true with almost all old structures in small towns, legends rose and lore surrounded the old jail and the prisoners who passed through it and of their causes and cases, hopeless and lost.

Those prisoners fortunate enough to have survived the march, the Union conscripted to build their garrison. Prisoners crazed by what they had seen and done and endured. Prisoners who only wanted to escape and return home. Prisoners shot for their efforts by Union soldiers no longer fit to serve in the front lines because they too were crazed by what they had seen and done and endured and wanted only to return home.

Hanna villagers enjoyed telling each other, and any outsider who would listen, the legend of the prisoners shot while escaping for home, and who were buried by their brother soldiers beneath the stone walls built over them. Walls now turned gray by the dead buried beneath. Soldiers not permitted even in death to return home by walls built over them of stone culled from Cemetery Hill and carried in man-pulled sledges to the garrison rising a mile away at the opposite end of Court Street.

Once when he was a boy, Calvin and his friends had camped in Hoovers' Woods within sight of the jail walls. That night they sat around their campfire until long past midnight roasting marshmallows and frightening each other with ghost stories. One boy, Gary Petoskey, they all held in especially high regard because his older brother, Daniel, had served six months in the jail for joyriding in Dr. David's Lincoln. His brother said that all of the prisoners, without exception, swore that when the wind whistled through the jail-wall cracks and crevices, it carried with it the whispers of the Confederate dead buried beneath. Whispers of their anguish at never returning home. Whispers of the Lost Cause.

Calvin stood at the booking desk and studied the wanted posters on the wall opposite until Deputy Smith passed down the corridor. He asked if Calvin needed to see a prisoner and escorted him up to the fourth floor.

Inside the visitors' room there was only a steel table bolted to the floor and two straight-back chairs. To ensure no visitor received the impression the county coddled its criminals, the commissioners required the walls and floor be painted a hard, gunmetal gray with the surplus paint wrangled by the county's assemblyman from the Ohio National Guard.

Sometimes on weekends, when the regular cells were full, the sheriff used the visitors' room as an overflow cell for the county's drunks. Because it lacked toilet facilities and on weekends had only a bucket, even with the window open and a breeze blowing through the bars, Calvin could still smell the odor of disinfectant overlaying the stench of fermenting urine, and he was always careful when meeting with a client to inspect the chair before he sat in it. One village attorney nicknamed "Pissypants" and "Old Wet Bottom" was enough. He needed no twin.

Above the visitors' room, there was only one small cell, formerly the garrison observation post, but now used for special prisoners too wild from psychosis or drug withdrawals for the general jail population. During summertime, its window was sometimes left open for ventilation, and it was common during the day, but especially in the middle of the night, for villagers to hear the cries of some madman. Someone would telephone the Sheriff's Office, threatening to vote for another come the next election, and a deputy would have to climb the flights of stairs and crank the window shut.

After waiting some minutes, Calvin heard two men coming up the stairs, both laughing. The door opened to the outside, and the deputy motioned for the prisoner to go in. But as the deputy did so, he showed an uncommon deference to the prisoner. More the respect an overdrawn customer might give his banker.

The prisoner was Calvin's height and build, perhaps one or two years older, with dark hair freshly barbered and combed straight back. Except for a thin stiletto mustache, he was clean-shaven. When he entered, the prisoner shook his head and swore softly to himself. Only after Calvin stepped forward did the prisoner give him his attention, and he scrutinized Calvin with clear, iron-gray eyes that saw with great clarity the tenuousness of his circumstances.

"I'm your lawyer, Mark. Calvin Samuels." He offered Alexander his hand. The deputy nodded once more and closed the door, a cold ring of finality echoing between the stone walls as he locked the two men inside.

Alexander did not immediately take the hand offered, but his eyes never let go of Calvin either, and it was only after a moment that he reached out his own hand. "You wouldn't happen to have some smokes on you, would you, counselor?" he said, his voice soft and rasping. Not quite a demand.

Calvin reached into his suit coat pocket and pulled out the pack of Marlboros and laid it on the table with a book of matches on top. "Keep them."

Alexander looked down at the cigarettes and then to Calvin, as though judging the price to be paid at some later time. He smiled. "Thanks," Alexander said, and he picked up the pack and unwrapped the cellophane. He lit a cigarette and walked to the window where he looked out through the bars toward Cemetery Hill. He drew down hard on the cigarette and nodded outside, but without remark.

Calvin began as he often did. "I don't know if you've ever been arrested before, Mark. We'll go into that later.

But before we begin, it's important for you to know that, even though I've been appointed by the county, I'm your lawyer. No one else's. I work for you and only you. Whatever you tell me goes no further without your say so."

He waited for some comment, but Alexander only leaned against the stone window ledge and looked out over the jail walls. He said nothing, gave away nothing, by word or otherwise. He may have heard what Calvin was saying, he may have been somewhere else.

"But in order to represent you, in order to have any chance at all of getting you off, I've got to know everything you know," Calvin said. "And everything you can guess at. The good and the bad. Especially the bad so I can minimize it."

"Mitigate it," Alexander said, still not looking at Calvin. "You need to know all of the bad so you can mitigate it."

"Ah. So you've been through the system before."

"Or maybe I've just read Raymond Chandler."

He waited for Alexander to say something more, but he did not. "I'm impressed," Calvin said. "But that's exactly right. Mitigate it. Prepare for it. Minimize its effect. When we can, we need to get it out first before the jury in order to build our credibility. Many of my clients don't tell me. The stupid ones. The ones in prison. They didn't trust me. And when the bad news comes out in trial, well, about all I can do is shake their hand and ask them to look me up when they get out. If they get out."

He paused to give Alexander an opportunity to say

something, but Alexander only dropped his cigarette to the floor and rubbed it out with his loafer. Calvin had never before seen a prisoner wearing loafers. Prisoners wore work boots or sneakers. And he had not seen anyone wearing Gucci loafers since law school. Alexander nodded and then returned to looking out the window.

"I can see you standing there, trying to decide how to play this jerkwater lawyer. What version of the truth am I going to tell him? What am I going to leave out?" Calvin shook his head. "Mr. Alexander. Mark. Don't even think for a moment about telling me anything less than the whole, complete truth. Unless you find the thought of a life sentence to Lucasville to be an appealing one."

Alexander turned from the window again, his back to the world, and looked at Calvin, his eyes still taking their measure. He may have smiled. "Understood," he said.

"Good. Now let's get started." He flipped to a clean page on his legal tablet and pulled off the cap from his Bic pen. "First, Ohio no longer has capital punishment. The Supreme Court abolished it three years ago. So don't let that keep you awake at night."

"I'm not worried about it, counselor. I didn't do anything to be executed for," Alexander said, his voice quiet, reasonable. Perhaps even the voice of an educated man or at least a well-read man.

Calvin nodded. "Well, if you were, you wouldn't be the first, but let's get started. Thompson says you offed a couple of drug-runners two summers back. Peter Bonner and Taylor Heath."

"Didn't do it."

"Didn't do it because you didn't know them?"

"Yes, I knew them. Knew them quite well, in fact. They were friends of mine. Very good friends of mine."

"Well, tell me what you know, Mark. Tell me what you know about their lives and about their deaths, particularly about their deaths."

Alexander studied the concrete floor a moment before he answered. "That summer," he said. "That summer Jocelyn and I . . . Jocelyn's my"—he struggled for the proper label—"girl . . . would sometimes visit a farm where Peter and Taylor were living. We'd go out there for an evening or overnight and sometimes we'd stay for a few days at a time."

"Which is where? This farm?"

"Just outside of Goshen."

Calvin looked up from his legal pad. "Where outside of Goshen?"

"Some road. It's been a while, counselor. The name will come to me."

"You don't recall the address?"

"No, it'll come to me. As I recall, though, the address was on the indictment they handed to me when I was arraigned yesterday."

"Where were you living when you were not at the farm?"

Calvin said.

"Well, before my accident I was living for a while in a trailer in Davis's Corner. That's a few miles from the farm."

"With Jocelyn?"

Alexander shook his head. "No, I was living there with my old girlfriend."

"Your old girlfriend?"

"Yes. My old girlfriend."

"Your old girlfriend have a name?"

"Allison. Allison Morris."

"Why did you move out of the trailer?"

"Well, Psycho and I . . ."

Calvin grinned. "Psycho?"

Alexander chuckled. "Yes. Psycho."

"Uh-huh."

"Yes, yes, I know."

"Uh-huh."

"You know that old saying? Never eat at a place called 'Mom's.' Never play cards with a guy named 'Doc.' Never, ever, sleep with someone who has more problems than you?"

"I've heard it."

"Well, add to it never hang out with a guy named 'Psycho'."

"Psycho's his Christian name?"

"No. It's definitely not his Christian name. Not even his Druid name. His real name's Walters. Jimmy Walters."

Calvin stopped writing. "Go on," he said.

"Well, Psycho and I were in my car—I forget where we

were going, probably to get some more beer at Ernest's or something—when I lost control, wrecked it, and ended up in the hospital. I was there for about ten days."

Calvin nodded as he wrote.

"During the time I was there, Jocelyn, we'd met at a party a couple of years before, kept coming by to see me. And Allison was not happy about Jocelyn's visits. Not happy at all. You know how possessive some women can get," he said with a wink.

"I've heard."

"So Allison and I broke it off."

"So after your hospital discharge, what happened? You went back to the trailer, got your gear, and moved out to the farm?"

"No," Alexander said. "Like I told you, I never stayed there for more than a day or two. Never lived there. No, after my discharge, I did go to the trailer for my gear, but Jocelyn and I went to stay with my Uncle Ernest for a couple of weeks. He runs a bar and grill in Goshen. 'Ernest's'."

"When was this?"

"Late July. Early August."

"What about the farm?"

"What about it?"

"When did you live there?"

"Like I said, counselor, I never did."

"Never?"

"No, I never did. Oh, I had a stereo system out there

for partying and stuff, and I kept some clothes there. But I never lived at the farm."

"Psycho must be telling Thompson you were."

Alexander unfolded his hands as though within them he held the truth. "Psycho is not someone you should take seriously. He's not someone whose words should be given a measure of respect as one might give, say, to your words, counselor."

"Why? What's his motive for lying?"

Alexander shrugged. Then he laughed and shook his head. "As you might imagine with a name such as 'Psycho,' sometimes his motives are difficult ones to discern. His name alone should tell you that he is not someone to be believed, why he is not deserving of your respect. But let me tell you something about Psycho. An anecdote if you will."

"Please do."

"There were no indoor facilities at the farm. So when we partied, we would just go off the porch. You know, watering the weeds as they say."

"Yes. Go on."

"Well, Psycho would stand on the edge of the porch, arms outstretched like Christ, and fall face-first off the porch, wallowing around in the urine-drenched mud like a pig."

Calvin grimaced.

Alexander laughed. "Yes, I know," he said. "It's too disgusting even to think about."

"If this is Thompson's star witness, I don't think you have many worries," Calvin said.

A howl came from above them. Calvin looked up at the ceiling and at Alexander. "Another contented customer?"

"No," Alexander said. "That would be Psycho. I understand he's been up there for over two weeks. Deputy Smith tells me he's crazy. I myself believe he's only going through drug withdrawals and his loss of control is only temporary. But now, now he'd sell his soul for what it craves," Alexander said. "Now, he would sell even his own mother."

"Must get on your nerves. Especially at night."

"Yes. It does. It certainly does."

Alexander reached toward the table and picked up the cigarette pack. "It does get on my nerves. Especially at night." He looked up at Calvin. "So what about bail?"

"Not a chance. Not on a murder charge. Not in this county."

Alexander nodded. "I thought as much."

From above them came a peel of hysterical laughter.

"He must have the ears of a bluetick," Alexander said. "Matches his breath."

"So who was living out at the farm if you weren't?"

"Psycho. Some of his friends."

"Bonner and Heath?"

"Yes, they lived there also," Alexander said. "At first they were living in a tent out by our trailer. But after I had my accident and moved to my uncle's, they moved to the farm."

"When was the last time you saw them? Bonner and Heath."

"When they came to visit me in the hospital."

"When did you learn they'd been murdered?"

"When I read about it in the paper," Alexander said, his voice sure and steady, his iron-gray eyes looking right into Calvin's.

"So after your hospital discharge, you stayed at your Uncle Ernest's?"

"Yes. That's correct. I stayed there for some weeks. His house is actually behind the bar."

"Will your uncle testify to that?"

"Yes. Of course." Alexander smiled. "Why not?"

"Most people aren't all that enthusiastic about testifying."

"Believe me, counselor. He'll be enthusiastic. My uncle will be very enthusiastic about testifying."

"Anyone else who will be particularly enthusiastic to testify?"

"Myself. Jocelyn. Perhaps more if you feel more are necessary for an acquittal, but I wouldn't think so."

"Will they talk to me? Cooperate?"

"Yes. Of course. Why wouldn't they?"

Calvin looked down at his illegible handwriting on the white legal tablet. The cursing of the prisoners below drifted up through the open window.

"So what do you think, counselor?"

Calvin looked up from his notes. "I think we just might have a defense here. We just might. If you do a good job. No, make that: if you do an outstanding job on the stand, and if your witnesses come through as advertised, you got a shot—maybe even a good shot—at an acquittal. If we can destroy Psycho's credibility, we've got a better-than-good shot. But . . ."

"But?" Alexander said. "Oh, my. I don't care much for 'buts.' They contain within them so much . . . so much uncertainty."

"But an alibi defense is a risky one. If your witnesses are too discrepant, Thompson will tear them apart. If their stories are too pat, it looks rehearsed. It's a treacherous middle ground to find."

"So where do you start? Talking to my witnesses?"

"Yes. You get word to your people. Tell them to cooperate with me."

"Yes," Alexander said. "Of course. Consider it done."

Calvin rose from his chair. "But the very first thing I do before I talk to your witnesses is find out where this farm is and have a look-see. I'll be in touch. Soon."

Alexander looked at Calvin a moment. "It is important, is it not, that I should be absolutely honest with you?"

"Absolutely," Calvin said.

"In turn, it is vital that you be honest with me."

"Absolutely."

"Good," Alexander said. "Then let me ask you; I sense this is your first murder case."

"Yes, yes, it is."

"I appreciate your honesty." Alexander studied him and smiled. "I think you will do well. Which is good for both of us. Good for you because you will build your reputation by freeing an innocent man. And good for me because I'm that innocent man. And maybe then, you and I, we will become great friends. After this is all over. I may even have some work for which I could manage to pay you."

Calvin rang the buzzer, and in a few minutes Deputy Smith came up and walked him down to the front desk before he returned for Alexander. "What're you smiling about, Mark? You look like the cat that just swallowed the canary."

Alexander smiled. "Tell me, Smitty. If I told you I played the violin as a child, would you believe me?"

The deputy frowned. "Well, I'm not certain, Mark. Did you?"

"No," Alexander said and laughed. "And it's such a shame now I think. I would have been, perhaps, a child prodigy. Perhaps even a maestro."

CHAPTER 25

W HEN CALVIN RETURNED to the Public Defender's Office, he took Alexander's indictment out of the file. He walked into the storage room and took out John Rogers's file. He looked at the address for Harry Katz. He looked at the address on the indictment. "Damn," he said.

CHAPTER 26

THE TWO STROLLED in that slow, half-stagger lovers display when one is out of step with the other. She walked with her arm locked around his, and when she spoke her lips almost touched his neck. They could have been mistaken for the lovers they once had been, save that when she spoke, the temples behind Alexander's eyes creased.

Though this Sunday in May was visitors' day, because of the wind most of the prisoners had remained in the recreation room where they shared with each other the fried chicken and chocolate cakes and potato salad brought by their families. Outside, Alexander and the woman crossed the grassless exercise yard under an iron sky and made their way to the dilapidated stadium bleachers standing in the corner of two jail walls as dust devils swirled and crisscrossed their path.

They climbed to the top row and sat, her arm still locked around his, never letting him free. Another prisoner and a woman were already sitting in the bleachers, and the man turned around and looked at Alexander as he passed. Alexander gave a sidewise jut of his chin. The other prisoner nodded and turned and spoke to the woman. They rose without another word between them and walked back to the recreation room.

As Alexander watched them cross the exercise yard, the woman released his arm. She took out her cigarettes and offered him one. He looked at it. He looked at her, and then at the cigarette again. Finally he took it, and she took one also and lit them both.

They sat for a long time without talking, he looking out over the exercise yard, she watching the creases behind his temples. Finally Alexander said, "Well, I've got to admit it. You're the last person I expected to see inside here, Allison. The very last person."

"Yes," she said. "I expect that I am."

Alexander shook his head, but he still wouldn't look at her. "You have guts. I'll say that for you. First you turn me in and turn state's evidence to save your own skin. Then you sneak in to see me."

Allison laughed. "You did look surprised, lover, when you finally figured out who I was."

He tipped the cigarette ash into the dust beneath the bleachers. "The wig is great. Great. A great disguise. Never,

190

not in a million years, could I picture you with blond hair cut short. And with the sunglasses, you could pass for Marilyn Monroe's twin. The sinister one."

"I'm just glad you didn't give me away to the deputies. It would have ruined everything."

"Yes," he said. "It would have ruined my revenge." He looked at her. "You know I must, don't you? If I don't it would . . ." Alexander smiled. "Let's just say it would impinge upon my reputation in business circles if I didn't."

Allison reached over, and he allowed her to again lock her arm around his. "We should at least pretend to be friendly so the deputies don't get suspicious," she said.

The two sat a minute in silence, just watching the dust swirls as they dallied across the exercise yard before disappearing into the jail wall like revenants.

She leaned her head on his shoulder. "Before you take your revenge, maybe you should ask me why I went to the trouble of putting on this wig and risk coming in here to begin with."

"To enjoy your revenge. To see the look on my face. To see me dressed all in orange like some circus clown and smelling of Lysol soap. What else?"

"Oh, Mark, Mark, Mark. Oh ye of little faith," she said and laughed. "I have a plan to get you out, sweetheart."

Alexander drew his arm away from hers. He stood and walked down a row of bleachers and turned to face her. "You will excuse me if I am skeptical of your motives. Thompson has you and Psycho testifying to put me away for life. Plus you're still angry over Jocelyn. And you want me to believe you're here to help me after turning me in? After turning state's evidence?"

Alexander's voice was angry and loud and in the wind it carried across the exercise yard. A deputy carrying a pump shotgun walked out of the recreation room and looked toward the bleachers. Allison nodded toward him. Alexander turned and looked. He smiled and raised his hand and waved and walked back to where he'd been sitting. Allison again threaded her arm through his and leaned her head back on his shoulder. The deputy watched them a moment before he went back into the recreation room.

"Personally, Mark, you're right. Nothing would make me happier than for you to sit in prison until Hell freezes over. And then some. But what I want and what I need are two separate things. Two separate things entirely." She rubbed her cigarette out in the bleacher seat. "And what I need now is Psycho Jimmy Walters with me on the outside."

"Take my advice. If your stepbrother was stupid enough to plead guilty to a trumped up charge like conspiracy to the murders of Bonner and Heath, you should leave him on the inside. Why would you want him out for anyway? He's a doper maniac." Alexander shook his head. "Didn't you learn anything from me? Didn't you learn that if you're going to deal, you don't sample the merchandise? That's what got Bonner and Heath killed."

"I'll tell you why I want him out, lover. Because before he was arrested, we were making more than a fair buck running coke out of Miami using the same run as Bonner and Heath."

Alexander reached over and shook out another cigarette. He sat and smoked with his feet propped up on the seat below, his elbows resting on his knees. "No wonder you were so anxious to see them dead and gone."

"I get dressed to kill and the police only ogle me and don't even worry if I might be carrying drugs," she said. "But sometimes I need a little strong-arm muscle. And there's nobody better at it than Jimmy Walters. And besides, blood's thicker than water. With Jimmy I never have to worry about a knife snapped off in my heart or having my throat opened while I'm sleeping."

Alexander smiled. "That's cruel. Very cruel."

"Besides," she said. "You use my plan, both you and Jimmy walk. Within sixty days. Guaranteed."

A deputy stood again in the door, watching them, before he closed it against the wind.

"I'm afraid to ask," Alexander said. "It's against my better judgment to even ask. But, okay, Allison. Call me a sucker. Tell me your plan. And it better be good, or I'll break your neck. Right here." He looked at her dead even. "Right now."

"It's a simple plan," she said. "You get word to Jimmy's less than faithful wife to visit you. Maybe use Jocelyn to get Miza here. Give her a chance to prove she's more than a worthless lay."

"You are vicious. Did you know that?"

"You tell her to visit Jimmy next visiting day. She's to tell him to do a letter confessing to the murders of Bonner and Heath. Then she's to get the letter out to your lawyer. Not by mail, but by someone getting released who mails it to him."

"Won't they check him out when he leaves here and find the letter?"

"They check you when you're going into jail, lover, not when you're leaving. They don't care what you take with you when you check out."

Alexander shook his head. "Sweetheart," he said. "I told you before. Stay away from the merchandise. It addles your brains. Tell me, just why would your psycho step-brother write such a dumb letter?"

"Because if he doesn't, you'll cop a plea for Thompson to a lesser included in exchange for telling him about the little dick Jimmy wasted."

"Which little dick he wasted? There's been more than a few, you know."

"The one they don't yet have a clue about."

"Yeah, but which one?"

She shook her head. "You don't need to know. This is my blackmail, not yours. Jimmy'll know and that's good enough for our purposes."

"Okay. Fair enough. But still. Why should he cop to Bonner and Heath? If he does, he'll face a double murder rap. If he doesn't, he faces a single murder rap for your friend, Dicky. What's in it for him if he confesses to Bonner and Heath?"

"Because you're the man with the plan to get him out in sixty days, and not in nineteen eighty-eight. And that's the earliest. Nineteen eighty-eight. And he knows Miza isn't going to wait for him until no nineteen eighty-eight to get out. He'll be lucky if she waits as long as the end of the week if that long."

"Okay. Tell me. What's my plan?"

"Simple. Jimmy does a letter to your lawyer confessing to the murders. Thompson will have Jimmy at your trial to testify against you, but he won't be expecting him to confess to both murders. Thompson will say Jimmy's lying. I can tone down my testimony a bit. Be a little less than convincing. If the jury doesn't believe Jimmy, no problem for him. If the jury does believe Jimmy, what's Thompson going to do? Turn around and charge him right after he called him a liar? Uh-uh. I don't think so."

"So if the jury believes him, I walk. If they don't, I don't walk. Either way, Jimmy's still on his way to the big house."

Allison smiled and shook her head. "I was down at the track a couple of weeks ago, talking to your old bookie. Lester."

"So?"

"There's a deputy here who likes the ponies."

"Go on."

"He's the deputy who drives the prisoners to Lucasville. Same guy. Every time. Smitty. You know him?"

"Yeah. I know him. Go on."

"Well, number one, Lester has sort of accidentally on purpose let Smitty get in over his head. Way, way over his head, in fact. Sort of as an insurance policy you might say."

"Number two?"

"Number two is, as I recall, Lester owes you big-time for collecting a debt for him."

"Anything else?"

"And number three is Lester's scared of you out of his skull. I happen to know he'll give you Smitty's paper on a promise you'll repay with interest when you can."

"Go on."

"So whether you're convicted or not, when Jimmy, or you and Jimmy, are on your way to Lucasville, you arrange for Smitty to drop him off or to drop both of you off. Whichever. You can rough him up a bit so he can say some Pagans staged an accident, and he got out to render assistance, and they overpowered him. Smitty loses his debt, but keeps his legs. Later, maybe you give him a little something extra for his trouble."

"So won't my lawyer get suspicious when Jimmy's suddenly performing a civic service, other than wasting his fellow parasites?"

"He may, but Jimmy'll explain in his letter that a jail house lawyer was telling him about his rights to a speedy trial. Once Thompson knows about his confession, he can't just sit on it and proceed at his leisure. Jimmy has a right to a speedy trial. It's in the Constitution somewhere. Which is the reason he's writing to your lawyer because he's afraid Thompson will just sit on it. But once your lawyer brings it out, Thompson isn't likely to prosecute. So when he's out, he doesn't have to worry about something he's already done."

Alexander shook his head. Allison waited.

"Babe, you've been in here less than a month and look at you. It's already tearing you up. I can see it. And county time is the easiest kind of time you'll ever do. This is nothing like what it'll be like in Lucasville and you know it. You remember what Rock said about it. What're you going to do if you get life in the big house? Maybe your lawyer will get you off, but what if he doesn't?"

Alexander stood. He looked at the jail wall behind them. "You know, sometimes, sometimes after supper and before lockdown, I'll come out here for a smoke. I'll take a deep breath, and if the wind is just right, I can smell the grass outside. I can hear someone's children playing somewhere. I can close my eyes and for the moment I'm back at the farm." He shook his head. "But it's getting harder and harder to remember what a beer even tastes like or the touch of a woman or the smell of her perfume."

He looked down at Allison. "I'll tell Jocelyn to be here next Sunday. We'll talk then." He was silent a moment. "But I warn you. Any tricks and I'll hunt you down like the dog you are." Alexander looked at her and spoke with great sincerity. "And I'll burn your bitch eyes out. And you know

I will because I have."

Two blocks down from the jail, the bartender from Ernest's, John Allen Rock, sat in his car listening to the radio and waiting. When the DJ gave the time, Rock looked at his watch, the same watch John Rogers's mother had given him on some distant Christmas past.

CHAPTER 27
ACT 2

THE FOLLOWING EVENING, Calvin drove back down to the Old Church Road. On such a warm evening, Harry Katz should have been outside, hoeing his tomatoes, but he was not. Calvin slowed and looked. His farm, too, looked like it might now be abandoned. His rocker was gone from the front porch, and the grass had not been cut since he had visited with the old man. Someone had nailed a four-foot-square sheet of plywood over the front farmhouse window. Misspelled across it, in foot-high, spray-painted letters were the words LOSE LIPS.

He pulled ahead and off the road onto the gravel shoulder near a rusted mailbox at the end of the lane just across from Katz's farmhouse and got out. He walked over to the mailbox to see if there might not be a name on its other side. What Calvin saw was not the name of the family who had once lived there, but that someone had riddled the mailbox with over a dozen bullet holes. Inside was stuffed a decomposing cat, its teeth smiling out at him malignly in a Cheshire grin. Whatever name had been once painted on the mailbox, like the last family to live in the farmhouse, was there no more.

Calvin stepped back as he might from a sleeping serpent he had not quite tread upon and leaned against his car door. He lit a cigarette and looked up the rutted lane. The fields on either side had not been plowed in years. Everywhere the farm was thick now with silver-oak brush, and, though it was only May, the cheatgrass stood knee high. After the lane left the road, it twisted up a rise following the contour until it reached a farmyard obscured behind a grove of sugar maples and dying Dutch elms. Past the farmyard rose a ridge of hills. Beyond the hills a squall line of thunderheads drifted by far to the south.

He checked his watch and walked to the back of his car. While he waited, he scratched with a thumbnail from the rear window the last remnants of his college decal. Before he'd half finished his cigarette, he heard coming up from State Highway 154 the misfiring of cylinders to an engine in bad need of a tuning. In a minute a faded-yellow, early-1970s Buick appeared, slowed, and parked near where he stood. He flicked his cigarette into the road and walked over.

"Thanks for coming down this evening to show me around, Brad."

McLain smiled from his open window and nodded toward the farmhouse. "Glad to see you weren't crazy enough to try to drive up there yourself."

"No. Waiting on you. Just got here. Glad I didn't, though. I don't think my old Bug could navigate some of those ruts I saw."

McLain got out and didn't bother to roll up his window. "I keep hoping somebody'll steal this old clunker so I can use the insurance money for a down payment on a new one. But I guess the neighborhoods I've been frequenting aren't all that desperate." McLain turned in a half-circle and looked about. "But tonight I might just get lucky."

The two walked up the dirt lane, straddling as they negotiated the two-foot deep ruts, until they reached the top of the rise. There the lane formed a circle before turning back on itself like a snake and returning to the road. On its way it passed a single-story oblong farmhouse, gray and weathered, with uncommonly tall windows, like those sometimes seen in old-time country churches, and a covered front gallery running its length. Opposite the front gallery and across the lane stood the barn and other outbuildings, all in various stages of dilapidation.

McLain surveyed the farmyard and shook his head. "Brother," he said. "From what I've been told, two summers ago this old farm saw some truly hellacious biker parties."

Calvin, bent over and breathing hard, his hands resting on his thighs, looked about and nodded.

"Come on," McLain said after a minute. "But stay close

behind me. With these weeds, it'd be easy enough for you to fall into if you've never been up here before."

They walked toward the end of the farmhouse on the far side from the road. Even thirty yards from the pit they could smell decaying excrement, but as they stood at its edge looking downward, there was nothing to see but more weeds. It was a moment before McLain spoke. "I don't care what they did. Nobody should have to die the way those two did. Not even drug-runners."

Calvin looked up from the pit. "So this is where the police dug up the bodies?"

"Yeah. It sure is."

"Dumped down an outhouse?"

"Yeah. They sure were."

McLain stepped back from the pit's edge and walked uphill and behind the house, and Calvin soon followed. As McLain made his way through the weeds, he flattened a swath before him with the sole of his hiking boot as though he might find something the police and two or three dozen adolescent boys from Goshen had somehow missed. Calvin walked some distance behind also looking down until he came even with McLain. "You've been covering this story since it broke, haven't you?"

McLain nodded.

"So what can you tell me that Thompson hasn't?"

"What's Thompson told you?"

"Nothing. Not even the time of day."

McLain stopped and looked back to the pit. "Bonner and Heath were both out of Flint, Michigan. Supposedly they were the key men in moving dope from Miami up to Detroit. Supposedly. Two summers ago, they were holding up in the farmhouse here." McLain started down the hill. "Come on," he said. "Let's give you a look-see inside the old rat trap."

They walked down the hill to the other side of the farmhouse and onto the gallery. The two stepped over the rotted floorboards, testing their weight with each step until they reached a dust-covered window. Calvin looked in, but the room was empty save for some rags someone had left on the floor. He turned to McLain. "So do you have a motive yet for why someone would want them dead?"

McLain shook his head. "Right now I've got about a dozen more motives than the police do bodies."

"I'm listening," said Calvin.

"All right. Could be that Bonner and Heath may have been killed in some sort of a double cross."

"What kind of a double cross?"

"A smalltime fence in Goshen tells me he heard they were killed by members of the Pagan motorcycle gang on the night of a party out here. Killed either over drugs, or drug money, or both."

"That kind of testimony could be good for Alexander's defense. The more individuals with a motive for murder, the better for him."

"Yeah, it would, but I also got a call from a smalltime dealer up in Detroit who tells me it was pure and simple avarice by Alexander. Friendship be damned. They had a drug run, and he wanted it. That's the theory I'd run with if I were Thompson. Except . . ."

"Except what?"

"Except that's not usually the way I get my tips. Usually I've got to work my tail off and meet some dingy guy with an aversion to soap and water in some dingy bar. They don't just call me up that way, out of the blue. During a commercial during the playoffs, yet. In fact, it's the first and only time it's ever happened."

"Sounds planted to you?"

"As planted as Harry Katz's tomatoes across the road."

"Planted by whom?"

"Folks upset at Alexander."

"Such as the Detroit folks if they think he did in their guys?"

"Yeah. Such as."

"You think they're trying to use you to create some bad publicity for Alexander?"

"Maybe."

"So maybe he murdered those two," Calvin said. "Or maybe the real murderers told the Detroit mob that Alexander murdered them."

"Maybe that, too."

They walked to the gallery steps that led to the lane

and sat down. Two boys with baseball bats and on bicycles had stopped by the cars parked at the end of the lane. One was pointing up at them, and the other had cupped his hands around his mouth and was shouting something, but the boys were too distant for them to hear.

"So what've you heard about the bikers who were staying out here?"

"That summer the Pagans had picked Goshen as their focal point to move and sell drugs. Bonner and Heath would stop by on their way up from Miami and sell them some of the merchandise before moving on to Detroit."

"Sort of a traveling pharmacy?"

"Sort of," said McLain.

"Anyone lived out here since that summer?"

"No. Hell, no," McLain said and snorted. "Would you?"

Calvin looked back toward the road, but the two boys on bicycles had disappeared. He stood and walked out to the lane and looked up and down the road. Far to the east he could see the boys furiously pedaling their bicycles. He smiled after them and walked back to the gallery steps.

"No," McLain said. "Nobody's lived here since that summer. This house has been abandoned now. Probably abandoned for good. But that summer, Bonner and Heath stayed out here with the bikers and with what the Goshen PD calls their town burnouts."

"I've never heard of the Pagans before," Calvin said. "Where'd they come from?"

McLain took out a pack of cigarettes from the pocket of his T-shirt. He shook one out, offered it, and took one himself. "Most of the Pagans live near the Ohio–Pennsylvania–West Virginia border," McLain said. "They came out here that summer, wreaked their havoc, and left in August like an ill wind."

"Sounds queer they'd come to a small, out of the way town like Goshen."

"That's their *modus operandi*. Each summer they'll find some little town with no police force or an underpaid one that they can buy on the cheap. They'll sell their merchandise until some law-enforcement officer who can't be bought takes notice. Sometimes they'll hit three or four of these little towns in a summer. Usually dirt poor ones like Goshen."

"Where'd you hear all this at? You must've done some walking and talking."

"Man, you've got that right," McLain said. "And my fair share of being stared at and threatened too."

"I bet."

"I'll tell you one thing, lawyer man. Information don't come easy in Goshen."

"No?"

"Oh, no."

"You think any of the locals knew? Knew what was going on out here that summer."

"Oh, yeah," McLain said. "There're locals here who

knew all too well what was going on that summer."

"Like who?" Calvin asked.

"Like some of Goshen's finest who were on the take."

"You wouldn't think there'd be all that many secrets in such a small town."

"That's the way Goshen is," McLain said. "An outsider—someone like me or you—can talk with people who know what's going on here, and they'll lie to you. Straight out to your face lie to you."

"So how'd Bonner and Heath fit in to all of this, other than selling some of the merchandise on their way north?"

"They lived out here when they were passing through, and on weekends so did maybe fifty Pagans. They'd be sleeping in the house or in the barn or just wherever it was they were when they passed out. At about the same time Bonner and Heath showed up and the Pagans came into town, a lot of drugs suddenly started becoming available to the locals."

"What kind of drugs?"

"One kid told me that all of a sudden there were all kinds of heavy-duty drugs around that hadn't been here before. Crystal-T, lots of acid, black beauties. You name it, it was here."

"Goshen never had a drug problem before?"

"Some marijuana. Maybe just one or two sugar cubes of LSD some college kid would bring home from Kent. But they never had anything before like what they had that summer. There was anything you wanted. All you had to do was tell your local dealer, and he'd get it for you."

"Like drawing flies to honey."

"Teenagers in Goshen tell me the Pagans threw a lot of parties out here. You could pay thirty dollars, forty dollars, to get on the property; and afterward you could swallow, snort, smoke, or drink whatever was available."

"What about weapons?"

"You noticed the Swiss cheese kitty in the mailbox out front, didn't you?"

"I noticed."

"The Pagans were always heavily armed, and they didn't mind using them either."

"Did you hear anything else about Bonner and Heath?"

"No. Not much, really. From what I was told, they were just quiet, friendly guys."

Calvin nodded. "That would have been the smart play. Playing it low-key. Smart." He looked up. "Is there a phone here?"

"Don't be funny. There's not even indoor plumbing here. There's not even outdoor plumbing here anymore."

"Okay, then, so if there's no phone, how'd they stay in contact with their drug ring? Up in Michigan."

"The bar customers I talked to say Bonner and Heath were all the time receiving calls back at Ernest's."

A 1960s pickup truck came up from State Route 154 and stopped by their cars. After a minute it slowly continued onward. "I wonder what's up with that," McLain said.

But Calvin didn't answer. He may not have heard. He

seemed to be studying the outbuildings. After a while, he said. "You know, I think this is promising, McLain. I think I might have something here."

"How so?"

"Well, seems to me like there were all kinds of bad dudes out here that summer. We've got us an outlaw motorcycle gang. We've got us two dopers who must have carried large wads of cash. And we've got us the folks up in Detroit who maybe were getting more than a little upset. Maybe Bonner and Heath were dipping into the till. Maybe they were sampling too much of the merchandise. Selling too much of it down here and not turning over enough of the profits."

"Well, I'll tell you, Calvin. The regulars at Ernest's say Bonner and Heath, and the Pagans too, were welcome there. Probably because they were always buying rounds for everyone. But when I talked to the bartender, John Rock, he said he didn't know nothing about nothing."

"What's that tell you?"

"It wouldn't surprise me if the Pagans were dealing out of Ernest's and paying a percentage to Rock for the franchise. But I got the distinct impression that it wasn't healthy for me to pursue it, so I didn't. Maybe you'll have better luck."

"Thanks a lot," Calvin said. "You call that intrepid newspaper reporting?"

"No. I call it not busting my health insurance deductible this early in the year."

"So what happened after Bonner and Heath disappeared?

Out here I mean. The parties just kept rolling?"

"Nope," McLain said. "Nothing kills a party like a killing, I always say. Especially two killings. No, the partying was finished by the end of July, first of August. The Pagans skedaddled on out of here."

"Where to?"

"Some other little town further down the river. The police say they don't know where they went. They were just glad they were gone. At least the one or two of them not taking donations to their retirement fund. And Bonner and Heath and maybe a third person killed and buried."

"Third person? What third person?"

"All of the locals tell me there was no third person. Except for one kid who I talked to out here, Billy Whalen. Kids call him 'Smell Whalen' for some reason. Whalen says there was a third killing."

"Whalen give you a name?" Calvin said.

"Said he didn't know it, but I think he did. I think he was too scared to tell me."

"What do you think?"

"Could've been a third person murdered out here and dumped somewhere else," McLain said. "But could've been, too, that Smell just liked me buying his drinks for him. Could've been Smell was scared out of his skull. Hard to say for certain."

"Doesn't it seem to you like this is something that should have caused a lot of talk in Goshen?" Calvin said.

"You would think folks would be talking about it for months. Having two bodies dumped out here and all."

"It did and they were. Almost immediately after the Pagans left, rumors started flying around about bodies being buried out here."

"You talk to Walker?"

McLain nodded. "He tells me he heard the stories at least a couple of times even before Labor Day, but, like he says, who had time to pay attention to rumors. Even if the police believed the stories, they couldn't substantiate them. You're looking at better than a hundred-acre farm out here."

Calvin stubbed out his cigarette, and for a minute the two just looked out at the fields of weeds.

"So what angle you going to take?" McLain said.

"I think I can make some hay with what I've learned this evening."

"How so?"

"Seems like I could point my finger at a whole bunch of bad dudes just from what you've told me. Bonner and Heath were no choirboys. They bought drugs in Miami from bad people, and carried them up north to more and badder people in Detroit. Along the way they sampled the merchandise, sold some, and gave some away to their friends, the Pagans— who are also bad dudes in their own right. Then we have the Goshen burnouts, any one of whom could have tripped out or maybe were just a little bit upset or maybe some parent of a burnout who decided it's anybody else's fault but his own that Junior's snorting animal tranquilizers. Then we have the regulars at Ernest's who maybe decided to add a snort to their customary shot and a chaser and didn't want to pay for it. Or even one of Goshen's finest who was upset at the contributions to the retirement fund. Seems like there are a whole lot of potential suspects who had some reason for believing Bonner and Heath would be better off dead."

"Where you going from here?" McLain said.

"Up to Michigan. Dig up some more dirt on Bonner and Heath. Point the finger at them and place Alexander somewhere else. Discredit any supposed eyewitness by linking them to any of those others with a reason to see Bonner and Heath dead. Parade all those other misfits before a jury. Bring the jury out here and give them the creeps so they don't know who to believe. But also give them some reason to believe that maybe, just maybe, Alexander didn't do it. Maybe he's just a little bit better person. He was a lost lamb, but now he's been found. That's my strategy. At least for now. At least until it doesn't work and until I come up with something better. Maybe he is a lost lamb. Somebody looking for his niche, but he got sidetracked along the way. Maybe."

Calvin looked at his watch and stood. "Well, I better be getting back. My neighbor wrenched her back, and she asked me to come over and water her pots. If I'm not there soon, there'll be holy hell to pay."

McLain rose, and the two walked down the lane in silence. Midway to the road, Calvin stopped and turned and looked once more back at the farmhouse. "You know," he said. "There's something strange about that farmhouse."

"Strange? What do you mean strange?"

"It's construction. The architectural style. It just doesn't look to me like an Ohio farmhouse." He looked at McLain. "You know what I mean?"

"That's because it wasn't a farmhouse at first. Not when it was first built it wasn't."

"It wasn't?"

"Nope."

"Well. What was it then if it wasn't a farmhouse?"

"A church," McLain said.

"A church. No kidding?"

"Yeah. No kidding. That's the reason this is the Old Church Road, and this is the Old Church Road farm."

"So what happened?"

"They say it's cursed."

Calvin looked back at the farmhouse. "Go on, McLain. Get out of town. This is too much. Who says it's cursed?"

"The locals."

"You mean it's haunted, too?"

"No," McLain said. "Not haunted. Just cursed."

"Okay. You've set me up for this. You might as well finish it."

"Honest, Calvin. The locals say this whole hollow is cursed. Has been for years. Didn't you notice that other than this and the Katz place across the road there aren't any other houses until you're back at the state road?"

"Yeah. So?"

"So it's at the intersection where the land flattens with cow pasture that the Mennonites who broke off from their church north of Hanna farmed and then sold off when they moved on."

"Why'd they move on?"

"This branch lived communally. So when the nineteen eighteen influenza epidemic hit, they were hit hard. One of them came down with it, they all came down. Quite a few died. Those who didn't just couldn't quite seem to cope. Over the next few years, no fewer than six were found to have hanged themselves."

"Where?"

"In the barn back there. After that, the few who remained sold out. Some moved back north of Hanna. The rest set up Goshen, which is a pretty spooky place in and of itself."

Calvin looked back toward the barn for a moment before he turned and walked the rest of the way down the lane. McLain followed. When he reached his car, Calvin looked toward McLain, who was opening his door. McLain looked back. "You know who you should talk to about this hollow being cursed?" he said.

"No. Who?"

"The psychic Sheriff Conkle and me had out here last winter. He lives in Goshen, you know."

"I don't have time to waste on talking to a psychic. I've got a murder trial to prepare for."

McLain nodded. "Then there's something else you should do."

"What's that?"

"Be careful. Alexander's no John Rogers."

As McLain was pulling out into the road, Calvin started to open his own door, but dropped his keys. When he stooped to pick them up, he saw that at the bottom of the door someone had misspelled in the dust, LOSE LIPS. Calvin stood and looked back down the road where he had seen the boys pedaling their bicycles. If they were watching him now, they were keeping themselves well hidden.

He opened his car door, but turned to look again at the farmhouse, at the barn collapsing in upon itself. He shook his head and got into his car and started home.

CHAPTER 28

INSIDE THE VISITORS' room at the jail, Calvin took a seat in one of the straight-back chairs. Because of the ammoniac smell, he had opened the window, and as he waited he watched the vapor from his breath appear and disappear. Spring had returned to winter.

After he left the farmhouse the night before, Calvin had driven to where the Old Church Road joined State Route 154. He turned north for Goshen, McLain a hundred yards in front. He had traveled not a mile before great sheets of rain fell so thick that after it was upon him he could not see McLain though he was certain McLain must have turned on his car lights. For the minute before the rain reached him, Calvin watched it approach. It swallowed him and McLain like some leviathan.

In the morning he rose and looked out his bedroom window. The rain had ceased during the night, but the day was gray and cold, the sky so low it seemed to him he could reach out and touch it. A last call from winter. In the back of his closet, Calvin found his herringbone tweed jacket, now badly in need of dry-cleaning from the winter, and though he wore it over a heavy, navy-blue turtleneck sweater, still he shivered.

When he entered the visitors' room, Alexander was wearing a pink sweatshirt under his jumpsuit. Calvin stood and wished him a good morning. Alexander nodded, but said nothing. Calvin reached into his jacket pocket and laid a pack of unwrapped Marlboros on the table and pushed it across. "So how are the deputies treating you?"

Alexander picked up the cigarettes and unwrapped the cellophane with no word of thanks. "No complaints," he said. "No complaints."

Calvin waited for him to say something more, but he did not.

"I was out at the farm last night."

Alexander lit a cigarette. "Yes?"

"Yes," Calvin said. "Interesting place." Alexander shrugged.

"I think your jury is going to find it to be a scary place. A place they'll want to protect their children from."

Alexander had started to lift his cigarette to his lips, but lowered it again. "Why would they ever see it, counselor?"

"Thompson will request a jury view. Judge Biltmore will grant it as a matter of course."

"I take it we can't stop it. Prejudicial and all that."

Calvin shook his head. "And the jury—good Christians one and all—will wonder why a group of young men and women in their twenties and thirties would be hanging out there. Hanging out at a scary, isolated, dilapidated farmhouse instead of holding down good-paying jobs in a shop somewhere and raising their families. Young men with motorcycles. Young men and women using and dealing drugs. It'll make sense to them that you'd want to hang out there only if you didn't want to be bothered by the police. If you were doing something you didn't want anyone else to see. It'll make sense if you were using drugs and dealing them to pay for your habit."

"But, as I keep telling you, I never lived out there," Alexander said. "Partied there some? Sure. So what? What of it? Does that make me a murderer?"

"Picture this," Calvin said. "Your trial starts. Jury selection begins. Opening statements are made. Then a jury view. And you'll be right there with them too. Back at the farm. The jurors will be looking about, poking around. And you'll be standing there. Standing by a deputy, perhaps even in handcuffs. And the jurors will look at you, and they'll see you there that summer. And if a juror can see you there, in his mind's eye, see you there during that summer, on a motorcycle, surrounded by the gang, drinking, smoking, Thompson will be halfway to a conviction before his first witness even testifies."

Alexander twisted his unsmoked cigarette into the tin

ashtray and scooted back his chair. He stood and walked to the barred window, his hands in his pockets, and looked out. "Not good," he said.

"No. Not good. Thompson will bring them back to the courthouse and tell them you offed those two drug-dealers so you could be the one running drugs out of Miami and up to Detroit."

"Thompson saying it's so doesn't make it so."

"No, it doesn't."

"Peter and Taylor were my friends. My *compadres*. I'd no more off them than I would . . ." He looked at Calvin, but didn't finish.

"That's what we must convince your jury," Calvin said.

Alexander nodded. Calvin watched him. "There's a rumor floating around of a third murder, Mark."

Alexander didn't answer.

"Know anything of a possible third murder?"

"I don't know anything about the first two except that two of my friends are dead. I know even less about any third murder. Who told you there might have been a third one?"

"Do you remember a Billy Whalen who hung out at the farm that summer? Kids called him Smell Whalen."

Alexander shook his head.

"Well, is there anybody missing that you know of from your group of acquaintances from that summer?"

Alexander looked down and smiled. "Yes, quite a few, in fact."

"Oh?"

"You see, many of my friends lead what some might call a nomadic life."

"A what?"

"A nomadic life. A life where, for a while, we will be together, and then some will be gone."

"Gone where?"

"Sometimes they'll be gone for perhaps only a few days. Sometimes for perhaps much longer. Sometimes they'll be gone forever. But they are not necessarily dead. They find love. They discover the comforts of middle-class life. Some would say they have disappeared, but it's just that they are no longer nomads. Or perhaps they only acted like nomads. Enjoyed the nomadic life for a time. For I say a true nomad is a nomad at the heart." Alexander evened his gaze at Calvin. "And a true nomad remains so until he dies."

"All the same, it would not be helpful if a third body turned up."

"But, counselor, you told me you received a letter from Walters confessing to the murders of Peter and Taylor. Isn't that enough to establish reasonable doubt? Enough for you to get my jury to find me not guilty?"

"It might well be. That's our ace in the hole. I wouldn't, however, want Walters's letter to be our sole defense, should our hole collapse in on us."

"What's our problem? How might it collapse in on us?"

"He might die while he's waiting to testify. Or he may

change his mind or Thompson might successfully impeach his credibility in the eyes of the jury. And if we just sit back and let Thompson develop an overwhelming case against you, even Jimmy Walters's letter may not save you."

"So what do you suggest?"

"We need to turn the farm around so it works for you and not against you."

"And how do we do that?"

"That summer the farm was populated with a rogue's gallery of potential murderers. Lots of lowlifes with more than sufficient motive to kill two drug-dealers. We need to point our brush at each of them and paint them as such."

"All right."

"Unfortunately, we'll be dripping some on you while we're painting them, so we've got to have testimony that you were somewhere else as much as we can. Somewhere close by, but also somewhere with less of a taint to it."

"Such as my Uncle Ernest, perhaps?"

"Yes," Calvin said. "Such as your Uncle Ernest."

Alexander walked back to his chair and sat down. He picked up his stubbed-out cigarette, but did not light it. "Well, I guess you'd better talk to my uncle then."

"Will he cooperate?"

"You asked me that before. Like I said, not a problem."

There was a knock at the door. Deputy Smith asked if they would be much longer because another attorney wanted to speak with his client. Calvin said they were done. He told

Alexander he would let him know how it went with his uncle.

He stood to leave and Alexander also stood and took Calvin's hand in both of his. "I am counting on you, counselor, not to let me down."

After the deputy had walked Calvin down and come back, Alexander asked him if he could use the telephone immediately rather than wait until his designated telephone day.

"Not a problem. Sheriff's down at the courthouse this morning, so not a problem. Just don't go letting anyone else know. One of them finds out you made your call out of turn, they'll all want to make a call out of turn, and I'll be in the soup."

"Not a problem, Smitty," Alexander said. "Not a problem."

CHAPTER 29

THE SATURDAY FOLLOWING, Calvin was hanging new cupboard doors in the kitchen when his mother telephoned. It was the first time she had called him since her commitment more than a decade before. In the past when she wanted to talk, she'd always written and asked that he visit. He didn't even know the sanitarium gave her telephone privileges. He had never asked.

She'd been there too long, his mother said, much too long without going out. Without coming back. She asked Calvin if he couldn't come by the following Saturday and take her out to lunch in Hanna. When he said he would, she asked if after lunch he wouldn't mind taking her to Cemetery Hill so she could again visit the memorial for his father. Calvin of course told her he would be glad to, but as he spoke he twisted the head of the screwdriver he was holding back and forth into the kitchen counter, as though turning a screw. When he hung up he saw he'd ruined the finish by gouging a hole in the wood an eighth-inch deep. "God damn it, Calvin," he said.

The next Saturday, he drove the thirty-odd miles to her sanitarium. When he pulled up to the front steps, she was already out front, waiting, graying white gloves in hand, and smiling.

The day was bright, and she was in good spirits and after a while so was Calvin. She spoke animatedly, but absent the old mania. She asked after Mrs. Ferguson and about how his practice was coming. She asked if he still tried to grow roses as she had once tried.

It was late when they got to the Country Kitchen for lunch and only a few patrons on their way out walked by their booth. They nodded at Calvin and smiled without recognition at the older woman seated across the table. In the twelve years she'd been gone, Esther Samuels had grown thinner and frailer, which her tailored suit disguised only a little.

The two finished their lunch, and Naomi took away their plates. "I'll be back with your coffees. Just give me a minute."

His mother leaned over the table, her eyes shining. "Why don't you have some pie, honey?" she said. "You always loved mine when you were growing up, and I always loved making them for you. My little 'pie face,' I used to call you. Your face smeared red with berries. I thought you'd get sick you gobbled it down so fast."

Calvin smiled, but shook his head. "No. That's okay, Mom. Their pie just isn't the same as yours."

"Oh, you mustn't be so fussy, dear. So what if it's not as good as mine? I'm sure it's very tasty all the same." Then she frowned. "And besides, you're too thin. Some pie would do you good."

Naomi returned, and Calvin sat stirring his coffee. "Do you mind if I ask you something?" he said.

His mother smiled. "Why, after all these years, did I finally ask you to come take me home for the day?"

"Yes. Why? After so long?"

His mother looked down at her hands. She twisted her wedding band around her finger, first one way then the other. "I just got to thinking about Henry. The night before I called, there was a special on public television about Korea. And I wanted to be some place close to him again for a little while."

"May I ask you something else?"

"You can always ask," she said. "You may not get the answer you expect, but you can always ask."

"How did you and Dad meet?"

Mrs. Samuels gave her son a blank look. Then she laughed. She laughed so loud the few nearby patrons turned. An older couple in the back leaned their heads closer over the table and whispered.

"Okay, what's the joke?"

She removed a tissue from her purse and wiped her

eyes. "It's not a joke. But I think if I told you that you'd be properly shocked. Quite properly shocked."

"So shock me."

She shook her head. "Not here," she said in a whisper. She looked around. "Too many ears."

"So let's go where the ears can't listen."

"Where dead men tell no tales?"

"Exactly," Calvin said as he rose from the booth.

"Fine, but let's take the back way, shall we? It was always so much prettier than Main Street."

Calvin reached down and took his mother by the hand and helped her from the booth and left a tip. He paid their bill at the register while she waited by their table and looked about for anyone she knew. Anyone from her past. Anyone at all. Calvin came back, and she placed her hand on his elbow. They walked to the back door that opened onto Friendship Street and began their walk to Cemetery Hill.

Along Friendship Street, villagers were out mowing their lawns or washing their cars so they'd be spotless for church the next morning. The two walked slowly, first down hill and then up after they had crossed the grass-filled tracks of the Baltimore and Ohio. His mother looked from one side of the street to the other, and she remarked on the changes since she'd left, but she also tried to see it all again as it had once been. "Do the Jacksons still live here?" she asked. "And whatever happened to those Metzgers?"

Calvin thought she would bring it up on her own, but

she did not. Finally, he said, "So when are you going to shock me?"

She smiled. "Well, if you're certain you really want to know."

"Yes, of course I do."

"I'll bet you didn't know your mother was a whore for the better part of a week, did you?"

Calvin stopped dead still in the sidewalk. He looked after his mother, but she just kept walking on as though she had confessed to no more than being elected prom queen during her senior year. After a few steps she turned back. "There," she said and giggled like a schoolgirl. "I knew I would shock you. What do you have to that, hey?"

Calvin didn't have anything to say, though his mouth was open. She rakishly winked her eyebrows at him and still he said nothing.

"Oh, Calvin," she said. "It wasn't all that bad. I was doing it for academic credit, after all." She watched him a moment longer before she walked back and took him by the arm and led him up the sidewalk.

"Academic credit?"

"Yes. Of course. Why else would I have done it?"

"You majored in prostitution in college?"

"No. Don't be such a goose. Sociology. I majored in sociology. You know that."

"Oh. Well. That explains it. That explains everything."

"Explains what?"

"Nothing," he said. "It explains absolutely nothing."

She shook her head. "Would you like me to tell you what happened?"

"I'm not certain. I'm not certain I really want to know."

"Why? What's the worst that can happen?"

"I'm not certain."

"In fact, it might even be romantic."

"Okay, Mother," Calvin said. "You've had your fun tormenting your only child. Now tell me the story before you burst."

"All right. I will since you insist." She patted his elbow. "It was the spring of nineteen fifty-one. It was quite a few years after Daddy and Mother had divorced, and we had moved away from Hanna. I was a senior up at Baldwin College. For the last sociology class before graduation we were required to team up with another student and write a joint term paper. Well, Nancy Faraday and I were both in the same sorority, and we were both taking the class so we teamed up, of course."

"Of course," Calvin said.

"But we procrastinated on selecting a topic. And we procrastinated and procrastinated. We procrastinated a while longer. And it was midterm, and we still hadn't decided upon a proper topic."

"But it was only a term paper. What was the big deal? And when did prostitution ever become a proper topic?"

"Oh, honey," she said. "It was our last term paper before graduation, and we wanted to go out with a bang."

"So you decided to go out with a bang by getting banged?"

"Don't be crude."

"Sorry. Please continue. By all means. Please continue."

"Thank you. As I was saying, it was midterm and we hadn't decided upon a subject with enough . . ."

"Bang," Calvin finished for her.

"Well, one Saturday night, we got a bottle of wine, locked the door, and started brainstorming."

"Oh, this ought to be good."

"Don't be rude," Mrs. Samuels said.

"Sorry."

"Anyway, Nancy and I were brainstorming. And we'd been studying that semester that in some cultures, in some times, prostitution was an acceptable profession for some women. So we thought we'd research why some women in our culture turn to prostitution. I think we were two-thirds to the bottom of the wine bottle when we thought, *Wouldn't it be great if we could give a firsthand account of what it feels like to be treated like a prostitute?* You know. Sort of a day in the life."

"Your prof gave you permission for this of course."

"Don't be silly. This was nineteen fifty-one. If the professor had any inkling of what we were up to before, he could have been terminated. No, of course we didn't tell him. Or anyone else for that matter."

"So exactly what was it you two did to obtain your

firsthand experience of prostitution? You and Nancy."

"We decided that the next weekend we'd take the bus into Cleveland, get a hotel room, and pretend we were professional women just to see what it would be like. To see how we were treated. Then, before any money changed hands or anything, we'd find some gracious way to back out."

"Like how?"

"Oh, I don't know. Maybe like telling them that they were such nice men we just couldn't give them the clap. You know. Something gracious so as not to hurt their feelings."

Calvin shook his head.

"I know. It sounds naïve now. But we were still really just children. Seven years younger than you are now. And it was nineteen fifty-one, after all."

"I don't know if I want to hear the rest of this," Calvin said.

"So on that Friday in May we cut our classes and took the bus from Baldwin College to Cleveland and took a room at one of the nicer downtown hotels. I don't even recall the name anymore. It may have been torn down by now. But the first thing we did was to go to Strauss's Department Store and purchase the proper outfits."

"What was an appropriate outfit for pursuing a career in prostitution?"

"Lord, we didn't know. But we both bought black cocktail dresses that were low in the front *and* back, and we put on a lot of makeup. A lot of makeup," Mrs. Samuels said, raking her eyebrows up and down again at her son.

"I get the picture."

"After we took our purchases back to the hotel and got all dressed up and all made up, we went down to the lobby and waited to be picked up."

"You went to the lobby and not the bar?"

"Ladies didn't go to the bar by themselves then, Calvin."

"But you were supposed to be hookers, not ladies."

"Then it would've been obvious we were just cheap hookers."

"Right," Calvin said. "Why didn't I think of that?"

"There we sat for the longest time. Waiting for someone to come over and proposition us. We waited and waited, but no one came over."

"How embarrassing."

"Yes, it was, and we were about ready to give up in disgust when your father came in."

"And the plot thickens."

"Shush you," his mother said. "He was wearing his uniform, and he and another soldier were making their way to the bar. His friend looked over our way, and he nudged your father in the side with his elbow. Nancy told me to look vampish."

"Vampish? My mother looked vampish?"

"No. I don't suppose we really did. No matter how hard we tried, we probably still looked like college girls. But we did try. Lit cigarettes and everything. Your father looked over his shoulder at us as they walked into the bar. I wanted to quit right then and there and go back to Baldwin that night, but Nancy said no, let's give them a few minutes to have a drink and work up their nerve. Well, we just sat there, trying to look vampish, and I could see out of the corner of my eye where they kept looking us over. Finally, after they had their drinks and probably talked it over, they came over and introduced themselves and asked if we would join them for drinks."

"So what happened?" Calvin said.

"Just like that Nancy told them it was going to cost them more than that because we were professionals. And then we watched their faces. This was to be the crux of our paper."

"And they said?"

"Your father said, 'Professionals? Professional what'?"

"Oh, no. They didn't get it?"

"And I thought *we* were naïve," Mrs. Samuels said. "And Nancy hissed at them, loudly hissed, that we were hookers."

"Oh, no," Calvin said.

"Oh, yes."

"And then?"

"Your father and his friend looked at each other, and your father smiled. Oh, what a beautiful smile he had. I think it was when he smiled that very first time I began falling in love with him."

"What happened after Dad smiled?"

"He turned to his friend, and then he looked right at me and said that our meeting was indeed fortuitous because he and his friend had been looking all evening for two professional women, and they were beginning to despair, and they asked us again to join them for a drink."

"And you said?"

"Nancy said, 'Sure, why not?' and got up. Your father's friend held out his arm and off they went to the bar and sat at a table for two. Your father held out his arm for me, and we started walking toward the bar. After several steps, though, he stopped and looked at me and smiled his smile and told me there was really a much nicer bar on the corner and would I mind leaving my friend for a bit."

"What'd you say?"

"At first I was hesitant to leave Nancy with a stranger and go off with another in a city I didn't know all that well. But I thought, *Oh, it's just around the corner.* And your father," she said looking at Calvin, "your father was a perfect gentlemen. Just the perfect gentleman."

They walked on. He waited for his mother to continue, but she looked lost in her thoughts. Finally, he said, "So just what did you two talk about?"

"Well, me, I hardly said two words after we left the hotel. But your father talked nonstop. Like the old do sometimes because they know their time is running out, and they want to get it all in while they can. And not in a bad way. Not bragging. Not boasting. But very patiently, in a very patient way he had, telling me who he was and where he was from. Telling me about his dreams and where he had hoped to go in life prior to being drafted into the Army."

"Not the truth I hope," Calvin said. "I hope he wasn't telling his life story to a hooker. Not on your first . . . meeting."

"Yes. The truth. And nothing but, as Judge Ferguson would have said. But as I told you, he was a soldier and he was shipping out to Korea the next week. He told me about his growing up and about Hanna and about the little cottage he'd bought there right before he was drafted and about his neighbor, Mrs. Ferguson, who had sold it to him. And he went on and on like that for maybe two hours. Maybe even three hours. After those two or three hours, I felt like I'd grown up in Hanna and known everyone here all my life."

"I thought you did grow up here?" Calvin said.

"No, dear. I was born here, but Daddy and Mother were divorced soon after, and I hadn't been back since I was three. Later I told your father, and we laughed at such a coincidence, but that night I just let him talk on."

"Fortuitous the two of you should have met like that in the big city. Both of you being from here. Originally, anyway."

"Predestined I think is a better description."

"Why predestined?"

Mrs. Samuels started to answer, but a crow cawed ahead of them from out of the cemetery, and she never did say why she thought their meeting was predestined. They walked on.

After a while, Calvin said, "Why did he tell you all this? I would think most men would cut to the chase. Buy a drink to fortify their courage and take you upstairs."

"And what would you know of pandering, Calvin Samuels?"

"Well. That's just what I've heard. In law classes and courtrooms and stuff. I don't really know. I . . . I . . ."

"And you just better not know either."

Calvin grinned and patted her hand. "You're not the only one who can tease, you know."

Mrs. Samuels shook her head. "Young people anymore."

"Yes, Mother, but why did Dad spend those hours spilling his guts out to someone he thought was a hooker?"

"After Henry told me about Hanna and himself, he sat for a long time not saying anything. Just looking into his whiskey glass. And he must have seen something because he said he supposed I was wondering why he'd been going on like that."

"And what did you say?"

"I looked at him and smiled and just shook my head. He told me the reason was he had a premonition he wasn't coming back. That he wouldn't be coming home. And he had thought for a long time about it, and while he'd been fortunate in life to have been born in Hanna and to have had a good life, he didn't want to die not knowing what it was like to be loved. He said while it was now too late for him to know, he'd like to pretend."

"Pretend?" Calvin said.

"Pretend is as good a word as any. So, to cut to the chase, he said he had a business proposition for me."

"Business proposition?"

"He was so sweet and so serious about it I had to struggle not to laugh, and I asked him just what it was he had in mind."

"And," Calvin said, "just what did he have in mind?"

"He said he had a week before he needed to report for shipping out, and would I consider going to Virginia Beach with him for the next week. He'd pay all of my expenses plus my time."

"You're making this up," Calvin said.

"God as my witness. At first I thought of saying no, but realized doing so would just crush him. He was so sincere and so earnest, and his smile was so sweet. I thought I would just tell him I was a two-thousand-dollar-a-night hooker, and I knew he couldn't afford me."

"So what'd you tell him?"

"In the end I just said yes."

"Yes?"

"Yes. I looked at him, and I knew his premonition was true. He wouldn't be coming home. And he was so sweet, I thought he should have a chance to know what it was like to be loved even if it was only for pretend. Even if it was only for a week."

"So what'd you two do?" Calvin asked. "You and Dad."

"We went back to the hotel, and I packed my bag while your father waited in the lobby."

"What did you tell Nancy?"

"I left a note for her saying I was okay, but I'd be gone

for a week and not saying where I was going and for her not to worry. We took a cab to the station and a train to Richmond. Henry fell asleep soon after the train pulled out, and he slept the sleep of the dead all the way there. He had the look of a man at peace."

"What happened when you got to Richmond?"

"We went to a diner for breakfast, and afterward we walked to the bus station and went on to Virginia Beach. On the bus, your father talked to the driver and got the name of a place for us to stay right along the ocean. And you know something?"

"No, Mom. What?"

"In a crazy sort of way, it did feel like our honeymoon."

"Mother!"

"Calvin," she said. "Honestly, sometimes you're just such a prude. But we got to the bus station in Virginia Beach and took a cab to the motel, which was just a group of cottages. And it was still early in the season. Not cold. But just barely warm. Just. So we were the only ones there. And the cottage was cute and quaint, and we were having so much fun. We changed right away into the swimsuits we'd bought, but the water was still much too cold to stay in for more than a minute, and the rest of the afternoon we just lay out on the beach. I slept most of the afternoon. I was exhausted from the trip. And I woke up and opened my eyes. Above me was an albatross hovering, and I thought to myself, *That's my life.* Just hovering. Just blowing this way and that from life's jetties and currents. I closed my eyes, and I felt very happy. I told myself I wasn't going to spoil this happiness, and I wasn't going to disappoint this boy. And if his premonition was right and if he wasn't coming back, I wanted him to have something to smile to himself about."

Calvin looked at his mother and touched her hand. "That's okay. I can imagine the rest."

"But I don't want you to imagine. I want you to know. I haven't told this to anyone. Ever. In almost thirty years. And I want someone to know."

"All right. If you'd like to tell me, I'd like to hear it."

"When we came back from dinner, it became evident very quickly we were both inexperienced, and your father realized at once I wasn't a professional woman, and I just cried and cried because your father was mortified, and my crying just made it worse."

"So what happened?"

"I cried, and he held me, and I fell asleep crying. But the next morning when I woke up, your father had gone to the store, and he was cooking the most wonderful breakfast I think I've ever had. He served me in bed, and we had a wonderful day, just laughing and carrying on. Nothing was said about the night before, and that night we did lose our virginity. Together, which made it special. That we did it together. It was a marvelous week together, and at its end we were both very much in love. On the way home, we stopped in Maryland and were married because they had no waiting period, and we caught the next train to Hanna."

"Must have been some homecoming."

"You know," Mrs. Samuels said, people just couldn't have been any nicer. Your father set me up in his cottage and introduced me to Mrs. Ferguson and left early the next morning. I remember him lightly kissing me on the forehead, but I was so exhausted I didn't wake up. That was the last time I was with your father. I didn't see him or speak to him again. Not in this life, anyway."

They had entered the cemetery, and they walked toward the war memorial at its center.

"When did you receive word about Dad?"

"It wasn't long. Not long at all. Less than six months. I hadn't received any letters for a while, but I wasn't concerned because I knew your father was right. He wouldn't be coming home. His letters finally arrived after I received word. But I couldn't read them for the longest time."

"So what did happen to Dad?"

"I don't really know. I don't believe even the Army knows. I received a letter from his company commander, who said he'd been left in a foxhole on a ridge and there'd been an attack that night, and the next morning he was just gone without ever having given word to the Army. He may have wandered off and been blown up in the bombardment, or he may have been captured, interrogated and killed, or sent north. We don't know. We simply don't know. Perhaps no one does."

"It must have been very hard on you. Not knowing."

They had walked to the memorial. A bronze plaque darkened by rain and snow and weather and time, the names only legible were the reader to stoop and sit on her knees.

"Even after he began haunting the cottage, Henry never said what happened to him."

Calvin looked down at his mother, her hand touching his name. "Haunting?"

She didn't answer immediately, but stooping on her knees, she traced her index finger back and forth along his name. The five letters of his first name. One for each day they had been together. "H." Honor. Honorable. That he had certainly been, and more. The seven letters of his last name. One for each night they had known each other. "S." Sweet. Yes, sweet. Or perhaps savagery for how he was taken.

"A year or so after the Army reported him missing, while I was asleep, there was a kiss on my forehead, just like on the morning when he'd left for Korea, and when I awoke in our bedroom, there he was, standing in the moonlight, wearing his uniform with his service hat beneath his arm, and smiling his beautiful smile. He smiled his smile, and he told me he had missed me. That was the reason he had returned. He had missed me."

"You must have been terrified," Calvin said.

"No. Not terrified. More curious than anything. At first I thought it must be his ghost—but then I suspected that maybe he'd been found and wanted to surprise me. I asked him what had happened. It was all I could think to say; but he only smiled, shook his head, and was gone. Faded away. That's when I knew he was a ghost."

"What did you do?"

"Oh. My heart just sank when he disappeared, when he faded back into nothingness. It was like losing him a second time. Like losing him all over again. I thought maybe he was here, at the memorial, and that he was waiting for me here. So I got up. I checked on you. You still slept in a crib in my room. You were wide awake and just smiling and cooing so I knew you'd seen him, too. I covered you up again and set out for here in my nightgown. I didn't even put on my coat, though it was November. Just my slippers."

Esther Samuels rubbed her finger along her husband's name, touching her finger to her lips. "I guess you know I didn't make it this far," she said. "A police officer on night patrol stopped to ask if anything was wrong."

"What did you say?"

"I was so excited I just blurted out that I was going to see my husband again, and if I could just make it here I could see him one more time. That he must have come back because he had a message to tell me. Well, you can imagine what happened. And after the fourth time your father visited me at night, and I rushed out of the house clad only in my night-gown . . . well, you know what happened."

Calvin nodded. "The snowballs."

"I was always sorry I didn't make it to the memorial that

night. Or the other nights he visited."

Mrs. Samuels turned back to the memorial. "Do you still see him on occasion?" Calvin said.

"No," she said. "Not since I moved out of the house."

"That's good. That's good, I suppose, that he doesn't haunt you anymore."

"No. It's not so good."

"Why is it not so good?" Calvin said.

"Because he's still there, you know."

CHAPTER 30

AFTER CALVIN AND his mother left Cemetery Hill, he took her back to the sanitarium. Neither one hardly spoke on the drive back, and it was dark when they got there. He walked her to her room and kissed her on the cheek. For a moment she held onto both his hands, studying his eyes and whatever it was they held. She told him that she loved him and how proud she was. Calvin smiled, nodded, turned, and left. He never saw his mother again.

He drove back to Hanna, and from Hanna he drove on to Goshen to see Ernest Alexander. As Calvin took the last turn on State Route 154 before the Goshen village limits, he saw up ahead a parking-lot light that from far off seemed to just hang in the blackness, beckoning him as might a false pole star. So dark was the night he would have missed the roadhouse entrance altogether were it not for someone starting his car and switching on the headlights. He turned in and rolled down his window and looked about. The hard-packed dirt parking lot was full, and he circled around and drove back out the way he had come in. He parked on the road's graveled shoulder, and when he got out, he double-checked he had locked both car doors.

As Calvin crossed the parking lot, a bat passed overhead, and he looked up and followed its path. It crossed beneath the roof eaves of the roadhouse; below, on an unlit and paint-faded sign, he was just able to make out by the parking-lot light the lettering reading ERNEST ALEXANDER, PROPRIETOR and underneath, DANCING WEDNESDAY AND SATURDAY NIGHTS, and then at the bottom, ERNEST'S, ESTABLISHED 1949.

Ernest's was the sole standing wing left from a now-dismantled auction house. Between the World Wars, however, it had been the commercial center for the farmers in south county. Not every week, nor even every month, but on two or, at best, three special occasions a year, a farmer, following a day's work and after supper, would pack up his wife and children in the flivver and drive to the auction house.

Out in the parking lot, the farmer might pull out a ratty change purse and give a nickel to each child for candy. If a boy or girl were old enough, they might walk about on their own, and, if they met, he would spend some of his nickel on the candy she said she liked. When they went home that night, each would take some wonder of someone new, someone not a sibling or from their church or school who they had known all their lives.

Inside the auction house, the farmer's wife would compare the quilts and craftwork to her own at home, and her husband would inspect the livestock and tools and swap lies with the other farmers. Someone might pull out a pint bottle of homemade corn whiskey from his hip pocket, and they would pass it around and none would bother to wipe the mouth of the bottle before taking a drink and passing it on to the next. Someone might point to a family of Mennonites, the father got up like a carny bumpkin in his straw hat and bib overalls and a row of stepladder children strung out behind him, struck dumb with mouths open by some sideshow featuring grisly human disfigurement.

While a few townsmen from Goshen might also be found at the auction house, they would be only backyard farmers and not seriously considered. They were remarkable by their trousers without patches and their unfrayed shirt cuffs, and the countrymen ostracized them with a viciousness appropriate for Gnostics.

For those in south county of a larcenous predilection, the auction house had always been salutary as somewhere they could fence stolen goods and, until the repeal of prohibition, as somewhere safe to sell and purchase bootleg corn whiskey. After World War II, however, there were almost no farmers left, and those who remained were worse off than they had ever been during the Depression. Even the illicit auction-house business fell on hard times. So its owners disassembled it and sold the weathered wood to war millionaires in the East for their dens when rusticity was all the style, except for one wing, which the Alexander brothers from neighboring New Hope had bought and converted to a roadhouse.

Even as a roadhouse, though, it was still somewhere for those of a larcenous predilection to fence stolen goods. When the former bootleggers with their newfound white powder to merchandise were searching for a safe house, they remembered the old auction barn that, while still close to Pittsburgh and Cleveland, was far away from any honest sheriff.

Outside the door to the roadhouse Calvin paid his admission to a middle-aged dwarf seated on a brown metal folding chair behind a raised card table. He put Calvin's dollar in a cigar box and handed him back a red ticket already torn in two. The dwarf nodded in acquiescence, and Calvin turned and walked down a tunneled entrance lined with sawdust.

When he reached the bar at the end of the tunnel, he stood a moment and looked about. Many sitting at the tables were old, or at least worn out old, holdouts from an agrarian society played out thirty years before. Their clothes worn thin, their eyes devoid of hope. One man with a gray, spittle-thickened beard looked deep into his glass, suggesting his misspent life was somewhere at the bottom. The younger patrons were the recapitulations of their elders, but they nonetheless eyed him as he stood in the entranceway, the light behind him, with the same suspicion they accorded all outsiders. The barman looked at Calvin as he reached under the bar, but he may only have been drying his hands. Behind the bar was a staircase, but no room where Ernest might have his office.

Calvin walked up to the barman and ordered a whiskey with water back. He walked with his drinks to the same table where he and John Rogers had always sat. To his left was a pool table covered by a tarpaulin splotched with paint. Next to it was a pay telephone.

Calvin listened to the country-western band playing until the end of its set. Their lead singer was trying hard to imitate Charlie Daniels, but was not much good. When they broke, Calvin finished his whiskey and washed it down with the glass of ice water that tasted like nickels and walked back outside.

As the dwarf listened he studied Calvin's hands or looked over the table and down at his shoes. He searched Calvin's eyes. When he seemed satisfied, he pointed to a flight of stairs hidden in the shadows from the parking-lot light. "Be careful," the dwarf hissed at his back. "The way is treacherous."

Calvin walked up the set of stairs to the first landing slowly as he had only the light from inside the bar, and every second or third step was missing or deeply cracked. He turned from the landing and walked up the second set of steps that led to a low door to what had once been a hayloft. At the top landing outside the door there was no railing to prevent someone who might lose their balance, accidentally or not, from falling twenty feet and being impaled on the picket fence below.

Pale light slivered from between the weathered wood siding, and Calvin heard a murmur of voices from men whose lives and livelihoods depended upon their not being heard, upon their failing to be understood. Calvin stood to the right of the door on the top step and knocked. "Mr. Alexander," he said, neither loud nor soft, but as clear and steady as he could make his voice.

The voices inside fell silent. A zipper unfastened. A drawer opened and closed. Calvin looked down over his shoulder at the gray picket fence pointing at him.

"Mr. Alexander," he said and knocked again. "It's Calvin Samuels, Mr. Alexander. Mark's lawyer." He waited a few seconds before adding, "Mark. Your nephew?"

After a moment a voice said, "Come in," and it, too, was neither loud nor soft.

Calvin stooped to enter the door. In the shadows before him, behind a never-painted handmade pine table, sat two men, their hands in the shadows beneath the table. Above and behind them hung a low-wattage light bulb covered by a wire cage so that when the balers threw in the hay they would not break a burning bulb and set the barn on fire. The light bulb hung above a floor door leading to the steps he had seen below behind the bar. Calvin watched as the door closed upon a woman with long, crow-black hair, her back to him. She disappeared as Lucifer might in some childish nightmare.

"Mr. Alexander?" Calvin said, looking from one man to the other.

Neither spoke for a moment, but finally the older of the two said, "Yes, what is it, Mr. Samuels? Is there something I can help you with, sir?"

He wore a mustache and a goatee that must once have been soot black. With the light behind them, both men looked flat, all face and front, cutout men with no substance to them. The voice of the man addressing him now—the older man—was not the voice of the one who had invited him to enter. The first voice was neither hard nor soft, but it was one out of Creek County. This one, the older voice, came from somewhere out of the South, out of a hard learned courtesy where all adult men are addressed as "sir" beneath a pretended graciousness.

"My name is Calvin Samuels. I'm your nephew Mark's lawyer."

"Yes, Mr. Samuels. I know of you. Mark called me from jail several days ago and told me to expect you." He placed his hands upon the table before him and folded them. "How is it I can help?"

"I need to talk to you."

"Yes. Yes, of course you do."

"Alone, if I could."

Ernest looked at Calvin for a moment before turning to the other man. "Perhaps, Rock, you should ensure that our guests downstairs are being well taken care of."

The younger man, his hair close-cropped, and his full beard carefully trimmed, watched Calvin as he took his hands from his pockets and zipped up his jacket. Without speaking a word, he rose and walked toward the light bulb and bent over. As he opened the floor door that led to the steps below, the shadows between the cracks of the floorboards shifted. He looked at Calvin once more before he, too, disappeared into the floor, his right hand holding the door as he walked down the steps, watching Calvin, stopping for a moment, and then closing the door overhead, and when he let go of the floor door, it fell half a foot, raising a small cloud of ancient hay dust and desiccated rat feces.

Ernest opened up his hands. "We're alone now," he said. "Tell me how is it you believe I can help you help my nephew?"

"You know, of course, that the reason Mark's in jail is because he's charged with murder. Two murders, in fact."

"Yes, I know that, of course," Ernest said. "Very unfortunate. A very unfortunate business."

"Yes, it is."

"He is . . ." Ernest hesitated, and then he smiled. "He is missed by his friends here, one and all. He has many friends here, you know."

Calvin nodded. "And you know Mark goes to trial for the two murders in only a few weeks. If he's convicted . . ." the shadow beneath the floorboards shifted once again, and Calvin lowered his voice. "If he's convicted, he'll be missed by his friends for a whole lot longer."

"Ah, so time is, how do you lawyers put it, of the essence?"

"Yes. Time is of the essence to Mark. In building his defense."

"What is his defense?"

"He says he was here, with you, recuperating from his car accident. Not out at the Old Church Road farm where the bodies were found."

"Yes, that's true," Ernest said. "I remember that summer well. Three years ago."

"Two years."

"What?"

"The murders were two summers ago."

"Two?"

Calvin nodded.

Ernest smiled. "Ah, you're quite right. So it was. Two summers ago he was here, recuperating in my home from the auto accident he was in with Jimmy Walters."

He smiled and shook his head. "Walters walks away without a scratch, and my nephew is almost killed. Haven't you always found it interesting, Mr. Samuels, the manner in which the Fate sisters twist and spin out our lives for us?"

Calvin didn't answer whether he found the spinning by the three sisters Fate to be of interest, and Ernest continued.

"But I digress, and you didn't come to me for philosophy or lessons in Greek mythology, but for hard facts with which to help my nephew. So, yes, the boy was here. Barely able to walk, he was. Bad shape. Very bad shape. After his release, his friends—the two boys he is accused of murdering, in fact—brought him here. To my home actually, which is behind here, and he was there and sometimes up here for a full month. Perhaps more. But for some considerable time."

"What did Mark do while he was here?"

"At first he didn't leave my home at all. Hardly came out of his bedroom. Mark was in considerable pain and taking Percodan and did little more than sleep for the first couple of weeks. Then, as his pain lessened, some of his friends would come into the bar, go down to my home, and bring Mark back up here. They'd hoist him up on a stool, and he would nurse a beer and watch television. The soaps and the game shows. Flirt with the girls who came in. In time he could again negotiate himself around the pool table."

"Mark would want you to testify to that," Calvin said. "Testify he was here and not down the highway at the farm at the time of the murders."

Ernest nodded and scratched at his beard. "Do you think my testimony is really necessary?"

"From what I've seen, the state doesn't have a great case, but Mark can't simply rely upon that factor if he wants to be acquitted. I've seen Thompson win even bad cases. Mark needs to put on the best case he can. Leave nothing to chance."

Ernest bowed his head. He looked down at the ledger

book that lay opened before him. After a moment he closed the book slowly and looked up. When he spoke, the hardness in his voice had lessened somewhat. "Yes, of course," he said. "I must, but what is it you would want me to say? What is it Mark would want me to say? I wouldn't want to say something . . . something not appropriate."

"Just what happened," Calvin said. "Simple as that. Just what happened. Just what you told me only in much more detail. So much more detail the jury will see him downstairs on a barstool and not out at the farm. From the time he arrived here until the time he left, and where he went when he left."

"Yes. What happened." Ernest tapped the cover of the ledger book with the eraser at the end of his pencil. "Yes, of course."

"For now, Mr. Alexander, why don't you tell me in your own words exactly what happened that summer. From the moment Mark arrived until the minute he left."

Ernest stopped tapping his pencil. He turned around to look at the floor door, but turned back. When he spoke, his voice was not much more than a whisper. "You know, Mr. Samuels, it's been long enough, two years now, that before we speak, maybe I ought to stop in at the jail and talk to Mark a bit. Maybe restore my memory. You know, it's not what it used to be, my memory," he said, and he smiled the faintest of conspiratorial smiles. Just such a smile as Brutus might have smiled on a mid-March afternoon.

Calvin started to speak, but stopped. He, too, looked at the shadows beneath the floorboards. Finally, he said, "Maybe we should talk later, Mr. Alexander."

Ernest smiled. "Yes. An excellent suggestion. We should talk later, you and I. After I speak with Mark. In person. Not over a phone where, who knows, there might be someone listening in."

Calvin rose to leave. "Mark tells me he used to work here."

"Yes. Yes he did. That's true."

"Doing?"

"Doing whatever," Ernest said. "Whatever needed to be done. Cleaning up. Unloading hooch. Moving merchandise."

"Moving merchandise?"

"Yes. This used to be an auction house, you know. And sometimes one of my old time customers will have something he wants sold, so we'll find him a buyer and move it for him."

"How long did this go on? Mark working here."

"Oh, off and on for maybe a year. He's my brother's child, you know. Working here was just a way of getting him some pocket money after he quit college where he should never have gone to begin with." Ernest shook his head. "College kids."

The country-western band began a new set. Calvin looked behind the table and saw below the light the dust rising from the cracks in the floorboards. "I appreciate your time, Mr. Alexander."

"My pleasure," Ernest said, not standing. "Like I told you, he's my brother's child. I'm happy to do what I can for Mark. And for my brother."

"Where's Mark's father?"

"Ah, he's dead, unfortunately. Died right before Mark quit college. A most unfortunate accident. Another one of the queer twists by the sisters Fate. Who knows what causes them to spin what they do. Did some fickleness visit one of them? Who knows? Who can say?" He looked to Calvin for some negation.

"How soon do you think it'll be before you'll get up to County to see Mark?"

"Maybe this coming week. This coming week, if I can. Maybe even tomorrow. As soon as I can get away. Don't worry, Mr. Samuels. I am a man of my word. Truly. I won't let you down. My word is my bond. Truly."

"I'll call."

"Excellent," Ernest said. "We'll speak then."

Calvin opened the door and squatted in the low hayloft door a moment as his eyes adjusted to the darkness. He negotiated the stairs.

"You be careful," Ernest called.

Calvin looked back.

"You could fall," Ernest said. "You could fall and be severely injured. You must be careful."

CHAPTER 31

EARLY THE NEXT morning Calvin drove through the cold, gray Hanna drizzle to the jail where he had to wait for almost a quarter-hour in the visitors' room.

"You can't interrupt their breakfast, for Christ's sake," Smitty said. "We'd have the whole goddamn ACLU down our throats like we did last year. Remember?"

He didn't say whether he remembered, and the deputy took his silence as acquiescence and closed the door behind him on his way out and locked it.

While he waited, Calvin sat on the table, propping his feet up on the seat of a chair. He lit a cigarette and looked out the window. Overnight, a second Canadian front had moved south over Lake Erie, and a cold, persistent rain fell, drowning all hope winter would ever quit. Because of the low clouds, Calvin couldn't even make out the trees opposite on Cemetery Hill, but he sat and looked out the window all the same and waited. His cigarette had burned almost to his fingertips before he heard the jailer's key unlocking the door.

Alexander shuffled into the visitors' room, wearing a different pair of loafers than before, his black hair neatly combed back. Calvin started to speak, but Alexander raised his finger to his lips, and he looked down so as to better hear. After a minute he looked up and smiled. "You're up very early, counselor. You make me optimistic working so early on my defense, and on a Sunday, too. We will enjoy success yet."

Calvin rose from the table and sat in the chair where he had propped his feet. He reached into the pocket of his herringbone jacket, still not dry-cleaned, and pulled out a pack of Marlboros. He laid the pack on the table and pushed it forward. Alexander walked to the table and palmed the cigarettes as dexterously as would a shoplifting child and placed them in the shirt pocket of his jumpsuit. He nodded.

"I didn't rush your breakfast, did I?"

Alexander shook his head. "No, you didn't."

"That's good."

"I don't believe in breakfast, counselor, so it would be an impossible thing for you to rush."

Alexander sat down and, without asking, reached over for Calvin's cigarettes and matches that lay on the opposite table corner. He shook one out and lit it and shoved the pack and matches back. "When I was not here," he said looking around the room. "When I was not in this horrible place, I never rose before noon. Do you believe that?"

"Sure, why not?"

"Lucky if I even had lunch, let alone breakfast. And I would start out my day with a vodka gimlet. The same way many start out with an orange juice. I would start out with a vodka gimlet."

"So I only rushed your beauty sleep."

"No. You didn't."

"Good."

"You didn't because it's impossible to sleep here. At least to sleep soundly. These buffoons are always," and he raised his hand in appeal to the patron saint of prisoners, "being buffoons."

There was just then a loud, long wail from the holding cell above. Alexander looked at Calvin and smiled and shook his head. "That's Walters. He did that all night. I wished they'd quiet him. It makes thinking most difficult. And a man in my circumstances," he said pointing his finger to his temple, "must think."

"I talked to Ernest last night," Calvin said.

"And?"

"Like you said, he remembers two summers ago you staying there for about a month."

Alexander smiled, his black mustache spread wide. "Ah, so you see. It is as I said. An ironclad alibi."

"No," Calvin said. "Not quite so ironclad."

"What do you mean, not quite so ironclad? What's the problem? What's the problem with my alibi?"

"The problem is I suspect your uncle's a little light on details of that summer."

"What kind of details?"

"Details such as the exact dates of your stay. Details such as the names of your visitors during your stay. Details such as what the weather was like. What the wallpaper-print pattern was in the room in which you stayed. How you spent your time. You know, details. Details, in general. The kind Thompson will ask him about. The kind he will ask you about to see if you and Ernest remember the same details. The kinds of details that can split open an ironclad alibi."

Alexander leaned back in his chair and nodded.

"Ernest says he needs to speak to you to refresh his memory about those details. Wants to be certain your stories are consistent."

"Yes," Alexander said. "I can see where consistency might be called for. Where it would be the prudent course here. Where, in this case, it would not be the hobgoblin of little minds."

Calvin shook his head. "Don't even think about it, Mark. Ernest isn't smart enough and neither are you. You might think you are, but you're not. Nobody is. You try to manufacture an alibi, you'll only hang yourself. There'll be too many inconsistencies for you to cover."

"Yes," Alexander said after a minute. "I can see. Details.

The Devil and God inhabit them, they say."

"Yes. Details. And if you tell me you're manufacturing testimony, you hamstring me. I can't call your witnesses. I can only let you testify, and I can't even argue your testimony to the jury."

"Says who?"

"Says the State Bar. I'd lose my license and go to prison along with you. So you and Ernest don't even think about manufacturing testimony."

Calvin began to write in his legal tablet.

"Or perhaps," Alexander said after a while, "Ernest and I should keep our conversation to ourselves so as not to cause you any unnecessary embarrassment."

Calvin looked up, and he and Alexander studied one another. They studied one another for a long time. Finally, Calvin returned to writing in his legal tablet. He hadn't agreed, but he hadn't disagreed. Alexander smiled. From above them came another wail.

"Ah, not to worry," Alexander said. "When I'm able to use the telephone this afternoon, I'll give Ernest a call and invite him up for a chat."

Calvin looked up.

"Just a chat. We'll just put our heads together and remember it all just as it was. Nothing made up. Nothing manufactured." Alexander held up two fingers of his left hand. "Scout's honor."

"Were you ever a Scout?"

"Would it be useful if I had been?"

Calvin tapped his legal pad with his pen. "All the same, another supporting witness would be helpful. Someone else who saw you there would make Ernest's testimony all the more convincing."

Alexander smiled broadly and held his arms out wide. "Hey, counselor, I can get you all the supporting witnesses you need."

"What about Allison? Will she testify you were living at Ernest's and not out at the farm after your accident?"

"I don't know with certainty, but my guess is she would not testify to anything even remotely helpful to me."

"Why's that?"

"I was living at Ernest's right after Allison and I broke up."

"What happened?" Calvin said.

"Before Walters and I wrecked my car, and I ended up at Ernest's, Allison and I were having, shall we say, some problems. I had started to see this other woman. On the side, you might say."

"Jocelyn?"

"Yes."

"Go on."

"Jocelyn was, until then, Peter's girl. She had stayed with him when he and Taylor pitched their tents by the trailer."

"So how was it that his girlfriend came to be your girl-friend?"

"Well," Alexander said. "For a couple of months before

the accident, Jocelyn and I kept running into each other pretty regularly. When Peter and Taylor were gone, she'd stay at her mom's in Weirton. In fact, I was the one who introduced them, Peter and Jocelyn, but I would still see her at bars and parties and such. You know. We'd met at a party some years ago. See each other every once in a while. Then we started seeing each other more and more often. I took her home a couple of times."

"And Allison suspected."

"Oh, yes. She suspected. Whatever else Allison might be, stupid she is not. I wouldn't get back until sometime in the afternoon of the next day. Told her that I'd stayed at a friend's house."

"And she wasn't buying it."

"When she'd go with me to parties and bars and Jocelyn would be there, Allison would see how she'd be hanging all over me."

"What about Bonner? Didn't he suspect?"

Alexander laughed and shook his head. "Peter was my friend and a nice guy, but he was about as bright as a rock. He couldn't tell you the day of the week if he were singing a hymn while kneeling in a pew."

"So what happened to set Allison off?"

"I was in the hospital for about a week. Allison came to visit once, and Jocelyn sat on the bed next to me. Poor timing on our part."

"And she was upset over that."

"Very. Big-time. So after my hospital discharge, Jocelyn and I stayed at Ernest's. So, to answer your question, no, Allison would not testify that she ever saw me at Ernest's. The further from the farm, the less likely it is she would testify that she saw me there, whether she did or not."

"And Jocelyn will testify to this. That she stayed with you at Ernest's after your hospital discharge?"

"Not a problem."

"Will she talk to me?" Calvin said as he wrote.

"Counselor, she will do anything you ask. That I can promise you. Anything at all."

Calvin looked up from his legal tablet. Alexander smiled and winked and licked his upper lip with his tongue.

"When will you see her again?"

"Today is visiting day. She'll be here from two to four. If she knows what's good for her. And I think she does by now."

"Can you ask her to stop by the PD office tomorrow afternoon? I'll be in trial tomorrow, so sometime after four."

"You got it."

Calvin looked down at his tablet a moment and smiled and shook his head. "Well, Mark, I think we're through for the day. I've another client to talk to. So unless there's something else, I'll give you an update next time I'm up."

As he rose from his chair, Alexander said there was nothing else he could think of for them to discuss. He raised his index finger to his temple to salute Calvin before turning and ringing for the guard. After the guard had led Alexander away and shut the door behind them, Calvin stared at it for a long time. After some minutes he stood and walked downstairs and asked Smitty to bring up another client.

CHAPTER 32

CALVIN STOOD JUST to the side of the window in the Public Defender's Office looking out, his hands sunk deep into his trouser pockets. The rain that had begun almost two days before had finally stopped sometime after noon. It was still cold, though, more the false spring of March than the promise of May. As he waited he watched the village green across the street from the courthouse now circled by empty parking spaces. The courthouse clock struck four-fifteen. Calvin pulled his hand from his pocket and checked his watch and continued to study the street below.

Some minutes later, a 1974 Chevelle, over-painted flat black with headers but no hubcaps, pulled into one of the empty parking spaces. Out of the passenger's side door stepped a woman with thick, henna brown hair. She wore a half-halter-top and very short jean shorts, and when she bent over to speak to the driver, even from the distance between them, Calvin blinked at the fleshiness of her bottom cheeks.

After a minute, the woman handed the jeans jacket she carried beneath her arm through the passenger's side window. She turned and jaywalked across Court Street before she disappeared from view in her walk alongside the courthouse. The black Chevelle backed out and sped off, skidding sideways, back in the direction from where it had come.

Calvin heard the rear courthouse door open and close three floors below, and he listened to the jangles tapping up the stair steps. There was a knock on the opened hallway door followed by "hello."

He walked from where he stood beside the window to the anteroom door. "Jocelyn?"

The woman nodded and pulled at the legs of her jean shorts to somehow hide even a little of the fleshiness of her thighs. In her platform shoes she stood almost as tall as he, her face cadaverous white under makeup so thick it cracked like sizing.

"I'm Calvin Samuels," he said. "Please. Come in."

Jocelyn looked about the anteroom. "Where's everybody at?" she said when she seemed satisfied there was no one else there.

"Gone home. County pretty much closes up at four o'clock."

She raised her eyebrows and smirked. "Must be nice. Maybe I should get me a job here."

"Please, come in and have a seat," Calvin said, and he

walked back to the chair behind his desk.

She walked into his office and again looked about before she sat in one of the chairs before the desk. "Mind if I smoke?"

"Please," Calvin said.

She had no purse, but carried her cigarettes and lighter in her hand. She lit a cigarette and without offering one to Calvin laid the pack and lighter on the chair adjacent. When he handed her an ashtray, she set it next to her cigarettes and slouched back in the chair. When she exhaled, she made no effort to blow the smoke anywhere but into Calvin's face. "So what is it I can do for you?"

Calvin smiled. "You're not from around here, are you?"

Jocelyn frowned through the smoke. "Nope. Are you kidding me? Weirton is more than enough of a hick town for this girl. But Hanna?" she said, and looked out the window shaking her head. "I'm afraid I'd be just too much for poor little Hanna. Preachers' wives would be throwing hissy fits about my hussying their men before the first week was out."

"You're originally from Weirton?"

"Yeah. Sure am."

She sat with her legs crossed at the knees, and when she spoke she fidgeted her right foot up and down.

"Long drive to Hanna, isn't it? From Weirton."

She shrugged and tipped her cigarette.

"Did you drive up alone?"

"Yeah. Sure did," she said. "Just me, all by my lonesome. Kind of hate the thought of driving back tonight, though. By myself and all, you know."

Calvin nodded. "The reason I wanted to talk to you is that we need to back up Mark's alibi. He says you were with him two summers ago, beginning just about the time he got out of the hospital after his car accident. Sound about right to you?"

"Yeah. That's right. That's about when we got together. Right after he got out of the hospital."

"When the two of you were staying at his Uncle Ernest's?"

"Huh-huh."

"You want to tell me about that summer?"

"Just what do you want to know, honey?"

"Let's start with your seeing Mark before his accident."

"What about it?"

"Mark was, up to then, still living with Allison, right?"

"You mean the bitch? What if he was?"

"What about it?"

"He was going to tell her to take a hike anyway."

"Was he?"

"He'd been talking about it for a month. Maybe more. I don't know what was taking him so long to give her the boot."

"Did he give you a reason for breaking it off?"

"Yeah," Jocelyn said. "He did. You've been eyeballing her for the last five minutes."

"So he broke it off over you."

"Yeah. That and Mark said she was smarter than him, which he didn't care for."

"Did he say why?"

"Said it was a good way for him to end up dead. Or in jail. Either dead or in jail. Funny he said that, don't you think? Either dead or in jail."

"Is she? Is she smarter than Mark?"

"Don't know. Only talked to the bitch once."

"Just once?"

"Yeah," Jocelyn said. "Just once. At the hospital."

"Sparks flew, did they?"

"Did they ever, honey."

"What happened?"

"She come into his hospital room and saw me sitting on the bed with Mark. Well, the bitch lost it. Out and out lost it. She come at me, and if Preacher hadn't been there to hold her back, I'd of taken her bitch head off."

"Preacher?"

"Yeah. Mikey Boy."

"Why do you call him 'Preacher'?"

"On account of him sending away and getting his preacher's license from the State of West Virginia. Did it as a joke. Said they didn't even ask him if he believed in God, which he don't." Jocelyn laughed. "Ain't that a kick in the butt?"

"Mikey Boy got a last name?"

She shrugged. "Ask Mark. Guess it was him that married . . ."

"Married?"

"Forget it. Nobody you'd want to know."

Calvin waited for her to add something more, but she didn't. "Okay," he said after a while. "So Mark leaves the hospital, and you go with him. Right?"

"Yeah."

"And you go straight to Ernest's from the hospital. No side trips."

Jocelyn shook her head. "One tiny side trip."

"Where?"

"Back to the trailer in Davis's Corner where Mark and her'd been playing house, so we could collect his stuff."

"I thought Mark's Camaro was totaled in the wreck?"

"It was, but he borrowed Bonner's pickup."

"Bonner's pickup?"

"Yeah. White one," she said. "Ford, I think. Bonner and Heath drove in separate cars to the hospital the day Mark was discharged. Bonner loaned the pickup to us so Mark could pick up his stuff before Allison burned it."

"Burned it?"

"That's what the bitch said she was going to do if he didn't come and get it. Immediately, she told him."

"What happened?"

"When we got there, she already had his stuff stacked up in front like she was fixing to make a bonfire of it."

"What did Mark do?"

"When he saw all his stuff piled up like that, he got real mad and told me to stay in the truck, which I did, but I could still tell one helluva fight was going on in the trailer. Finally, he comes out and points at me and tells me to stay where I was, and Bonner gets out and packs up Mark's stuff. And about that time Heath arrives and in a few minutes we was gone."

"To?" Calvin asked.

"Mark's Uncle Ernest's. Aren't you listening?"

"Do you remember when all this happened? What time of the summer?"

"Late July. Early August, I guess."

Calvin nodded. "Do you remember ever going out to the Old Church Road farm that summer?"

"Oh, sure," she said. "Lots of times. I'd go out there for parties and stuff before Mark's accident. A lot of us went out there."

"And after his accident?"

Jocelyn shook her head. "Not until a couple of weeks after we got to Ernest's. Maybe longer."

"Were Bonner and Heath there after Mark's accident? At the farm?"

"No. Last time I seen them was when they dropped off me and Mark and Mark's stuff at Ernest's."

"Do you know where they went?"

"Somebody at the farm said they'd gone to Florida."

"Do you remember who? Who it was who told you?"

"No. Just some kid who was hanging out there."

"Before he went to Florida, weren't you living with Bonner in a tent by the trailer?"

"Yeah," Jocelyn said. "What if I was? You some kind of preacher, too?"

"No, but didn't Bonner care about his girl moving in with his buddy?"

"No," she said and laughed. "He didn't know, and he was so strung out on coke he didn't suspect. I was going to tell him when he got back, but I never got the chance. Just as well."

"Why's that?"

"Because, honey," she said as she leaned over pushing her breasts into the desktop, "I like men. I like to be with men, and not just the same one all the time. That's so boring—and I hate boring. You know what I mean?"

"Must be hard on you now. With Mark in jail and all."

"Very hard, honey. But I get by. I get by. Do what I gotta do to get by."

"I'll bet you do."

She winked a blue-black-mascara-laden eye at him.

"So you had no suspicions they'd been dumped out at the farm? Bonner and Heath."

"Nary a one. Not until I read it in the papers."

Jocelyn picked up her cigarettes. "I've heard rumors of a possible third murder," Calvin said. "You hear anything?"

"Nope. Bonner and Heath are the only two hit-vics I've heard of."

"Is there anyone who used to hang out at the farm you haven't seen since?"

She looked across the desk to Calvin's legal tablet for a moment before she answered. "You know, now that you mention it, there was this guy."

"What guy?"

"Used to hang out some with Walters," she said.

"You remember his name?"

"Don't know if I ever heard it. Had a nickname, though. Some pirate nickname Mark gave him. Like Bluebeard or Captain Kidd or something. But funny sounding."

"Funny sounding?"

"Yeah. Now what was it Mark used to call him? Funny name. Funny kid, too." She shook her head. "Maybe it'll come to me." She smiled at Calvin. "Maybe, after I have a drink."

"Maybe. So how long were you two at Ernest's?"

"About a month I guess."

"You and Mark have your own room?"

"Yeah. That's right."

"Go anywhere for that month?"

"Nope. Neither of us. Not even out to buy cigarettes. After a while, Mark would go up to Ernest's, but other than that, nope. Ernest and Denver—that's Mark's aunt—took care of everything."

"So just the four of you," Calvin said.

"Plus some visitors we had."

"Visitors?"

"Yeah," Jocelyn said. "Some of Mark's friends."

"Mark's friends?"

"Yeah."

"Do you remember their names?"

"John Rock was one."

"What can you tell me about Rock?"

"Used to be president of the Pagans," Jocelyn said. "But he just tends bar for Ernest now."

"Anyone else?"

"Miza Siran."

"Who is?" Calvin asked.

"Jimmy Walter's wife. Common-law wife, anyways."

"Anyone else?"

She shook her head. "No. If I think on it, something might come to me. But I think they was the only two that come down. Mark wasn't real up for visitors, him being all stoved up and everything."

"Have you ever been arrested?"

"Not even a speeding ticket, honey."

"During that summer were you doing drugs?"

Jocelyn shrugged.

"I have to know. Thompson will ask you when you're up on the stand."

"A little coke," Jocelyn said. "A little grass."

"And now?"

"A little."

Calvin sat back and read over his notes. Jocelyn watched him a moment before smiling and again leaning forward over the desk. "I sure could use that drink," she said. "Isn't there someplace you can take me? I really could, you know."

Calvin looked up into her bold eyes.

"Wouldn't have to be a bar or nothing."

After a moment he grinned. He raised his arms as though he meant to stretch, but he winced and rubbed his right arm instead.

"What's the matter, honey?" she asked.

"Nothing, really. My arm's just a bit sore."

"Sore from what?" She smiled. "You need me to rub you somewhere or something? I'd be glad to do it for you."

"Just a shot I got yesterday."

"A shot?"

"Yeah. Penicillin. A million units. Doc said that should be the last one, though. So long as it doesn't come back."

CHAPTER 33

AFTER JOCELYN LEFT, Calvin stood again just to the side of his window looking out until he heard the back courthouse door open and close. She must have walked some other direction from the way she had come because he didn't see her cross the street. After he'd waited and watched several minutes more, Calvin locked up and walked again up the hill.

When he reached the jail, the prisoners had already eaten their evening meal. Some were outside in the exercise yard where they gathered in groups of threes and fours talking among themselves. One was hitting a plastic ball with a plastic bat. When Calvin inquired, the night jailer pointed toward the gray stadium bleachers where Alexander sat alone, watching the other prisoners who stood away from him on the opposite side of the exercise yard. Calvin walked out the back door and across the muddy field. He had almost reached the bleachers before Alexander took notice of him, and when he did, he betrayed no sign of surprise.

"Counselor," he said and raised his hand. "To what do I owe the privilege of two visits in two days?"

Calvin didn't answer.

"I remain impressed. Your dedication to my case makes me believe that we will truly prevail, that we can truly persevere."

Calvin walked up the bleacher seats and sat down next to Alexander. "Jocelyn just left."

Alexander cocked his head and nodded, but said nothing.

"I thought you'd like to be kept posted as to how your defense is proceeding."

Alexander reached into the chest pocket of his jumpsuit and pulled out the near empty cigarette pack. "Indeed."

"Outwardly, on its face, not bad. We have two witnesses who can corroborate that from the middle of July to the middle of August you were either in the hospital or at Ernest's. Today I received your hospital records confirming your stay."

"What's the problem?" Alexander said. "There must be one. Otherwise you wouldn't be working so hard in my defense. Am I not right?"

"The problem is that we have your testimony about having been at Ernest's. We have Ernest corroborating your testimony. We now have Jocelyn corroborating the testimony of both of you."

"Outwardly then, on its face, as you say, there would

seem to be no problem. Yet there must be one or you wouldn't be spending your time with me," Alexander said, and then he smiled and winked. "And not with someone else."

"The problem is the Pagans."

"What about them? They're just my beer buddies."

"To start with, their name doesn't help," Calvin said. "Not in Creek County, it doesn't. If it weren't for your friendship with the Pagans, our chances of success would increase. Considerably. But because of them, our chances decrease. Considerably."

"Why considerably?"

"You're going to have twelve jurors, all of whom will consider themselves Christians after a fashion. Even if they haven't been inside a church in years, they're going to consider themselves Christians. And Thompson will be painting for them a picture of motorcycles, drugs, booze, guns, sex, and hedonism run rampant."

"Yes," Alexander said. "I can see the truth of what you're saying. What's your suggestion?"

"Any Pagans who might make a good appearance before a jury? Convince them they're not a bunch of twowheeled thugs. Just a bunch of working class stiffs who only play at Hell's Angels and drink beer on the weekend."

Alexander dragged on his cigarette. He turned back to Calvin. "Talk to Rock. He will know of someone."

"Jocelyn mentioned Rock."

"Used to be president of the Pagans. Now he just tends

bar for my uncle."

"How do I get him to talk to me?"

"I'll have Jocelyn set it up."

The jailer walked outside from the recreation room and put two fingers to his teeth and whistled and waved the prisoners in. Alexander said he had to go, and he rose and walked down the bleacher steps and on across the mud field.

Even after the prisoners had all gone in, Calvin continued sitting in the bleachers. He lit a cigarette and watched the last of the sunset and listened to the wind whisper to him through the cracks in the stone walls. A long wail came from the jail tower. It was followed by shouts from below and then silence.

Calvin flicked his cigarette away. He stood and walked to the back jail door and then out and back down to the courthouse.

CHAPTER 34

THE FOLLOWING EVENING, Calvin pulled into the empty gravel parking lot behind the Goshen Police Department. Although he had called ahead, the station did not appear to be open. The building was dark inside, and after he got out of his car, he stood there studying the windows. Just enough daylight remained for him to read the inscription above the windows and beneath the roof eaves:

WORKS PROGRESS ADMINISTRATION

1936

He walked up a brick stoop to the back entrance, knocked, waited, stood on his toes, and looked through the six-inch-square door window. Calvin stepped back and studied the adjacent houses. There were no lights on inside. Even the streetlights were dark when they should have been burning thirty minutes before. From the surrounding houses came no sounds of televisions or radios, and although there was considerable stillness and mugginess, there was not even a whirl from a window fan.

He went to his car and opened the door and leaned three times on the horn. He walked back up the stoop and knocked again until flecks of blood speckled his knuckles. "Come out with your hands up," he yelled.

In a minute a blind in the corner window twitched, and in a minute more the door cracked open. Big Jim Walker stood inside, holding his hand to his mouth covering a yawn. He told Calvin to get the hell inside and to stop making so much goddamn racket. After he came in, Walker shut and re-bolted the door, and Calvin followed him down a hallway. From somewhere in the station came the chatter of a police radio.

"Village trying to cut down on its electric bill, is it?"

"No," Walker said. "I'm afraid it'd take more than turning off the lights around here to balance our budget. No, the storm that marched through here half an hour ago knocked our power out. Radio's on emergency batteries."

At the end of the hall Calvin followed Walker into an office. Walker sat down in a swivel chair behind a gray metal, coffee-stained desk, and he proffered a two-finger wave for Calvin to sit in the lone other chair. Save for a wire basket on top of the desk half filled with out-of-date police dispatches, only partly covering a woman's exposed breasts on a magazine cover, the desk and office walls were bare.

"You the only one on duty in the evenings now?" Calvin said.

"Yeah, and the village aunts will likely eliminate even this shift once your client is locked away and the good towns-people aren't scared out of their wits anymore."

"So I guess you'll keep having some overtime once Alexander's acquitted."

Walker shook his head. "You've always been an optimistic sonnuvabitch," he said. "I'll give you that."

Calvin grinned.

"You know I could get canned for talking to you like this."

Calvin nodded.

"I figure I tell you what I know, we're square for you helping me put away that pedophile preacher a couple of years back when you was still was working for Thompson and the good guys."

"I appreciate the risk you're taking."

"Just so you are."

Walker tapped his lower lip with his finger. "But, Calvin, tell me this: why did you ever leave the Prosecutor's Office? You could've been the best of them. Could have taken over for Thompson when he runs for judge someday. None of them other assistants was even interested in taking on the preacher. None of them excepting you."

"You just meet a better quality of people in the PD office."

Walker snorted. "Yeah. Like Alexander, I bet."

Calvin smiled and reached into his jacket pockets. From one pocket he pulled out two juice tumblers, each with a different, faded NFL-team decal, given to him for filling up at the truck stop that used to operate between Hanna and Goshen. From his other pocket he pulled out a pint of Seagram's Seven. He twisted off the bottle cap and filled both tumblers half full and pushed one across the desk. Walker sat up. "Well, well, well. What have we here?"

"To a long life," Calvin said as he raised his glass.

"Long life, Calvin."

The two clinked their glasses. Calvin refilled them and leaned back his chair against the wall behind him. "So what can you tell me about the deaths of Peter Bonner and Taylor Heath?"

Walker sipped at his drink and swiveled back in his chair.

"And I hope you'll embellish the story considerably less than when you last told it down at the Eagles," Calvin said.

"Ah. Now that hurts," Walker said. He pointed his finger at Calvin. "I'll have you know this is the first time, the very first time mind you, I have ever told this story outside of official channels. Ever. And as I said, if I didn't owe you for taking on that preacher who was diddling retarded little girls I wouldn't be talking to you now. Even if we did play ball together once on the Legion team."

"So you just going to whine and drink my whiskey or you going to tell me what happened?"

Walker swirled the whiskey around in his glass. "The regular dispatcher was on her break, and I was filling in. It was a Sunday afternoon. Just. Just a little past noon. Year ago last December. I'd brought in my portable TV from home, hoping it would be a quiet afternoon, so I could just sit and watch the game."

"And no such luck."

"And no such luck is right. I took the call. Tipster said we could find two bodies buried at the Old Church Road farm, beneath where the outhouse used to stand."

"Who do you think your tipster was?"

"No idea," Walker said. "No idea whatsoever."

"Man or woman?"

"Man. Man's voice did the talking anyway."

"Say anything about Alexander?"

"Nope."

Calvin sipped at his whiskey. "Still, could've been someone trying to set Alexander up. Get the ball rolling," he said. "Not seem too anxious. Not expose himself too much at first."

"Could've been."

"Why do you say that?"

Walker put down his drink and stood and walked over to the window and looked out. After a minute he turned back. "The tipster sounded not so young. I'd guess maybe late twenties to mid-thirties. But very matter-of-fact. I'm not certain of this because of the bad connection, but there may have been someone in the background whispering to him, and the whisperer might have been a woman."

"I don't suppose a tape was made."

"No," Walker said. "Maybe next year we'll get the federal funds for it, or maybe the year after; but on that day, no."

"So why'd you believe him? Your tipster."

"I don't know that I believed him, but it was too odd a thing not to take seriously," Walker said. "Oh, we'd been hearing rumors for months about bodies buried out there. Someplace. Started right after the Pagans pulled out of here in August. Bodies buried somewhere out at the farm or weighed down and dropped in Bear Cross Creek. And I thought when I first heard them, yeah, could be."

"Why could be?"

"Because for some weeks them Pagans had been hanging around out there, and we'd been picking up a lot more of our own kids high on dope than we ever did before. A few days before the phone call, we get an inquiry from Flint, Michigan, asking for any leads we might have as to the whereabouts of Bonner and Heath."

Walker thought a moment. "Maybe it was just the voice. I don't think in my life I've ever heard a voice so hard, so cold, talking about bodies. Even when I was in the Army. Talking about killing. Like it was nothing to him."

"So you get the call on a Sunday last December, just after noon, and you go out with the village backhoe," Calvin said.

"Yeah. Tracked down and got one of our maintenance boys out of bed and notified the Sheriff's Office, and off we went."

Walker chuckled. "I'll tell the world, old Jackson was none too happy about being rolled out of the nice warm bed he was sharing with Betty Mailer on a cold Sunday afternoon just so he could go dig up where an outhouse used to stand."

"Is she the one they call Knockers Mailer?"

"The same."

"Well, I guess Jackson's attitude is an understandable one to hold," Calvin said.

"So me and Jackson are out there with Sheriff Conkle, and we're finding nothing. Because we had about two feet of snow on the ground, we wasn't even sure at first exactly where the outhouse had been. Seems like somebody had burned it down, along with a few other small buildings. Then the dispatcher radios us after we'd been out there digging for a couple of hours. Says she just got a phone call telling her we was digging in the wrong place and to move closer to the house. Sure enough. Five minutes later we hit pay dirt."

"What you'd find?"

"Most of a skull. Turned out to be Bonner's. We kept on digging. Brought out a dump truck to take all the dirt and bones and excrement back to the village garage to be sifted later."

"You see anybody drive by while you were out there digging?"

"Nope," Walker said.

"Your tipster seemed helpful."

"Yeah. Well, like I said, when I talked to him he seemed real intent on helping us find the bodies."

"Think he might have been watching you from Harry Katz's?"

"That's the Sheriff's suspicion, but that's all it is. Just a hunch."

"Is Katz gone now?"

"We think so. Haven't been able to track him down yet anyway."

Calvin pulled out his bottle and refilled their glasses. "What can you tell me about Bonner and Heath?"

"Not much. Bonner was born in nineteen fifty-five or -six; I forget which, up in Flint. Vice president of his senior class, they said. Graduated in nineteen seventy-four. Michigan folks told us Bonner was the All-American boy 'til a brain injury he'd gotten playing football changed him somehow. Altered his personality is what they said."

"What happened to him after high school?"

"Attended Ferris State in western Michigan before going to work for his daddy in the plumbing business."

"Ferris State?"

"That's where Thompson thinks he first hooked up with your guy."

"How long it take you to identify Bonner?" asked Calvin.

"We was able to ID him right off the bat. Within a couple of days, after we got his dentals."

"And Heath?"

"He's been the real bitch for us. Still don't know whose all bones were in there with Bonner's."

"They're not Heath's?"

"Coroner says they're not."

"So you have a third victim?"

"Looks that way."

"What seems to be the problem with identifying them?" Calvin said.

"Problem's been we just don't have enough of him, or her, to make an identification. At first we thought the only part of the second body we'd found was an upper arm bone, and we didn't even know if it belonged to a guy or a gal."

"That can make it tough, all right."

"Another thing making it tough is there was these damned animal bones mixed in with the human ones."

"Animal bones?"

"Yeah. You might recall reading how the *Hanna Morning Journal* was making out like we had some kind of satanic cult running around down here sacrificing animals and people and aliens and such. Probably because the name of the gang is the Pagans and all. But it was just critters out there that got to gnawing away."

Calvin shuddered and took a long drink from his tumbler. "That's a sweet thought."

"You know what else was strange, too?" Walker said.

"You tell me what isn't strange about this case."

"We was certain, I mean we was dead certain, Bonner and Heath was just two no good for nothing dope dealers down here poisoning our youth. Turns out, though, Heath was calling his mom every day up in Flint from Ernest's. Told her that him and Bonner was down here on vacation.

What do you make of that?"

"Goshen, the garden spot of Appalachian Ohio," Calvin said. "Any of the regulars at Ernest's able to shed any light here?"

"Well, we all knew the locals who'd been hanging out at the farm that summer. You know, the town burnouts."

"Doesn't narrow it down much from the general population, does it?"

"And it's your guy's name that keeps cropping up with the burnout crowd over and over again as Mr. Numero Uno. They tell us he ran the whole show out there that summer."

"And of course you checked him out."

Walker nodded.

"And?"

"The West Virginia Smokies tell us your guy is the president of the Pagans."

"And?"

"And they also tell us you don't get to be the Pagan president by kissing babies. You've got to of wasted some Pagan enemies. The more, the better. The nastier done the better."

"So where's Thompson taking the investigation?" Calvin said.

"Like I was saying, we still don't know if the bones the coroner has is Heath's. The jawbone we have don't match his dentals. Some of the burnouts are saying it's really some local who was out there at the time Bonner and Heath was killed, and Alexander decided he could do better with one less witness. So he murdered all three and dropped them in the outhouse."

"Bizarre."

"Oh, it gets better, good buddy. Later that night there was a wedding and party out there with all of them Pagans in attendance and with the outhouse still smoldering."

"Have the burnouts given you a name for the local they say was killed out there?"

"Nothing," Walker said.

"John Rogers's name come up at all?"

"Not yet."

Calvin nodded. "So Thompson's theory is that Alexander did in Bonner and Heath for money and drugs?"

"Could be. But the Michigan folks also said they suspect Bonner and Heath might have double-crossed the Detroit mob, and maybe they hired your guy to teach them a lesson."

"What's your theory?"

"My own suspicion is Alexander mostly wanted the Miami-to-Detroit drug run all for hisself."

Calvin swirled his whiskey around the bottom of his glass. "You know, Jim, I'm feeling better and better about this case. Sounds to me like there were a whole lot of people with a motive to do in Bonner and Heath."

"Yeah, that's true. There was lots of people with a motive, but that's true with most murders because most victims are not nice people themselves. It almost always comes down to who had the most motive and the best opportunity. And your guy had both the most motive and certainly the best opportunity for doing them in."

"When did their families last see them?"

Walker scratched his chin. "Well, as to Bonner, I don't recall if I ever did know. But Heath's family said they last saw him just a couple of weeks before he turned up missing. He was home for a family reunion when Bonner calls and tells Heath to get the hell back down here. Last time his folks talked to him was a couple of weeks later. Collect call from Ernest's."

"What about their vehicles?"

"What about them?"

"Were they ever found?"

"Nope. Not yet anyway."

"Alexander have any priors?" Calvin asked.

"No prior convictions, but he was tried and acquitted for a nineteen seventy-seven knifing murder in back of the Club Paddock across from the track down in Weirton."

"Who'd he knife?"

"Just some lowlife doper who didn't want to pay Alexander the freight for the merchandise. Your guy stabbed him in the heart when he wouldn't pay up. Same way Walters is telling Thompson your guy did in Heath. Stabbed him, and after he stabbed him, he snapped off the handle with the knife blade still in his heart."

"So how'd Alexander get off the first time?" Calvin said.

"D.A. down there suspects some jury intimidation. Early-morning telephone calls. Following their kids home from school."

"What about Walters? When'd he get out of town?"

"Soon after the murders," Walker said. "Trouble was he kept calling his mom when she was down at Ernest's."

"No?"

"Yep. So Conkle arranged for a number tracer."

Calvin pulled at his whiskey. He looked out the window for a moment. "You know, there's one thing that just doesn't add up in all of this."

"What thing's that?"

"Why did Bonner and Heath pick Goshen to hang out? You're not even on the AAA maps. They stuck out down here like sore thumbs."

"I wondered that, too, and you know what I come up with?"

"No. What?"

"If you think of Bonner and Heath as just two party boys, you're right. Goshen don't make a whole lot of sense. But if you think of them as astute businessmen, it was perfect."

"How so?"

"After almost four days of straight driving up from Miami, this is a place for them to stop before their last leg up into Michigan."

"So?"

"So remember, the most dangerous part of their job is the delivery, and they needed to be sharp as tacks for that."

"Why the most dangerous?" Calvin asked. "They were just delivering it to their bosses."

"No way. Their bosses weren't as stupid as all that. They didn't want to be anywhere near that white powder if they could avoid it. No, when they ran the coke into Detroit, they were delivering it to the buyers it'd been promised to. When they got the money and gave it to their bosses, that's when their run up from Miami ended."

"Why so long a drive up from Miami?"

"Because they were becoming a little too well known to the DEA boys. They didn't even take the state routes, let alone the interstate."

"What'd they do?"

"Drove the county roads," Walker said. "Some were just gravel paved. Just."

"Jesus."

"Yeah, no kidding. Jesus. They was driving roads that often as not wasn't marked along a route that must of taken them at least three months of trial-and-error to work out. At least."

"Who'd have thought of it from a couple of dopers?" Calvin asked.

"And it must of been a good route for them, too, because there's no record of them ever being stopped. If they ever had trouble with any of their competitors, you'd of never found out where they was buried. But it had to be one mean bitch of a route that would've required their full-time attention for four days straight. So by the time they reached Goshen, they both must of been exhausted."

"And probably high on coke all the way," Calvin said.

"No, sir. I don't think so. What they told the locals was that while they might do drugs with a vengeance when they partied, they were straight when they worked. Drank only coffee is what they said."

"So how'd Alexander and Bonner hook up again after college?"

"Don't know the answer to that one. I wouldn't be surprised, though, that Bonner and Heath stopped in at Ernest's one time and there he was. Or maybe he had told Bonner about Ernest's, and Bonner knew where to look, but when they did hook up again, Heath was in tow, and Alexander was living in a trailer in Davis's Corner with his girlfriend."

"How long did this go on?"

"For some months in the spring and summer of eighty. They wouldn't stop in Goshen on their way south. Going south they carried no drugs or cash so they could take the Interstate. Cash would be there waiting for them in a locker at Miami International."

"How'd it get there?"

"Detroit mob would wire it to their lawyers, and they'd pass it on."

"So they'd picked up the cash . . ."

"Usually they'd make the buy right there in the airport."

"Then they'd take the long way home."

"And almost always lay over with your guy."

"So what happened?"

"The nearest bar to Davis's Corner was Ernest's. Alexander had taken to wandering in daily with some merchandise for sale. One of his best customers was Psycho Jimmy Walters. One hot afternoon in early July of eighty, Alexander was driving through Goshen in his Camaro convertible. Walters waves him down and suggests they go swimming at Bear Cross Creek out on his granduncle's farm. They went and got a case of beer at Ernest's and both were fairly drunk when Alexander missed a turn on 154. He crashes his Camaro and was hospitalized. When he gets out of the hospital the trailer owner wants him gone, and Walters suggests the farm as a great place for him to recuperate."

"What can you tell me about John Allen Rock?" Calvin said.

"Runs Ernest's."

"And?"

"Not much else that I know of. Not now leastways I know of. Better not be."

"What about before?" Calvin said.

"Before, he was in Lucasville. Still on parole."

"What was he in for?"

"Manslaughter. Supposed to have been president of the Pagans, but when I talked to him one time about it during the investigation he denied it. It was just about the time when he went off to prison that Alexander took over so Rock has a credibility issue with me. Since he's gotten out, he's been at Ernest's. Ostensibly tending bar. Anything more, well, it's difficult to speculate. Could be nothing. Then again. He could just be biding his time."

"If Alexander's truly president of the Pagans, I'd think he'd be concerned about a predecessor so close by." Calvin said. "Wouldn't you?"

"A little too suspicious if he was to just turn up deceased, don't you think?"

"Why wouldn't he just tell Rock to move on?"

"What was it L.B.J. used to say? He'd rather have some pain-in-the-ass politician inside his tent pissing out than outside pissing in."

Calvin smiled and shook his head. "What you've been telling me didn't come from Alexander."

"Nope."

"And it didn't come from Walters."

"Nope."

"Bits and pieces from the burnouts?" Calvin asked.

"Bits and pieces."

"But from what you've told me, most of it could only have come from Allison Morris."

Walker sat up. "You didn't hear me say that, Calvin. Did you hear me say that?"

"Thompson loses her credibility, he's lost his case."

Walker didn't answer.

"Wouldn't think she'd be all that difficult to impeach. Living in sin. No doubt using drugs herself. And jilted by her lover, to boot. If she's Ben's big gun, he could be in trouble."

"Or you could," Walker said.

Calvin didn't reply. He may not have heard. He twisted his now empty glass in his palm. He looked up. "That about it, Jimmer?"

"Yeah," Walker said. "No. I take that back. There is one more thing."

"What's that?"

"I'm telling this now to you as a friend. As someone I went to school with. Someone I played ball with. Someone I worked with in the summer baling hay."

"Go ahead."

"Be careful. Alexander's not your ordinary drug punk. Not your ordinary hoodlum. He's not even your ordinary murderer. He's one mean sonnuvabitch. And I'll tell you something else."

Calvin looked across the desk. "Tell me."

"He don't forget. Nothing. And he don't forgive. Anything. You lose his case, you better hope he dies in the penitentiary."

CHAPTER 35

THE FOLLOWING EVENING Calvin was standing at his desk in the Public Defender's Office packing his briefcase to go home when the telephone rang. Jocelyn, all honey spent now from her voice, told him John Allen Rock would be working tomorrow. At Ernest's. Then she hung up without so much as a goodbye.

Calvin looked at the receiver. "Lord," he said to it. "A person would think I actually gave you the clap from the way you're behaving." He shook his head. "Women. Go figure."

The next morning Judge Biltmore was holding arraignments. Each month arraignment day shortly followed the adjourning of the Creek County grand jury. The prisoners had only been picked up over the weekend, and they still looked befuddled when the deputies herded them into the courtroom wearing their overly large, orange county jumpsuits, shackled and shuffling their feet so as not to lose one of their laceless work boots or sneakers.

Two deputies escorted the thirty-one prisoners into the courtroom. Some, with no sense of irony, sat in the jury box, and the rest in the gallery. There they waited until the bailiff called their cases, waited in silence except for one halfwit boy who for a while addressed everyone and no one until one of the deputies rose and stood before him and slapped his baton in the palm of his hand until the halfwit, too, fell silent.

Thompson was sitting at first counsel's table and Calvin at the table behind. Judge Biltmore called each case in turn, beginning with the A's. As each prisoner stood, Calvin approached him, notepad in hand. In a whisper he introduced himself and told his new client to say nothing more than to enter a plea of not guilty, promising to meet with him as soon as he could, probably no more than a day or so.

A few prisoners shook their heads and said no, they wanted to enter their guilty plea today, not understanding they would get home no sooner, and Calvin had to prevail upon them to wait. They could reach a better deal later if they would only wait and play hard to get.

Thompson would recommend either bail or a recognizance release. If Thompson recommended bail Calvin would ask his client if he could make the bail amount, if he supported a family, and if he held down a job. Judge Biltmore followed Thompson's recommendation for all of the prisoners, except for one for whom he ordered bail rather than recognizance.

The arraignments dragged on from late morning past the dinner hour and on into the afternoon, and it was almost three o'clock before they finished and after four before Calvin pulled once again into Ernest's parking lot. He walked down the tunnel entrance, past the advertisements from decades before of brands of soda pop and cigarettes and patent medicines no longer sold, here or elsewhere.

When he reached the bar entrance, Calvin stood there a moment, his eyes gauging the shadows just beyond. Out of them he heard the murmur of voices and then the ivory crack of pool balls, and he turned. In the back stood two pool shooters. They were wearing dark business suits, rare in Goshen even on Sundays. They had removed their coats and carefully draped them over a chair, but had not loosened their ties. One shooter was leaning over the table and measuring his shot. The other was chalking his cue and studying Calvin. Their eyes locked, but each looked away to watch the other shooter. Overhead, a ceiling fan churned the muggy, early-summer heat. His tan poplin suit coat slung over his shoulder and his tie loosened, he watched their game for a minute, sweat beading on his forehead. It was more than the heat making Calvin sweat, however.

The pay telephone hanging by the pool table rang. The shooters looked at each other before the one chalking his cue stopped and leaned it against the table and picked up the receiver, his back to Calvin, his voice silent. From the kitchen behind the bar, drying his hands on a tea towel, came the same man who two weeks before had been sitting with Ernest in the hayloft, the same man Calvin had asked to leave.

The bartender looked back toward the telephone. He nodded to the shooter still standing beside the pool table, and turned to Calvin. He was wearing black jeans and a black T-shirt with a pack of cigarettes rolled up in his left sleeve. Under his sleeve rode the tattoo of a coiled serpent, forked tongue protruding from its mouth, wrapped around a panther, squeezing its life out. Beneath the tattoo were the initials USN. "Something I can help you with?" he said. "We're not really open yet. Cleaning up still. Getting ready to open up in about another hour if you care to come back then, unless you're just here for carryout."

The two were about the same height, but the man's chest and arms under his black T-shirt were those of a weightlifter. A prison weightlifter who killed the hours pressing a bent iron-gray bar up and down, back and forth. Hour upon hour. Day after day.

"I'm looking for Rock," Calvin said. "John Allen Rock?"

The man stopped drying his hands. After a moment, he smiled, but there was no welcome in it. His eyes, born of years of seeking and finding the weakness in other men and of hiding his own, never left Calvin. "You got him," he said. "You're Mark's lawyer, ain't you? We met a few weeks back."

Calvin nodded. "That's right. There someplace we can talk?"

Rock pointed with his chin to a table, two tables from the pool shooters. "Why don't you grab us that one over there, and I'll get us some coffees. Fresh brewed. You look like maybe you could use it. Long day?"

"Yeah," Calvin said. "Long day."

He walked back to the table and sat where he could watch both the front door and the shooters. Though they continued with their game, they had ceased speaking, ceased even to call their shots, but pointed with their cue sticks to a ball and to the intended pocket. After a minute Rock returned with two handleless mugs on a tray.

"Thanks," Calvin said. He picked up the mug and sipped at the coffee, quickly setting the mug back on the table and flapping his hands.

"Too hot for you?"

Calvin shook his head. He picked up the mug again, blew and sipped at the rim, and set it back on the table. "You must be a Navy man?"

"Yeah. How'd you know that?"

"The tattoo. The mugs without handles. How long've you been out?"

"Six years. In for six, out now for six."

"Six years is kind of an unusual enlistment stretch, isn't it?"

"Not if you're a nuclear engineer on a sub it's not. It's what they require when you sign up."

"Don't get many of those in Goshen."

"You were maybe expecting a longhaired biker with a

302

beer gut down to his knees?"

"Maybe."

"I've got family just across the river. And after six years on subs with a bunch of guys, well, this is okay. I like it here."

The shooters had stopped their game, though pool balls remained on the table. One sat tipping back a bottle of Coke.

"So how can I help you?"

"Mark's in trouble. I'm sure you've heard."

Rock only nodded.

"What can you tell me?" Calvin said.

"About what?"

"You know he's charged with the murders out at the Old Church Road farm."

"Yeah," Rock said. "I know that."

"And you know Jimmy Walters has pled guilty to conspiracy."

"Yeah. I read it in the papers."

"Mark says he was nowhere near the farm when Bonner and Heath were murdered."

"Where's he say he was?"

"Out back," Calvin said. "Says he and Jocelyn Murphy were staying with Ernest back behind here, and Jocelyn and Ernest back him up. But the more witnesses backing him up, the better."

Rock said nothing.

"Mark says once he got to feeling better, he'd come up here from the house and hold down a stool. Played some pool after a while."

Rock looked over his shoulder at the pool shooters, who were shooting no pool. He turned back to Calvin. "How can I help Mark out?"

"I may need you to testify about what you saw that summer. What you remember."

Rock looked down at his coffee mug and turned it slowly counterclockwise. "Mark says he and Jocelyn were hanging out up here after the accident? Up here in the bar?"

Calvin nodded.

Rock ran his index finger around the rim of his cup. "I do recall seeing Mark that summer," he said. "And I recall seeing Jocelyn."

"Good."

"But what I don't recall is seeing Mark with Jocelyn. Not here. Not in the bar. Not that summer."

"No?"

"No," Rock said. "As I recall, Mark was still seeing Allison Morris that summer."

"Do you remember seeing Mark in here with her?"

"Can't say I saw a whole lot of Mark anywhere that summer; but if I saw anyone with him, it would always have been her, not Jocelyn."

"Yeah?"

"Seems to me the first time I saw Mark with Jocelyn was when he brought her in here on a Sunday, and they was drinking beer and watching a football game. Which would have put it in the fall."

Calvin glanced toward the pool players. The pool players were watching him. "I see," he said.

"Sorry I can't help you. I'm not saying Mark's wrong or lying or nothing, mind you. I'm just saying I don't remember it that way. The way he said it all went down." Rock shrugged. "Maybe he's right."

"Not a problem," Calvin said. He reached into his shirt pocket. "Here's my card. Anything comes to mind, I'd appreciate a call."

"You've got it."

Calvin stood to leave. "So were you a Pagan before you joined the Navy or after you got out?"

"Never was. Not then, not now. Never was."

"No?"

Rock shook his head. "No. Where'd you get the idea I was?"

"Oh, one of the Goshen PD."

"Yeah. Don't surprise me none. I serve so many Pagans, cops just assume I'm one myself, but I'm not."

"Yeah, that sounds like cops. Always jumping to conclusions."

"Yeah, especially the misfits they have here."

"So what are they like? The Pagans."

"Some are okay, some not. They're just weekend bikers."

Calvin nodded. "Well, I need to be getting back, but I do appreciate your time."

"Not a problem."

"Just one more thing, though, before I go."

"Sure," Rock said.

"There was a local boy hanging out at the farm that summer."

"There were too many local boys hanging out there that summer."

"Did you know any of them?"

"A few."

"Did you know John Rogers?"

Rock looked at Calvin's card and turned it over in his hand. "No," he said. "I can't say I did. Was he someone you'd want to talk to?"

"No," Calvin said. "I appreciate your time. Thanks for the coffee."

"Anytime. Come back some Saturday again or even Wednesday, why don't you? We have dancing them nights. Place is packed. Lots of fine-looking women here. Plenty who would be pleased to make your acquaintance."

Calvin said he would. He turned and walked down the tunnel and back to his car.

Rock rose and walked to the window and looked out through the slatted shutters. After a moment he nodded to the shooters. One looked at the other who went to the telephone and dropped in a dime.

"Yeah. He just left. You're on now, sweetheart. So break a leg, will you?" he said. "Break a leg or we may have to do it for you."

CHAPTER 36

THE NEXT MORNING, Calvin was up at the jail interviewing the prisoners who had been arraigned the day before. Even before they had finished their breakfasts of cornbread and beans, Calvin had parked his Volkswagen opposite the jail wall on what would be the shady side of Court Street when he left. All morning and for most of the afternoon he met with almost half of his new clients, listening to their stories and explanations and excuses while he read over their arrest reports, often deciding all too readily which cases to try and which to deal.

It was after five o'clock when he drove back down the hill. He parked in the back parking lot and used his passkey to enter the rear courthouse door. When he reached the third floor, Calvin found the door to the PD office open. In the anteroom sat a thin, pale man, not much older than himself, his hands folded before him like a man in prayer. His overalls were oil-stained, his fingernails broken.

Calvin stood in the doorway. "May I help you?"

The man looked up from his hands slowly, as someone reluctant to surrender his petition, and stood. "Your girl said it'd be okay if I was to wait," he said. "You Mr. Samuels?"

"That's right."

The man held out his hand, dirt and grease embedded deep into the crevices of his knuckles. "I'm Tony Roberts. Jim Walker said you might be wanting to talk to me."

"Oh?"

"My boy, David, was run off the Old Church Road farm two summers back. Jim told me to come on in. Said you'd be wanting to talk to me."

"Yes," Calvin said. "Quite right. I do. Very much so. Actually, it'd be your son David I'd like to talk to if I could, Mr. Roberts."

"I know it, and I told him to come in with me, but he wouldn't do it."

"I see," Calvin said. He turned and shut the door. "Please. Come on back."

After Calvin hung up his coat and loosened his tie, he sat in the chair next to Mr. Roberts. He reached into his shirt pocket for his cigarettes and offered one, but Mr. Roberts held up his hand and shook his head. "No, I'm trying to quit," he said. "On account of David. I don't need him to be picking up any more of my bad habits."

Calvin smiled. "So David's afraid of lawyers, is he?"

"He's afraid of Alexander, Mr. Samuels."

"Has he said anything to you? About what he saw that's making him afraid?"

"David fancies himself a kind of junior private detective," Mr. Roberts said. "Likes to read the Hardy Boys and stuff."

"Yeah. I did, too, once upon a time."

"Yeah, I did, too. In fact, it's my old books he'd been reading that got him into this."

"Oh?"

"Found them up in his grandma's attic. I'd of thought she'd threw them out or give them to Goodwill years ago. And you know how Goshen is. Not much else for a boy to do except to find his way into mischief."

"Yeah. I know how that is," Calvin said.

"And even with his reading the Hardy Boys, he still found his way into mischief."

"How so?"

"Well, as I said, David fancies himself a kind of junior private detective, and he probably overheard his mom and me talking about those Pagans who was hanging out there that summer and was most likely up to no good. So I think he decided to hike on out there and snoop around and see if he couldn't turn up something."

"Seems like I might have done something similar to one of my neighbors once," Calvin said.

"Yeah, I did, too."

"Except I didn't see anything except one of the neighbor

ladies in her underwear." Calvin shook his head. "Sure wished I hadn't. Some things just aren't meant for little boys to see. I take it David saw considerably more."

"Yes, sir. I think he must of, too."

"What can you tell me?"

"It was a Saturday. I was just getting home. Probably a little after six o'clock. We closed the garage at six, and it's only a couple of blocks to where we live. This was before the garage closed down for good. Hot summer day. Busy day in the garage, for a change."

Calvin nodded and tipped his cigarette ash into the wastebasket with his little finger.

"As I was coming up the walk to our house, my wife come sailing out the front door and says she ain't seen David since lunchtime and she's worried. Saturday's pork chop night at our house, and pork chops are his favorite. So I gives her my lunch bucket, and I look in the backyard, and I climb up and looked into his tree house. I figured maybe he climbed up there and was taking hisself a little nap. But no David. So I climbed down, and I checked around the neighborhood, but still no David. Walked to an old field where the kids sometimes played ball, but nothing. My wife started calling the folks of his friends, and she can't find him neither. Nobody's seen him since lunchtime. Finally, she calls Jim Walker who's there at the house when I get back. You know Jim, don't you, Mr. Samuels?"

"We played ball together some in school."

"Jim's a good guy."

"Yes," Calvin said. "The best there is."

"Anyway, I get back. And my wife's near hysterics, what with them Pagans hanging out there and all, and Jim asks me if we'd looked in the boy's room, and Janice says that's the first place she did look. Well, he says, maybe he'd come in while we was out looking. So we all went up to his room."

"Was David there?"

"We went up, but we didn't see him at first. Then Jim went to the closet door and opened it."

"He was in their asleep or playing some kind of joke on you?"

"No," Mr. Roberts said. "He was standing there screaming, but nothing was coming out of his mouth. He just stood there, his arms wrapped about hisself, but not making no sound."

The Public Defender's Office was still, the courthouse silent save for the creaking of the sandstone blocks as the evening cooled.

"What do you make of it, Mr. Samuels?"

Calvin stood and walked to one of the windows and looked out into the quiet, deafening evening.

CHAPTER 37

THE FOLLOWING FRIDAY was again motion day. Like a secular Sabbath, the day Judge Biltmore set aside once each week for sentencings and uncontested divorces and motions that would each take no more than a few minutes to argue. No more than a few minutes to lose or win and to change lives forever. A day set aside for supplication and repentance, for vengeance and sometimes forgiveness.

Calvin appeared at five hearings between ten and three o'clock. At noon Judge Biltmore adjourned court for an hour. Calvin walked next door to Wilson's corner grocery where he purchased the *Hanna Morning Journal* and a carton of milk and an apple. He walked across Court Street with his purchases to the village square and found an empty bench under a shade tree, its paint curling off in thick blue peels. He ate his apple and drank his carton of milk while he read the paper. He watched the young woman who worked in the courthouse look into the store windows and dream dreams of he did not know what.

The afternoon while bright and hot was nonetheless pleasant in the shade. Calvin lowered his chin to his chest after he finished reading the paper and fell asleep. When the courthouse clock chimed one o'clock, he woke with a start from a dream he could not remember but which left his heart pounding in his chest and his breath rifling in and out. He rose from the bench and brushed the paint peels from the seat of his trousers and returned to the courtroom.

When he finished his last motion for the day, he drove up to the jail with papers for one of his just-convicted clients to sign before Deputy Smith drove him to the penitentiary that night. Calvin could have just mailed him the documents, but he had learned through hard experience that appeal papers were often lost when mailed to the penitentiary, not being found until it was too late and his client had lost all hope for a reversal of his conviction.

When he had his client's signature and was ready to leave, the jailer took a long time in coming after he rang the buzzer. When he finally did come, his eyes gleamed like those of a cat. Calvin asked him nothing. If the eyes were for him, he would find out soon enough.

He walked down the back jailhouse steps. When he stepped outside, heat waves shimmered over the black asphalt pavement, and behind them, at the far end of the parking lot, a group of deputies surrounded the rear of a brown Chevy van. Calvin didn't need to ask to whom the van had once belonged. He looked up at the cellblock. Prisoners filled every window. Though he could not see him, Alexander would be at one of them too.

Calvin crossed the parking lot to the van. One deputy looked up. He said something to the others, and they all fell silent. None even smiled as he approached. He walked to the rear of the van where Sheriff Conkle sat inside, his hands a deep crimson from the iodine tincture he still used when dusting for fingerprints. He looked up, smiled, and returned to his dusting.

"Well, howdy there, Calvin. You 'bout ready to knock off for the weekend, are you?"

Calvin looked inside the van and shook his head. "Can't afford to, Don. Not if I don't want to let you get too far ahead of me. And it looks like you're picking up some speed heading down the back stretch here."

"Now that's a fact, son. That's a fact indeed."

Conkle looked up from his dusting toward his deputies. "Boys, why don't you all go inside where it's a might cooler for you? I suspect me and Attorney Samuels here got some jawing to do."

The deputies looked at Calvin. One spat onto the pavement.

"That's a fact," Calvin said. "We certainly seem to have some topics for conversation."

Calvin watched the deputies as they crossed the parking lot. He looked up to Alexander's window. He squinted against the sun and nodded, though he could still not make out Alexander, hidden within the shadows of his cell. He turned and watched the sheriff dust as would a woman with her makeup brush, each stroke meticulous and with some special meaning and purpose. "Well," Calvin said. "It looks like you might've struck the mother lode here."

"Yeah," Conkle said and chuckled, but he did not cease the whisk and sweep of his brush. "You might say I fell into it real good this time."

"Yes, sir. That's exactly what I'd say. That you fell into it real good."

Calvin walked around the van. He stopped a moment to look into the open driver's window and walked back to the rear of the van. "This van looks to be in awful good condition for you finding it after sitting in the bottom of a hole in Bear Cross Creek for two years."

"Now, Calvin. Do you take me for a complete fool? If I'd of found this here vehicle in the bottom of some hole in Bear Cross Creek, do you think for one minute I'd be sitting here on a Friday afternoon, sweating like a pig, dusting for prints?"

"I've got to confess that the vagaries of law enforcement have always been more than a bit of a mystery to me."

"Ain't nothing vagrant about it. It's all scientific."

"Then don't hold me in suspense. Where'd you find it?"

The sheriff grinned. "Pittsburgh airport."

Calvin stooped and looked at the license plate. "So the

van's been sitting in the Pittsburgh airport for two years with Heath's plates on it, and you never found it?"

"Nope. Found Heath's plates inside under the passenger's seat."

"Whose plates are these?"

"Nineteen eighty Michigan plates issued for a nineteen seventy-seven Dodge pickup owned by a Fenton, Michigan, man. Last seen alive and well no more than a month ago."

"You find him yet?"

Conkle smiled and dusted. "We're working on it right this minute," he said. "Don't you worry about it none."

"How'd you locate the van and identify it as Heath's if it had somebody else's plates on it?"

"Can't say. Can't say just now, good buddy."

Conkle stopped his brushing for a moment and looked up. "I can't recall now, but did I sell you some of those lottery tickets for the drawing we're having next month?"

"Yeah. You did. Got me for five dollars worth."

"That's right. I did. Now I recall."

A howl came from the holding cell. Calvin looked up, but saw nothing but fifty pairs of hands coming out from between cell bars below it. He looked down to ask Conkle another question. Conkle started to whistle. "Any success on the prints yet?"

Conkle grinned and shook his head. "I'll let you know when I do."

"So how long was the van parked at the airport?"

"Security there says within three weeks either side of September first two years back."

"What was it like when you found it?"

"Unlocked," Conkle said.

"Maybe whoever left it there was hoping someone would hotwire it?"

"Maybe."

"Good mechanical condition when you found it?" asked Calvin.

"Yeah, excepting for a flat tire and a dead battery."

"Anything missing?"

"Heath's dad says a radio and table top his son kept behind the seat was gone."

"You find anything else?"

"A map of the eastern half of the United States. Funny thing, though."

"What's that?"

"Map was torn in half, and the top half was missing."

"So what're you doing with the van once you're through with it?" asked Calvin.

"Mr. Heath said he'd take it after we was through dusting and all."

"What's he say about his son?"

"He's an optimistic son-of-a-gun," Conkle said. "I'll give him that. Says there's still no clear cut evidence his son's dead."

"What do you say?"

Conkle stopped smiling. "My gut tells me Heath's gone,"

he said after a minute.

"If he's dead, most logical place to find him would be with Bonner, wouldn't it?"

Conkle nodded, but said nothing. Calvin looked down at his watch. "Well, I'd better scoot if I'm going to file these before Karl closes up the clerk's office for the weekend. I'm sure you'll be letting me know if you find anything of interest."

"You'll be the first one to know, good buddy."

"And don't worry about finding Taylor Heath," Calvin said. "Maybe our coroner in one of his many less than lucid moments sent the wrong jawbone back to Michigan or something."

Conkle shook his head. "Nothing in this life could be that easy," he said. "You take care, Calvin."

"You take care too, Sheriff."

As Calvin crossed the parking lot, Conkle stopped smiling and looked after him. "I wonder," he said.

When he reached his car, Calvin opened the door and looked back, but still he could not see Alexander with the sun above and behind the jailhouse blinding him. It was a dog sun. A sun circled in rings of blue. Unusual for so early in summer. Common enough in August, but rare in June. His grandfather had once told him some superstition the Indians had about a dog sun, but what it was he could no longer recall.

Calvin lowered his hand from his forehead and drove back down to the courthouse.

CHAPTER 38

THE NEXT MONDAY, Calvin rose before dawn. He had slept fitfully during the night, drifting in and out of a restless sleep. The unseasonably warm, muggy air, even with all of the windows in his house open, hung over him.

Once, after midnight, while still half asleep, he was certain someone was in the room. Someone standing in the shadows, just to the side from where the moonlight fell through the window. He raised himself on his elbows, but he saw no one. He fell back on his bed, and he lay there a long time before he returned to his fitful half-sleep, drifting in and out of some world he could not name.

At four-thirty he opened his eyes. He looked at the florescent clock hands, and he knew sleep was useless and would not be coming no matter how long he lay there. He sat up. His T-shirt clung wet to his chest, and his mouth tasted of ashes. Even at this early hour, he knew the day would be without mercy. Hot and long and without mercy.

He bathed in the coldest water he could stand, and he enjoyed his shivering because he knew it couldn't last. He ate breakfast and read until seven. He debated whether it would be better to walk up the hill to the jail or to let his Volkswagen sit outside all morning in the sun before lunch, and he opted for walking and having lunch at the jail. Much as he had heard his clients complain, he had never actually had one meet his demise after one of Sheriff Conkle's meals.

After a clear sunrise, though, the morning had turned dark and threatening. All day in the visitors' room, Calvin prepared Maggie Borgstrom for trial. She was, the court psychologist said, borderline retarded, and accused of abandoning her two-hour-old son. While he had not died, a dog, in eating the afterbirth that still covered his head, had also eaten a part of the little boy's face.

By noon Calvin's shirt was sweat-stained under his arms and down his back almost to his waist. No matter how many times they rehearsed her testimony, each time it came out different. Sometimes only a little different, sometimes a lot. By four o'clock, her testimony was as solid as it would ever be, and he asked Deputy Smith to bring Alexander up after he returned Maggie to her cell.

While he waited, Calvin reviewed his day's notes, making additional notations in the margins. Outside the steel-barred window, the sky in the west grew ever darker. The wind was rising, and the temperature had dropped. Thunderless lightning flashed, and a mile away the cemetery trees swayed.

When Alexander came in, his back was to Calvin, and he was speaking to the deputy in a voice Calvin could not hear. After the deputy closed the door, Alexander turned and raised his hand. "What's new, counselor? You've been making new friends here all this week, or at least so I've heard. And you still have time for me."

"I've always time for you, Mark."

"Impressive. Each day I gain more hope that we will prevail. That we will persevere."

"That's good."

"I've been reading Mr. Hemingway. *The Old Man and the Sea.* Santiago is right, you know. To persevere, to persevere is everything. Don't you agree?"

Calvin gestured to the other chair and reached into his pocket and pulled out a pack of cigarettes. He looked at it and smiled, but nevertheless laid it down along with a book of matches. He pushed them across the table. Alexander picked up the matchbook. He looked at Calvin.

"Virginia Slims?" Alexander said. "You are fooling me, aren't you? You're turning feminist on me, are you? One of those bra-burners?"

Calvin shook his head. "Sorry, Mark," he said. "I must've gotten mine mixed up with Maggie's. I'll drop off two packs of Marlboros for you tomorrow."

"Forget it," Alexander said, but he said it with a half-smile that said he forgot nothing, forgave nothing. Not even the faintest of slights no matter how unintended. A half-smile saying he was forever keeping score.

"How'd it go with Rock?"

Calvin laid his pen on his legal tablet. "Not bad. Not catastrophic, but not as well as I had hoped."

"What's the problem?"

"Rock didn't have anything helpful to say about the Pagans. Nothing harmful really, but nothing very helpful either."

"Anything else?" said Alexander.

"He also says he doesn't remember seeing you with Jocelyn that summer after the accident. With Allison, yes, but not with Jocelyn."

Alexander studied Calvin. His eyes, a cold iron gray, filled with more than a little hate, and not just for Rock. "Well," he said after a minute. "If that's what he's saying now, he's a liar."

"Perhaps."

"Perhaps? Perhaps? You think he's telling the truth?"

"No, but he might not be lying either. It's been two years. Two years is a long time. A long time to forget. A long time in which his memory might fade. To mingle with other memories. He may honestly not remember. Especially if he was a heavy drug-user two summers ago."

Alexander shook his head and looked at Calvin as he would a fool. "When Joc—" he said and stopped. He stood and walked to the barred window and looked out. The darkness was almost upon them, the lightning no longer without thunder.

Calvin tapped his pen up and down on the table. He started to ask a question, but stopped in mid-sentence. Alexander stared out the window, blowing cigarette smoke the approaching storm only blew back in upon him. Finally Calvin said, "Rock, on your side, in your corner, might have been helpful, or not. Witnesses with prior convictions experience difficulty establishing their credibility with jurors."

Alexander didn't answer.

"His not corroborating your testimony isn't going to break your case. But I'm talking to someone tomorrow who could."

"Who's that?"

"Allison Morris."

Alexander looked at Calvin and turned back to the window. He shook his head.

"Thompson's playing this one close," Calvin said. "Closer than I've ever seen. He's got Psycho Jimmy Walters, who has no credibility; and besides, we have his letter. Thompson can't even rely upon Walters taking the stand, let alone telling the same story twice the same way in the same day. She's his only witness who can place you at the farm the morning Bonner and Heath were murdered who might have any credibility with a jury. And you've got you and Jocelyn and Ernest to say otherwise."

Alexander nodded.

"So tell me about her. How you met. How you seduced her into living with you. Or how she seduced you. Mostly,

323

tell me why she's turned on you."

Alexander rubbed his cigarette into the concrete windowsill. At the rumble of distant thunder, he raised his head to look out. After a moment a curve of a smile cracked at the edges of his mouth. "Not much to tell really, counselor. Two years ago we met down at the Weirton track. She worked as a groom. I like playing the ponies."

He reached into his pocket. He looked at the label on the pack, but shook out a cigarette and continued. "We dated a few times; three, maybe four times before she moved into my trailer. We stayed there until my accident. After I was in the hospital, we separated. Separated about as fast as we'd gotten together."

"How were you supporting yourself that summer?"

Alexander looked at him.

"Get used to it, Mark. Since Thompson isn't going to let you off easy, neither can I. Details. The truth is in the details. And if you give them to him, you damn well better expect him to check them out."

"Like I told you," Alexander said after a minute. "Allison was grooming horses at the track. Me? I had some money saved up from working at Ernest's over the winter. Doing some odd jobs now and again. Did well on the ponies that spring. And my trailer was not exactly the Ritz. My cash needs were minimal."

"You can substantiate this?"

"Yes. If you need it substantiated, I can substantiate any

324

of it. I can substantiate all of it if need be."

"Thompson will ask you what you did during the day."

"Tell him I fornicated with myself," Alexander said.

"Is that what you want your jury to hear?"

Alexander shrugged. "Slept in late. Hung out at Ernest's. Shot some pool. Maybe did some odd jobs now and again. Maybe go swimming out at the farm until the old lady got back from the track."

Alexander continued to look out the window, out into the blackness. If Calvin had asked what else, Alexander would have only repeated what he had just said.

Calvin lifted his worn leather satchel from under the table and put away his tablets and pens. He stood up and buckled the satchel shut and looked out the window. "I should have brought an umbrella."

Alexander shook his head. "Umbrella would do you no good. The wind would only rip it inside out."

"Yes. I suppose you're right. It would only be ripped inside out."

"Damn straight," Alexander said.

Calvin looked at him. "Tell me something about her."

Alexander drew down on his cigarette. He turned toward Calvin. "She's smart. She's sweet when she wants to be. She may seduce you even. She may have you believing I'm guilty. You be careful. She's a temptress."

Calvin nodded. He watched Alexander. "Thanks," he said. "I will."

Calvin walked to the door and rang for the jailer who came up in a minute to take him back down. While Alexander waited for the jailer to come back, he stood at the window and watched Calvin cross the parking lot. "You be careful, counselor," he said. "Because you belong to me now."

CHAPTER 39

CALVIN AND THOMPSON took the entire next day to try a narcotics-sale case. After the day's session, Thompson told Calvin he could talk to Allison Morris in Thompson's office.

The West Virginia narks who planned the sale had planned for it to occur on their side of the Ohio in Weirton. Calvin's client, though, smelling a rat, had insisted at the last moment that the sale go down on the opposite side of the Ohio in Creek County, erroneous in his belief that if his buyers were in fact West Virginia police, they couldn't arrest him for a sale in Ohio.

He was almost right, but after the buy on the Ohio side, the narcotics officers had driven to Hanna where they obtained a warrant from Judge Biltmore and a deputy from Sheriff Conkle. The three drove back across the river to Weirton and arrested Calvin's client, his protests that the three were trampling his rights notwithstanding.

He refused to waive extradition from West Virginia; refused to enter a plea of either "guilty" or "not guilty" following his extradition; refused even to talk to Calvin. His trial was, consequently, an abbreviated one. Jury selection and opening statements in the morning; presentation of evidence and closing arguments in the afternoon.

The courtroom gallery remained empty except for a newspaper reporter, who Calvin had dated off and on and who sat in the middle front row, and a woman who sat in a corner in the back. The same woman who some weeks before had sat in the gallery and watched as Jimmy Walters entered his guilty plea. The woman with eyes very dark, her hair crow black.

At both the morning and afternoon jury breaks, Thompson ignored the reporter and walked back to speak to her. Ignored a reporter in an election year. During the course of the trial, though, it was Calvin she watched. Even when Thompson was questioning a witness or speaking to the jury, it was Calvin she watched.

Early on in the trial, Judge Biltmore made it clear he was anxious for the trial to end by overruling every objection raised, unless it was Thompson raising the objection. This trial was to be a one-day affair and no more because Judge Biltmore was anxious to get out of town. As a jurist in a country courtroom, his services were in demand in the busy Cleveland courts where he received one hundred dollars a day and a paid hotel suite downtown, away from his wife, while still receiving his Creek County salary and benefits.

Following closing arguments, Judge Biltmore ordered the jurors immediately to begin their deliberations. He sent his bailiff over to the Country Kitchen for carryout and told the jurors they would go home just as soon as they reached a verdict.

After two deputies led his client away to await the verdict, Calvin packed up his briefcase. When he turned to leave, Thompson was holding the door open for the woman who had been watching the trial from the back of the courtroom. He left the courthouse and jaywalked across Main Street to his private office. While he waited for the jury to come back with their verdict, he prepared for Maggie Borgstrom's case he was trying the following week.

His hopes for an acquittal rose when he telephoned the bailiff sometime after nine o'clock and learned the jury was still out. The bailiff telephoned Calvin a few minutes later, however, and told him a verdict had been reached. From the tone in his voice, he guessed his client had been convicted. Three summers before, when Ohio still had a death penalty, the bailiff had volunteered his vacation time to act as a witness to an electrocution in Columbus and was so distraught when the Governor stayed the sentence he vowed to a group of attorneys standing outside Judge Biltmore's chambers he would never vote for another goddamn Republican as long as he lived. The bailiff's remonstrations continued until Judge

Biltmore called him into his chambers and told him to shut the door.

Calvin repacked his briefcase. He clipped his pen to the pocket inside his suit jacket and removed a clean tablet from a desk drawer. He shut and locked his office door and walked down the steps and back across Main Street. Even wearing his suit jacket, though, he shivered in the unseasonably cold night, and his breath vaporized before him as though it were October. A ground fog, no more than eight inches above the earth, was rolling in from the country and creeping through Hanna like a pride of phantom cats. Like white-ghost cats. Silent, white-ghost cats. As silent as death herself.

The foreman stood and announced they indeed had convicted Calvin's client, and he was sentenced and led away almost before the foreman could sit back down. After Judge Biltmore dismissed the jury, Thompson waved for Calvin to follow him as he made his way for the front courtroom door. Midway up the stairs Calvin caught up. "A little late, isn't it, Ben? Can't this wait until tomorrow?"

Thompson shook his head. "It's now or never if you want to talk to her."

"Why now or never?"

"It's the only way I could convince her to come back before Alexander's trial. She didn't have to come, you know."

"Yeah, I know it all too well."

"She's scared to death one of the Pagans might be watching the courthouse and will follow her and find out where she lives. Which is, by the way, one of the ground rules. You can ask her anything you want about the killings. You can ask her anything within reason about her background. You may not ask her about where she's working or where she's living."

At the top of the stairs, Thompson rapped at the door to his office. A deputy wearing a bulletproof vest under his blouse unbolted and opened the door. Ten feet behind him stood a second deputy, his right hand at rest on his holstered pistol. Calvin nodded to the first deputy, but the deputy only eyed him and said nothing.

Calvin followed Thompson to the end of the hall. Thompson knocked and spoke, and the two of them entered. Inside, Deputy Smith sat in front of Thompson's desk, an opened newspaper spread across it. His right hand also rested on his pistol, and he looked behind the two of them as they entered. On the couch, reading a coverless paperback, was the woman who had waited most of the day in the courtroom gallery.

When Calvin and Thompson came in, she did not immediately look up. Only after a moment did she dog-ear the page and close her book. She glanced at Calvin, and then she looked at Thompson and laid her book on the couch armrest next to an ashtray filled with lipstick-smudged cigarettes.

"Smitty," Thompson said. "Would you mind waiting just outside my door for a few minutes while we talk?"

The deputy folded his paper. Without speaking, he stood and left the office, his paper in his back pocket. Thompson bolted the door behind him and turned around.

"Allison," he said. "This is Calvin Samuels. Alexander's PD. Calvin, Allison Morris."

The two smiled and nodded. Thompson walked behind his desk and sat. He laid down the files he had carried up from the courtroom, and he leaned back in his chair. Calvin turned around and sat in the chair where Deputy Smith had been sitting.

"Allison, Calvin's agreed to the ground rules you and I discussed earlier. All questions before, during, and immediately after the murders are fair game. You are to answer the question asked, but only the question asked."

Allison nodded.

"Calvin, I will tell you that Allison is living now somewhere on the East Coast. She works as a sales clerk in a department store. Other than what I just said, she isn't going to tell you where she lives or where she's employed. Fair enough?"

"All right," Calvin said. "For now, anyway. Shall we get started?"

"Please do. It's been a long day," Thompson said and placed his hands behind his head.

"Ms. Morris. It's late. Mr. Thompson and I are both exhausted, and I'm sure you're tired too. You've a long drive ahead, so let me get right to it. Did you see Mark Alexander murder Bonner or Heath?"

"No. No, I did not, Mr. Samuels." It was the first time he had heard her speak. Her voice was low, and her enunciation betrayed a woman of education.

"But you believe he did kill them."

"I know he did."

"How?"

She looked down and fidgeted with a cuff of her blouse. When she looked up, her eyes were swimming. "Several days before," she said. "Several days before Peter and Taylor disappeared, he asked me what I would do if he killed them. When I asked him why he would want to, he said if he did we'd have two thousand dollars, Bonner's truck, Heath's van, and a pound of THC to cut and sell."

"And you said?"

"I told him it didn't matter what he did. I loved him, and I would always love him, and I would stand by his side no matter what he did. No matter what."

"Did you believe him at the time? Did you believe he was serious about killing them?"

"No," she said. "No. I didn't take him seriously."

"Why not?"

"People often say they're going to kill someone when they're only angry. I thought Mark was only angry."

"Did he have cause to be angry?"

"I suppose so. In his eyes."

"Why was that?"

"Taylor had gone to Florida with money from Mark

and with his own. He was supposed to buy THC," she said. "When he came back, he had only Peruvian cocaine. They argued about it. A bad argument."

"What happened to the cocaine Heath brought back?"

"We ended up snorting it that night."

"Who's 'we'?"

"Me," she said. "Mark. Peter and Taylor. Walters. One of the Goshen townies who was hanging out at the farm. All of us."

"Do you remember the name of the Goshen townie?"

She studied Calvin a moment, but finally said no, she didn't remember. Calvin moved on with his questions. Allison sat back in the couch.

"Did Mark ever admit to you, or did you ever overhear him say he'd murdered Bonner and Heath?"

She shook her head. "No, he didn't, but when I came back to the farm, they were gone."

"Where was it you were coming back from?"

"The day after he asked me what I would do if he killed them, Mark drove me into Goshen and told me to stay with Mike and Barb Hanket," she said. "Friends of his. When I left the farm, the outhouse was still standing. When I returned it was . . . it was . . . burning."

"How old are you, Ms. Morris?"

"Twenty-three."

"When did you meet Mark?"

"April. April of that year. Nineteen eighty."

"And how soon after you met did you begin living together?"

She looked to Thompson. Thompson nodded. "Later that spring," she said. "I moved into his trailer later that spring."

"Were Bonner and Heath living there, too?"

"They would pitch their tent nearby. When we moved to the farm later that summer, they would stay there. At the farm."

"Why do you think Mark was so upset about Heath buying cocaine instead of THC?"

"It wasn't only the THC Taylor was supposed to get, Mr. Samuels."

"What else?"

"Mark had been in an auto accident a few weeks before. He was still in a lot of pain. In addition to the THC, Heath was supposed to buy some marijuana and Quaaludes for him."

"And he didn't."

"All he brought back was the cocaine."

"And when did Mark talk to you about killing them?"

"When we went to bed that night. The night Taylor returned with the cocaine."

"After he drove you into Goshen to stay with his friends, when did you next see Mark?"

"The next day. He drove into town in Peter's pickup. Barb and I were sitting on her front step. Drinking iced tea. Talking. When he pulled up, Barb got up and went inside, and Mark asked me if I wanted to get married."

"Get married when?"

"The next day."

"And you said?"

"I said okay."

Thompson opened his eyes. "Alexander thought he'd figured out that if he married Allison, she wouldn't be able to testify against him, which would leave only Jimmy Walters with any knowledge of the murders."

"And by then the outhouse had burned down?" Calvin said.

Allison nodded. "It was still smoldering when I got back. Mark said Walters had been behind it smoking and set it on fire."

"You said Mark was driving Bonner's pick up when he drove into Goshen to propose to you?"

"Yes, that's right."

"What about Heath's van? When was the last time you saw it?"

"A few days after Peter and Taylor disappeared, I drove it to the Pittsburgh airport with Miza Siran."

"Who is Miza Siran?"

"She's Walter's common-law wife," Thompson said.

"And where was Mark?"

"He and Mike Hanket followed."

"What happened at the airport?"

"When we got there, I parked the van. We wiped our fingerprints off and left."

"Why the airport?"

"Mark said if the police ever recovered it, they'd just think Taylor took a plane somewhere."

"You said he asked you to marry him. Were you ever in fact married?"

"The day I returned to the farm we were married in a Pagan wedding ceremony."

"A Pagan wedding ceremony?"

"Yes, Mr. Samuels. A Pagan wedding ceremony."

"What's that like?"

"We had a regular wedding procession. Took our vows, and got drunk after the wedding. There was a tank of laughing gas, and we used garbage bags to inhale it. After we were married, Mike and Barb Hanket renewed their wedding vows. It was their tenth anniversary. We were almost like real couples."

"Ms. Morris, do you recall the approximate date all of this took place?"

"I would guess July thirtieth or thirty-first."

"We've located the marriage certificate," Thompson said. "They were married on the thirty-first."

"Are you still legally married?"

"Allison obtained a divorce some months ago," Thompson said.

"When did you finally leave Mark?"

"November. November of that year."

The telephone rang. Thompson picked up the receiver

and turned around. "Yes, Renate. I know it's late."

Calvin made a note in his legal tablet. When he looked up, he saw out the window mists of ground fog drifting past the bottom of a streetlamp. Beneath the streetlamp stood a figure looking up at him. The courthouse clock chimed.

Thompson hung up the telephone and yawned and sat up. "Anything else?"

Calvin shook his head. He placed his legal tablet inside his briefcase and his pen inside his jacket pocket and stood. "No. I've nothing more to ask."

He turned to Allison. "I appreciate the trouble you've taken in coming back, Ms. Morris."

Allison nodded, but said nothing.

Outside the courthouse, Calvin stopped a moment at the bottom of the steps and lit a cigarette. He saw no one beneath the streetlamp, but he walked over to it anyway. When he reached the corner, he looked back to the lighted window in Thompson's office. There, watching him, stood Allison Morris.

CHAPTER 40

CALVIN ROSE EARLY the next morning. Since he had no client appointments or court hearings that day, he pulled on an old pair of canvas trousers and the thin, patched work shirt he had kept from his summers roofing houses and barns with the Mennonites. He walked in the dark to the Country Kitchen and by six o'clock had ordered breakfast. As he drank his coffee, he read the account in the *Hanna Morning Journal* about the narcotics-sale case he and Thompson had tried the day before. Calvin shook his head. He should have called the reporter after their last date like he had promised her he would. "Hell hath no fury," he told his coffee cup.

Though it was early, the restaurant was already three-quarters full, and the waitress serving him wore a mustache of perspiration. In the back sat the wise-men. They were mostly the older men of the village who, seven days a week, gathered early around their table. As some left for their offices or shops, others took their places. Some would stay and sit and talk until it was time for them to go home to lunch where they would bring their wives abreast of the village gossip since the morning before.

Holding court that morning at the table was Brad McLain's editor. For years it had been common for some or another villager to see him walking about town as early as four o'clock, waiting for the Country Kitchen to open at five-thirty. Some villagers said he was just an old newshound in pursuit of his craft, but Mrs. Ferguson once told him that years ago the editor had gotten some local girl into trouble, and she had bled to death from a backstreet abortion botched by an alcoholic physician who had lost his license. Now, she said, the editor walked the streets at night because he couldn't sleep. Could barely stand to live with himself.

He was, though, a fine newspaperman, because having seen depravity in himself, he could spot it readily in others. He saw the evil that lurked in the hearts of all men and believed the only thing needed to unleash it were the right circumstances. Circumstances such as those which had befallen him. Men and women among the unfallen, he said, had simply not yet been sufficiently tempted.

Also sitting at the table was the town's new young doctor, just back from the hospital in which he had worked all night. Calvin later heard he had been successful in keeping a premature baby born to one of Hanna's few families of color alive until the baby could be rushed to the Cleveland Clinic. Mrs. Ferguson said he most likely was the bastard son of the abortionist, but Calvin attributed her conjecture to an old woman with not enough to keep her occupied and to her general romantic nature.

When he came into the restaurant, Calvin had walked back, said hello, and joshed and exchanged lies for a minute before going to his table and reading the paper during the wait for breakfast. As he read an article in the editorial section about the need to replace Hanna's sewer system, Big Jim Walker came in. He looked about and came back. "Calvin," he said.

Calvin looked up from his paper. "Hey, Jim. Have a seat. You're up early. You digging up more work for me?"

Walker sat down and shook his head. "I don't know," he said. "I may have."

"What's up?"

"I was talking to Smitty up at the jail. You know Smitty?"

Calvin nodded. "Sure. See him almost every time I go up to see another customer you brought in for me."

"Seems he fished a boy out of the Ohio River last evening."

"They identify him yet?"

The waitress came over to their table, but Walker ordered only coffee.

"Kid from Goshen. Billy Whalen. Called him 'Smell Whalen'."

"How'd he die?"

"Shotgun blast to the stomach."

Calvin flinched his brow. "Messy?"

"Very. Smitty says it was suicide."

"Suicide?" Calvin said. "You think that likely?"

Walker shook his head. "Whalen was a strange kid."

The waitress brought over Walker's coffee, and she refilled Calvin's cup. Walker stirred his coffee.

"How do you mean strange?" Calvin said.

"Whalen was one of those kids always hanging out on the fringes. Kids who want to be accepted, but don't know how to go about it."

Calvin nodded. "I know the mold."

"He was one of the hangers-on out at the farm two summers back."

"How involved was he?" Calvin said.

Walker shrugged. "Who knows? At the very least he was one of those showing up for some of the forty-dollar parties they was holding."

"Anything else?"

"Not that I ever heard of. Smell wasn't a mean kid. But the only other people he fit in with were the other town burnouts."

"Why do you call him 'Smell'?"

"When he was a kid, he spent quite a bit of time in foster care. In foster care, you don't always bathe as often as you should."

"No," Calvin said. "I guess not."

"And of course the name stuck. So there he was. Eight years old, and already branded an outcast."

The two sat, sipping their coffees.

"I take it you're not buying into the suicide explanation," Calvin said.

"No, I guess I'm not."

"Why's that?"

"Doesn't fit," Walker said. "Suicide's usually an act of desperation. Smell was never desperate. And to use a shotgun?" Walker shook his head. "A shotgun shows some real anger, and Smell was just a sweet, mixed-up kid. If you're going to do yourself in, you're going to do it quick. Smell didn't live long after he was shot, but while he did, he suffered plenty."

"And it doesn't seem you'd be finding a suicide killed by a shotgun floating in the river," Calvin said. "His home. His car, maybe. But not the river."

Walker nodded.

"There's something else bothering you, too, isn't there?"

"Yeah, there is."

"What is it?"

"It was Smitty who found him."

"So? Last time I heard he was a deputy."

"Yeah, but he don't go out on patrol no more. Fridays he transports prisoners to the penitentiary, but most of the time he's just the jailer up at County."

The waitress came over and told Walker he was needed

back at the station. Walker nodded, but didn't get up to leave. "What else is bothering you?" Calvin said.

"During the investigation, it turned out Smell kept going back to the farm, even after the parties stopped and rumors was flying around that Bonner and Heath was dead. Which isn't what you'd expect from Smell. He was just a scared little shit."

"So why'd he keep going out, you think? The drugs?"

"No. I asked him that. Said it wasn't drugs."

"When'd you talk to him last?" asked Calvin.

"About a week ago."

"What'd he say?"

"Whalen, I think, knew more about the murders than he was letting on to me," Walker said. "He didn't see anything, but him and one of the other burnouts hanging on out there had spent some time together in a foster home about ten years back."

"Who was that?"

"The kid you come see me about a couple of years ago. The kid who was missing and later turned up dead. John Rogers."

Walker looked up at the clock on the wall behind the counter. "I better be going before the station calls me here a second time," he said. "Calvin, you take care."

Walker stood and walked to the cash register. Calvin looked out the window to the hills south of town. He, too, stood and paid for his breakfast and walked to his office to prepare for trial.

When he went home that evening, Mrs. Ferguson was walking between her rose bushes with her pruning shears hanging from a string tied around her neck, and Calvin walked back to ask after her.

"You've been working with that Alexander for a few weeks now," she said. "What's your opinion of him?"

"Can't decide. Some days he seems like he's okay. Other days?" Calvin shook his head. "Can't decide."

CHAPTER 41

CALVIN HADN'T GONE a hundred steps from his front gate when it was plain he'd made a mistake in wearing a suit for the mile walk up Cemetery Hill. He stopped under the broad shade of a sugar maple growing in the devil strip that ran adjacent to Mrs. Ferguson's lawn and loosened his tie. He took off his coat and removed his father's gold cufflinks and placed them in a trouser pocket. After he rolled up his shirtsleeves he continued on, his coat slung over his shoulder.

Past him drove a score of motorists. Some still wore their church clothes and were on their way to Sunday dinner with their families; some already had changed and were driving to picnics and little league games. A few honked their horns, and Calvin raised his free hand and smiled even if he didn't recognize the car. Mrs. Ferguson had more than once accused him of being a natural-born politician. She said he was wasting his talents being a lawyer and that he should lose some more of his principles and run for office.

Halfway, a '64 Dodge Dart pulled up to the curb. With the front fender less than a half-inch off the pavement, it looked held together by wire and Black Magic and little else. Calvin looked at the driver and shook his head. Judge Biltmore had placed him on probation just the Friday before. The driver leaned over the seat and rolled down the passenger window and asked Calvin if he could offer him a lift. "Take you anywheres you care to go, Mr. Samuels."

Calvin looked behind the driver. The ignition was missing, and the radio lay on the floor, its red and black wires still running back into the dashboard. Calvin thanked him for his consideration, but said no, and asked where he was headed. When the driver answered to Pennsylvania, Calvin said that was probably prudent.

"You might want to consider sticking to the county roads and keeping off the state highways, though" he said.

The driver said he would and pulled back out into traffic. The car had no rear license tag.

"If you're going to go back to prison for car theft, idiot, at least make it worth your while by stealing a Cadillac."

With the start of Alexander's trial only four weeks from Monday, Calvin should have been in his office preparing, but he'd made a promise. At the cemetery entrance, Calvin stopped and retied his tie and took the cufflinks from his pocket. After he put his coat back on, he passed through the stone arch and into the cemetery beneath the hundred-foot summer canopy.

Calvin walked by the cemetery church, built of stone by the Lutherans who were the first denomination to settle in Hanna, and past the weathered, teardrop markers quarried from the limestone beds found to the south and west, near New Hope. The markers nearest the cemetery entrance dated back to the founding of Hanna. Most, the rain and snow had long ago scoured clean, but those few Calvin could read bore the names of families still common in town: Fox, Stacey, Frost, Wright.

As he passed deeper into the cemetery, he came to the tombstones dating from the Civil War. Most remained legible. Along with the name of the soldier was the battlefield where he'd fallen: Antietam Creek or Gettysburg. The slaughterhouse of humanity historians called Cold Harbor. When he reached the markers for the soldiers who had died in Korea, he stopped and looked back to the church. Mrs. Ferguson had once told him when his father shipped out, it was from there he had left for the Hanna train station in the early morning.

Henry Samuels had been born on a dairy farm only a half-mile away, just across the pasture adjacent to the cemetery, and it was to this cemetery church Calvin's grandmother had brought his father when he was not yet a week old. In those days Hanna still had its own clockmaker, and the Lutherans had elected him one of their deacons. They held him in high esteem, due in no small part to his having long been addled from listening for over half a century to the constant reminders of eternity's passing. When Calvin's grandmother entered his shop several months before the birth of her son, the clockmaker told her that death often arrived early and without notice, especially to the very young. Sin, he said, lurked everywhere, and it was never too early for a child to get right with God.

When Calvin was but ten, his uncle showed him the place in the woods not a hundred yards away where the two of them, his father and uncle, had built a diving platform and dammed the steep ravine below to create a swimming hole during summer floods. His hand that day had touched the weathered wood, and he had closed his eyes and seen his father and uncle, about the same age as he was then, swimming naked in their hole. When his uncle took him home, his mother had been taken for the first time to the sanitarium. He remembered sitting very small in a sofa chair, looking out the large picture window of their cottage. On the brick sidewalk, Reverend Barker was shaking his uncle's hand, both men smiling.

He walked on. As Calvin crested the summit of Cemetery Hill, he stopped in mid-step. Standing next to the marker for his dead friend, wearing a black penitent dress, was Allison Morris. She must have heard his footsteps clicking on the asphalt path before he came over the summit because when he saw her, she was watching him.

Calvin looked at her, turning from where he'd come to see if she were watching another, but there was no other in the cemetery but him. He hesitated but ultimately walked to where she stood, stopping when the jasmine of her perfume reached him. Calvin looked at the ground under his feet, the earth not yet sunk back in upon itself.

When he looked up, his question must have appeared on his face because, without his asking, she told him John had told her Calvin would be here today.

"John?" he said.

"Yes. John Rogers."

Calvin swallowed. "When?"

"Two years ago," she said. "Two years ago tomorrow."

"But how?"

"How?"

"How did you know him?"

She smiled, not unkindly. "He lived for a while at the farm with Mark and me," she said. "And with Bonner and Heath."

Calvin looked down.

"You didn't know, did you?"

"Not for certain. I suspected, but I didn't know for certain. I'm not sure I wanted to."

He fell silent again, but after a moment, he asked, "What was he doing at the farm anyway? How did he end up down there? With Alexander?"

"After he lost his job at the carwash, he took to hanging out with Walters. He needed a place to stay because his grandmother had gone back to Pennsylvania. Walters was staying there. I think it belonged to their uncle or granduncle or something."

"Yes. Granduncle," Calvin said.

"They didn't need to pay rent to old Harry, and they could swim in Bear Cross Creek. Forget their problems. With Bonner and Heath passing through, they didn't need to worry about a lack of dope. Walters said if they needed some cash they could always pull some penny ante burglaries or sell some dope to the locals."

"Was John still there when Bonner and Heath were murdered?"

"Yes," she said. "He was still there."

"Why didn't he get out?"

"Too frightened. No place to go. And he was too strung out to think clearly. We both were, really."

Calvin looked off to the south. The cattle that had been grazing along the fence had moved nearer the barn, and beyond them a thunderhead came over the horizon.

He turned back to her. "When was the last time you saw him?"

"When I dropped him off at the Travelers' Hotel in Weirton. A week after the murders he asked me to help him get out. Last time I saw him, he was in the rearview mirror, waving goodbye. Smiling."

Calvin shook his head. "Smiling," he said.

"After we left Goshen, he told me what was in the letter

he mailed to you. Told me about his asking you to visit his grave each year."

"Yes, he did."

"I told him he was crazy. Told him there was no way a lawyer would go out of his way like that. He told me I was wrong. Told me if there was anybody I could count on it was you."

"He was a good kid," Calvin said. "Special."

"Yes, he was."

"He'd overcome so much, and he was so close to breaking out of his past. Then he was dead."

Allison nodded. "Some scumbag came upon him soon after I dropped him off."

"What did you do? After you dropped him off."

"Went to my parents in Weirton, but they were done with me. I had no place to go. I didn't have the courage to go nowhere. So I went back, to Mark, until I found the courage."

"So why are you here today?"

"I wanted to tell you what happened to your friend. To John."

"Yes, thank you."

"I didn't think you'd talk to me if I called you or if I just walked into your office."

"No," Calvin said. "Probably not."

"I didn't want to tell you this in front of Thompson."

Calvin didn't answer. As they were talking, the thunderhead had come upon them, and the cemetery nightlights flickered on.

"I also came today to warn you," Allison said.

"Warn me?"

"You think you can atone for the loss of your friend by getting Mark Alexander off. You can't."

Calvin shook his head. "Is that what you think I'm doing?"

"Listen to me. I know him. I know how manipulative he is. He sees your need. He saw my emptiness and took advantage of me. He sees yours, too."

Calvin didn't answer.

She touched his hand, and he looked into her eyes. Eyes so dark whole worlds could be lost forever within them. So what chance one lost soul?

"We should talk again before the trial. Anytime you like. Anywhere you like. Perhaps even here again." She turned and walked back over the hillcrest.

Calvin looked down. "Was there any truth in what she said?"

He was silent a moment. "What if there was?"

CHAPTER 42

FOR A LONG time, Calvin stood watching where Allison had disappeared back over the crest of Cemetery Hill. After a while he took off his coat and laid it on the grass next to the grave of his friend and sat and waited. He waited until long after the sky had darkened above him, darkened as though it was the dead of night, as though it was death herself who had stolen upon him. Waited even as the storm broke and the ground shook beneath him from the thunder and long after he was soaked and he trembled from the cold, but she did not come back.

"I'm sorry, John," he said as he stood up. "I'm sorry I let you down." Then he picked up his coat and disappeared himself back over the crest of Cemetery Hill.

He walked once more under the stone entrance and out of the cemetery to Court Street before starting downhill. Motorists passed by him once again as he walked home, their headlights umbral behind the great sheets of rain, making their own way through the dark as best they could. None honked their horns as they had earlier. None stopped to offer Calvin a ride. Some, no doubt, didn't see him, but some did and those inside only looked at one another and shook their heads and kept going.

The next morning, and for the whole of the week through Saturday, Calvin worked out Alexander's defense. He rose early each day and walked to the Country Kitchen while it was still dark. He would buy a coffee and perhaps a sweet roll; and he would stop next door to pick up a *Cleveland Plain Dealer* at Reash's Newsstand; and he would carry his purchases to his private office and kick the door closed behind him. Then, until the telephone or a client interrupted or until it was necessary for him to cross Main Street to attend a hearing, Calvin worked on his trial outline.

He planned out Alexander's defense on a half-dozen white legal tablets, writing with an antique Italian fountain pen willed to him by one of his first clients when she had died, heirless and alone save for him. Her father had purchased the pen during his service at the Venetian consulate, and he in turn had willed it to her. The pen was talismanic, she told Calvin on the afternoon she had executed her will with it, and when he wrote his legal briefs and thought of her, he would see that exactly the right words flowed from her pen. He would see.

He wrote slowly, deliberately. Some days he wrote no

more than a few lines or half a page. Other days he scribbled out page upon page. Always, though, he listened, not just to the logic of what he would say, but to the rhythms and cadences of his words as would a Chautauqua minister.

During the week he visited Alexander but once. Calvin told him about his meeting with Allison in Thompson's office, but not about their second meeting. Alexander had stood at the window of the visitors' room and looked out across to Cemetery Hill. He said nothing, betrayed nothing, of what he knew or of what he perhaps suspected. When he finished, Alexander only nodded and asked if Calvin could spare him his half-pack of cigarettes.

After he left Alexander, Calvin walked back to his car that he had parked in the shade along Court Street, just outside the county jail. He was unlocking the door when McLain pulled in behind. Calvin shook his head when McLain asked about Alexander's defense. He said perhaps McLain had been right. Perhaps it was time for him to talk to the psychic who had been out to the farm the winter before.

On Sunday he attended services at the cemetery church, and even at that morning hour, the day promised to be unforgiving. Men wearing short-sleeved shirts and ties, but abandoning their suit coats altogether. He arrived late, just as the final hymn before the sermon was ending, and he sat in the back. The pew was empty except for two boys who sat fidgeting by the aisle, looking like they planned to make good their escape before the sermon's end and would do so if only their mother would stop eyeing them over her shoulder. When the hymn ended, Reverend Barker rose to the pulpit and smiled at the boys. They quieted and straightened and sat back with more than a little resignation.

The sermon came from Job. Calvin closed his eyes, as might a pilgrim at his sojourn's end, hoping at long last to receive the wisdom of the ages. Midway through the sermon, however, he opened them. He looked to the other end of his pew. It was empty. The two boys had made good their escape while their mother was in prayer, perhaps asking Him to look over her two scoundrels. Calvin checked his watch, nodded at Reverend Barker, and stood and left.

The road from Hanna to Goshen was deserted, the countrymen either still in church or still asleep, or more likely both. Calvin turned left at the village's abandoned gas station, and did so again at the first cross-street. He parked in front of a two-story house, three houses down from the corner. He checked its address against the note in his shirt pocket, and got out and walked up the front steps. A note was thumb-tacked next to the screen door. Its writer stated he would be returning soon after he finished his sermon, sometime between twelve-thirty and one o'clock, and he told Calvin to make himself comfortable on the porch.

Calvin folded his coat over the porch rail and sat in a bleached oak rocker. Tied to it was a handmade quilted seat, and someone had left the *Sunday Hanna Journal* lying there, folded and unread. He laid it on the porch floor and studied the neighborhood.

It was common in Goshen for the lots between adjacent houses to be an acre or more, so that someone standing on his own porch would not have understood his neighbor without his neighbor shouting. The lots had once accommodated prodigious vegetable gardens and small orchards when housewives still filled their cellars during the summer and fall with their own preserves. Now, though, the gardens had been plowed under and the orchards cut down and only a wasteland of weeds surrounded the houses.

He sat and rocked and looked up and down the street. After a while Calvin closed his eyes. He could hear remnants of some hymn coming through the treetops, the words to which he had long ago forgotten and which were coming from too far for him to make out, but he found himself humming along all the same until he fell asleep.

In his sleep, he heard children's voices. They seemed very distant, but when he woke and looked up, he saw a couple in their early forties with five children coming up the walk. Calvin stood and walked to the porch steps. The husband smiled. "Mr. Samuels?" he said. His voice sounded friendly, but weary. Not tired as from standing two hours at a pulpit, but weary. Life-weary.

"Yes, sir. I am."

"George Barnhouse," he said, and reached out, and the two shook hands.

"And this is my wife, Elizabeth."

The woman smiled, but she wavered on her feet as the two youngest children pushed each other to hide behind her dress.

"Elizabeth, can you manage the children for a few minutes while we talk out here? I'm certain Mr. Samuels would like to be on his way so he can be with his own people on Sunday."

Again the woman smiled, but did not speak. She walked up the steps with her children, who either tried to escape into the folds of her dress or walked close behind. Calvin held the screen door open and said it was a pleasure to have met her, and she and her children disappeared into the cool darkness.

"Please," the minister said. "Make yourself comfortable." He held out his hand toward the porch rocker where Calvin had been sitting.

The minister took off his own coat and laid it over the porch rail next to Calvin's. His shirt was dark with sweat stains, not only under his arms, but also down the yoke of his back, as though he must have struggled with some great burden that morning. The minister looked down at the porch floorboards for a moment. When he looked up, he tried to smile.

"You must pardon my wife. I don't want you to think her rude."

"Excuse me, Reverend. Rude?"

"She can't speak, my wife. Or won't. I've not yet decided which."

Calvin shook his head. "I'm sorry. I don't understand."

"No. Of course you don't. How could you? You've only just got here. I should explain."

"There's no need," Calvin said.

"But I should."

"All right."

"When I visited the Old Church Road farm last winter, Elizabeth came with me. I was walking about, not paying much attention to her, but just trying to sense what had happened out there that summer."

"Yes, sir."

"It wasn't until late in the afternoon it came to me how upset she was, barely speaking."

"Upset at what?"

"We came home, ate dinner, and read in our parlor after we put the children to bed, as we always do, not discussing what we had sensed or felt or deduced that day. Elizabeth didn't say much that evening either, but I assumed she was as exhausted as I was—as we always are after such an encounter—and we turned in early. She slept fitfully at first, but after a while she seemed to settle down. Then, right before sunrise, I woke. She was sitting straight up in bed. Silently screaming."

"Silently screaming?" Calvin said.

"Her mouth agape, her eyes wide at something she'd seen, either real or imagined, but making no sound. She was asleep, I thought, and so I held her. After a while her trembling stopped, and she lay down and went back to normal sleep. Or at least a quiet sleep. But she hasn't spoken a word since."

"Has she seen a physician?"

"Yes. Three or four, really."

Calvin started to ask another question, but the minister raised his hand and looked away in mid-sentence, straightening and walking to the opposite end of the porch. He stood there, hands on hips, suspenders crisscrossing the sweat-stained back of his shirt, looking out over the field of dandelions and skunkweed separating his and his neighbors' houses. He turned back to Calvin, but the minister said nothing, and after a minute he returned and leaned against the porch rail next to their coats.

"This house used to be Elizabeth's parents', and before that her grandparents'. When her grandfather returned from the Great War, he, too, did not speak."

"Wounded?" Calvin said.

"No. Nothing physically wrong with him, he was never wounded, but emotionally." The minister shook his head. "He didn't speak. Shell shocked they called it back then."

"How odd. Such a coincidence."

"It was his way of forgetting what he'd seen done to other men, I think. Forgetting what he himself had done. If he didn't have to talk about what he'd seen, about what he'd done, he could begin to forget."

"Did he ever speak again?"

"Oh, yes."

"That's good."

"But not for six years."

"Six years?"

"Yes. Six years of his family wondering if he ever

would. Wondering if he was going mad, or perhaps already was. Elizabeth's own father was five years old before he heard him speak."

"When was that?"

"They were attending Easter services, and he said he heard a voice singing he'd never heard before. He looked up, and it was his father. He'd finally found a way to deal with his war, to deal with what he'd seen, with what he'd done, and he was finally able to work it all out."

The minister studied the parallel cracks in the porch floorboards. "Elizabeth's grandfather only spoke to me once about it. It was shortly after Elizabeth and I were married, shortly before the old soldier died."

"What'd he tell you?" Calvin said. "About the war."

"It was September of nineteen fourteen. He lived here, in Goshen. In this very house, in fact. The other houses you see about were not yet built. This was all one big farm he and his father worked before his father had to start selling it off. Just the two of them. No hired hands. Couldn't afford to hire any, he said. All of the other children, all of his brothers and sisters, had died in childbirth or shortly after.

"One Saturday he and his father drove their wagon into Hanna for supplies as was their weekly custom. The Creek County fair was going on that particular weekend, so his father gave him two bits. But he never made it there."

"Where'd he go?" Calvin asked.

"He walked instead to the newsstand. Purchased a

penny's worth of licorice candy and a Cleveland newspaper. Never should have bought the paper, he said. Should have stopped with the licorice candy."

"Why's that?"

"War'd broken out in Europe. The Cleveland paper was full of it. Germans marching through Belgium with babies hoisted on their bayonets. Raping nuns, the paper said. That was just British propaganda. But there on the last page was an article about Canada entering the war and how they'd set up a recruitment office in Cleveland for any Americans who might care to enlist. Paid them an enlistment bonus, even, just because they were Americans."

The minister shook his head. "He said his buying that paper was the biggest mistake of his life."

"What happened?" Calvin said.

"The Sunday following, he told his parents he was too ill to attend services. Had a sore throat, he said. After they left he got up and got dressed. Under his bed he had a gunnysack full of clothes he'd packed the night before. A friend from town drove him to the train station in Hanna.

"Instead of going directly to Cleveland, he went first to Pittsburgh to confuse any would be pursuers, not that there would have been any. He doubled back through Hanna that night on a milk train and rode on into Cleveland the next morning. He still carried the week-old Cleveland newspaper with him. By pointing out the address to passersby he finally found his way to the recruiting office. By noon he'd joined up with His Majesty's Royal Canadian Expeditionary forces. The recruiters said they were only too glad to have him even if he didn't look sixteen, let alone eighteen."

"How old was he?"

"Sixteen. Just. Just turned sixteen."

"What happened after he enlisted?" Calvin said.

"They gave him a voucher for food and a train ticket for Ottawa where he did his basic training. He was there for about four weeks he said, and when he was through, he went by troop train to Halifax, by steamer to Liverpool, by train to Dover, and across the Channel to France."

"What happened to him there?"

"He never spoke much about the fighting, the killing. Said he spent four years in the trenches. Four years living like a rat with the rats. Rose to the rank of sergeant. But the day after the Armistice he woke up and couldn't speak."

"That must have been unnerving."

"No," the minister said. "He told me it didn't bother him all that much, his not being able to speak. He figured it to be a judgment on him. A judgment on him for God having let him live through what he had when so many others hadn't. When he'd deserted his parents to run the farm by themselves in their old age, forcing them to sell it off in pieces in order to get by, leaving them only a note. For having killed so many men in four years he had stopped keeping count of them in the spring of nineteen fifteen. For having sent so many of his own men off to what was often an inglorious and lingering death. He told us this in nineteen sixty-five, and he said some of his men were still in veterans' hospitals up in Canada and had been since the war. Wrote to them still. So it was a judgment on him, he thought. He had used his voice to betray God. Now it could betray no one else."

He looked at Calvin. "The doctors say whatever it was Elizabeth saw in her dream, or whatever it was she sensed out there, she has to sort it out on her own. When she does, they say she'll speak again. Like her grandfather, she must sort through it all. They tell me she expends the minimum amount of mental energy in living day to day as is necessary. As though she needs to focus all of her remaining energies in sorting through what she saw, what she sensed."

"When do the doctors say that'll be?"

The minister shook his head.

"How did you become involved in this anyway?" Calvin said. "With the murders out there?"

The minister turned and looked out across the street. "It was last winter," he said. "Right after New Year's when I received a call from this reporter in Hanna."

"Brad McLain?"

"Yes. That's right. Do you know him?"

"Yes, sir," said Calvin. "I run into him fairly often at the courthouse."

"Yes. I suppose you would," he said. "Well, I received this call from Mr. McLain. Told me the Sheriff's Office was having a difficult time identifying a body and would I consider driving out to the murder scene sometime soon and having a look-see."

"Why you?"

"I often find myself asking that same question, Mr. Samuels."

The screen door screeched, and Mrs. Barnhouse came out carrying a pitcher of lemonade and two glasses on a wooden tray. After she placed the tray on the three-legged table that was between the porch rocker and swing, she touched her husband's shoulder and smiled and nodded toward Calvin.

"Yes, of course," the minister said to her. "Mrs. Barnhouse would like to know if you could stay for dinner. We've got plenty, and you won't find a better cook in Creek County. That much I can guarantee you."

Calvin smiled at Mrs. Barnhouse and shook his head. "That's very kind of you, but no. I need to be getting back as soon as I can. Trial starts three weeks from tomorrow, and I still have more preparation to do than I'll ever get done, even working on Sundays. But I do thank you."

She smiled and disappeared inside again. The minister reached down and filled their glasses.

"You were saying, Reverend Barnhouse."

The minister handed a glass to Calvin. "I said I often find myself asking the same question," he said. "But that wasn't the answer to the question you asked. The reason why me is that Mr. McLain was told by a Cleveland reporter I'd helped out the police up there with a case that'd been giving them fits some years ago."

"In Cleveland?"

"Yes. Before I moved back to Goshen, I was minister to a congregation there, and the niece of one of my members had disappeared. It was in all the papers at the time. The killer dumped the body along Lake Erie. I was able to show them where. As to why I have this . . . this ability, I can't say. At times I think it more curse than gift."

"So the Cleveland reporter told McLain about you, and McLain called, and the two of you visited the farm last winter?"

"Yes."

"What happened out there?" Calvin said.

"It was on a Monday. We had postponed the trip twice before because of bad weather. Icy roads. Worst winter we'd seen in years. You remember it, don't you? Even worse than the winter before. They called it the five-hundred-year winter."

Calvin nodded. "It was horrible."

"But by the end of the first weekend in January, the county had cleared the main roads. So we bundled up and got in our old pickup truck with sandbags in the back for ballast and drove out there. The county had plowed the Old Church Road, but it hadn't been salted, and packed snow still lay on top."

"Desolate place, isn't it?"

"It is. I remember as we turned up the lane to the farmhouse how lonely it all seemed. Like a white desert. Like a white desert with snow ghosts swirling across it.

"When we managed to make it up the lane to the farmhouse, the coroner and Sheriff Conkle and McLain were waiting for us. They were all standing around outside, shivering in the cold, stamping their feet just to keep their circulation going."

"So how did you begin?" Calvin said. "Looking for whatever it is you were looking for."

The minister laughed for the first time since Calvin's arrival. "That's all right," he said. "You can say it. Ghosts. Call it what you will, at the end of the day, Elizabeth and I were out there looking for ghosts."

"All right, ghosts."

"After being introduced all around, we just started walking. At first together, but after a while we parted and most of the time each of us was alone."

"Didn't the coroner or anyone else follow you?" Calvin said.

"At first McLain did, first me and then Elizabeth, but after a while the cold was so bitter it drove even him inside the farmhouse along with the two others, which is where they stayed for the rest of our visit. We just walked around by ourselves."

"What is it, exactly, you do while walking around?"

"I don't know if I can really explain it," the minister said.

"Well, tell me something it's similar to."

"Most of the time what we do is like watching someone whispering who's a hundred yards away on a cold day, and we're trying to figure out what he's saying just by watching the rising vapor of his breath. On most days, I'm afraid, what we sense are mere ghosts of meaning rather than meaning itself."

"I see."

"Or it's like chasing after these—I call them ghost-dancers—little whirlwinds made of loose snow kicked up and swirled about by the winds blowing across the fields. That is what it is like for us, Mr. Samuels. It is like chasing after ghost-dancers."

"I see."

"Unless what we sense is particularly strong, which is rare."

"Was it particularly strong?"

"Yes. Frighteningly so."

"How's that?"

"Right away, right after I started walking around I felt, and Elizabeth felt, there were five "emotionalities," personalities you would call them, directly involved in one way or another with the murders."

"That would make sense," Calvin said. "Alexander, Bonner, Heath, and Walters. And there was Allison Morris."

"No," the minister said shaking his head. "Not her. I received the distinct impression that all five emotionalities directly involved in the murders were men, and Elizabeth felt the same."

"Who was the fifth?" Calvin said.

"I don't know his name, but he seemed to want to be a guide figure. He wanted me to see, or at least to understand, what had happened."

"Interesting."

"What was more disturbing is that he also wanted to be what I would call a protector."

"Of *you*?"

"No," the minister said. "Not a protector of me."

"Then of who?"

"I don't know. I just don't know, Mr. Samuels. This is what I mean when I say what we do is similar to trying to understand what someone is saying by watching the vapor rising from his breath on a winter day. We can tell he's speaking, but most of the time we just can't understand what it is he's saying. Even when the emotionalities are strong, we can seldom grab on to everything."

"Were you able to grab on to anything else?"

"Well," the minister said. "I told you we felt five emotionalities to be involved directly in the murders in one way or another, either as participants or as spectators. Or as victims."

"All men, you said."

"That's right. But there was another—and this one was definitely a woman—who didn't take part directly in the murders, but who hovered about. In the background. And she had a strong personality. Very strong, indeed. And I sensed that while she didn't participate, she was a moving force both in the murders of Bonner and Heath and in the later murder of the fifth emotionality. In fact, I sensed part of the reason I couldn't understand the guardian better was that she was interfering."

"What can you tell me about her?"

"I sensed a woman of about twenty-four with fairly long and very thick black hair."

The minister paused. "I didn't sense she was dead, but I did sense she was in danger."

"In danger when?" Calvin said.

"That part wasn't clear to me either. Maybe at the time of the murders. Or maybe it was at the time I was out there."

"Or maybe both?"

"Or maybe forever in danger," the minister said.

"Forever in danger?"

"Maybe. And maybe some of those around her are, too."

"In danger of dying?" Calvin said.

"No. Not of dying."

"Then in danger of what?"

The minister looked at Calvin. "In danger of oblivion."

Only after a minute did the minister begin again. "May I tell you a theory of mine?"

"Yes," Calvin said. "Please."

"I'm sure you've heard the theory that all of us, even a minister, under the right set of circumstances, will kill."

"Yes. I've heard that."

"The theory's proponents assume there's some little push that shoves someone over the brink. It's not just the push, of course, but a whole lifetime and then the push. A loss of a job, the discovery of an unfaithful wife. Some confrontation. Something. Some push that causes the murderer to kill."

Calvin nodded.

"Well, I have a corollary theory."

"What's your corollary theory?"

"That sometimes the push comes not from some present stress, or from some person, but from some act of violence in the past of which the murderer is unaware. Sometimes, because the act of dying was so horrific or the emotionality of the deceased or of the killer was so strong, they never leave the scene of the killing. More like a stress of place rather than a stress of events or of persons. Do you see?"

"Like a haunted house?"

"Indeed. Like a haunted house, except it's more than a haunted house. Stronger than a haunted house. If a person who's already predisposed to murder comes into a stress of place, it can push him, or her, over the edge. It's the events of the past, not the present, which are the catalyst. It's as though a hand reaches through a curtain to give the killer a shove before quietly, and sometimes completely, disappearing."

"Is the farm one of those places?" Calvin asked.

"It may well be."

"Why's that?"

"I received the distinct impression that another violent death, or deaths, occurred there some years ago. Perhaps many years ago. And as I walked about, that earlier death and these deaths were all jumbled together. I felt like the cat who enters a room trying to sense who's just left, except for me, those who left had done so months, if not decades, before."

"So what came through about the murder of this fifth emotionality?"

"Nothing about his physical appearance or the details of his death," the minister said. "Only his determination to guide me through. To sort it out for me, and, as I said, to also act as a guardian or a protector."

"Protect you from what?"

"Not necessarily as a protector of me."

"Then who?"

"Perhaps of someone I might speak to, such as one of my congregation. It could be that one of them was more involved with the goings on that summer than he, or she, has let on to me."

"Did Mrs. Barnhouse sense anything similar?"

"Yes, but again it wasn't clear if what she sensed was the recent murders, or the deaths from some time ago. Since Elizabeth cannot speak, she wrote out for me what she sensed."

"What did she write about?"

"Of a woman lying on a table."

"Where?"

"Maybe a cooling board in a morgue, or perhaps in a funeral home. Or maybe just an ordinary kitchen table. She could see only the woman's throat. Her body was covered to the neck with sheeting. The face was indistinct except Elizabeth is certain it was a woman she saw. Only her slit throat, wide and agape, was clear and distinct, she told me."

"But there's been no indication of any woman killed there," Calvin said.

"As I told you, Mr. Samuels, sometimes what we sense are persons, but sometimes what we sense is an evilness of place. And when we are in an evilness of place, what we may sense is the evilness of the recent past, or perhaps of the distant past. And sometime, if the evilness is sufficiently strong, it is an evilness of the future. An evilness that is yet to be."

"Do you think what Mrs. Barnhouse saw had anything to do with the recent murders?"

The minister didn't answer. Calvin studied him. After a minute, he said, "You don't believe the woman's death Mrs. Barnhouse sensed was a death in the past, do you?"

"No. I guess I don't."

"You think what she sensed is a death yet to come."

"Yes," said the minister. "I think what she sensed is a death yet to come."

"Is that why she cannot speak?"

"I think it is more that the evilness she sensed won't permit her to speak."

"Won't permit her?" asked Calvin.

"Yes."

"Forever?"

"No," the minister said. "I don't think forever. That would require too much energy on its part."

"Then until when?"

The minister leaned forward and looked across the street for a minute, his hands folded before him. "I think she will speak again when the evilness has again been set in motion so it cannot be called back," he said. "When there is nothing Elizabeth can say or do to halt the evilness that will be set in motion." The minister turned to Calvin. "That is when I believe she will again speak. And I believe the time is fast approaching."

"If you were me, Reverend Barnhouse, where would you go from here in trying to unravel what happened?"

"I've often found history to be useful. With enough history you can begin to add some substance to what before were only ghosts of meaning. If you must, I would talk to some family member, perhaps Mr. Alexander's family. Are they nearby?"

"Yes. His mother still lives just outside of New Hope."

"To understand more, I suggest you speak to her," the minister said.

"All right."

"But let me tell you something else."

"Please do."

"I've worked a number of investigations since my first one. I was even invited to Atlanta several years ago during their hysteria when they were digging up all those Negro children."

"Yes, sir."

"I've never, ever, experienced such a suggestion of evil as I experienced out at the farm that day. It truly frightened me. Whoever is dealing with it should be very careful. In fact, my suggestion is for him to walk away as quickly as he can, though it may already be too late."

Both men fell quiet. After a minute the minister raised his head, listening. Calvin waited. When the minister said nothing more, Calvin stood, and they shook hands, and he thanked him for his time. The minister walked him to the porch steps, but when Calvin was halfway down the sidewalk and he turned to wave farewell, Reverend Barnhouse was no longer there. He had not even heard the screech of the screen door.

Calvin walked back to his car, but as he was unlocking the door he look up to a second-floor window. There stood the minister, his arms around his wife—who was looking down at Calvin, her mouth open, screaming silently.

CHAPTER 43

CALVIN DIDN'T RETURN directly to Hanna after he left Reverend Barnhouse. He drove through Goshen, the streets all but deserted on a Sunday afternoon, and when he reached State Route 154 he went right and continued on to the Old Church Road.

At the end of the lane leading up to the farmhouse, he again parked next to the rusted and riddled mailbox. He switched off the car ignition and sat there a moment just looking out his car window. How had it been that day last winter? The swirls of snow ghosts arising out of nowhere and dancing across white, barren fields only to disappear into nowhere.

A Model-A Ford pickup, chugging back toward the way he had come, pulled up beside him. Except for the restored cars in the Founders' Day parade, Calvin had never seen a Model-A. A toothless woman of some indeterminate age and looking hard used by life leaned out her window. She told him he had best stay away from the farmhouse if he knew what was good for him. "No good luck ever come to nobody who ever took up there," she told him. "But an awful lot of bad sure has. An awful lot." She spat into the road. "I should know." Then she drove on.

Calvin watched her in his rearview mirror until she disappeared into her own cloud of summer road dust, and he got out and walked up the lane to the top of the rise and around to the back of the farmhouse. He found the path that led to Bear Cross Creek and followed it down, and there he sat on a patch of brown grass above a sheer drop over the water. For the rest of the afternoon he sat there and watched the creek pass below him, watched until the sun set and the sky bled out a rich, wine red behind it.

With all the publicity about the murders reported in the *Hanna Daily Journal* last winter, Alexander might well have been nearby as George and Elizabeth Barnhouse walked the farm that day. He could have stood on the hill that rose across Bear Cross Creek, binoculars in hand and bundled against the cold, as might a deer hunter or some other stalker of prey. If someone had later asked, Alexander could not have said why he had gone there. He would not say, would never say, he believed any psychic would really find anything worth finding, find anything incriminating. Alexander would have asked himself if the sheriff could really be that desperate. Or was it all a sideshow? To get him to let his guard down, to show himself? Fat chance.

Calvin opened his eyes and watched the creek roll by until it grew dark. With the coming of night, the wind off Lake Erie rose, and it seemed as though it might have carried with it the voice of a baseball announcer. If there was a voice within the wind, though, it soon died away and for a while, except for the passing of water, he heard only a solitary mourning dove, but as the wine red sky bled out into the darkness it, too, died away.

As he sat in the darkness, there seemed to be someone watching him from across the creek. Whoever it was did not move, but only studied him as he studied him back. It was so dark, though, what he saw could have been nothing more than a tree stump or a bush or a boulder or something other than someone watching him. But it could have been someone watching him. It could have been.

On just the other side of Bear Cross Creek were the foundation remnants from the first settlement in the county. The settlement founded almost a century before Hanna and whose inhabitants the Native Americans said had disappeared, disappeared as mysteriously as they had appeared.

Finally Calvin stood and brushed off the seat of his trousers with his hand. He walked to his car and drove back to Hanna.

CHAPTER 44

A S CALVIN CRESTED the last rise, he wiped the vapor from the windshield with his shirtsleeve and looked out through the drizzle to ridge upon ridge of coal-dingy low hills. Hills never leveled by the great glacier, stretching out before him like ripples in time to the horizon and beyond. He shifted gears and coasted downhill for the better part of a mile until he entered what remained of the village.

New Hope, Ohio, lay to the south and east of Hanna. It may have had a population of a thousand, but the village was a census-taker's nightmare. No county official would venture for certain whether the population was indeed a thousand, or any other number, because it dwindled from month to month. Not since the 1920s had anyone actually moved there. Calvin might in fact have been the only outsider that day to drive through the village's remnants. The

County Recorder, who had held office for six consecutive terms, once told him it was a rare year for him to record even one deed, and then almost always a probate document, for a parcel transfer there. The sheriff had stopped all tax foreclosures because no one ever appeared at the bidding.

When the last great glacier crept south out of Canada, it had stopped two miles north of New Hope. As it melted, rocks and boulders taller than a man washed all the way to the Ohio, making the land in and around the village impossible to farm. It was land good only for men who knew how to mine it for coal. Good only for men willing to live lives despairing, desperate, and short. When the last of the mines closed after 1929, the mine owners, and those miners who could, moved on. Those who remained either converted to subsistence farming, where they somehow scratched out a crop, or they found work as truck drivers or machinists in the small shops in Hanna.

No villager ever moved out of New Hope of their own volition. They simply succumbed to old age or were sentenced to long prison terms by Judge Biltmore and never returned. Those who remained were remnants of the coalminers whose pits had long ago played out. As he drove along Main Street, Calvin passed between two short rows of gray houses on either side. Houses not painted in decades. Dwellings just this side of dilapidation and whose dwellers had long since passed beyond the far edge of desperation.

When he reached the far edge of New Hope, Calvin

downshifted for the mile long upgrade. At the top, though, the rain abruptly ceased, and he drove into sunshine, the road not even wet.

He drove on and turned left at the second road outside of town and into the first driveway a half-mile farther down. Calvin stopped. The house at the far end of the asphalt driveway was not a graying, turn-of-the-century dilapidation, but a modern brick ranch house.

After a minute he pulled ahead and parked in front of the garage. He got out and walked to a side door where he was greeted by a woman whose hair was pulled back tight in an iron bun. She smiled. "Would you like to talk outside or in?" she said.

"Outside, if you don't mind, Mrs. Alexander."

"Why don't we sit under the big maple by the barn, where we can catch the breeze?"

The two crossed the yard and walked past a horse stable. It was built in the Dutch style, and an ornamental Amish hex sign hung over the door. Behind the stable was a pasture enclosed by a whitewashed wooden fence. To the side of the barn were two lawn chairs beneath a maple tree. Exactly half of the tree was in leaf; the other half was bare enough to suggest it was the dead of winter.

"Struck by lightning two summers ago," said Mrs. Alexander. "Broke my heart. Such a beautiful tree. I've asked Ernest to cut it down for me and plant another." She shrugged. "But, you know men."

"Beautiful place you have here."

Mrs. Alexander looked about her. "It's quiet. Pretty."

"Very."

"Did you know you can see both Pennsylvania and West Virginia from here? The three corners."

"Really?"

"Right out there. That's New Hope behind you," she said and pointed over his shoulder. "And there's Pennsylvania and over there's West Virginia."

Calvin looked to where she was pointing and then he looked back at the cloudbanks. "You know, when I was driving here, it was the strangest thing," he said.

"What was?"

"It rained all the way from Hanna through New Hope. Then outside of town the clouds and rain just stopped, and it was clear."

"It does that," Mrs. Alexander said.

"Interesting."

"I've heard it told that it used to drive the Indians crazy. None of them would live down this way."

The two sat, and Calvin again turned to take in the farm. "Yes, I really admire your place here."

"We worked hard for it. Not just the mister either, but myself, too. Used to drive twenty miles to the hospital in Weirton. Each way. Every day. No matter what the weather."

"Really?"

"I was a nurse, you know."

"No, ma'am. I didn't. Mark never said."

"Not such a big deal now anyways, what with women doctors and all. But in my day, let me tell you, if a girl became a nurse, well, that was something, and there wasn't much more she could hope to accomplish in this life."

"No, I expect not."

"Anyway, as I was saying, with me and the mister both working, we managed to get and hold on to this."

"What was it Mr. Alexander did?"

Mrs. Alexander frowned. "Well, that's kind of a sore subject with me."

"I'm sorry," Calvin said. "I didn't mean to intrude."

"You're not. It's not a secret or anything. It's just a sore subject."

"Yes, ma'am."

"He and his brother owned Ernest's Bar & Grill."

"I thought it was always run by Ernest."

"He has always run it," she said. "Ernest ran it, managed it day to day. But until he died, both he and Mark's father owned it. Fifty-fifty partners."

"Oh."

"Ernest ran it, and the mister took care of what he called the back office matters, though he never really explained exactly what they were."

"I see."

"Of course the police were convinced they were just using it to move stolen goods and to sell dope on the side.

Never arrested either one of them, mind you. They were always very generous with their political contributions."

"That can be helpful."

"But every once in a while, somebody whose house had been recently robbed would wander upstairs and spot something of theirs, and they'd call the police, and the police would talk to the mister and Ernest and convince them to give it back. I begged him to give it up when that happened, but he just said it was a cost of doing business."

"Yes, ma'am."

"Our son, as it turns out, is now a cost of doing business."

"Perhaps not," Calvin said. "We've a good chance at an acquittal."

She shook her head at the irrelevancy.

Calvin stood and looked over the stable and fence. "You sure do a nice job of keeping the place up. On your own and all. Must take considerable work. Without Mr. Alexander about."

She looked where Calvin was looking and nodded. "I take a pride in it."

"What breed of horses do you raise here?"

"Quarter horses," she said.

"That's a good, solid breed. Especially if you can't find the time to ride them every day. They don't spook as easily as might an Arab, say, or an American Saddlebred."

"Yes, I suppose that's so."

"Mark a rider is he?"

"Mark? Goodness no," she said, and laughed. "The horses

are pretty much just there to look at. Like the ornamental Japanese cherry tree out front you drove past when you came in the drive. It's pretty to look at, but the fruit would poison you."

"I see."

"No, Mr. Alexander kept them just because he liked them. They reminded him of when he was a boy."

"Was he a rider then?"

"Oh, you young people," she said, and shook her head, but she smiled too. "You think machines have always been here. No. His family were farmers. Before they got their first tractor, Mr. Alexander plowed with Belgian draft horses."

"But Mark was never a rider?"

"Oh, in the summer he might ride two or three times, and I will say that for several years he got involved in 4-H. But he lost interest once he got his driver's license."

"That happens. Boys lose their interest in a lot of things once they get their license."

"Mark was big enough to have played football in high school, but he was lazy and lacked the discipline. His grades were so-so, though, and he managed to get admitted to college."

"How'd he do?"

Mrs. Alexander shook her head. "Not so good, I'm afraid."

"What happened?"

"He started using marijuana. Then LSD. He didn't think I knew, but I'm a trained nurse. I saw that sort of thing all the time in the hospital."

"Yes, I suppose you would."

"And it was there he met Peter Bonner and Taylor Heath."

"Did you ever meet them?"

"No. I never did," Mrs. Alexander said. "I do remember Mark mentioning their names not long after he started college. And they telephoned here when Mark was home on break. But I never met them."

"And Mark never graduated?"

"He dropped out before they could flunk him out. The alcohol. The pills. The marijuana. All of it made concentration impossible. So he came home again. Even more directionless than when he'd left."

"What'd he do?"

"We let him keep on living here. Which was a mistake."

"It must have been difficult," Calvin said.

"I made Mr. Alexander give him an occasional odd job at Ernest's just so he'd have some pocket money, but that was just another one of my mistakes."

"How so?"

Mrs. Alexander drew a breath, and it was a moment before she answered. "I think all he did was gamble the money he earned shooting pool with the riffraff that would bring in their stolen goods, claiming it to be their own junk."

"Is that how he got involved with the Pagans?"

"I've got my suspicions," she said. "Maybe I shouldn't say so, but since you asked, I will if you'd like to hear it."

"Yes, I would."

"Some fellows from the Ohio Bureau of Investigation

were up here once. Not long after the mister passed on. One was a real nice gentleman who said he had a son a lot like Mark. Said his heart just went out to me." She looked at Calvin. "From what he and others have told me, I've got my suspicions."

"Anything you can tell me?" Calvin said. "If I'm to do Mark any good, I need to know the bad right along with the good."

"A lot of bikers—oh, they're just smalltime thieves who like that Harley-Davidson, Marlon Brando outlaw image—fenced more than an occasional item with the mister and Ernest, and they'd go downstairs to the bar afterward. Mark would be there, of course. He is a great talker. Charming, really."

"Yes," Calvin said. "That he is."

"Even the quietest, shyest barfly you've ever met could spend hours talking to him. Give Mark their life's story in an afternoon."

"Yes, they could."

"I suppose at some time some biker must have asked Mark how he was doing, and Mark would have allowed he was doing middling to fair. Not bad. Not great, but okay with the part-time jobs he was able to pick up here and there. The biker would have asked Mark if he were interested in picking up a few dollars on the side by holding onto some merchandise for him. And it might have been cocaine just run up from Miami."

"That's how you think it started?"

She nodded. "From there, Mark became more and more involved with drugs and the bikers. From starting out and just holding the merchandise, to transporting it, cutting it, selling it. Finally to using it, and then all the other that went with it."

"I guess that's what happens. Little by little. Walking down the primrose path one step at a time."

"Mark must have been well paid for his work. I suppose he wasn't home more than three or four months before he had his own Harley."

"Expensive bike," Calvin said.

"The BCI gentleman told me it wasn't long before they think Mark committed his first murder."

She looked down for a moment. "The BCI gentleman said it was almost self-defense. A customer who couldn't pay or who just didn't want to and knew he would have to hurt Mark if he wanted the cocaine."

"My clients have told me drug buys can get real crazy."

"An informant who was there told them the purchaser was so far gone that when he drew his gun he dropped it, and Mark picked it up and shot him."

"And even though it was self-defense, it's not the type of discussion you want to be having with the police," Calvin said.

"He loaded the body in the dead man's car, drove it to a stripper cut, and rolled the car in."

"Was the car or body ever found?"

She shook her head. "No. Stripper cut water is pretty

acidic. Body wouldn't last long, especially in the summertime."

"How long after that before he ran into Bonner and Heath again?"

Mrs. Alexander shook her head. "I don't know, but by the time Mark met up again with them, the BCI suspects he was already involved in the deaths of ten others."

"Did they tell you who they were?"

"No, not really—but I imagine competitors. Customers planning to double cross him. And just plain ordinary thieves trying to steal from him."

"Your son doesn't seem to be the murdering type. I don't see the viciousness."

"After the first, I suppose the second murder is easier; and after the second, well, after that, probably no qualms at all."

She looked at her watch.

"I should be getting back, Mrs. Alexander."

The two stood and walked back. When they reached the house, Mrs. Alexander went inside, but she still stood looking back through the screen door. Calvin was walking toward his car when he stopped and looked again at the maple tree that was half alive—but at the same time half dead.

As he stood there, an Irish setter came up to him and rubbed against his leg. Calvin stooped and rubbed its fur and scratched behind its ears. He looked up at Mrs. Alexander, her face faintly shrouded by the screen. "You've got a well trained dog here. Most country dogs bark their heads off at strangers."

"He used to."

"Good boy," Calvin said.

"Until somebody slit his throat."

Calvin dropped his hand.

"About a week before the mister was killed."

Mrs. Alexander stepped back, the shroud of her face disappearing as she shut the door.

CHAPTER 45

THE FOLLOWING SATURDAY, Calvin began the day working on the case files of his private clients he had been neglecting. He drafted a will, and he typed up two small-claims petitions. He outlined a buy-sell agreement for a metal shop three of his high-school classmates were starting up. By one o'clock he had moved on to his public defender files, studiously avoiding those of Alexander he kept in a three-quarters-full banker's box. At three, he tuned the radio to KDKA for a Pirates doubleheader. The day following, he would have to look in the *Pittsburgh Press* to find out who had won the second game.

At seven o'clock the telephone rang for the first time all day. It rang three, four, five rings. Calvin stopped writing, but he did not look up. Thirty seconds later it rang again and continued to ring until he answered.

Brad McLain was calling from a pay phone outside the

abandoned gas station in Goshen. He told Calvin to meet him where Bear Cross Creek emptied into the Ohio. *Now*, McLain told him, and hung up.

Half an hour later he stood next to McLain at the top of a thirty-foot bluff over Bear Cross Creek. Beneath them were two sheriff's cars, a van, and perhaps another half-dozen deputies. On the creek bobbed two scuba divers.

"How many divers total?" he asked McLain.

"The two you see. One still down."

"So what've you got?"

"Divers found a pickup. Sheriff thinks it might be Bonner's."

Calvin squatted. "White Ford?"

"Can't be certain. Too dark. Too murky."

"When'd they find it?"

"About an hour ago. Right before I called you."

"I appreciate the call," Calvin said. "I owe you a scoop sometime."

"Yeah, right. A scoop of ice cream. Maybe."

Calvin grinned. "Can I help it if all my juicy stuff is privileged?"

McLain shrugged.

"So how long've they been out there?"

"Since dawn."

"You come out here with them?"

McLain yawned. "Yeah."

"It took them twelve hours to find something as large as a pickup truck?"

"Give them a break, Calvin. The water's thirty feet deep, and visibility is about eight inches, if that. They're exhausted. They've had to crisscross the entire creek bed."

"Yeah, I suppose."

"And they found more than just the pickup," McLain said.

"Yeah? What else?"

"An AK-47."

"A what?" asked Calvin.

"An automatic rifle."

"Where?"

"In the cab."

"I suppose they'll run a check with Alcohol Tobacco and Firearms to see if Alexander owned one."

"Even if he didn't, Heath did."

"Yeah?" Calvin said.

"Yeah. He and Bonner had a practice firing range set up on some farm property his family owned up in Linden."

The third diver surfaced, removed his mask, and said something to the other two. All three disappeared under the water.

Calvin and McLain watched and waited. After a while, Calvin said, "Is the coroner even close to identifying those remains as Heath's?"

"No. He suspects they are, but he can't verify it."

"Have they determined anything about them at all?" Calvin said.

"Male. About twenty-five years of age. Dentist is working with the lower jawbone. Two molars missing. Some of the other teeth looked like someone tried to yank them out with pliers."

One of the divers surfaced. He shouted something to the creek bank and dove again.

"I also heard Heath's father was offering a twenty-thousand-dollar reward, but changed his mind," McLain said.

"Why'd he change it?"

"Got a three-o'clock-in-the-morning phone call. Said he had his family to think about. Said he should be considering the health of his grandkids. Couple of days later, he received some photographs of them taken at their school playground."

A gust of wind pushed the two back a step from the edge of the bluff. Calvin was wearing only a T-shirt and he crossed his arms and shivered. "So they found nothing in the pickup except for the rifle?" he said.

"Nada. But Bonner's brother says his Sportster was also around the area, so it could be down there, too."

"Or in a chop shop."

"Yeah, there, too."

All three divers surfaced. McLain raised his hand to skylight them. The divers turned over on their backs and paddled to shore. The deputies gathered together in a line below the embankment.

Calvin and McLain walked down a steep path that led to the creek bed, but one of the deputies told them to stand back if they didn't want to be arrested for interfering with the investigation. The divers came on shore and took off their equipment, which the deputies helped them load into the sheriff's van, and all of them drove off and were gone in less than sixty seconds. McLain said he should follow them back to County to pick up the rest of the story, and he started to walk back to his car.

"Hey. McLain," Calvin shouted.

McLain turned.

"Bear Cross Creek is a big stream. How'd the sheriff know where to look?"

"You'd have to ask him that yourself to know for certain," McLain said. "My guess would be Allison Morris might be his answer." McLain turned and continued up the path and disappeared into the night. After a while, Calvin heard the still un-tuned engine turn over.

He lit a cigarette and looked out at the creek where he could hear the water ripple in the darkness. He looked across the creek to the other side, and he tried to make him appear again, but he could not. He flicked his cigarette out into the darkness and walked back to his car and drove home.

The following Monday, Calvin was coming down the courthouse steps as Sheriff Conkle was coming up, and he stopped the sheriff.

"Now that you mention it, Calvin, the cigarette lighter was missing from the truck. Why do you ask?"

CHAPTER 46

ALEXANDER'S IRON-GRAY EYES glared at Calvin as Deputy Smith unlocked the manacles cuffing his wrists, but Calvin did not turn away. The deputy hooked the manacles to his belt-ring and left the two of them, shutting the door to counsel's room in the courthouse behind him.

Alexander walked to the wired window, his fists in his jumper pockets. "This is not good, counselor. This is not good at all. I'd hoped you would do a better job of convincing Judge Biltmore not to try my case in front of these . . ." Alexander turned and looked at him. "In front of these farmers."

"Mark, try to keep today in perspective. This was just one arrow out of your quiver. Out of all your arrows, you only need one to hit home, and you walk. We don't know which one it's going to be, so we keep shooting away. We keep trying."

Calvin waited a moment for Alexander to say something,

but he didn't, so he went on. "And we're building a record for your appeal if one's going to be necessary. Maybe this arrow didn't hit home and maybe the next one won't. But before the Appeals Court, enough of these arrows and Thompson's case against you will begin to look full of holes."

Alexander stood at the wired window, listening. After a moment he said, "You know what I think?"

"What?"

"I think you intentionally lost my motion for a change of venue because you want to try this case."

"I what?"

Alexander turned and looked at Calvin. "If my case is transferred to another county, I'd be represented by the State PD and not you. I think you pulled your punches today so you will be the one trying my case."

"Now, why would I want to? For eight weeks I'm getting a measly hundred sixty dollars a week for eighty hours a week of work and a whole lot of aggravation thrown in. Since I've been assigned to represent you, my private practice has gone to hell in a hand basket to boot. I haven't paid my office bills for a month now. So tell me. Just why in hell would I want to try your case?"

Alexander shook his head, but his eyes did not let go. "I don't know. But I can tell it's not because you believe in me. There is something else going on."

Calvin waited for Alexander to say something more, but he did not. After a while, he said, "It's been a long afternoon. Is there anything else?"

Alexander said nothing and walked to the door and knocked and told Deputy Smith he was ready to go back up. As the deputy re-cuffed him, Alexander turned to say something to Calvin, but changed his mind and left with the deputy's hand on his elbow.

Calvin walked upstairs to the Public Defender's Office and stood at the window and watched as Smitty helped Alexander into the cruiser. He turned and looked at the door to the storage room, and then he looked back to the street. "I'll find out before this is over, John. I promise. One way or the other, before this is over, I'll find out."

CHAPTER 47

SOMETIME AFTER MIDNIGHT Calvin surrendered all hope of falling asleep. He got up and pulled on a pair of well-worn jeans and the undershirt he found lying on the floor, already worn during the day. He walked out the back door and into his yard.

He looked across to Mrs. Ferguson's house, but it was silent and dark. Calvin walked back to the alley which ran behind their houses. A half-mile beyond the alley he could see a ground fog creeping up the rise from the countryside toward Hanna.

He walked back and sat in a lawn chair and watched the fog's approach. He lit a cigarette and smoked and waited. When it had almost reached the alley, the summer crickets ceased their chirping and a specter stepped out.

Calvin reached over to crush out his cigarette, but he must have dropped it sometime before because now it lay sullen and wet in the dewy grass. When he looked up, the specter was close enough Calvin could see him smiling, but not so close he would have recognized his face.

"I thought I might see you tonight," Calvin said.

The specter placed his hands in his coat pockets, but came no closer. "Why was that, Calvin?"

"It just felt right. Or not right. I'm not sure which."

"You're not afraid, are you?"

"No. Should I be?"

"Yes," said the specter. "You should. But not of me."

Calvin leaned forward, but still he could not recognize the face. Nor could he recognize the voice. He was not even certain the specter was speaking.

"If I shouldn't be afraid of you, then of what?"

"Of yourself," the specter said.

He waited for the specter to say something more, but he did not.

"I'm not understanding you," Calvin said after a minute. "Why do I need to be afraid of myself?"

"I remember once, years ago, reading a story where a woman gives the detective hero the name of a museum curator who can describe a piece of stolen art. After she does, she asks the detective if he was going to lead him into trouble. He shouldn't, she said, because he was one of the good people."

The specter looked at him. "Are you one of the good people?"

Calvin sat back in his lawn chair. "Why is it if I was, I don't feel that would be a compliment?"

"There are, unfortunately, in your line of work, bad guys who accept evil and try to profit by it."

"Such as Alexander?"

The specter shrugged.

"Go on, please," Calvin said. "What about the good guys?"

"The good guys are those who take some small stand on principle. Who, perhaps only once in a lifetime, find the courage to stand above everyone else."

"The good guys are good people then?"

The specter shook his head. "No. On the edges, apart from the bad guys, are the good people. The good people are the vast majority of good, ordinary people who are innocent, but they are innocent only because they've never been tempted. Not morally tempted. They have not yet spent their forty days in Sinai."

"I see," Calvin said.

"The criminals are evil because they want to lead those people, the good people, into the desert."

"And the detective?"

"The detective," the specter said. "The detective is like a guardian. He wants to save them from a moral trial they will certainly fail."

"Which am I?"

"Which are you, Calvin Samuels?"

The two looked at one another for a moment. Then the specter nodded and walked back into the fog from which he'd come.

CHAPTER 48

SUNDAY AFTERNOON OF the following week, Calvin was working alone in the Public Defender's Office. All was quiet save for the drone of the fan he had wedged into the window. The compressor to the air conditioner in his office above the Hanna Bank & Trust had finally died midmorning, so he had packed Alexander's files into the banker's box and carried them across Main Street. Before he had even reached the back courthouse door, however, perspiration dripped off his forehead, stinging his eyes, and onto his nose.

Calvin set the box down on his desk and took his legal tablet and the top file from the box. He removed his pen from his shirt pocket and picked up where he had left off.

Late in the afternoon, someone knocked at the office door. "Go away," he mumbled. "Please, just go away."

After a moment, the door lock turned, and Thompson

came in. "Calvin," he said, "Calvin?"

He walked back to Calvin's office. "Calvin. I hoped I'd catch you. Didn't you hear me knocking?"

Calvin pointed. "Fan running," he said.

Thompson looked at the window.

"Don't tell me the Prosecutor has a key to the PD office?"

"Why do you think we always win?"

"I thought it was because you were just a good prosecutor."

"I am a good prosecutor," Thompson said, and he held up his key chain. "But a great prosecutor has a key to the PD office."

"Since when?"

"One of the perks of holding elective office is that all of the officeholders have keys to all of the courthouse offices."

Thompson dropped into one of the chairs in front of Calvin's desk. "I thought you should know we found Heath."

Calvin straightened. "Where?"

"Had him all the time. He was buried with Bonner, after all."

"I thought your coroner ruled that out months ago?"

"My coroner kept Bonner's jaw, but sent Heath's back to Michigan with the rest of Bonner's bones and then couldn't figure out why it didn't match Heath's dentals."

Calvin shook his head. "No way."

Thompson grinned.

"No way."

"Sheriff Conkle says to say thank you. He says you were

the one who thought of it while you were helping him dust Heath's van a few weeks back."

"No way."

"Says not to worry. He won't let on to Alexander you've been helping him out on the side."

"Tell the sheriff I said thanks."

"Will do."

"But, Ben, how could your coroner have made a mistake like that?"

"Says it was the unorthodox burial. Also the unusual way the bones were recovered. Plus Bonner's family wanted him buried again as soon as possible. Add to that the condition of the few bones we did find, burned and covered with quicklime, and all mixed up together with animal bones."

"Plus, your coroner is incompetent when he's not drunk."

"If the truth be known, he's incompetent even when he is drunk," Thompson said.

"He'll make a great witness."

"Only in your dreams, Calvin, will our esteemed coroner be testifying in this trial. In fact, I think he plans on being on vacation during the week of trial. Fishing up in Ontario."

"So what'd you do? Go up to Michigan and dig them up?"

"Yeah," said Thompson. "Conkle went up to a cemetery near Heath's hometown and had them exhumed."

"Exhumed?"

"First time in county history we've ever had to exhume a body."

"And the longest time in county history a murder victim hasn't been identified."

"Don't remind me."

"And is this an election year?"

Thompson raised his hand to cover his eyes and groaned. "Don't remind me," he said. "Please, don't remind me."

"So for nearly two years now, Conkle's been spinning his wheels."

"Until you helped him out."

"Don't remind me."

Calvin got up from his chair and walked to the door and shut it. He walked to the window fan and turned it up to high speed and walked back and sat in the chair next to Thompson. "So the Bonner family gave you permission for an exhumation."

"Nope. Conkle and Donna Lacy, the Assistant Coroner, drove up on Thursday."

"How'd they exhume the body without the family's permission?"

"While they were there, they got a search warrant from a judge in Genesee County, and they exhumed it at Flint Memorial Park."

"Went to the cemetery the same day?"

"Yeah," Thompson said. "Cemetery crews removed the vault and placed it in a tent at graveside. Lacy opened the vault and the infant casket. Said it held only fifteen bones."

"And the Bonner family?"

"Mr. Bonner looked on."

"So what did Donna bring back?" Calvin said.

"Upper jawbone. Lower arm bone."

"Why the arm?"

"Bonner broke his as a kid," Thompson said. "We wanted to be certain it wasn't Heath's."

"And you brought them back for your coroner to look at?"

"Not on your life. Jawbone we gave to a Cleveland dentist. Arm bone we sent to BCI."

Calvin nodded. "I appreciate your letting me know."

Thompson rose and walked to the door. "No harm done," he said. "It'll be in the papers tomorrow anyway."

"I can't wait."

Thompson stood and went out to the hall and locked the door behind him.

"Damn," Calvin said.

CHAPTER 49

A LITTLE AFTER SIX o'clock on the Monday morning one week before the start of Alexander's trial, Calvin pulled onto the Ohio Turnpike where it passed some twenty miles north of Hanna. He reached up from the gear shift and cranked back the canvas sunroof and let the heavy summer air roll over him. He turned off the radio and left it off.

He had told only Brad McLain where he was going. With what once seemed like a can't-lose case slithering through his fingers like so many worms, Calvin told McLain he'd better go up and talk to the families of Bonner and Heath. Something might turn up. Might.

Near noon, he pulled up in front of a squat yellow tract house in bad need of a coat of paint. Gravel driveway, but no garage. A lawn more weed than grass, but no garden. Calvin leaned over and checked the address against the note in his glove compartment. When he got out, he left his pen and legal pad on the passenger's seat. As he shut his car door, a curtain moved by an unopened window. He watched a moment longer, but it didn't move again.

Across the street, a neighbor pushing his lawnmower stopped in mid-yard. Marine Corps tattoos drooped in flabs from each arm, and his American Legion belly hung out of his stained undershirt and dropped so far over his belt that his urinary directional flow must have occasionally been problematic. He removed his plastic-tipped Muriel panatela from between his teeth and frowned. He looked at the license plate on the Volkswagen and at Calvin before turning and spitting a thick brown wad into the grass. Calvin nodded, but the neighbor only put the cigar back between his teeth and frowned some more.

Calvin walked up the gravel driveway and up a crumbling concrete walk to the front stoop. A woman in her fifties wearing shorts that exposed her porcine thighs crisscrossed by lumpy varicose veins opened the screen door without his having to knock.

"You must be that lawyer feller come up from Ohio." She didn't smile, but neither did she look displeased.

"Yes, ma'am, I am. My name's Calvin Samuels."

"Well, come on in then."

"Thank you."

The small living room was overfilled with furniture, and tables and shelves were crowded with knickknacks like the kind children win at county fairs. Walls covered with photographs. While one yellowing picture was of a smiling soldier wearing an Eisenhower jacket and pointing back with his thumb at rubble-laden buildings, the rest were of children at all ages.

"Just let me get off the phone, and I'll be right with you, Mr. Samuels," the woman said, and she walked to another part of the house, the floor creaking beneath her, while Calvin stood just inside the front door.

"Yes, it's him. I'll have to call you back later. No, I don't think that'll be necessary."

A door opened and closed somewhere, and after a minute the woman came back. "Would you like some coffee?"

"Please," he said. "It was a long morning's drive."

"I'll bet it was. Instant okay with you?"

"Yes, ma'am."

"I always have to ask. Some people just can't stand the taste. Can't stand it."

"Yes, ma'am, but I can't tell the difference."

"Me either. And who cares about the taste anyway. It's the jolt, right?"

Calvin nodded. "Absolutely."

She turned and walked out of the room again, and Calvin waited by the screen door. The neighbor's lawnmower was no longer running, and now he could hear a television set from somewhere in the house.

"And let's go to contestant number three," a television announcer said. "She dislikes men with tattoos and beer guts."

Calvin looked out at the neighbor across the street.

"Now she's going to tell us what other kinds of men she doesn't like."

There was a pause followed by a woman's voice, shrill as a cat in heat who had just learned to speak. "And I hate men who treat women like they're nothing but mindless, steaming sexpots with no minds of their own."

After the canned studio audience laughter, the announcer came back. "A woman who's a mindless, steaming sexpot with no mind of her own. Where can I find one of those?"

Someone turned down the volume. Mrs. Bonner returned and handed him a cup of coffee. She motioned toward a green-print sofa, and she herself sat in a matching stuffed chair. Behind her were handmade cards with crayoned landscapes inhabited by stick people and stick animals standing on red grass beneath purple skies. Calvin sipped at his coffee.

"So how's Mark, Mr. Samuels?"

"Mark?"

Mrs. Bonner nodded.

"Oh," Calvin said after a moment. "He's doing about as well as can be expected, I guess. Under the circumstances."

"Well, at least his circumstances are that he's not dead. Not dumped down an outhouse and poured over with gasoline and set afire. At least I hope his circumstances would be that he was dead before he was set afire."

Calvin placed his cup and saucer on the coffee table. "Have you met Mark?"

"Have I met him?" Mrs. Bonner said.

"Yes, ma'am."

"I should say indeed I have. I have indeed."

"Where was that?"

"Well, right here, of course."

"Here?"

"He collects topazes just like I do. He would sometimes come over with Peter, and I'd show him the newest additions to my collection since I showed it to him the last time, and he'd go to a gem show somewheres and maybe send something back to me."

"He was here in your home?"

"Oh, my, yes. He and Peter often came over here for supper. I didn't mind, though. Peter didn't have many friends after his accident."

"Accident?"

She looked up at the photographs on the wall next to her. "Peter Bonner was an All-American boy. Everyone—his friends, his teachers, his schoolmates, members of the Methodist church, everyone—we all expected that when he finally got to college, he'd go on to be a real All-American. Get to meet the President and everything."

She nodded toward the table next to Calvin. On it was a photograph of a boy of about sixteen with a black cowlick looking self-conscious and holding his helmet in his left hand by the faceguard. Red jersey, white pants. Number fifty-four. A concrete stadium in the background, the grass greener than grass could ever be except in a photograph.

"He was playing football when he fractured his skull," Mrs. Bonner said. "He was in the hospital for a month. Laid on that couch for another three. He was never the same, though."

"That's a shame. A kid so young with so much promise."

"I've often felt, after his accident, that the Peter I knew, the one I gave birth to and raised, died the night he fractured his skull. After that, it was just waiting until . . . well, it was just waiting."

"When did Peter and Taylor meet up?" Calvin said.

"They never really did. Not the way you might think. They'd known each other since kindergarten, I suppose. Probably before kindergarten even. But it wasn't until Peter fractured his skull they began seeing much of each other."

"Oh?"

"Before, Peter was just shy, but he was never what you'd call a trouble maker. Afterward, he was still quiet. Polite. But when he couldn't play football no more, he started hanging out with the wrong crowd. Beer led to wine to marijuana to . . . well, you know."

"Yes, ma'am."

"After he stopped playing, Peter had no real friends anymore. Then he had one. Taylor. T-Ray they sometimes called him. For Taylor Raymond."

"What was Taylor like?

"They was the opposite sides of the same coin, as people say. Peter, like I was telling you, was big and quiet and shy."

Mrs. Bonner studied the black-screened television set for a moment. "Did you see that Hallmark Hall of Fame show that was on last month? *Of Mice and Men*. By that fellow Steinway."

"No, ma'am. But I remember reading it in college."

"After his accident, my Peter would have reminded you a lot of that Lenny. Maybe a little brighter."

"And Taylor?" asked Calvin.

"Taylor was shorter and louder. More arrogant, if you know what I mean. More of a ladies' man than Peter."

"Did he play football, too?"

"Oh, no. Besides having no ambition, he lacked Peter's height and weight and speed, so football was out of the question for him. Besides, he didn't have the discipline."

"I see."

"No, he just watched from the stands, more at the girls who were watching the players than the game. Of course Taylor needed money for the ladies, but he lacked the initiative to go out and find a real job. Dealing to his schoolmates was a whole lot easier, and he made a whole lot more than he would have pumping gas or bagging groceries."

"When did they become buddies?"

"It was after Peter recovered from his injuries—or at least recovered as much as he was going to—and he was up and walking around and gone back to school. It was probably about the time he had moved on from wine to marijuana, and he was buying from Taylor."

"They wouldn't seem to have had much in common."

"Taylor could see the advantages of having someone of Peter's size and reputation along when he met some of his tougher customers. The ones who wouldn't think twice about shaking him down, but might if Peter were along."

"What happened to them after graduation?" Calvin said.

"Peter tried college, but the concentration just wasn't there. I've often thought that if he hadn't of gone off, he would of never of met up with Mark, and he might still be with us."

"Yes, ma'am."

"But I tell myself, no, Page Bonner, if it hadn't of been him, it would have been someone else. Or something else."

Calvin nodded.

"After the accident, my Peter was gone, and he was never coming back. We was just passing time until what little was left was taken, too."

She looked at Calvin. "It was as if I had two sons," she said. "One before the accident and another after. The one I had before was gone. The son that was with me after was not to be with me long. I knew that. But still, I loved my second son. And I always hoped the first would come back to me."

Calvin again heard television laughter from somewhere in the house, but it quickly died away.

"Mr. Bonner," she said. "Some days he just don't feel

much like going out to work."

"What happened after his first year of college?" Calvin said.

"Oh, he quit and worked in his dad's plumbing business for a year or so. Mr. Bonner liked that. He hadn't seen much of the kids while they was growing up, and he felt real bad when he couldn't spend more time with Peter after the accident—we had some horrendous hospital and doctor and medicine bills to pay. He was working seventy, eighty hours a week for over a year. So it gave him some time with Peter. To make up for his not being there before."

"What about Taylor?"

She shook her head. "Taylor didn't even try college. He just kept dealing. Kept on seeing the ladies. He was always real popular with them. Had lots of cash to spend. Nice cars to show them off with."

"And the very best dope in town."

"And that, too," she said.

"So after Peter quit college and started working with Mr. Bonner, Peter hooked up again with Taylor?"

"Mr. Bonner figures it wasn't too long after Peter began working for him that Taylor saw the advantages of riding along to transact his own business."

"Taylor would've been almost invisible," Calvin said. "At least until the police caught on."

"I suppose that's so. By that time I imagine all of Taylor's cars were pretty well known to them. The plumbing van wasn't yet. And you're right. He was almost invisible to them. A blue work shirt, white overalls, a cap on his head; and Taylor was just another working joe."

"So he started dealing out of the plumbing van."

"Peter must of told him his schedule the day before. Taylor would tell his customers where to meet him the next day."

"So he'd just hang out at the work site and socialize with Peter until a buyer came by. No steady stream of disreputable customers into a good neighborhood for the police to pick up on."

"Taylor, they tell me, became one of the largest dealers in Genesee County, and his suppliers began to take notice."

"In what way?" Calvin said.

"When there were runs up from Florida that needed to be done and there was a shortage of couriers, they'd ask him to fill in."

"He must have been good at what he did."

"Because of his speed and reliability, after a while he was doing it full-time," Mrs. Bonner said. "And of course where Taylor went, Peter was sure to follow."

"Peter stopped working for Mr. Bonner?"

"Yes. Peter and Taylor were inseparable."

Calvin turned his coffee cup in its saucer. "Has anyone from Creek County been up to see you?"

"Yeah. Can't recollect his name, though."

"Conkle?"

"That's the gentleman," Mrs. Bonner said. "He said they

was good. 'Took no unnecessary chances' is what he told us. Stayed off the interstates. Slept during the day. Drove only at night."

"How did Peter and Alexander reconnect?"

"One time after they'd got back after a run, Peter told me they'd stopped in a little town called Goshen, Ohio, for something to eat, one of those out of the way stops Conkle told me they preferred. And guess who they saw while they was there? I couldn't guess, and he said it was Mark from college."

Calvin nodded.

She looked down at her hands. She looked up at him. "You're probably wondering why I'm going on like this. Blabbering on about family history and secrets to someone who's trying to get Peter's killer off the hook. Trying to keep him out of the penitentiary."

"You miss your son, ma'am."

"And it was Mark Alexander who killed him," Mrs. Bonner said. "Your client, Mr. Samuels. Your client who slit his throat open is what Conkle told us. Like he was no more than a dog. Then shoved him down an outhouse. Set it afire." She looked at the photograph beside Calvin. "I can only hope Peter was dead when he dumped him down there."

Mrs. Bonner looked down at her hands again.

"Ma'am. Could it have been . . . ? Did Peter have any enemies? Might he have mentioned someone to you?"

"I know you come here to ask me if it might've been someone else. That's your job, and I can appreciate that."

418

Calvin nodded.

"But it wasn't no one else, Mr. Samuels. It was Mark. When you called and asked if you could come up, I almost hung up on you. I was expecting your call and that's what I planned to do. Hang up on you. But after you started talking, I thought, *No*. You didn't know nothing about our Peter. You didn't know he was more than just a drug-dealer. You didn't know that he was somebody's son. My son."

Calvin looked at the photograph, too. "Yes, ma'am. I can see there was a real bond between you."

Mrs. Bonner looked at Calvin. She looked back to the photograph. After a moment, she said, "Now, I must ask you to leave, Mr. Samuels."

He looked into her eyes, eyes like shattered pier glass. He tried to smile.

When he stood, Mrs. Bonner did also. As Calvin was going out the door, she followed, taking the photograph off the table. "Mr. Samuels," she said. Calvin turned to face her. "I want you to take this with you. I want you to place it on your desk, and I want you to look at it while you're working on getting him off."

Mrs. Bonner shoved the photograph frame under his arm and stepped back. Calvin walked outside and let the screen door softly close behind him. He looked at the face smiling out at him through his shyness. When he turned to say something, he saw that Mrs. Bonner was sitting on the floor a few feet behind the screen door, weeping quietly.

He studied the picture for a minute more. He looked down at the woman sitting on the floor. Then Calvin placed the photograph in the mailbox and walked back to his car.

CHAPTER 50

A S CALVIN HAD several hours to kill before Raymond Heath would be quitting his shift at the Chrysler assembly plant, he drove around until he found a McDonald's. He doubled back toward the Bonner home to a park he'd passed along the way. He parked and carried his purchases to a bench near a little league baseball diamond. Across from the baseball field stood the stadium pictured in the background of the photograph Mrs. Bonner had shoved under his arm.

He ate his hamburger and drank his soda. The french fries were overcooked, so he tore them in bits and threw them out to the sparrows, seeing how close they would come to him. He dozed until cars began pulling into the parking lot and boys pedaled in on their bicycles and parked them behind the backstop. Two men in baseball caps unlocked their trunks and a group of boys surrounded each car and carried away canvas bags holding bats and balls and mitts to their respective dugouts. Calvin spread his arms on the back of the park bench and for a while he just watched nine- and ten-year-old boys pitch and hit and catch.

He sat close enough to their game that he could hear their chatter. In the second inning a boy called Paul came to bat. He was smaller than the others, and baseball must have come harder to him because his team and the crowd seated behind them rooted for him with a special ardency. They told Paul to come on, to knock the cover off, to come on.

He swung, swung with all the might a young boy might have, but he missed, and he swung so hard that when he missed he fell to the ground on his knees.

"Come on, Pauly," the crowd behind him shouted. "You can get this next one. You can do it."

When the ball came, Paul swung again, and again he swung with all the might he could muster, but again he missed.

"Come on, Pauly. Don't strike out. You can do it. You can."

Paul choked up on the bat. He stood square with the plate, and he looked at the pitcher with much determination and with much fierceness. He growled. The pitcher eyed the bases over his shoulder. He looked over at his coach and threw the ball, hitting Paul squarely in the ear.

Paul's knees buckled, and he hit home plate with the same soft thud as a slingshot robin. His teammates emptied their bench and gathered around him, and the coach shouted at them to stand back, to give Paul some air.

After a minute Paul stood up on wobbly legs, but he dusted off the seat of his jeans and trotted to first base to the cheers of his team and the crowd. The pitcher, who had not moved from the mound after he knocked Paul down, watched him as he took first base with a "Who, me?" look on his face.

Calvin looked at his watch. He stood and walked back to his car and drove to the Heath home. When he knocked at the front door, no one answered. He knocked again and followed the sidewalk to the rear of the house.

He found Mr. Heath sitting on a concrete stoop by the back door, his legs hanging down, his shoes untied and lost in grass long uncut. Next to him was an open Schlitz can. He was smoking a cigarette and looking toward the setting sun at a group of children cooking hot dogs over a campfire.

"Mr. Heath?"

He didn't answer at first. After a moment, he turned. "You must be that lawyer feller."

"Yes, sir."

Mr. Heath looked down at the grass and spoke to it, spoke in silence.

He looked up. "Well, what time's it getting to be?" He raised the hand holding the Schlitz can and looked at his watch. "Gosh, I'm sorry, Mr. Samuels. I didn't realize it was getting on so. I should of been up front to meet you instead of sitting back here drinking my suds. And here you drove all the way up from Hanna, Ohio, just to talk to me and the missus."

"No harm done, sir."

He nodded. "I like to come out here in the evening when it's nice like this to think."

"Yes, sir. I can see why. It's pleasant back here."

Mr. Heath sipped at his beer. "I've already put Marilynn to bed," he said.

"That's okay."

"After supper she'll take her Valium and pour herself a big glass of vodka. I'll do the dishes, and we'll sit in the living room and listen to records from when we was kids. We never talk much. Just sit there and listen until she falls asleep. I'll help her up to bed and undress her and tuck her in. Then I like to come out here."

He looked at Calvin. "That's really a lie I told you."

"A lie?"

"I don't come out here to think. Only not to."

Calvin nodded.

"No," shouted a woman, her voice coming from an open window above them.

Calvin looked up, but Mr. Heath only looked out to the sunset over the children.

"Marilynn'll toss and turn all night until almost dawn. Often she'll sit up in bed and shout 'No,' like that, at the top of her lungs."

"Do you need to check on her?"

Mr. Heath didn't answer.

"Has she seen a doctor?"

"In the mornings I'll ask her about what she'd been dreaming. She'll tell me she don't remember, but I know she does. You may not remember your dreams, but you never forget your nightmares."

"What do you think they're about?"

"Probably the same as mine. Taylor floating in a hole full of filth. His arms and legs and hair all stretched out on the surface, and somebody covering him up with lime and setting him on fire, and he shrivels up like a . . ." He looked out at the children by the campfire. "Like a marshmallow on the end of a stick."

"Does it come often?" Calvin said.

"Every night. Same dream. Sometimes over and over. Without end it seems like. Forever. Sometimes the dream'll wake me, and I'll not be able to go back to sleep, and I'll just lay there 'til morning. Thinking about Taylor. I'll hear Marilynn, and I'll know she's dreaming it, too."

"I'm sorry."

"You know, I was in one of the Army units that liberated Dachau."

"No, sir," Calvin said. "I hadn't heard that."

"It's true, though most folks around here don't know it; if any did, they'd say the Jews got what was coming to them. I suppose I might of thought the same way when I left here, but not by the time I got back."

"No. I guess not after you saw what you did."

"Even though they hadn't burned up any Jews for quite a while before we got there, the smell of them they had still clung to everything. Hung in the air like it was their ghosts. And you know what?"

"No, sir," Calvin said. "What?"

"I smell the same smell in my dreams about Taylor. Isn't that strange? After all these years, having long ago forgotten it, the smell come back to me like that. In a dream."

"Yes. It's strange."

"Marilynn's taken to sleepwalking, you know," Mr. Heath said. "Sometimes in the middle of the night I'll hear her shouting downstairs, and I'll get up and bring her back to bed. Once I woke up, and she was sleeping soundly, but I saw there was muddy tracks leading up to her bed, and her slippers was caked in mud. I went outside, but I couldn't tell where she'd been or gone to. I managed to clean up the mud without her noticing. Had to throw away her slippers, though. The ones I'd bought for her one Christmas."

He pulled a pack of cigarettes out of his pocket. He watched the children playing by their campfire for a while before he spoke again. "It wasn't supposed to be like this for us, you know. It wasn't supposed to be like this for Taylor."

"No, sir."

"When I was discharged in forty-six, I took my savings and my bonus and opened up a small machine shop. It wasn't much, I didn't make much, but it was enough to support a family for a few years until I got hired on at the Chrysler plant. They had to take back the returning vets first before they could hire on anyone who hadn't worked there before the war."

"That's something," Calvin said. "That's something to be proud of all right. Your own shop and all."

"Those early years after I got out of the service, thems was the best ones. Why, on Thursdays, sometimes I didn't know where the money would come from for us to pay for Saturday's groceries. But it always did, and we had hope and fun and happiness. Finally we had Taylor after we had our four girls."

He looked at Calvin. "What went wrong?"

It grew dark, and they watched the children's campfire burn down to only embers.

"I worshiped that boy," Mr. Heath said. "I wasn't home much. Often I put in double shifts and sixteen-hour days. But T-Ray, that's what his mama took to calling him, stole every minute with me he could when I did get home."

"A special boy to you," Calvin said.

"He 'specially liked reading the Sunday funny papers with me. Sometimes after services we'd start to walk home from church while Marilynn caught up on the week's gossip. We would sit on the cement bridge that was on the way home and toss in stones and look for crayfish and snails and such. T-Ray would ask me where'd the creek come from, and I told him it come down from the farms north of here. *Where's it go to?* he'd ask me. Milford Creek, I'd say. Then on to Little Creek, then Lake Huron to Lake Erie, Lake Ontario, the Saint Lawrence, and finally out to the Atlantic.

"Then one Sunday T-Ray says to me, he says, you mean if he was to spit in the creek, it'd end up all the way out in the Atlantic Ocean? I told him most likely it'd of evaporated long before it ever got there. The next Sunday, he says to me, supposing he was to drink a whole milk bottle full of water and supposing he was to pee in the creek? *What then?* he says. 'Supposing you just don't,' I told him."

Mr. Heath chuckled and shook his head. "I had to try hard not to laugh. You know you got to be careful not to laugh at a child so as not to encourage them."

"Yes, sir."

"Marilynn would come by and pick us up and drive us home. We'd change out of our Sunday best, and we'd read the funny papers together while Marilynn finished up the roast she cooked every Sunday and had started before we'd left."

"Sounds like a good life, Mr. Heath. A nice life."

"Yes, it was. At least until T-Ray got to be about thirteen it was. Then we was at each other's throats."

"It's a disease most of us go through at that age all right."

"He wanted his independence, and I wanted him to have it, too. Hellfire, I remember what it was to be young, but I wanted him to have the benefits of some of my mistakes so'd he live long enough to enjoy his youth."

Mr. Heath shook his head. "You know, if they're lucky, fathers and sons grow back together again."

"Yes," Calvin said. "If they're lucky."

"Most boys dance on the wild side while they're growing up. At least I did. Didn't you?"

"Some. Not much. But some."

"Sometimes they'll dance over the line, but come back to where they belong, and they never cross over again."

"Yes. That's the way it most often works out."

"Other times, a boy'll dance over the line and go further and further away until he's finally lost for good. You know?" He looked at Calvin. "You know what I'm saying?"

"Yes, sir. I've seen it go that way, too."

"Taylor. He was a lost one."

"I'm sorry for your loss. To you and Mrs. Heath. You seem like good people."

"Good people."

"Yes, sir."

Mr. Heath flicked his cigarette butt far out into the dewy grass, where it spit for a second before dying.

"When Taylor was thirteen, I think he just picked the wrong crowd to start hanging out with. At first I suspected, and then I knew. Knew for a fact. The sudden drop in grades. The odd hours. The money, but never a job. Hell, sometimes it seemed like he had more money than me, and he wasn't but a teenager. What could I do?" He again looked at Calvin.

"I don't know, sir," Calvin said. "Wait for the crazy years to pass. Hope for the best." He was quiet a moment. "Prayer, maybe?"

"I've never been a good disciplinarian, even though I was in the Army like I told you. I know if I'd of told T-Ray to clean up or get out, he'd of gotten out. But I didn't. Then it was too late to do anything."

He picked up his Schlitz can and twirled around the beer left in the bottom. "Almost empty," he said. "You want a beer, Mr. Samuels? I don't know what's got into me. Here I've been running my mouth, and I forgot my manners. We got some Schlitz. It's good and cold."

"No, sir. I've a long drive ahead of me tonight. But thank you."

Mr. Heath shook his head. "You and the goddamn FBI." He leaned and spat into the grass. "I was hoping to get them boys drunk when they come by. I bet you I could of gotten some wing-dinger stories out of them, too, if I had."

"Yes. I bet you could of, too."

"Goddamn FBI wouldn't take nothing. Not even a glass of water."

A child unseen shouted somewhere out in the darkness.

"Last time we seen him was at Marilynn's family re-union. She scolded him on account of his hair being too long and his beard being all scraggly. His frame was too thin, she told him. And then she spoiled him and made a fuss. Reunion was right in the backyard here. All of Marilynn's brothers and sisters and their husbands and wives and all of their children and Taylor's sisters and their husbands and their children were all here."

"That sounds nice, sir," Calvin said. "Something nice to remember."

"And then Peter Bonner called him up from down your way and said Taylor had to leave right away. As soon as he hung up the phone. That was the last time we seen him. After that he was gone."

"Yes, sir."

"It's not supposed to be this way, you know. Not your only son dying before you do."

"No, sir."

"Marilynn still talks about nursing him. You know how women are."

Calvin nodded.

"She knew her T-Ray would be our last one, and he would be her only son, and she and his sisters spoiled him. Spoiled him good."

"Yes, sir."

"Spoiled him rotten is what I should say."

"Yes, sir."

"Sometimes his sisters would dress him up like he was some kind of doll with clothes they'd found up in the attic. Marilynn took some pictures of him dressed that way, and she'd bring them out years later; and T-Ray, he screamed bloody murder about it."

The telephone rang. Mr. Heath let it ring. He may not have heard it.

"Taylor was born in the same year our youngest daughter started first grade. The weight from her pregnancy with him was more difficult for Marilynn to take off than it'd been with our others."

Calvin turned around and sat on the step to the concrete stoop, his back to Mr. Heath, and closed his eyes.

"So Marilynn took to taking long walks, him riding in a wagon in the fall and in a sled after it'd snowed. She'd sing and talk to him just as though he could understand what she was saying. But maybe he could, maybe he could at that because I'd watch her, and she'd get down on her knees and point to a robin and say 'bird' like that and his eyes would watch her lips and follow her arm and T-Ray would smile and gurgle and raise his arms as though he were trying to fly.

"Marilynn loved her T-Ray walks. That's what she called them, Mr. Samuels. Her T-Ray walks. They kept on long after she took off her extra pounds. She finally had to stop them when he started walking and wouldn't stay in the wagon or the sled. Afraid he'd get hit by a car. She was real sorry when they stopped.

"Ever since they found Peter, I figure Marilynn must be dreaming of her T-Ray walks again. Reenacting them. You know what I mean? With her sleepwalking and all."

Calvin neither nodded nor answered.

"Sometimes Marilynn'll sit straight up in bed and say 'tree,' and it's like she's pointing to some huge maple in leaf, and T-Ray's arms would be open wide as if he were imitating the branches."

Mr. Heath fell silent.

After a minute, Calvin said, "I understand after Taylor's van was found, you went down to drive it back."

"Yes. That's right. I did. Your Sheriff Conkle called me. Wanted me to go down and positively identify the van. 'ID it,' he said."

Mr. Heath shook his head. "Hell, drove all that way, and when I got there those cheap sons of bitches even made me pay the parking fee to get it out of the airport parking lot for them. We fixed the flat, and one of the deputies drove it back to the sheriff's where they dusted it for prints."

"And?" Calvin said.

"Nothing but T-Ray's and Peter's. They told me I could take her home, and that's what I done. I was relieved when I left there, I'll tell you. With no fingerprints excepting theirs, I thought we still had a shot. That there was still a chance T-Ray was alive somewheres. I was glad to be driving the van. Lately I'd been dreaming it was at the bottom of a river somewheres with T-Ray floating inside her. When they hadn't been able to identify the second set of bones as his, I thought for certain the dream was true.

"When I was in the war, especially after Dachau, I'd be dreaming of what I'd seen, about the bodies and such. Maybe I'd be sleeping in my bunk or, if I were on leave, dozing off in a park, and the bodies would be right there with me when I first woke up. Some of them lying across my legs, even. Scared the hell out of me. I thought I was cracking up for sure. I went in to see one of them Army docs, and he said it wasn't all that uncommon, and in time they'd go away. And they did. After a while.

"After they found T-Ray, those kinds of dreams started up again. I'd wake up, and I'd see him sitting at the foot of my bed looking at me, smiling, or maybe if I fell asleep in my chair, floating over the TV with his arms all stretched out, like he's still floating in that filth. Sometimes he'll be crying.

"I know it's only a dream, and after a minute it goes away. I know if I close my eyes and count to twenty and open them again, T-Ray'll be gone. But I don't. I keep them open and try to make T-Ray, the T-Ray in the dream, last as long as I can make him last. Even if it's only T-Ray who's dead. It's still T-Ray.

"When I was driving his van back here, I felt closer to him. I thought if I could drive it, maybe I could find some peace. T-Ray was not the one in the bottom of the outhouse. He was not drowned in the van. T-Ray was alone somewheres. He was hiding out from Alexander somewheres.

"With Peter dead, who could blame him for hiding out? I asked Marilynn. He hears Peter's dead and high-tails it to the airport and drops out. Doesn't write. Doesn't call. Hell, that's just what I'd do if them boys was after me. Drop out. Just disappear into some city or some small town down south or out west. Maybe even go down to Mexico."

Mr. Heath grasped his empty beer can in both his hands. "As I was driving back, I said to myself, maybe it'd all work out for the best. Maybe Peter's death had put the fear of God into T-Ray. Maybe he'll clean up his life and quit them drug rackets."

He looked at Calvin, his eyes large behind his thick glasses. "Taylor was good with his hands. Did you know that, Mr. Samuels?"

Calvin shook his head. "No, sir. I hadn't heard that. Was your son good at repairs?"

"You betcha. He could fix anything. Anything at all. I thought he could of found his way to a small town and maybe get a job in a fix-it shop or as a handyman. Settle down. Maybe meet some nice girl who could keep him on the straight and narrow." He laughed quietly. "Yes, sir, my Taylor was quite the ladies' man. Did you know that?"

Calvin smiled. "Yes, I bet he was."

"A year. A year at most, I thought, and we'd be getting a call or a card saying he was okay and for us not to be worrying none."

Mr. Heath took a deep breath. "I knew, I just knew, Taylor couldn't be gone for good."

He was quiet a minute before he spoke again. "There're a lot of hard lessons in this life."

"Yes, sir, there are."

"But I think the hardest is that when someone's gone, they're gone."

"It must've been hard when you did hear," Calvin said.

"When we finally learned he was really gone, I didn't know

if our nightmare was finally over, or if it was just beginning."

"Yes, sir."

"I knew he hadn't drowned. At least not in water. I hoped he was dead when they dumped him down that outhouse."

"Yes, sir. I hope so, too."

"The thought of Taylor choking to death on . . . on . . . but supposing his feet and hands was tied together, and he just sunk to the bottom?"

"I don't know, Mr. Heath," Calvin said. "I don't know."

"But that couldn't be, could it?"

"No. I guess not. No, I'm certain it wasn't that way."

"We was told Walters said Alexander stabbed him in the heart and broke the blade off. Snapped it off while it was still in his heart. That should have killed him right then and there, don't you think?"

Calvin closed his eyes. "Yes. I'm certain he died immediately. That he didn't suffer."

"Dead for twenty-two months before we knew. I oftentimes wonder what I was doing at the time, at the exact moment he died. Was I working, sleeping, watching the Tigers and enjoying a brewski? Did Taylor die right away or did he hang on for a few moments? Or even longer? Hang on long enough that he knew he was going to die."

"I don't know," Calvin said.

"Did he wish he could of done better?"

"I don't know."

"What was his very last thought before he died? Me?

His mother?"

Calvin covered his ears with his hands.

"Some girl we never even met?"

After a while, Calvin uncovered his ears and laid a hand on Mr. Heath's shoulder. "Goodnight, Mr. Heath. Thank you for talking to me. Thank Mrs. Heath for me."

Mr. Heath neither spoke nor acknowledged Calvin had spoken, but only looked out into the oblique nothingness of a black Michigan night.

Calvin could still hear the voices of children coming from somewhere, children not yet willing to surrender their perfect summer night to sleep. For which of them knew if there would ever be another?

He took his hand from Mr. Heath's shoulder and walked down the concrete walk to the corner of the house where a young woman stood.

"You the lawyer?"

"Yes, I am." He looked back to Mr. Heath. "I hope my coming didn't disturb him. Sometimes it helps, though, to talk to a stranger."

"He probably didn't even know you were here. I have to come over every night to take him inside. Otherwise he'd sit out here all night, telling his story whether or not there's anyone here to listen."

She looked up. "One time I came here and found him sitting out in the rain. Just talking to the dark."

CHAPTER 51

CALVIN DROVE BACK to Hanna that night without turning on the radio to keep him company, without stopping for something to eat or even for a cup of coffee. When he pulled back on to the Ohio Turnpike, he rolled down his window and listened to whatever counsel the rush of wind had to give him, await whatever omens might present themselves.

Sometime past two o'clock, midway between Toledo and Cleveland, his right front tire blew. Calvin turned out of the skid and spun in two complete circles across the turnpike and into the medium strip. After he came to a stop, he closed his eyes and laid his forehead on the steering wheel, shaking his head. It took a long time for him to stop shaking and get out.

Eight hours after he left Raymond Heath sitting on his back stoop, he pulled into the alley off Main Street that ran behind his house and turned into his driveway. He was bone tired. It had taken him more than two hours to change the flat. The batteries in the flashlight he kept in his glove compartment were corroded and dead. So he had only the light coming from passing cars and trucks to work by in the moonless night, and he had sometimes to wait ten minutes and more between them.

He switched off the ignition. It was just breaking dawn. Calvin sat in his car a minute, looking at the door to the garage. He finally got out and walked up his back steps. While he was unlocking the door, he heard his telephone ringing. He did not rush to get inside, but the telephone kept ringing until he picked it up.

"Where have you been?"

It took him a moment to place the voice. "Allison?"

"Yes. It's me. I've been trying to call you all night. And all morning." She paused. "I was worried. I thought something had happened."

"No. Nothing happened. Just a long night."

"A long night?"

"Of talking."

"Oh."

He waited.

"Listen," Allison said. "I thought of someone you should talk to."

"Why?"

"Because maybe if you won't believe me now, maybe you will after you speak to her."

439

"Her?"

"Miza Siran. She should be working at Ernest's the night after tomorrow, if I got her schedule right."

"Look, Allison, I don't think that's such a good idea."

"Listen to me."

Calvin leaned back against the wall from where his telephone hung.

"Are you still there?"

"I'm still here."

"If you care about the truth, if you care about what happened, you'll talk to her." Then she hung up.

Two evenings later, he drove to Ernest's beneath a hard, iron-gray sky that had steadily darkened as he neared Goshen, the air heavy and electric from the coming storm. He parked in an empty parking lot and walked down the tunnel entrance, where, at its end, the stench of urine and stale beer common to old roadhouses hung in the air, the stagnant summer heat only augmenting its pungency.

Calvin took a seat by the cash register and laid his suit jacket across the next barstool. He took out his cigarettes from his jacket's breast pocket and put them up on the bar and turned around. Ernest's might not have even opened yet. No shooters stood by the pool table. When Calvin turned back around, no one came out of the kitchen behind the bar even after he drummed his knuckles so loud that it echoed. The bar was empty save for him. The television set was black and the jukebox silent. Only the ticking of the White Owl cigar clock over the cash register disturbed the taciturnity of the roadhouse.

He was putting his cigarettes back into his jacket pocket when he heard a flush of water. A woman dressed in jeans and a halter-top, her hair of some indeterminate color cheaply dyed darker and tied back in a bun at the nape of her neck, walked out of the restroom. She looked toward the kitchen. She looked at Calvin and blinked.

"Howdy," she said.

"Howdy."

She walked behind the bar.

"Hope you weren't waiting long."

"Not long."

"What'll you have?"

"I'll take a Bud. On tap if you have it."

She nodded. "We do. You want that with a shot?"

"Yeah. Why not? Old Thompson if you have it."

The woman scanned the rows of bottles behind her. "I believe we do," she said. "Let me look, but I believe we do."

She turned and took a mug off the drying rack. As she was filling it, she studied Calvin's reflection in the back-bar mirror until she saw he was watching her too, and she looked down at the mug. She topped it off and set it in front of him.

"Thank you."

She nodded, turned, and reached for a dusty bottle in back, filling a shot glass and setting it next to his beer. "You're Mark's lawyer, ain't you?"

Calvin nodded as he lifted the shot glass and tossed back the whiskey and brought his glass back down hard on the bar, his eyes watering. "I am," he said in a husky voice, not quite a gasp.

The woman smiled. "I thought you was. I seen you up at the county jail when we was up there on visiting day couple of weeks back." She dried her hands and reached over the bar. "Miza Siran."

The two shook. "Pleased to meet you, Miza."

Calvin leaned over to his suit coat and opened the breast pocket. "What do I owe you?"

She shook her head. "First one's on the house for Mark's attorney man."

"Thanks."

She leaned against the back-bar and crossed her arms. "What you doing down this way? Investigating for Mark, are you?"

Calvin grinned and shrugged as he lifted his beer mug. He took a long swallow and wiped the foam from his lips with his shirtsleeve. "You get up to County much?"

"Yeah, since my old man's been sitting up there I get up every visiting day I can."

"That's good. Good of you to take the time. Make the effort."

"I think he appreciates it."

"It'd drive me crazy sitting up there. Day in, day out. Like a kid trapped inside under punishment in the summertime. Not being able to help myself. Relying on a stranger to get me out. It'd drive me crazy."

"Yeah, me, too," she said. "But Mark seems to be taking it pretty good."

She turned to ring up a No Sale on the cash register. Calvin glanced up at the White Owl clock, its eyes twitching back and forth between them. "So how long have you known Mark?"

"Oh, about two years now. Maybe three. He and my old man like to ride together. Or did."

"You hang out at the farm much that summer?"

"No. Not really. I was out there for his and Allison's wedding. I was her maid of honor, if you can believe it," she said, and she threw back her head and laughed. "And maybe one or two other times we was out there."

"You and Allison friends then?"

"No, I wouldn't say friends."

"No?"

"We'd only met that summer, but she was sure crazy about Mark, I'll tell the world. Or at least that summer she was. So I saw a lot of her and Mark because, like I said, he and my old man like to ride together."

"Seems a little strange they would get married so soon after just meeting, though."

"Yeah. It does. Until you get to know her."

"How so?"

"She had this, I don't know, this big emptiness inside her.

Like she had this bottomless pit where her heart should've been that could never be filled. Mark must of seemed like the answer to her prayers."

"Why'd she turn on him?"

"Second oldest reason in the world."

"Which is?"

"Jealousy. She found out he was two-timing her."

"Over?"

"Jocelyn Murphy. Who else? You must of heard of her."

Calvin nodded. He drained his mug and pushed it across the bar. She picked it up, and he reached over and took out a five-dollar bill from his wallet and laid it on top of the bar.

"Yeah," she said, pulling back on the tap. "Jocelyn and Mark was always flirting with each other. Even before he and Allison met, him and Jocelyn was always coming on to one another. Nothing serious, mind you. Just innocent stuff. After Allison moved into his trailer, he and Jocelyn weren't so obvious about it."

"Were Mark and Jocelyn sleeping together before Bonner died, you think?"

"No," she said, putting the mug down on the bar. "I don't think so. Not then, not before anyways. They were both just a couple of flirts who enjoyed flirting. I don't think Mark would two-time a friend while he was alive. But after Bonner was dead? Well, as they say, why not?"

Calvin sipped at his beer. "So when'd you hear Bonner and Heath were dead?"

"When I read about it in the papers."

"Any suspicions before then?"

"Yeah," she said. "I've gotta say I did."

"Why was that?"

"Saturday afternoon. The Saturday following their wedding, Mark walks in here and says he's got to get to the airport and would I mind riding along with Allison. Keep her company. And I says, 'Yeah. What the hell? My old man can mind the store'."

"Slow on Saturdays, is it?"

"Yeah. Just some old duffers come in from the country to watch their baseball. So I goes out to the parking lot and there's Allison driving Heath's van with some kid sitting in front with her. Bonner's pickup was sitting in the parking lot, too, so I guess Mark drove that in. Mark said he'd follow us to the airport with Mike Hackett. He's the one they all call Preacher. The one who married them."

"So she drove Heath's van to the airport, and you rode shotgun with her?"

"Yeah."

"While Mark and Preacher followed in Bonner's pickup."

"Yeah, that's right. They was behind us."

"What about the kid?"

"Oh, he hopped on out of the truck and came in here."

Calvin turned his mug first one way, then the other. Outside, the wind had risen, and it was whistling through the siding cracks, rattling the glasses and bottles behind the bar so they jingled like the keys to a hundred doors dangling from a ring.

"Anyone say why you were riding separately?" Calvin said.

"Allison said Mark was flying down to Florida on some business. Said he was going to meet up down there with Bonner and Heath, but they might be staying awhiles longer than he had intended. Which made sense. He just wanted some wheels he could get to quick when he come back."

"What happened when you got to the airport?"

"Me and Allison pulled into long-term parking, and Preacher and Mark drove on up to the terminal. We parked, and she handed me a rag and told me Mark wanted us to wipe down the van for prints before we left."

"That seem a little odd to you?"

"No, not really."

"It didn't?"

"No. She said it was just a precaution so we wouldn't all be pulled in if Bonner and Heath was busted and the cops traced the van."

"So you wiped it down and then what?"

"Me and Allison could see the pickup way up at the terminal. Mark got out and Allison said, 'You dirty sonnuvabitch.' And then she went to the front of the van and stood on the front fender. I could see Preacher pulling away from the terminal, and I could see Mark. Right next to him was Jocelyn."

"Jocelyn?" Calvin said.

"Yeah. Ain't that a kick in the butt? Couldn't confuse

that long, flowing red hair with anything."

"What'd Allison say?"

"After calling Mark a sonnuvabitch for five, ten minutes, she didn't say nothing. Just stood on the fender. She must of touched the windshield while she was standing on it. I figured that's how the cops tracked her down."

"Why's that?"

"She'd got herself arrested for drunk driving about a year before so they was probably able to match her prints."

"What'd Allison say on the drive back?"

"She didn't say nothing. All the way back in Bonner's pickup. Nothing. Just did a slow burn. I sat next to Preacher and she sat next to me, arms folded, looking out the window."

"Not happy, huh?"

"If looks could kill, I'll tell you what, Mark would've been six foot under right there and then that afternoon."

"What happened when you got back?"

"Preacher dropped us off back here. Said he had some business of his own he needed to be attending to."

"He say what?"

"Said he was meeting up with a buddy of his, so he'd be leaving the pickup for Allison to get back to the farm in."

"What'd you two do?"

"Came in here. Saw where the kid who rode in with Allison that morning was sitting over there by the pool table. Talking to Rock. Looked like maybe the kid was crying, or maybe had been, I don't know which."

Calvin turned and looked at the table near the pool table. "Any idea who the kid was?"

"Just one of the locals. I'd only been here a year or so, and I didn't know nobody. Still don't. Hardly even met any of my old man's family. Said he had a cousin around, but he never introduced us or nothing."

"So the two of you walked in here after you came back from the airport?"

"Yeah, and like I said, the kid was over there talking to Rock when we come in, and the kid looks up at us, like he was kind of hoping we wouldn't be here."

"What'd Rock do?"

"He turns around, sees it's us, and gets up and goes back behind the bar."

"What'd you do?"

"Then me and Allison sits down at the bar, and we orders us some seven-and-sevens. While we're talking to Rock, Allison looks back at the kid. I look over, and see he's on the phone, and that's when she scoots off her stool, lickety-split, and starts walking over to him, and he sees her coming and hangs up."

"What'd he do?"

"She starts talking to him, and after a while they sat back down at the table."

"What were they doing?"

"Just talking. But real quiet-like so's nobody could hear."

"Even you?"

448

"Yeah. Even me."

A couple of metal shop workers came in and stood at the other end of the bar. She walked down and gave them each a shot with a beer and came back.

"Go on," Calvin said.

"Not much else to tell you, really. She and the kid just sat at the table for a couple of hours. I guess she needed a shoulder to cry on, and so'd the kid. They got up to leave. She had the keys to the pickup. Allison talked to my old man a bit, and she and the kid left on out of here."

"Any idea what she said to your old man?"

"I asked, but he shrugged me off. I knew better than to push it. We split up earlier that spring, and we'd only gotten back together the week before. Even when he left a few minutes later, I didn't ask him where he was going. Anyway, that was the last I saw of Allison."

The two men who'd been at the other end of the bar moved to a table by the window. When Calvin heard their laughter, he turned toward them and saw it was now dark outside. He stood to leave. "Well, I thank you for the beer and the conversation, Miza, but I need to be getting back."

He picked up his suit jacket and slung it over his shoulder. He crushed his cigarette and walked toward the exit.

She waited until Calvin was almost to the tunnel entrance. "Hey, I think I remember the kid's name."

Calvin stopped and turned.

"I remember it because Mark walked in here not long

after they left."

"I thought he was in Florida?"

"He was, but it's only a two hour flight each way. Guess he got down there, did what he had to do, and caught the next plane back."

"What about taking Jocelyn with him?"

"Guess he just wanted some company, or maybe he thought Jocelyn would give him better cover than Allison. She's less antsy, you know."

"He say anything to you?"

"Yeah. He comes in here and asks my old man about the kid. Called him by a funny name. A pirate's name. Jolly Rogers, he called him. But I think his first name was Jim. Or John, maybe. Yeah, I think it was John. John Rogers."

Calvin looked at her.

"Then he and my old man left."

One of the two metal workers sitting at the table raised his mug, and she walked back toward them. Calvin looked up at the clock over the cash register, the White Owl eyes flicking back and forth. After a minute, he turned and walked back down the tunnel entrance and out to the parking lot.

As soon as Calvin left, Rock came out of the kitchen and walked to the window. He watched as Calvin pulled onto the road, and turned toward the table where the two metal workers were sitting. Miza looked back at him, and he held up his thumb and smiled.

CHAPTER 52

AFTER HE LEFT Ernest's, Calvin drove back to Hanna. When he came to the village square, he pulled off to the curb. He looked straight ahead Main Street toward home, glancing left and up Court Street. After a while he put his car in gear and turned.

The streets of Hanna were empty except for a pair of headlights he saw in his mirror that were far behind. He parked on a side residential street and walked to the cemetery with only the thunderhead bearing down upon him from the west providing illumination.

He stood at the gravesite a long time before he smelled the jasmine of Allison's perfume. When he turned, she, too, was looking down at the marker. Calvin had not even heard her come up, and he did not know how long she had stood beside him.

"How did you know where to find me?" he said.

"I was driving to Goshen when you passed me going the other way."

She looked up at him. "Do you come here often?"

"My grandfather first brought me here. When I was growing up and felt I'd no one to talk to and no one who would understand, I would often walk up here. Pretty grotesque for a kid, I guess."

"No," she said. "Not really. Your grandfather's buried here. Your father's memorialized nearby. It's quiet. Peaceful. You gain a sense of perspective here, I think. About what's important, or what should be. About what matters. Truly."

Calvin reached out and took her hand. "We should go."

"I guess," she said. "I just hate leaving you."

"Then stay. Stay with me tonight, Allison."

She looked at him, not refusing, but not acquiescing either.

"I know," he said. "I know. It's a mistake, and I know I'm going to regret it. If not tomorrow, then another day, but tonight I don't care. Tonight I feel betrayed and alone and except for you I don't feel as though anyone cares."

Calvin touched her hand to his cheek, and then he kissed it before he let it go. "He's guilty, isn't he? He really murdered them."

"Yes. He really did."

"I still might get him off with Jimmy Walters's testimony. Or even just a hung jury. I would only need to convince one juror to hang all of them."

"Yes," she said. "You probably could convince one."

"What I can't figure out is why Walters would be willing to confess to even one murder he didn't commit, let alone two. What kind of man is he anyway?"

"You didn't talk to Miza?"

"I did."

"Then you didn't understand what she told you."

Calvin shook his head.

"If Alexander ordered him to murder John Rogers, what kind of man do you expect Jimmy Walters to be?"

Calvin looked into her eyes, but it was too dark to tell if the truth was shadowed there. All he could see were the dark sockets her eyes should have filled, and he suddenly shivered as though from a chill caused by the storm coming down upon them.

CHAPTER 53
ACT 3

HE LAID NEXT to her, she all pale and slender, her long, crow-black hair cascading in a procession down her back. He lay awake for a long time while she slept. Twice before dawn he rose, crossed the room, and looked out his bay window. He was craving someone who would not come, and all he saw was the falling rain and the close grayness of a morning arriving all too soon.

It rained off and on all night, and finally he did sleep. When he woke, Allison was sitting on the cushioned cabinet before the bay window, her legs folded beneath her under the shirt he had worn the night before and had hang-dried from a chair near the bedroom radiator. She was looking out at the rain and the grayness where her life had led her. Where his life had led him.

He watched and did not speak. He barely breathed. He only watched, as if by studying her through half-closed eyes he might somehow see their future.

When she saw he was awake, she stretched out her long legs from under her and stood and walked to the bed and sat down beside him, taking his hand in both of hers. Calvin looked into her eyes, deep and dark as the world itself, and when he could not find the answer he sought, he asked how it was she had come to be with Alexander. Allison looked back at the window, as though her past was something she must conjure from the world outside.

People, she told Calvin, were drawn to Mark. All kinds, really, but especially those with an emptiness inside them. He had a way of smiling and laying his hand on your shoulder and convincing you that he believed in you just as much as you needed to be believed in, just as much as you had always wanted to be believed in.

They had met in the spring of 1980. She was working as an apprentice-groom at the track in Weirton. Mark loved playing the ponies and considered himself to be something of an *aficionado* of racehorses. Almost every day that spring he drove out early to the track, two hours or more before the first race, just to look over the horses running that day. Sometimes Jimmy Walters came with him. Mark would buy the race papers and walk through the paddocks and study the horses, and often he would stop and talk to the trainers and the jockeys, sometimes exchanging a dime bag for a tip.

That spring she was the happiest she'd been in years. Allison loved her job as an apprentice-groom. She loved horses.

She loved all animals, really, but she especially loved horses.

Someone had told her once, it might even have been Mark, that people who do not connect with people will sometimes connect with animals. As a child, she had never connected well to any adult, except to her Aunt Ellen. It was she who had raised Allison's own mother after their mother died. Allison's mother, though, soon found her older sister's home too confining, too restrictive. She guessed her mother, too, must have been a wild one.

Her mother escaped when she eloped with a handsome, sweet-talking salesman passing through Weirton she'd met in a bar when she was two days past her eighteenth birthday. She'd not wanted to marry, not really; she certainly hadn't wanted a child. She just wished to leave Aunt Ellen's house behind. To leave Aunt Ellen and her rules behind. Her mother really just wanted to have fun. When a year later she found herself pregnant at twenty, however, the fun stopped.

Allison was born at the county hospital in Atlanta where they just happened to be passing through. Her father never saw her. He checked her mother into the hospital and walked past the waiting room and kept on walking. A week later her mother returned to Aunt Ellen's, but she forever blamed her daughter, forever held her daughter responsible, for her own irresponsibility.

Her mother remarried some years later, but Allison was never close to her stepfather. So all of the love she had to give, she gave to animals. First to cats, then to horses. When she was an adolescent, she would have sold her soul, she said, to own her own horse. Her best friend Francine owned one, though, and every day during one glorious spring the two of them took the after-school bus out to the stables where, they told their parents, they were grooming and caring for him. But their real reason for going there was to ride.

While cats appealed to her need for love and security, horses appealed to her own wild side. When Pegasus would canter, it was as if the two of them were of the wind. It was as if they had left the earth and all of her hurt far below. She held so much power under her heels and between her thighs and grasped within her hands that no one could touch her anymore.

"Yes," Calvin said. "I can see why that would appeal to you."

"I liked brushing him after we rode. Making his coat shine, him rubbing his head against my shoulder."

"Like kindred sprits."

"Like sprits akin," she said.

She gave her love to her cats and to any horse she rode. They never betrayed her. They never threw her out of the house as did her mother after the Weirton police arrested her for public drunkenness. Threw her out when she'd no idea of how to support herself.

She learned. She cooked pizza, and she cleaned hotel rooms. One winter she washed police cars so she could collect food stamps.

"How'd you end up at the track?"

The spring after her mother threw her out she was reading the help-wanted ads, and she came across one for apprentice-grooms. They offered room and board and a small salary. They offered a chance for her to be around race horses and barn cats day and night.

While she loved the work, at first it was hard for her to take to the track bums and they to her. In time, though, she came to understand and to love them too, she said. They were much like the carnie bums she saw at fairs. The dregs of society. Most had been in and out of jail all their lives, and one old track bum told her what he liked about her most was her openness. Her openness to accept people just as they were. No questions. No conditions, but just as they were.

"And when did Alexander walk into all of this?"

"We met," she started to say, but then she looked out the window before she began again.

"It was after work, on a Thursday I think, when me and some of the other track bums went across the street to one of the bars. I don't even remember which one anymore. That's where I met Mark. In a bar catering to track bums. To the *aficionados* of horseflesh. *Aficionados* of human flesh, too, if the truth be known."

"What happened?"

"He and my stepbrother came in. As you can see I'll tell my life story to anyone who'll listen. And Mark can be a very sympathetic listener."

That very first night he made her feel special. Made her

feel like she was not a failure, and when she left the bar with him that night, she thought she was in love. Three days later she moved into his trailer at Davis's Corner.

She let go of Calvin's hand. She stood and walked again to the window and into the pale gray light of morning and held her hands to her face. After a while she came back, and the two sat together in silence until finally he spoke. "I need you to do something for me, Allison."

She nodded, but she would not look at him.

"I need to know if what Jimmy wrote to me, about him being the real murderer of Bonner and Heath, is truly a lie."

"You don't believe me then."

"It's not that I don't believe you, but you could be mistaken. You weren't actually there, but I must know, to a certainty, that Alexander was truly the murderer. Do you understand? If I'm going to betray him, I can't go on anything less than dead certainty."

"And what if Jimmy won't admit he isn't the real murderer?"

"Between now and his trial, something may break. Alexander may reveal it was he who murdered them."

"What if he does?"

"I'm going to use the trial to find out if he was truly behind the murder of John Rogers. If Alexander was, and if Jimmy admits he's not the true murderer of Bonner and Heath, I might be able to get that to Thompson."

"What do you want me to do?" she said, still not looking at him.

"I need to know—I've got to know—if Jimmy is telling me the truth. He won't tell me if he's not, but he might tell you. His stepsister."

"What do you want me to do?"

"Go to Jimmy on the next visiting day. This Wednesday. See if he'll open up to you. See if he'll tell you the truth. Tell you he wasn't the one who murdered Bonner and Heath. That it really was Alexander."

"Trial starts a week from today, Calvin. If Jimmy does decide to open up and admit to me his letter's a lie, he won't do it right away. He'll draw it out. I know him. If he does it at all, he'll wait until the last minute. What do you do in the meantime? How do you prepare not knowing?"

"As though Jimmy's letter is the truth. Anything less and Alexander will be suspicious, but I've got to know if it is the truth."

He looked at her. "Will you do this for me?"

She nodded and turned and walked back toward the window. Calvin rose from the bed and walked to her and put his arms around her and pressed his face into the back of her neck. "Thank you," he said.

As they stood there, Allison watched the others being reflected back in the milky-blue window glass like a cataract-infested eye. "You fool," she said silently to their others. "Oh, you stupid fool."

CHAPTER 54

AFTER ALLISON HAD dressed, Calvin offered to buy her breakfast, but she shook her head no. It would not look good for either of them to be seen together so close to Alexander's trial; he did not insist.

He started to walk her to her car, but at his back door she turned and placed her hands on his chest. She reached up and kissed him on his cheek where he had touched her hand the night before, and ran through the rain to the Camaro parked in front of his garage. He watched as she pulled out, and long after she had disappeared he was still looking down Main Street after her.

Calvin shaved and showered. He did not bother with a suit or even a tie, but wore only an old pair of khakis, his faded work shirt, and a sweater. He walked up the alley wearing his fishing hat and hiding beneath an umbrella. When he reached the Hanna Bank & Trust, he entered by the back entrance where the musty oldness always present hung mustier and older with the rain. Calvin walked down the hall to his office and locked the door behind him. He took off his fishing hat and hung it on the doorknob to dry and turned the umbrella upside down.

Sitting at his desk, he poured himself a cup of coffee from the thermos he had brought from home and waited for his eyes to gray the darkness so he could write without turning on a light some client might see from the sidewalk. He switched off the telephone ringer and tuned in the Cleveland PBS station and turned down the volume very low.

Calvin took out a legal tablet from where he kept a stack of them in his top drawer, and he looked down at the blank white page a minute before he began a third draft of his closing summation. Next, he outlined the evidence needed to substantiate his argument: the names of his witnesses and the subject areas they must cover. He outlined his opening statement. Finally, he wrote out his jury *voir dire* questions.

After several hours, Calvin laid down his pen and outstretched his arms. He poured himself another cup of coffee and walked to the window. The few pedestrians he saw were wearing their autumn coats and hats. One woman even wore gloves. Solid rain, neither heavy nor just a drizzle. A cold front down from Canada, the radio announcer said, and the rain rattled the window in its frame.

As he stood watching the rain, he heard footsteps come up the steps, and a knock at his door. After a minute, the footsteps retreated. He leaned forward and tried to see who it was but could not.

Calvin finished his coffee and opened the window a crack so he could better hear the rain and sat down again.

He wrote out the closing argument he would make were he Thompson and he outlined the evidence and witnesses Thompson would need to present in support of his case. After a while, he stopped and read over what he'd written. He began writing out the points he needed to touch upon in his own cross-examination of Thompson's witnesses. Quick, simple questions. Just enough for a juror to look askance at the witness's credibility. He wrote out the cross-examination questions Thompson would ask Alexander's witnesses, and constructed their rehabilitation on his redirect examination.

It was almost nine o'clock when he finally turned on the office light. Before Calvin sat down again, he looked out. The sun was setting behind Cemetery Hill. From the sway of trees there, the cold front must have passed for the wind was coming now out of the southeast. In another day it would be so hot and muggy he might just as well be in Georgia.

Calvin went back to his desk, and it was past midnight before he again put down his pen. He leaned back in his chair and closed his eyes. Not far from the Ohio River, Calvin was walking down the road on which barely stood the brown-as-phalt-shingled shack where John Rogers had grown up before the county had taken him from his mother. The road was not paved this far back into the hills, and while the distances between houses sometimes was only a matter of feet, sometimes it was a quarter-mile and more.

Across the street from the shack where John lived, was a mobile home that would have collapsed in upon itself had its owner ever done anything more than just consider moving it. Behind almost every one of the shacks was a doghouse with one or more mongrels chained to it, and the stench from them was nauseating even as far out as the road. The yards were of dirt, but weeds grew high in the lots between the shacks, and it must have been summer because the weeds were brown the way they turn in August before the fall rains begin.

John was sitting beneath a tree he shared with a dog behind his mother's shack. It was the same dog that had lunged at them two years before when the two had walked down the alley toward the home of John's grandmother outside of Hanna. Both John and the dog were chained, but John's was secured to the tree by a large padlock. Because there were so many, Calvin avoided only some of the piles of dog feces as he walked back from the road.

When he got to the tree, he tried to twist the chain over John's head, but it was noosed too tight about his neck. As he pulled, the dog stood up, baring its teeth and growling, but John told it to hush and it lay back down again and was quiet. Calvin picked at the lock with a piece of wire he found in the dirt, but he could not open it. He tried again to wrench the chain over John's head, this time with all his might, but still it would not come.

Finally he told John he could not free him. He was sorry, but he could not. John smiled and said it was all right, he knew Calvin had done the best he could.

It was not until John looked up at him as he spoke that Calvin saw he had no eyes, just two crow-black holes burned into his sockets.

Then Calvin woke.

After he caught his breath, he looked at his watch. It was almost four o'clock. He put his legal pads away in their drawer and locked up. As he walked past the town square, Jim Walker pulled up in his squad car. He was coming back from the county jail where he had dropped off a drunken motorist who had totaled his car on the road between Hanna and Goshen. "What's wrong there, counselor? Some mean old pussy throw you out for the night 'cause you couldn't get it up no more?"

Calvin smiled and said he had only been working late and fallen asleep in his office. Walker laughed and shook his head. He told Calvin he'd better start getting in practice before he started lying in earnest next week. He drove off down Main Street, headed back toward Goshen.

CHAPTER 55

ON THE SAME night Calvin was working late on his trial preparation, Allison was waiting in the parking lot behind Ernest's. Near eleven o'clock, Rock stepped outside and stood on the back stoop as he lit a cigarette. She flashed her headlights. Rock looked her way and walked over and got in by the passenger door.

"What's up?"

She explained Calvin's request of her as Rock sat smoking. After a minute he told her it wouldn't be wise for her to visit County again. One more visit was one more visit too risky. He'd have Miza deliver a message to Walters.

"It won't be Samuels's message," he said and chuckled, "but it'll be a message."

He rubbed out his cigarette in the ashtray and got out and went back inside.

CHAPTER 56

AFTER JIM WALKER drove off, Calvin walked home in the faint light of the false dawn common to that part of the Midwest during the short summer nights. He entered his cottage by the back door and walked through pulling the blinds shut while he went. He took the telephone off the hook and dropped into bed and wrapped himself in the sheets that still held the presences from the night before.

He slept the sleep of the dead, so deep that when he woke he could not recall if it had been dreamless or if he had again shouted during the night from some nightmare. What woke him, however, was someone knocking at his back door, but before he could get out of bed he had to struggle to unwrap the sheeting that had noosed itself around him as he tossed and turned.

He found his wrinkled khakis lumped on the closet floor

and pulled them on as he hopped on one foot from his bed-room to the kitchen. Outside the curtained door, squinting through the window, stood Mrs. Ferguson. She wore a sum-mer dress patterned with some faded summer flower, and a wide-brimmed straw hat that must have once belonged to the judge when it had been in style in the 1930s. When he opened the door, he saw she had on canvas sneakers, a white, low-cut, yellow-paint-smeared one and the other a black high-top, and she held a bamboo fishing pole she had told him was older than even her brimmer.

Calvin smiled and leaned his head against the open door-jamb. "We going fishing this morning, Mrs. Ferguson?"

She looked up at him over her spectacles much as she had when he told her he was certain Charles Dickens had written *Silas Marner*.

"It's evening, Calvin," she said. "Past six o'clock, in fact. You haven't been sleeping the day away, have you, boy?"

He turned and looked at the kitchen clock. He looked behind Mrs. Ferguson and saw the sun was indeed sinking behind her.

"I must have."

"Isn't that kind of backward? Even for a lawyer."

"I worked until early this morning, preparing for the trial next week, and fell asleep in the office." He raised his hand to cover a yawn. "But I didn't think I was that tired."

"Well, then," Mrs. Ferguson said, "I guess it's a good thing I came along when I did. You need a break, even if it's only for an evening; and me, well, I need someone to take me fishing."

Calvin pretended to have fallen asleep again, and he started to snore. After a moment, he cocked his right eye open a little and grinned.

Mrs. Ferguson shooed him inside with her free hand. "Now hurry up. And don't keep an old lady waiting. You young people anymore don't have the manners God gives to stray cats in heat."

She turned and started cutting across their backyards toward her garage. Calvin went back to his bedroom and put on the shirt he had worn the day before and found his own pair of sneakers. He looked in the mirror and rubbed his day-and-a-half-old beard stubble, but he only brushed his teeth and combed his hair.

He found his fishing pole, the one Mrs. Ferguson had purchased for him on his ninth birthday. Ever since, several times each spring and summer, usually on their birthdays, but sometimes on no particular day other than one or the other needed a friend, the two went fishing.

Mrs. Ferguson was waiting in her 1955 Cadillac, the top already down. While Calvin climbed in, she punched the accelerator before he even closed his door, and she almost flipped him over into the back seat.

"You didn't sneak a drink before you came out, did you, Calvin?"

The fishing hole where they always started, and which

they seldom went beyond, lay along a narrow stream that crossed the farm Mrs. Ferguson's grandfather had once worked. She still owned it, though she only leased it now for pasturage to a Mennonite family rather than farm it herself with hired help. Along the way, they talked of the cool July weather and what a pretty evening it was now that the storm had blown through. Mrs. Ferguson told him how the town and the county surrounding the town had changed since she was a girl and especially how it had changed since the war. She told him Hanna was no longer merely the county seat for a few tradesmen who sold their wares to villagers and outlying farmers, but had changed into something different. Something she did not understand. Something she did not like much. Neither spoke of Alexander's trial.

Mrs. Ferguson parked in the gravel drive by the boarded up farmhouse. She had tried leasing it out years ago, but it was too far from town, and because the only potential tenants who showed any interest were riffraff who could not afford a house in Hanna, she let it stand empty.

Calvin opened the wood fence gate for them, and they hiked across open pasture for an eighth of a mile to where a line of trees, two to three rows thick and planted by Mrs. Ferguson's grandfather, bordered the creek on both sides the entire length of her property save for paths left open for the cows to get to water.

It could have been a good stretch of water for fishing. The trees gave shade to the insects that in turn fell into the water and provided food for the fish. The two of them, though, were not accomplished fishermen. Neither really knew how to fish. Usually they just baited their hooks with stale bologna and wiggled their lines in hopes a fish would bite out of curiosity. When he was younger, Calvin had once suggested they might have more success with worms, but Mrs. Ferguson replied she had proven a variation of her theory on the judge, and she didn't see any reason to fool with success. Calvin had often wondered since what variation of the stale-bologna theory of fishing applied to catching a man, but some mysteries of life, he finally decided, should remain so.

He unwound his line and baited his hook with the rotting meat Mrs. Ferguson carried in a sandwich bag in her pocket. He fixed the red-and-white bobber to his line and cast, watching the current carry it out from the stream bank. Mrs. Ferguson sat in an ancient folding canvas campstool she had brought along, and Calvin settled in a seat made by the forked roots of the tree behind him. He looked out at his bobber and wiggled his pole sideways, back and forth. "Try to imitate the movement of some insect," she had told him years before.

"So you were up until morning preparing for Alexander's trial, were you?"

"Yes, ma'am. Until I fell asleep in my chair."

"How's it looking?"

Calvin shrugged. "Could be worse."

"Could be better is what you're saying."

"Always could be better."

"That's what the judge used to say, too."

"He's got a chance," Calvin said. "He's got a good story; a credible story, at least."

"But?"

"But it just depends on how well he does on the stand."

"How do you think he'll do?"

"We've been rehearsing his testimony."

"And?" Mrs. Ferguson said.

"He seems to be doing okay."

"That doesn't sound like an overwhelming vote of confidence."

"It'll be different on the stand for him."

"Different how?"

"Depends if he tells the truth or not," Calvin said.

"What do you mean?"

"A lot of people try to lie on the stand, but I've never yet seen anyone do it convincingly. They even had me fooled until they got up on the stand. Something looks through them, and their heart's just not in the lie. It shows."

"You don't believe him," she said.

Calvin smiled. "Not much gets past you, does it?"

"A lot does. A lot has flowed right past me that I missed."

"I find that hard to believe."

"Believe this: when it comes to you, no, not much gets past me."

Mrs. Ferguson watched her line a moment. "You going

to tell me what's up?"

Calvin studied his bobber.

"Wouldn't have anything to do with your visitor who left by your back door morning before last, would it?"

Calvin smiled, but said, "I probably shouldn't say anything until I know for certain."

Mrs. Ferguson leaned over and opened a rusted, green tackle box. She reached in and fumbled and pulled out a marijuana cigarette she lit with a kitchen match. While she toked down on it, the wind carried the smoke to Calvin. He turned toward her.

"Cancer's back." She looked down at her chest. "Damned if I'm not going to lose my other tit."

She toked, a long drag. "Damn," she said and looked after her bobber as it drifted away.

"I'm sorry, Maude. Anything I can do?"

She shook her head. "No. Nothing anybody can do except maybe make it worse."

"What does your doctor say?"

"Says he could operate again. Then chemo."

"Again."

"But he said this time it most likely wouldn't be successful. My chances are between slim and none, he told me."

"So what're you going to do?" Calvin said.

"I know what I'm not going to do."

"What's that?"

"I'm not going to die in the hospital. That's no place for

anyone to die."

"Where would you want to?"

"When it's time I want to be sitting in a lawn chair in my rose garden," she said. "On a hot August afternoon, listening to the Hawkins children playing baseball two doors over in that little field they cut out behind their house while I brush away the flies who don't have the courtesy to wait a while longer."

"Yes," Calvin said. "In your own way, in your own time."

"I don't want to die in any goddamn hospital sedated after they cut off my other tit."

"How long?"

"Six months, if I'm lucky," Mrs. Ferguson said. "Three if I'm not."

"Are you in any pain?"

"Some. Doctor gave me some medication." She regarded her cigarette. "But I prefer my good old reefer here. I'm a simple woman at heart."

Calvin watched his own bobber as it drifted downstream, a little behind Mrs. Ferguson's. "You remember John Rogers?"

"Yes, of course." She took one last drag before she arced the butt into the creek. "I remember all my pupils. Especially the ones who die young. The ones doomed to die young."

"Could you tell that?"

"I didn't see it then, or I didn't want to, but looking back I should have."

"How?" Calvin said.

"He had that look about him of someone born to lose."

"Is that why you were reluctant to tutor him?"

She nodded. "I knew he wouldn't last long. So why bother?"

"So why did you bother?"

"He got such joy from it. Not so much from the learning. That was just a means to staying out of Lucasville. But he got such joy in someone touching his life. In someone caring what happened to him."

"But you could tell? That he wasn't going to make it?"

"I should have."

"Why?" Calvin said.

"He had no foundation beneath him."

"No, not much of one, did he?"

"Without one, when life dealt him a bad hand—which it does to all of us at one time or another—he didn't know how to get back into the game, and some of his bad hands were doozies."

"Yes, they were," Calvin said.

"Anyone would have had trouble getting back into it when all they could expect was another bad hand."

"So it was only a matter of time?"

"There was nothing you could have done to save him," Mrs. Ferguson said.

"You think not?"

"If he hadn't died the way he did, when he did, it would have been something else. Sooner or later, and more likely sooner."

For a minute, she watched Calvin watching the stream. "So what about John?"

"Alexander might have had something to do with it."

"Might?"

"Might have been him who had his eyes burned out."

"But you're not certain."

"No, ma'am. I'm not. I'm hoping to find out during the trial."

"What do you do if you do find out?"

"Well, maybe he didn't."

"But what if you do?"

Calvin shook his head.

"What if your client, the one you've taken an oath to defend zealously, what if he did murder your friend and you find out about it before the trial's over?"

"My life will get more interesting."

"Could you defend him, though, if he were the one who murdered John?"

Calvin didn't answer.

"Could you? Could you keep your word, your oath, and defend him zealously?"

"Zealously," Calvin said.

"Do you remember where 'zealous' comes from?"

"The Book of Daniel. You taught me that. From the Zealots who allowed themselves to be impaled because they believed it would save Israel."

Mrs. Ferguson nodded. "And your duty is to the living,

not the dead. The only rights of the dead are the last ones Reverend Barker gives them."

Calvin didn't answer.

"Because if you betray Alexander, you'll be betraying your oath. More importantly, you'll be betraying yourself and all those who believe in you. And consequences will flow from your betrayal."

"From my betrayal of Alexander?"

"No, Calvin. From your betrayal of yourself."

Calvin didn't answer.

"You betray Alexander, you'll not only be betraying yourself, but John as well."

He looked back at her. "John?"

"Yes, because he believed in you, and your betrayal will haunt you until the end of your days."

It was almost dark. On the far bank of the creek, a ground fog had risen. "We should be going," he said.

Mrs. Ferguson nodded and stood. "Nary a nibble did I get this evening. How about you?"

"Unlucky in love, unlucky in fishing."

"Let's pack it in, shall we?"

They wound their lines back in, and he folded up Mrs. Ferguson's campstool and carried it back to her car. She held onto his free arm while they crossed the pasture, and when they reached the fence gate, she turned and looked back into the loaming, and she started toshudder.

"What is it?" Calvin said. "Have you taken a chill?"

"No."

"Then what?"

"Let's just get back, Calvin."

"Do you want me to drive?"

Mrs. Ferguson nodded. "Perhaps you should."

CHAPTER 57

UPON ARRIVING HOME, Mrs. Ferguson parked inside the garage where her father had stabled his horses when it was a carriage house. She bid Calvin goodnight, and thanked him for taking an old lady fishing. She told him it meant much to her.

He asked if she would like to go again once Alexander's trial was over, but she shook her head and said she thought not, thanking him one last time. She turned and shuffled up the slate sidewalk, her straw brimmer perched askew upon her head, the tip of her fishing pole scratching across the slate behind her.

Over the past three-quarters of a century, how many times had she crossed this same walk and walked up her back steps? It must have been there, on an evening just such as this, that Judge Ferguson had first kissed her goodnight, with the air heavy with summer and the perfume of vermillion flowers, and a million lightning bugs about, and the promise of one hundred thousand tomorrows to follow.

She closed the door behind her, but as Calvin crossed their lawns to his own back door, he saw the ground fog again creeping in from the country. He went inside and put away his pole; but as he was closing his closet door, he saw the Jack Daniels on the shelf. Calvin reached up and took down the bottle and walked into the kitchen. He poured a tumbler two fingers full, held it up, and poured in a little more for good measure.

He walked outside and sat in a lawn chair he had left on the brick walk. He sipped the whiskey, rested his head on the back of the chair, and studied the firmament unscrolling until he closed his eyes.

Calvin dreamt he was a guest attending the marriage of Alexander and Allison two summers before at the Old Church Road farm. They were holding their wedding ceremony beside the cemetery on the hill that looked down upon the farmhouse, which had once been a church to the Mennonites—before they began murdering themselves. Someone had freshly cut the lawn using Harry Katz's push mower, paying particular attention to the grass between the graves. Behind Calvin and off to the farthest upside corner of the cemetery rose small mounds upon which weeds grew high and wild and where no tombstone stood. It was here the suicides were buried, scorned and to be forgotten, but who were remembered most of all.

Alexander and Allison stood at the edge of the cemetery before a Bible-holding man wearing a black smock and white collar. Snaking down from them ran two lines of Pagans, their common-law wives and girlfriends, and some empty-eyed locals. The two groups stood six feet apart to allow the wedding couple a path to walk down the hill to their reception. Other than the individual mocking a man of God, none had taken any effort to dress for the occasion, wearing only jeans and T-shirts.

On the back porch sat galvanized washtubs full of ice and beer, and next to them a large cylinder of nitrous oxide and a dozen boxes of Glad garbage bags. A picnic table held dishes filled with marijuana and hashish, cocaine and Quaaludes. There were plates with blue pills and plates with white pills, and Allison, in her childish script, had written little signs, like nameplates for a formal dinner, so none of her guests overdosed by accident.

The Pagans had parked their motorcycles, thirty or more in number, where the serpentine lane looped in front of the house. What remained of the outhouse still smoldered, and the smell of seared flesh hung in the air. Off to the side of the front porch, where men stood and even some women stooped to urinate, Walters rolled like some insane porcine into which Christ had driven the demon of some other, more fortunate, madman, and he gleefully smeared himself in an ammoniac sizing of mud. The burnt-flesh smell hung heaviest over him.

Near Alexander and Allison sat John Rogers, tailor-style,

rocking back and forth and nodding in his intoxication from some combination of substances. Alexander whispered to her, and she giggled into his shoulder. When John seemed about to pass out, Alexander bent down and spoke to him. John looked up, eyes wide, and Alexander pretended to slit his own throat with his index finger while Allison laughed at the joke with the maniacal guffaw of a madwoman.

Calvin started to run from the porch up to them, but fifty pairs of arms reached out from the two lines and grabbed hold of him. Alexander yelled for them to put him into the pit too—and to throw in the Jolly Rogers for good measure. Calvin twisted to get free as they carried him over their heads, and he turned back and looked at Allison for deliverance, but she was sitting on the ground, bent over with laughter, waving goodbye.

Calvin woke when his whiskey glass shattered on the brick walk. Its breaking echoed forever in that hour of dark Ohio summer emptiness, when sounds are as clear as consequences oblique. He looked down for a minute, studying the glass shards as though he might fit them back together. Finally he rose, but when he stood, he saw Mrs. Ferguson standing in a lighted second-floor window. She was in her robe, her hair undone, watching him. They looked at each other for half a minute, neither acknowledging the other by even so much as a nod.

Finally, he stooped and picked up the pieces of the shattered whiskey glass. When he looked up, the window was dark, and Mrs. Ferguson was gone.

CHAPTER 58

AS THE GREAT oak door swung shut, its brass hinges echoed in the empty courtroom. For a moment, Calvin stood inside the door, his eyes graying the darkness in the early-morning light. Early morning, not yet past dawn. He could have reached out and switched on the lights, but he did not. He heard a click above him, and when Calvin looked up, he saw that the hands of the illuminated clock on the back gallery wall had just struck the hour. Three hours. Then it would begin. In three hours.

Though more than a week had passed, he had not yet heard Walters's answer. He had not heard a word from Allison. Calvin had met with Alexander the evening before to complete their trial strategy. He would, he told Alexander, cross-examine Walters the first go-round as though he had never received his letter admitting to the murders. Only after both sides had presented all of their other witnesses would he call Walters back to testify a second time, and it would be then he would elicit his confession. Bringing it out so late at trial would make it all but impossible for Thompson to recover.

Alexander agreed his strategy provided them their best hope of success, and the two shook hands on it. If Alexander sensed Calvin's reticence when he took his hand, it did not show.

At second counsel's table, Calvin took off his suit coat and draped it over the back of one chair and twisted the other sideways so he would catch what little light fell through floor to ceiling windows behind the jury box. He laid on the table an already filled legal tablet, and he took his antique pen from his briefcase, rolling it in his fingers for a moment before turning to his legal pad.

Judge Biltmore's bailiff arrived at eight o'clock, and it was he who switched on the courtroom lights. He saw Calvin sitting at second counsel's table, his head bowed, his lips moving. As the bailiff opened the bar gate, he asked if he could bring him a cup of coffee. Calvin opened his eyes and looked up and smiled and told him a cup of coffee would be most welcome, thank you. Then he turned to his legal tablet.

By eight-fifty no gallery seat remained unclaimed. The ceiling fan circled, but could not dissipate the early-morning heat rising from the press of bodies already moist and stale with sweat. Even along the back and side walls, there seemed to be no space left to stand. Still, when the courtroom doors opened and another spectator entered, he would look about and spot someone he knew well enough, and stomachs were sucked in and somehow space was found for the newcomer to squeeze into.

A few minutes before nine o'clock, the double court-room doors swung wide open. Several spectators lining the nearby wall jumped from the crack of the doors against it as two deputies hustled in Alexander, dapperly dressed in a navy pinstripe suit, looking more like a lawyer for the defense than an accused double murderer, smiling, though at no one in particular, enjoying his spectacle.

Calvin reached over for his brief bag and moved it to the floor on his opposite side. After greeting Alexander good morning, he turned to continue reviewing his notes, but he heard a murmur behind him. When he looked, seven deputies were seated just inside the bar, their chests inflated by their bulletproof vests, their arms crossed before them, coats open. None smiled.

The front courtroom door opened, and Calvin turned back around. Thompson and his chief trial assistant had entered, speaking to one another in quiet voices, eyeing the gallery. They sat at first counsel's table, setting out their files and arranging their notes until some minutes later when Judge Biltmore took the bench.

Calvin and Thompson devoted the first half of the morning to their various preliminary motions to suppress evidence and to amend the indictment and to compel additional discovery. At a little past ten-thirty, Judge Biltmore ordered the bailiff to bring in the jury of eight men and four women whom Calvin and Thompson had picked the day before. "State may make its opening statement," he said.

At the podium Thompson unwrapped the rubber band holding together his stack of three-by-five cards. "Your Honor. Mr. Samuels. Members of the jury. As you'll recall from yesterday, my name is Ben Thompson, and I'm the County Prosecutor.

"Ladies and gentlemen. Those chairs you're now sitting in are fitted with armrests. Before this trial is over, you're going to be putting those armrests to good use. Good use because what you're going to be hearing will make you want to hold on as though for dear life. What you'll be hearing you're going to find disturbing. So disturbing some of you may even become ill.

"And what you'll be hearing will be testimony under oath coming from this witness stand. Testimony that will shock you. Shock you because the witnesses you'll be hearing from will be giving you a guided tour down the black and bloody roads of Creek County. Roads many of you maybe didn't know existed. That you'll not want to exist so close to your homes. To your children and to their children."

Thompson pivoted and pointed at second counsel's table. "This man, Mark Alexander, has been a sojourner on our back roads—and off of one of them, just a little over two years ago at an abandoned farmhouse south of Goshen he murdered two men."

Calvin looked up from taking notes. All of the jurors were staring at second counsel's table. Alexander was watching Thompson, his eyes clear iron gray.

"Who is this murderer among us? He is one of the founding members and the current president of the Pagans, a motorcycle gang running out of West Virginia, Pennsylvania, and eastern Ohio.

"Who are the Pagans? It's not a large gang as motorcycle gangs go. Not like the Hell's Angels out there in agnostic California. But we will show you that they are a particularly ruthless and brutal brotherhood for whom murder is a livelihood as well as a way of life. They kill for profit, but they kill for fun.

"Finally, we will show you that Alexander murdered Peter Bonner, and that mere seconds later he murdered Taylor Heath. Just outside of Goshen, at the Old Church Road farm.

"In closing, ladies and gentlemen, let me say I am confident that after you've heard all of the evidence in this case, you'll find the defendant, Mark Alexander, guilty of the aggravated murders of Peter Bonner and Taylor Heath. Thank you."

Judge Biltmore leaned forward. "Defense may make its opening statement, Mr. Samuels."

Calvin pushed back his chair and rose. "Thank you, Your Honor."

He walked to the podium and laid down his legal tablet.

"Judge Biltmore, Mr. Thompson, ladies and gentlemen."

He looked up at the two great windows before him, nodded, and lowered his eyes and began.

"What Mr. Thompson has told you is his opening statement. It is not evidence. What he has told you is only a story, and it's based upon the stories told to him by others. Told to him by liars. By criminals. Mr. Thompson chose to believe those stories, those liars, those criminals; but you have no similar obligation to do so."

The juror seated before Calvin crossed his arms and frowned. Calvin looked at him.

"Now you might be saying to yourself, but Mr. Samuels, why shouldn't I believe Mr. Thompson? He seems like a bright fellow. A hardworking, honest man. A man of integrity. Why, I might even have voted for him in the last election.

"And so he is. Ben Thompson is indeed a man of integrity. This county is lucky to have a man like him working for them as their prosecutor, and you're going to be hearing from Sheriff Conkle later in this trial. The citizens of Creek County are lucky to have a sheriff like him working for them.

"But, ladies and gentlemen, Mr. Thompson and Sheriff Conkle are men, and even honorable men, even men of integrity, make mistakes of judgment. Mistakes of judgment you, the jury, are here to prevent."

A woman at the end of the first row nodded, and Calvin walked to her side of the jury box, his hand gliding along the banister.

"As I said, what Mr. Thompson has just told you is not evidence. It is a story based upon stories told to him by other individuals; it is those individuals who will be testifying, and it is only what *they* say from this witness stand that is evidence. It is only what they say when they are in this jury box that you may consider.

"After hearing from Mr. Thompson's witnesses, you will be hearing from Mark Alexander's. Most of these witnesses Mr. Thompson has not spoken to. Had he done so, his belief as to what actually occurred at the Old Church Road farm two summers ago might be different. It just might be different. I think—no, I know—that before this trial is over, all of you will have serious questions about the believability of Mr. Thompson's witnesses.

"After hearing from *all* of the witnesses, your decision at the end of this trial, as to guilt or innocence, is extremely serious. How serious?

"Maybe you remember your decision to purchase your very first home? Or maybe your very first car. Do you remember the time you spent? The people you spoke to? The opinions of people you trusted, and that you considered in reaching your decision?"

Several jurors nodded.

"Well, for Mark Alexander, this is just such a serious question.

"And even now when you buy a car, you don't just purchase it sight unseen. You drive it around. You kick the tires. When you bought your house, you walked through it. You poked around. You might've even had your brother-in-law come over to take a look at the plumbing. Before the bank gave you a loan to buy it, they sent out their expert, an appraiser, to be certain you weren't paying too much for it.

"Now, none of you were present when Peter Bonner and Taylor Heath were murdered. So if you're going to convict Mark Alexander, you're going to have to rely on witnesses. Individuals who purportedly were there, witnessing the murders. You're going to have to rely upon what they tell you. And you're going to have to trust they're telling you the truth, which is a little bit like your buying a car without driving it or purchasing a home without seeing it, relying only upon what someone else has told you. How many of you would be willing to dothat?

"Well, you might. You might purchase a car without driving it first. You might even purchase a home for you and your family sight unseen. Depending upon what others told you. Depending upon their credibility. But would you rely upon what was told to you by criminals? I'm certain you would not, and I'm equally certain, ladies and gentlemen, at the end of this case, you won't be buying the state's story because you won't be buying their witnesses's stories.

"The only witness, the only one, who'll be testifying that he in fact saw Mark Alexander murder Peter Bonner and Taylor Heath will be Jimmy Walters. Known in Goshen as Psycho Jimmy Walters."

At the mention of Walters's name, there was a snicker in the gallery, and Judge Biltmore glared in its direction. His courtroom was immediately still.

"Psycho Jimmy Waters is a convicted criminal. He is a criminal who panicked after he was arrested and made up a story to save his own skin. He's the kind of criminal who, if he ever came up to you on the street and told you the time of day, not only would you not believe him, but you would turn and run away as fast as you could, as far as you could. You would never, ever, purchase a car from Psycho Jimmy Walters. You would never, ever, purchase a home for you and your family from him—and if you're not willing to purchase a car from Psycho Jimmy Walters, and if you're not willing to purchase a home from Psycho Jimmy Walters, how in the world, *how in the world* can you buy his story? A story upon which turns the fate, upon which hangs the life of Mark Alexander.

"And if you don't believe the testimony of Psycho Jimmy Walters from the witness stand, the rest of the state's evidence doesn't matter," said Calvin, and he waved his hand in what was both a summation and a dismissal.

"This trial is the first opportunity Mark Alexander has had to confront his accusers, and I want to remind you that he is cloaked with a presumption of innocence, the same as anyone else would be were they charged with a crime. The same as each of us would want to be. He doesn't have to sell you that car or sell you that house. It's the job of the state to do so, and by the end of this trial, I don't think you're going to be buying the state's case.

"This trial is a test of the state's evidence." Calvin held up a document. "At the meeting of the grand jury which returned this indictment, Mark Alexander was not even allowed to be present. He was not even allowed to question witnesses or to present evidence."

A juror in the back row, the Hanna High School history teacher, shook his head.

"The state, ladies and gentlemen, doesn't even know the exact date of the murders. Think about that, if you will, for a moment. The most serious crime with which a person can be charged in our society, and the state doesn't even know the exact date of the murders over two years after they occurred. And if they don't know the date of the murders, how much else don't they know?

"Why is Mark Alexander on trial? The reason he sits before you is because Psycho Jimmy Walters and Allison Morris are pointing their own dirty fingers at him. But Psycho Jimmy Walters is a convicted criminal. He was drunk and doped out of his skull almost every moment of that summer. I want you to ask yourselves just how much credibility you can give to the testimony of a man whose own friends refer to him as 'Psycho.' Enough to convict another man of murder?

"Both of them, both Psycho Jimmy Walters and Morris, as you will hear, have questionable motives for testifying against Mark Alexander. Walters was permitted to plead guilty to a lesser felony and the state has given Morris total immunity. Total.

"By the end of this trial, the state will not have proven to you who is guilty of Peter Bonner's murder," Calvin said. "The state will not have proven to you who is guilty of Taylor Heath's murder. I want you to listen to the state's evidence. I want you to listen to our testimony. I want you to take everything you hear spoken from the witness stand with a grain of salt. I want you to weigh what you will hear from the witness stand. I want you to ask yourselves just how far the police, just how far the sheriff, and just how far Mr. Thompson went to find the real truth? How far did they go to find the real murderers? Did they go far enough? By the end of the trial, I think you'll be telling Mr. Thompson he needs to keep looking.

"In closing," Calvin said as he picked up his legal tablet, "I want to remind you that under the American way of justice, Mark Alexander is not required to prove his innocence. He doesn't have to say a word to save himself. He doesn't have to prove a thing to you in order to be found not guilty. And while the physical evidence that will be introduced at this trial by Mr. Thompson will be extensive and gruesome, it will not show you that Mark Alexander killed Peter Bonner. It will not show you that he killed Taylor Heath."

Calvin stopped, and before he spoke again he waited until all of the jurors were looking only at him. "But, ladies and gentlemen, while Mark Alexander is under no legal obligation to do so, at the end of our presentation, we will reveal to you the true killer of Peter Bonner and Taylor Heath. In this very courtroom, before your very eyes. Thank you."

When Calvin turned around, Thompson was staring at him openmouthed, and Alexander was smirking. Even Judge Biltmore, who had grown weary from years of lawyers' antics in his courtroom, looked up from his note taking and studied him for a moment. "We'll break for dinner now," he said, and turned toward the jurors. "The state has made a motion for a jury view, which I have granted. After we've eaten, a bus will pick us up behind the restaurant and drive us all down to Goshen. Court's adjourned until then."

The gallery spectators stood to go home for the day, talking over among themselves the opening statements, especially Calvin's last remark. All except for John Rock, who was the first spectator out the courtroom door.

CHAPTER 59

DEPUTY SMITH ESCORTED the jurors out of the courtroom and across Main Street to the Country Kitchen where they ate alone in the back room. Since Judge Biltmore had admonished them not to discuss the case, and none knew any of the others, the jurors ate in silence except for two of the men who complained about how the Yankees had crushed their Pirates the night before. "Goddamn Newark empires," one said.

Calvin ate a sandwich and drank a carton of milk in the Public Defender's Office as he read over his morning notes. Once, he stood up and stretched and walked to the window. Alexander, his hands cuffed in front of him, and Smitty stood outside the restaurant, smoking and laughing. He watched them a moment and went back to his notes.

After dinner, the jurors gathered outside the back entrance where they boarded a waiting bus chartered by the county to drive them out to the farm for a view so they might better understand the testimony they would hear. Thompson and Judge Biltmore rode together in the front. Calvin sat in the back so he could watch the jurors. One read a paperback, but the rest only looked out their windows. He looked out the rear window. Following the bus in a patrol car were Smitty and Alexander.

Gathered behind Thompson and Judge Biltmore were half a dozen local reporters as well as one who had driven down from Cleveland the morning before and was staying with McLain. They talked about the weather and about how well the corn crop seemed to be maturing on the farms they passed. They exchanged county gossip and speculated about the upcoming elections. No one spoke about the trial. No one guessed that a little more than two years before, Bonner and Heath must have driven these same roads, seen this same farmland in crops.

When they reached the farm, the driver maneuvered the bus around the ruts as best he could and as far up the lane as he dared. He stopped and opened the door. Thompson and Judge Biltmore stepped out first and waited for the jurors, and all walked together the rest of the way to the farmhouse. Smitty and Alexander pulled in behind. After the last of the jurors reached the farmhouse, Smitty got out and opened Alexander's door and unlocked the handcuffs with Alexander still sitting in the back seat, his door open so the jurors could not see his handcuffs.

Calvin walked back to Alexander who still wore his blue-pinstriped suit, but the tip of his tie now hung out of one of his coat pockets. He told Alexander he needed to stay within earshot of the jury. "You never can tell when you might hear a remark worthy of a motion for mistrial."

Alexander nodded and said he and Smitty would wait by the patrol car.

Before they left the bus, Judge Biltmore instructed the jurors that, while they were not to enter the house due to its disrepair and the risk of injury, they otherwise were free to walk about as they liked. After he had spoken to Alexander, Calvin walked up the lane to where he could hear whatever remarks a juror might make, but all were silent as they walked about grave-faced.

One opened a shed door and poked his head inside, shyly, as though he were fearful of an accusation of voyeurism or some other crime of moral turpitude. He closed it, shaking his head in disgust if not incomprehension. Another walked up to the farmhouse and stood outside a window. She stood on her toes, her hands shading her face from the sun's glare, and looked inside, but if there was anything to see, she said nothing of it. She walked to the side of the farmhouse away from the road where she discovered a rose, its bloom a hand or more in width, growing out of the pit where the outhouse had once stood. "Isn't it pretty?" she said, but when she reached over to bring it closer to her nose, the ground at the edge of the pit gave way and she slipped in, screaming and kicking.

Judge Biltmore and Thompson and the other jurors rushed to where the woman had fallen in and a great many hands reached down. "I'm all right. I'm okay," she said.

After being pulled out, she and the rest of the jurors continued with their inspection, and Judge Biltmore took it upon himself to stand by the pit to guard against any more potential juror losses. "I don't even want to think about the headlines, Ben," he said. "And McLain. I don't want to be reading about this tomorrow in that Democratic Party rag you work for."

Over the farmyard hung an odor of rotting, burned-wood decay. Weeds knee high grew where there had once been a yard. A shattered farmhouse window looked like a spider's web in wait. From beneath missing porch floorboards rose the stench of rat feces, and it was this that drove Calvin across the lane where he stood beneath the shade of a great elm. McLain walked down from the pit and joined him.

"Good place to be standing," he said.

McLain took out a handkerchief from his rear pocket and wiped his face. "Man, this heat is blistering today, isn't it?"

"Some."

"Well, we won't be here much longer, I'll tell you what."

"Why's that?"

"Some of the jurors are already sweating. That air conditioned bus will start looking real good to all of them real soon."

Calvin nodded, but said nothing while he watched the jurors. Then he and McLain heard laughter behind them, and when they turned, they saw Smitty and Alexander standing in front of the patrol car, smoking. Thompson, who was still at the edge of the pit talking to Judge Biltmore, heard their laughter too, and when he saw who was laughing, his face reddened, and he trotted down the lane, leaving behind him little clouds of brown dust.

Calvin grinned. "Ben must be purely throwing a hissy fit over this. Talk about influencing the jurors. Just how dangerous can Alexander be if he's laughing and smoking a cigarette with a deputy sheriff?"

Thompson took Smitty, who stood a good twelve inches taller, by the arm and walked him a few yards away. After a minute, Smitty dropped his cigarette and rubbed it out with his boot. He walked back to Alexander and stood at rest. Thompson walked back up the lane. He turned around once, but then continued on up to the farmhouse. When he passed Calvin and McLain, he didn't even look in their direction.

"Now there's a queer bird," McLain said.

Calvin looked toward Thompson, who was standing again by Judge Biltmore, his hands in his pockets. "Oh, Ben's okay," he said. "He's just under a lot of pressure. Taking two years to catch a suspect to a double murder and all. Election coming up in November."

"I know Thompson's okay. It wasn't him I was talking about."

"Who, then?"

"Smitty."

Calvin looked back down the lane. "Smitty?"

"Yeah."

"What's so queer about him?"

"Well, you know Alexander likes to play the ponies."

"Yeah. Tell me something I don't know already."

"Did you know when he was arrested this spring, he was coming home from the track?"

"No, McLain. I have to admit I didn't know that. Does it matter?"

"Thompson told me that the day after his arrest."

"So?"

"So a couple of days later I went down there. Talked to some of the grooms. Some of the jocks. All of them knew Alexander. All of them knew Allison Morris."

"Learn anything of interest?" asked Calvin.

"About Alexander?"

Calvin nodded.

"No. Not really. Not about Alexander. He'd come around almost every day and talk to the grooms and the jocks, trying to get some tips. Never tried to dope a horse they said, but what would you expect them to say?"

"Yeah. I guess."

"About a week later, though, I went down there again."

"How come?"

"To see if there might be someone who hadn't been there the first time," McLain said.

"Was there?"

McLain shook his head. "Nobody interesting, but I did see Smitty down there. Both times."

"Tailing you?"

"I don't think so. He seemed embarrassed."

"About what?"

"Like he didn't want me to see him there. Which was funny."

"Funny how?"

"Funny he was down there both times I was."

"Yeah, that is funny."

"Funny he was embarrassed I should see him. Hell, Smitty knows I wouldn't say anything to the Sheriff, or to Thompson."

"So what happened?" Calvin said.

"After the second time I was down there, I was about ready to pack it in, but I decided to try some of the bars to see if any of the barkeeps knew Alexander."

"Did they?"

"None who would admit to it," McLain said. "I went to five or six near the track and got the same treatment at all of them. I'd order up a beer and try talking to the barkeep, who wouldn't know nothing."

"Guess getting their name in the paper wasn't worth dying over."

"After about six bars and six beers, I was beginning to get a little light headed. Then in the last one, in comes Smitty, and he sits down beside me and buys me a beer and asks me what I'm doing without asking me right out."

"What'd you say?"

"I just told him I'm working."

"So what'd you two talk about?"

"The ponies."

"What do you know about the ponies?"

"Nothing. But Smitty does, and he gave me an earful."

"Yeah?"

"I offered to buy him a beer, but he said no thanks. Said he had to be going and leaves, and I was just sitting there to give him enough time so he wouldn't think I was tailing him or something. Well, after he leaves, the barkeep comes over and asks me how I knew Smitty, and I told him. The barkeep smiles and says he didn't think I was no shark because he thought he knew all the ones who worked the track."

"You telling me Smitty's in over his head?" Calvin said.

McLain shrugged. "Could be. It adds up. Barkeep wouldn't say, but it adds up."

Calvin looked back down the lane again. "Well, I'll be damned."

Smitty was still standing in front of the patrol car, still in the at rest position he had learned in the Army. Alexander was standing in front of him and off to the right in the shade. He saw Calvin looking back. Alexander nodded and smiled.

CHAPTER 60

THE NEXT MORNING at ten minutes past nine, Judge Biltmore picked up his gavel and rapped the filled courtroom quiet. "Court will now come to order." He looked to first counsel's table. "Mr. Thompson, call your first witness, please."

Thompson stood. "Thank you, Your Honor. The state calls James Walters."

Judge Biltmore looked down to his right and nodded. Deputy Smith nodded back and turned and opened the front courtroom door behind where he stood and then quickly stepped aside.

Through the doorway Walters stumbled. He straightened and faced forward, his feral-dog eyes running wild all over the courtroom. Those in the gallery from Goshen who knew Walters, knew him since he was a boy and knew his family, watched him as they would a mental defective in a carnie side show brought out for their amusement, and they nudged one another with their elbows.

Deputy Smith took Walters by the elbow and led him past the bench and first counsel's table. The bailiff asked Walters to raise his right hand, but found it necessary to tell him to raise his other right hand. After the bailiff finished, Walters looked back at Thompson who nodded.

"I do," Walters said.

As Walters took the stand, Deputy Smith returned to the front courtroom door where he stood, beefy tattooed arms folded across his chest, eyes straight ahead. Calvin turned around. Two deputies stood in tandem before the main courtroom doors. One of the doors inched opened. A deputy looked to Judge Biltmore who shook his head no. The deputy hissed something into the crack and pulled the door shut.

Though Thompson had dressed Walters in a powder-blue, polyester-vested suit, purchased for fifty dollars from a Goodwill store, Walters still looked like a used-car sales-man, absent any residual credibility. After he settled in the witness chair, Walters glanced once toward Alexander, but thereafter kept his eyes focused on the gallery. He saw some-one in back, and he smiled and started to raise his arm as if to wave. Thompson, seeing the smile, immediately stood and stepped within Walters's line of vision. Walters lowered his arm in reluctant little jerks and his smile disappeared.

After questions about Walters's age and education and

where he had been born and raised, Thompson brought him around to the summer of 1980.

"Me and Alexander had gone into Goshen earlier that day, driving Bonner's pickup truck," Walters said. "And as we was coming back up the lane, it looked like Bonner had just gotten on Alexander's Harley and was getting ready to start her up."

"Why was he getting on Alexander's Harley?"

"I asked him that later on, and he told me he needed his truck back so he could get into Goshen to get some supplies, and he decided to go looking for us."

"What did Alexander say when he saw Bonner on his Harley?"

"He got mad."

"Real mad?"

"Yes, sir."

"What did he do about Bonner being on his Harley?"

"Nothing except to tell him to get the hell off. At least not right then he didn't do nothing. Didn't punch him or nothing. I thought the whole thing had blew over."

"Where was Allison Morris at?" Thompson said.

"She must've been still sleeping inside the farmhouse."

"Let's jump ahead a day, Jimmy. Did you hear Alexander give Ms. Morris any instructions?"

"Yeah, he told her that she had to move on into town."

"Into town where?"

"To stay with Preacher and his wife."

"Do you know Preacher's real name?"

Walters shook his head. "I just know he rides cycles with Alexander sometimes."

"You said you thought the argument between Alexander and Bonner had blown over. Had it?"

"No, sir. Right before Alexander told Allison she had to move into town, it started up all over again."

"What caused it to start up?"

"Bonner started ragging him about when he was to be getting paid for the drugs they'd bought for him when he sent Heath down to Miami."

"What did Alexander say to that?" Thompson queried.

"He told Bonner they'd get what was coming to them the next day."

"Alexander told Bonner they would get what was coming to them the next day?"

"Yes, sir."

"Jimmy, did you talk to Alexander after the argument?"

"Yeah, I did."

"When was that?"

"Later that afternoon."

"Where?"

"I'd gone into Goshen, where I got into an argument with my old lady. We wasn't living together no more because she'd thrown me out."

"Is that the reason you were living out at the farm that summer?"

"Yes, sir."

"Go on, please."

"Then I went to Ernest's. Stayed until I ran out of money, and I started out for my mom's. As I was getting there, Alexander pulled up. He was driving the pickup again, and he drove me back to the farm."

"Where was he coming from?"

"He was coming from dropping Allison off at Preacher's."

"Did he ask you anything on the way back to the farm?"

"Yeah. He did."

"What?" Thompson said.

"He asked me if I hadn't been in the service."

"And what did you say?"

"I says, 'Yeah, I been in the Army. So what?' I says. Then he asks me if I'd ever killed anyone."

"And what did you say to that?"

"I didn't know what to say. I didn't say nothing. I guess now maybe I should've. Bonner and Heath might be alive today." Walters looked at the jurors. "But then maybe I wouldn't."

Calvin stood. "Objection, Your Honor, to the last comment by the witness. It's speculative."

"Yes, sustained," Judge Biltmore said. "The jury will disregard the last statement by the witness."

"Go on, please, Jimmy," Thompson said. "Did Alexander say anything else to you as you were coming back to the farm?"

"Yeah. Then he said he was going to waste Bonner and Heath."

"Meaning he was going to kill them?"

"Yeah."

"And what'd you say to that?" Thompson asked.

"I told him if he was going to do them, he should take it somewheres else. I didn't want it at the farm, I told him. I didn't want nothing like that going down at my granduncle's."

"What did Alexander say?"

"He laughed. Said not to worry. Said he was only funning with me."

"After you and Alexander returned to the farm, what happened that night?" Thompson said.

"Me and him and Bonner and Heath played some poker."

"Anyone doing any drugs?"

"Bonner and Heath was popping Valiums."

"A lot?"

"Yes, sir."

"What about Alexander?"

"He drank only one or two cans of beer that I could see."

"Go on, please."

"About one-thirty, Heath and John Rogers drove to the Steel Trolley between Goshen and Hanna for a take-out order."

"What happened when they got back?"

"Don't know. I passed out before they come back, and I don't remember nothing 'til the next morning when Alexander shook me awake."

"What did he say when he woke you?"

"He told me to get up. Told me it was time," Walters said.

"Where were the others?"

"Heath was asleep on a couch in the living room."

"What about Bonner and Rogers?"

"They was sleeping on some couches they'd dragged out to the front porch."

"What happened after Alexander woke you?"

"I followed him downstairs and out to the front porch."

Walters stopped and swallowed.

"What happened on the porch, Jimmy?"

"Alexander sits down besides John and shakes him, but John is all groggy. It takes him a minute to come round, but when he does, Alexander asks him if he'd ever killed anyone. Just like he'd asked me the day before."

"What did Rogers say?"

"He didn't say nothing at first. I could see he was trying to pull hisself together. Trying to see where all this was going. But he answered no, he'd never killed anyone. He'd never wanted to kill anyone."

"What did Alexander say?"

"Told him to get up, but John didn't. I think he must of still been half asleep."

"Go on please, Jimmy."

"Then he opens up his switchblade and offers it to John. Asks John if he could kill Bonner."

"What did Rogers say?"

"He told him no, he couldn't."

"What did Alexander say?"

"He says in that case maybe John had better leave. When John started to get up, he changed his mind."

"What'd he change it to?"

"He tells John to just sit there and keep his mouth shut. Told him to keep out of the way."

The fan clicked overhead. Thompson told Walters to continue.

"Then Alexander gets up. He walks over to where Peter's sleeping. Places his one hand over his mouth and with his other, the one holding the knife, he slits Peter's throat open. Slits it open just like he would a hog's."

"Could you tell whether Bonner ever regained consciousness?"

"I think so. I think he might of woke up and tried to talk. Tried to say something. His eyes was looking at me, like for me to help him. But Alexander was holding his hand over his mouth, and there was only this sound from where he'd slit Peter's throat, like maybe a baby gurgling. That lasted for a few seconds. Then it stopped. I guess he was dead."

"What happened next?"

"Alexander turns and offers the knife to me."

"Did you take it?"

Walters shook his head. "No, sir. I sure didn't."

"Go on."

"I follows Alexander into the living room where Heath is sleeping on the couch."

"And?"

"Alexander knelt down beside him, and he takes his knife and raises it up over his head, as high as he could, in both his hands." Walters raised his own clenched fist. "And he brings his knife down, brings it down as hard he can into Taylor's chest," and Walters brought his own hand down hard into the palm of his other hand, the crack echoing in the courtroom, the juror closest to him flinching in his seat.

"Where did Alexander stab Heath?"

"In the heart, Mr. Thompson. He stabbed him in the goddamn heart."

"Did he remove his knife from Heath's chest?"

"No. After he stabbed him, he twisted the knife around, to make sure he was good and dead I guess, but he twisted it so hard he broke the blade off at the handle. Broke it off in his heart."

"What happened after Alexander broke off the knife blade in Heath's heart?"

"Alexander stands ups and walks to the corner where Heath kept his AK-47, and I followed him back out to the porch."

"What happened there?"

"He points it at John's throat, and I thought sure as the world he was going to do him, too. Shoot him in the neck or his head or something. He was my cousin, you know."

"Did you say anything?"

"I asks him if there hadn't been enough killing here. If there hadn't been enough out here for one day. John wouldn't say nothing, I told him."

511

"What did Alexander say?"

"Said John better goddamn well not say nothing. Said if he did, he wouldn't be living long. Then he puts the safety back on and slings the rifle on his shoulder."

Calvin glanced over toward Alexander, but Alexander only watched Walters, his face showing the same interest it might were he watching a rerun for the third time. He had heard it all before.

"Please, go on," Thompson said. "What happened next?"

"Alexander first said he wanted us to bury them, but then he changed his mind."

"What'd he change it to?"

"Told us to dump them in the shitter."

"Did you?"

Walters nodded. "He walked over to the tool shed and comes back with a crow bar. Tells me and John to carry Bonner over in his sleeping bag. While we was carrying him, he was prying off the seat with the crowbar. Then me and John dropped him in. Headfirst. Then we all walked back to the house and he had us carry Heath over, and we dropped him in on top."

Thompson looked at one of his three-by-five cards, flipped it, and read the next.

"Did the three of you go anywhere that day?"

"Yeah, we did."

"Where?"

"After we dropped them down the shitter, we took the

pickup to Schmidt's Hardware Supply."

"Is that in Goshen?"

"Yes, sir."

"Did you go anywhere first?"

"Yeah, we did."

"Where was that?"

"We stopped off at Ernest's."

"Why?"

"Alexander said he felt like a game of pool."

"Did you do anything besides play pool?"

"Me and John didn't, but Alexander did."

"What did he do?"

"First, he went upstairs, said he had to talk to his uncle about something, and then he come down and used the pay-phone."

"Who did he call?"

"He didn't say, and I didn't want to ask. He never was what you'd call a morning person."

"Go on."

"After he used the phone, we went to Schmidt's. Alexander told me to get out and buy five bags of lime, and he give me a twenty-dollar bill."

"Where was Rogers?"

"Sitting in the truck next to him."

"Did you ask for Rogers's help?"

"Yeah."

"What did Alexander say?"

"He leaned over and puts his arm around his shoulders and says no way. The Jolly Rogers would just stay in the truck with him."

"Did he say why?"

"He said that way he wouldn't get no ideas about talking about things he had no business talking about."

"Did you buy the lime?"

"Yes, sir."

"Where did the three of you go after you left Schmidt's?"

"We drove out to that gas station that's between Goshen and Hanna. The one across the road from the Steel Trolley."

"What happened there?"

"We bought us three dollars worth of gas. Filled an old gasoline can Alexander found in the barn."

"Did Alexander say anything to you, or to Rogers, during this time you were driving around?" Thompson asked.

"About what?"

"About what happened two days before? When Bonner got up on his motorcycle."

"Yeah, he did. I remember him saying, 'Now ain't you glad, Jolly Rogers, ain't you glad you didn't get up on my cycle, too? You should, because no one, no one, gets up on my cycle or wears my colors. Leastways not if he wants to keep on loving and living'."

"What happened when you returned to the farm?"

"Alexander had me pour the lime down the shitter and then the gasoline, and then John set it on fire."

"How long did it burn, Jimmy?"

"Three days. Maybe five. I don't rightly know. Made a god-awful smell, though, I'll tell you; but I couldn't tell you for certain how long it burned."

"Why's that?"

" 'Cause me and John got messed up that night. I didn't want to think about it no more. Still don't want to think about it."

"Do you?"

"Sometimes. 'Specially at night. Sometimes I wake myself up screaming. For a long time they had to keep me locked up, at the top of the jail, on account of I was screaming so much. Keeping everybody else awake."

"What happened after you set the outhouse on fire?"

"Alexander had us clean up the blood from the porch."

"What did you use?"

"Some paint scrapers and wire brushes."

"Did he help you clean it up?"

Walters snorted. "No. He just stood there watching us with Heath's rifle slung over his shoulder, like he was guarding us or something, flipping the safety on and off."

"Go on, please."

"When we was done scraping, he had us drag the two couches out into the lane and had us burn them, too."

"What happened after they burned?"

"Me and John shoveled up the ashes into the back of the truck, and we all drove to the dump on the other side of Goshen."

"What happened when you got back?"

"Alexander started going through their personal stuff. Keeping what he wanted."

"What did he keep, Jimmy?"

"He took a tent, Coleman lantern, .357 Magnum, and a briefcase."

"What was in the briefcase?"

"When he pried it open, I saw Heath's driver's license, personal papers, plane tickets, and two, maybe three thousand dollars in cash."

"Any drugs?"

"Not in there."

"Anywhere?"

"We walked over to a shanty they'd been using, and we found a thermos full of THC and another of cocaine."

"What happened to the items you found?"

"After we found the dope, we walked to the kitchen, and Alexander counted the money out. Offered me five hundred and John five hundred."

"Did you or John take it?"

"No, sir."

"Did he offer you anything else?"

"Bonner's motorcycle, but I didn't want that neither."

"Anyone come to the farm that day?"

"The head of the Pagans' West Virginia chapter, Dick, or Dicky maybe. I ain't certain which, and Preacher come out."

"How'd they know to come out?"

Walters shook his head. "Alexander must've called them while we was playing pool at Ernest's. Or maybe Ernest did."

"What happened when they got there?"

"They talked to Alexander for five, ten minutes maybe, and all three of them got in and drove away in Heath's van."

"When did you see Alexander again?"

"The next day."

"What happened the next day?"

"All them Pagans come out on their cycles."

"Do you remember talking to a Billy Whalen that day?"

"Yeah, I do."

"Did you tell Alexander about that conversation?"

"Yeah, I did."

"When was that?"

"Next day, after the Pagans had all gone, I told him I'd been so messed up that I went and told Whalen about what happened."

Calvin stopped writing. He looked up and watched Walters.

"He'd come out to the farm the day before, when the Pagans was all getting there, and he asks me where was Bonner and where was Heath."

"Why was he asking for them?"

"Said he needed to buy some dope."

"What did you tell him?"

"I told him they was in the shitter and they was dead."

"What did Whalen say to that?" Thompson said.

"Said he didn't want to know nothing about it. At all.

He got back in his car and tore on out of there like a bat out of hell. Just about drove over some Pagans, which ain't a healthy thing to do either. Didn't even stay for the wedding."

"What happened after you told Alexander?"

"He had me and John drive with him to find him."

"Did you?"

"Yes, sir."

"Where?"

"Standing in front of the house where he was living. In Goshen."

"Go on."

"Alexander told us to stay inside for a minute, and he gets out and walks up to him. The two of them walks over to the front steps and sits down."

"Could you hear what was being said?"

"No, sir, but it was Alexander doing all the talking, and Whalen doing all the listening, all right. He just sat there, not saying nothing, until Alexander gets up, pats him on the shoulder, walks back to the truck, and gets in; and we go."

"What was Whalen doing?"

"Just sitting there. Wouldn't even look over at us, and we'd been friends since before first grade, even."

"What happened to Whalen?"

"He died."

Thompson nodded. "How much longer did you stay at the farm after this?"

"Few more days."

"Why did you leave?"

"Alexander got mad at something I said to Allison. I told him I didn't mean nothing by it. I was only joking around with her, but he got mad, so I decided I'd better get out while I could. Before he got into another of his nasty moods."

"When did you leave?"

"That afternoon. I didn't want to stay there no more."

"Did you ever go back?"

"I come back the next day with my mom and my grandma for my clothes."

"Why did you bring your mother and grandmother?"

"I didn't think he'd do all three of us right there in broad daylight."

"Objection," Calvin said.

Judge Biltmore nodded. "Yes, sustained."

"Was that the last time you were at the Old Church Road farm?" Thompson replied.

"Yes, sir. Never been back there since. Never want to."

"What about your cousin, John Rogers?"

"He was still living out there when I left."

"Where's he at now?"

"He's dead, too."

Thompson gathered up his note cards. "No further questions, Your Honor."

He walked back to first counsel's table, but all of the jurors were staring at Walters. One woman held her hand to her mouth. A man in the back row slowly shook his head.

Judge Biltmore announced they would break for lunch. When they returned an hour and a half later, he told Calvin he could cross-examine Walters.

Calvin stood and walked to the podium.

"Why do they call you 'Psycho'?"

Walters grinned. "There was this guy in Goshen I used to hang out with. We called him 'Sicko.' And Sicko called me 'Psycho.' Everyone started calling me that."

"Why did Sicko call you Psycho?"

Walters shrugged. "Some of the crazy stuff I done."

"Like breaking beer bottles over your head?"

Walters grinned, but when his audience only looked at him, glaze-eyed, he added, "What I do to myself is my concern. It ain't none of yours."

"Mr. Walters, isn't it true that in a statement you made to the police on February third of last year you said Alexander had killed only Bonner, and it was your cousin, John Rogers, who had killed Heath?"

"Yeah. So what?"

"So your testimony today is that Alexander killed both of them."

"Yeah," Walters said. "So what?"

"So which time were you telling the truth? Then or today?"

"What I'm saying today is the truth."

"Were you lying to Mr. Thompson, or are you lying to this jury?"

"I ain't lying to nobody about nothing. What I said here

520

today is the God's truth."

"But you have lied about what happened that summer."

Walters did not answer.

"To the police."

Walters turned like he was about to spit, but did not.

"It's also true during that summer you abused alcohol, Quaaludes, and THC."

"Yeah," Walters said. "It's true."

"And it's true you've a felony conviction for aiding and abetting to aggravated murder?"

"Yeah. It's true."

"And it's true you've been arrested for marijuana possession and petty theft?"

"Yeah. So what?"

And so Calvin questioned Walters throughout the afternoon. At almost five o'clock, he looked up at Judge Biltmore. "No further questions, Your Honor. But the defense reserves the right to re-call Mr. Walters at a later time."

Calvin closed his legal pad and sat down. Alexander was smiling. Deputy Smith led Walters away.

"We'll break for the day here," Judge Biltmore said. "We'll reconvene at nine o'clock tomorrow morning. The jurors are instructed not to discuss this case with anyone nor are they to read accounts of it in the newspaper. Court's adjourned."

After the jurors left the courtroom, Alexander turned to go with the deputies, and he placed his hand on Calvin's shoulder. Calvin looked at the hand, but said nothing.

CHAPTER 61

THE NEXT MORNING, as Calvin sat at second counsel's table, studying his notes and waiting for the day's session to begin, the front courtroom door creaked. The spectators behind him fell silent. He looked up and saw Deputy Smith, holding the door open for Allison, staring lewd-faced down at her legs, the tip of his tongue on his upper lip.

Calvin had not seen her since she had kissed him in his back doorway the week before. He had not even talked to her by telephone, and he still did not know if she had spoken to Walters.

She had parked that morning a block from the courthouse and had waited in her car until she saw Calvin walking toward her down Main Street in the half-dark. After he had gone inside, Allison got out and entered the courthouse by the back door and went upstairs. She waited inside Thompson's office, alone except for a deputy. Another stood guard outside the door. From the sofa couch she looked out the window and watched the witnesses and spectators as they arrived, and she smiled when she saw Jocelyn walking down the sidewalk. "Number your days, honey," she whispered.

When it was time, the bailiff telephoned up from the courtroom, and the deputy outside Thompson's door knocked and said they were waiting for her downstairs. Allison stood and smoothed her dress. She reached into her purse and redid her lipstick. When she finished, Allison smiled at the deputies and said she was ready.

They escorted her down the flight of stairs, one in front to her left and one behind to her right. When they reached the second floor, they turned immediately right and then left. The deputy in front knocked at the courtroom door and gave her a wink when she passed him. After Deputy Smith opened the door, he walked her to the bailiff, and Allison raised her right hand.

She was wearing the same black penitent dress she had worn that first Sunday afternoon in the Hanna Cemetery. As she swore to tell the truth, the men seated in the jury box straightened in their chairs. One combed what hair strands he had over his liver-spotted scalp.

After he had sworn her in, the bailiff walked Allison to the witness chair. As she seated herself she looked at neither Calvin nor Alexander, but only at Thompson who, wearing a new yellow, polka-dot designer tie, already stood behind the podium, studying his note cards. When she had settled, Thompson looked up.

"Good morning, Ms. Morris."

She nodded.

"Will you please tell the jury where it is you're residing and where it is you're employed?"

Allison told them.

"Ms. Morris, I want to take you back to two summers ago."

Thompson paused. Allison smiled her assent.

"I want to begin by asking you under just what circumstances it was that you met the defendant, Mark Alexander."

Allison told the jurors about how they had met and how she had quickly fallen in love with Alexander. She told them about moving out to the farm after his accident and about their lives there. As she testified, she almost always referred to Alexander as the defendant, almost never by name.

"Ms. Morris," Thompson said. "After you moved out to the farm, do you recall ever hearing Alexander requesting of Bonner or Heath to purchase drugs for him?"

"Objection," Calvin said. "Leading."

"No," said Judge Biltmore. "I'll allow the question."

"Yes," Allison said. "Yes, he did."

"And when was that?"

"It was a week, maybe two, before he suggested that I leave the farm."

"What was the nature of his request?"

"I heard the defendant ask Taylor to go to Florida to purchase marijuana for him."

"Why Florida?"

"He said he was still in considerable pain from his car accident, and the marijuana he was getting from the local dealers wasn't potent enough to do him any good."

"When Heath came back from Florida, did he bring with him the marijuana he'd been sent to purchase?"

"No, he didn't. He made another purchase instead."

"And what was his other purchase?" Thompson asked.

"He returned with Peruvian cocaine."

"What did Alexander say about Heath's substitute purchase?"

"They had an argument. A very bad one."

"What eventually happened to the cocaine?"

"We snorted it that night while we played cards. Poker and blackjack and even crazy eights."

"All in one evening, you snorted up your noses a few thousand dollars worth of high-grade Peruvian cocaine?"

"Yes."

A woman on the jury looked at Allison's Pierre Cardin dress and shook her head.

"Did Alexander say anything to you about the cocaine?"

"Yes, he did."

"What?"

"After we went to bed he asked me what I would do if he killed Peter and Taylor."

"What did you say?"

"I asked him why he would want to."

"What did he answer?"

"He said if he did, we'd have Peter's pickup and Taylor's van. Two thousand dollars in cash, maybe more, and a pound of THC. Probably some cocaine, too."

"What did you say?"

She looked at Calvin. "I told him I would stand by his side. No matter what."

Alexander followed her look to Calvin. He followed his look back.

"What happened the next day?"

"The defendant told me to leave the farm for a few days."

"Where did you go?"

"He drove me to some friends of his in Goshen."

"When did you next see him?"

"The next day the defendant drove to where I was staying."

"What did Alexander say to you?"

"He asked me if I wanted to marry him."

"When?"

"The next day," she said.

"When did you return to the farm?"

"The next day."

"Did you see Bonner or Heath upon your return?"

She did not answer. She turned and looked toward the window, and Thompson had to repeat the question.

"No," she said. "When I got back, I didn't see them."

"Did you ask about them?"

"Yes, I did."

"Who did you ask?"

"The defendant."

"What did he say?"

"He said that they'd gone south the day before."

"Anything else?"

"He kind of smirked and gave me a thumbs-down, like this." Allison pointed her own thumb down. "And then he started to laugh."

So her testimony went that morning and after lunch and on into the afternoon, Thompson pulling from her the events of that summer, weaving them into Walters's testimony from the day before.

"Upon your return to the farm, did you notice anything out of the ordinary?"

"Yes."

"What?"

"The outhouse was smoldering," Allison said.

"Did you ask anyone about it?"

"I did."

"Who?"

"John Rogers."

"What did Rogers tell you?"

"He said Walters had accidentally set it on fire when he was behind it smoking."

"Did you ask Alexander about it?"

"No, Mr. Thompson, I did not."

"Why not?"

"I was afraid."

"Who was it you were afraid of? The defendant? Mark Alexander? Your lover?"

"Yes," Allison said. She looked at Alexander. "The defendant. My lover."

After their wedding, she had continued to live at the farm with the defendant until September. They talked about finding another place—a place with some heat—before the fall rains, before the winter snows.

"When you left the farm, Ms. Morris, did you leave with the defendant?"

"No, I did not."

The curtain by the open window next to her stirred, and Calvin looked out at the trees. There was no breeze.

"No further questions, Your Honor."

Thompson returned to first counsel's table. His assistant leaned over and whispered, his hand patting Thompson's shoulder.

"Defense may cross-examine," Judge Biltmore said.

Calvin stood and walked to the podium. He looked down so long at his legal tablet Judge Biltmore found it necessary to clear his throat.

"Ms. Morris, I have just a few questions. I don't want to take up much of your time. I'm sure you're anxious to return to Maryland."

Allison nodded.

"How did you get along with Bonner and Heath?"

She frowned. "I'm afraid I don't understand the question, Mr. Sanders."

"His name is 'Samuels'," Judge Biltmore said.

"I'm sorry. Mr. Samuels."

"Let me assure you it's not a trick question. It's a very straightforward question. How did you get along with Peter Bonner and Taylor Heath? Were you friends? Enemies? Indifferent?"

"They were the defendant's friends. His business partners. We were friendly if not friends. We partied together." She paused. "I'm still not certain what you mean."

"So when you guessed they had died, guessed they had probably been murdered by your lover, if we are to believe your testimony, you were not particularly upset?"

"No, that's not true. I was."

"But not upset enough to report your suspicions to the authorities. Not enough to go to the police."

"No. I did not go to the police. But not because I wasn't upset. I told you I was frightened." She shrugged. "I was a coward. I wished I hadn't been, but I was."

"In fact, you weren't even upset enough to leave the Old Church Road farm until another five weeks had passed."

Thompson stood up. "Objection, the question is argumentative."

"I'll withdraw it, Your Honor," Calvin said.

Thompson sat down.

"Ms. Morris, it's true, is it not, that you married Mr. Alexander even though you say you believed him to have murdered Peter Bonner and Taylor Heath. Is that correct?"

"Yes, that's true also."

"So you returned to the farm, married Mark Alexander, slept with him, even though you believed he was responsible for the murder of two people you knew and with whom you were at least friendly if not friends. Is that what you're asking this jury to believe?"

"Yes," she said. "I can't say I'm proud of it, but it's true."

"And before you left the farm for good in September, did you ever visit your family in Weirton?"

"Yes, I did."

"On how many occasions?"

"I don't know. Three. Maybe four."

"And did Mark ever go with you on these visits?"

"No," Allison said. "My parents didn't approve of him. I always drove down alone."

"So you did have the opportunity to leave him on any number of times prior to when you did in September."

"Yes. I suppose I could have. If I had wanted to endanger my family, I could have."

"You testified earlier today that when you left the farm for good, you left alone, is that correct?"

The ghost-gray curtain beside Allison again flapped and twisted.

"Ms. Morris," Calvin said. "When you left the farm for

the last time, did you leave alone?"

"Yes, Mr. Samuels. When I left the farm, left it for the last time, I was alone."

"No further questions."

CHAPTER 62

CALVIN SAT HUNCHED over his desk, reviewing his notes of Allison's testimony and making necessary changes to the strategy notes for the day following. Because it remained still warm on the third floor of the courthouse even this late in the evening, he had not turned on the overhead florescent lights, reading only by the light of his desk lamp. From time to time Calvin switched off the lamp and looked out the open window, but he saw nothing more than the darkness.

The courthouse clock had chimed ten o'clock some minutes before. The telephone rang. He stared at it while it sounded once, twice, three times. On the fourth ring he picked it up.

"What's wrong, Calvin? Trying to figure out if you wanted to pick up your phone? Figured it must be a crank call or a heavy breather at this time of night?"

Calvin smiled. "What are you, McLain? Psychic?"

"No, but I've got someone outside my office who is. You remember Reverend Barnhouse?"

Calvin leaned back in his chair and rubbed his forehead. "Not tonight, Brad. I really don't have the energy. I've way too much preparation before nine o'clock tomorrow."

McLain's voice dropped. "I know you're tired, but I wouldn't be bothering you at this hour if I didn't think it important. Trust me on this one."

Calvin looked down at his legal pad, the words all running together. "All right," he said. I'll meet you downstairs."

Outside, he sat on the courthouse steps, his coat, smelling pungent under the arms, folded across his knees. He took out his cigarettes and shook one out, but his shaking hand couldn't light it, and Calvin had to hold his match hand with the other.

Main Street was empty. He smoked and looked at his fun house reflection in the plate glass windows across the street and waited. In a few minutes two men passed beneath the halo thrown by a corner streetlamp as they rounded Court Street. He ground his cigarette into the pocked courthouse step and stood. "Gentlemen."

"Calvin," McLain said. He nodded to his side. "You remember Reverend Barnhouse."

Calvin offered his hand. "Yes, of course. How have you been, sir?"

The minister nodded. "I'm sorry to trouble you, especially so late and when you're so busy."

"It was my idea," McLain said. "He called this evening, and I told him to come in. He said he couldn't talk on the phone."

"It's my wife," the minister said. "You remember her condition? From the time you were at our home some weeks ago."

"Yes, I do."

"The least mention of this case upsets her so."

"She is no better?"

"Some days better than others. But no real change."

"I'm sorry."

"Yes. Thank you. But the reason I called Mr. McLain this evening was that I was in the courtroom today, sitting in the back."

"He read in my column that Morris would be testifying today," McLain said.

Before the minister could continue, four sheriff's squad cars, sirens screaming, raced past the courthouse. Calvin looked at McLain who himself looked puzzled. The minister waited until the squad cars had disappeared, and they could no longer hear their sirens.

"Actually, it was my wife who first read the article. I try to keep the papers away from her, but I was detained on my way home yesterday by a parishioner who's been ill, and the paperboy beat me home. By the time I got there, she'd read the story that Miss Morris was to testify today."

"Oh."

"She reacted very badly, Mr. Samuels."

"I'm sorry," Calvin said. "This trial will be over soon.

Perhaps she will begin to heal then."

"When I finally quieted her down and got her into bed and resting, I went back to the front porch to see what had upset her so."

"Yes."

"When I finished reading the story, I sensed something."

"What?" Calvin asked.

"I felt like I did on that winter day when Elizabeth and I were walking around the farm."

The courthouse clock struck the half-hour.

"There was something that bothered me today. In the courtroom."

"What was it?"

"I detected there three presences from the farm."

"Three?" Calvin said.

"One was Allison Morris, of course, and another was Alexander. The other I couldn't see, but was by the window. Next to her while she testified."

"You don't mean Deputy Smith, do you?"

"No, Mr. Samuels. I said I could not see the presence, but it's one that was alive at the farm."

"And is not alive now?"

"Yes."

"Who?"

"It was the guardian we talked about before."

Calvin turned to McLain.

"I thought you should know," McLain said. "I don't

know what it means either, but I thought you should know."

Calvin thanked them both for taking the time to come in so late in the evening. He slung his coat over his shoulder and walked away slowly, looking at the sidewalk. A block from his home he looked up at a lighted second-story window where a mother stood over her child who was kneeling in prayer by his bedside.

CHAPTER 63

T HE FOLLOWING DAY at midmorning, Thompson rested the case in chief for the State of Ohio. Judge Biltmore nodded to Calvin and told him to call his first witness.

"Thank you, Your Honor," Calvin said as he stood. "The defense calls Jocelyn Murphy to the stand."

Deputy Smith walked out into the hallway. There the witnesses who were to testify that day sat contorted like medieval gnomes on cushionless benches lining both sides of the second-floor corridor, only dimly lit by high windows at either end. When her name was called, Jocelyn did not so much stand as jump, and she followed closely behind the deputy back into the courtroom.

After taking the oath, she climbed the single step to the witness stand. Her eyes searched the courtroom for a moment before she fixed her attention on Calvin who was standing behind the podium. She grimaced more than smiled.

That evening McLain would tell Calvin that, as he was walking through the courthouse door, he had heard running behind him and turned and seen her coming up the front steps. He tried to speak to her to get a quote for the next day's edition, but she only rushed past him on her way to the stairs leading to the courtroom. McLain looked at the deputy standing guard inside the door and remarked on how it was strange some members of the public just didn't enjoy reading about themselves in the papers. The deputy laughed and said that having your car blown up for you can make the more cautious members of the public real hesitant about being read about in the papers.

When McLain asked the deputy what he was talking about, he said Jocelyn had been at Ernest's the night before, tossing down a few and talking to the boys, when her car exploded out in the parking lot at around ten-thirty.

McLain looked up the stairs. He told the deputy she should consider herself lucky even to be alive.

No, the deputy disagreed. The way Sheriff Conkle had it figured was that some of the friends of Bonner and Heath up in Detroit just wanted to rattle a couple of memories a little bit, but they didn't intend any real harm. Just their way of funning.

Jocelyn was on the stand for all of five minutes. Calvin had her confirm her stay at Ernest's home with Alexander after his accident and no more. After he sat down, Judge

Biltmore looked to first counsel's table. "The state may cross-examine if it wishes."

"Thank you, Your Honor." Thompson walked to the podium carrying no note cards.

"Miss Murphy, you love Mark Alexander, do you not?"

Jocelyn did not answer. She was looking into the gallery, all color so drained out of her face even her pancake makeup could not hide her freckles. Calvin turned around. The two pool shooters from Ernest's were standing against the back wall, arms folded. Thompson repeated the question.

"Yes, I do," she said.

"And you would do anything you could to help him, would you not?"

She looked at Alexander who turned his head to one side in a half-shake of his head. She looked to the back of the courtroom. She stared down. From the window behind that lay across the courtroom floor and separated her and Thompson, a single-routed dust mote reeled through the light. She nodded and looked up.

"Yes, Mr. Thompson. Of course I would. I'd do anything Mark asked me to do. Anything at all. No matter what."

"No further questions, Your Honor."

"Defense may redirect," Judge Biltmore said.

Alexander grabbed Calvin's arm, desperate as a man drowning, whispering rabid directions, but Calvin shook his head.

"No redirect," Calvin said.

Alexander looked at him. He released his grip on Calvin's arm, but only slowly.

"Defense may call its next witness then."

"Defense calls Ernest Alexander."

After a while, Alexander sat back, his elbows on the chair's armrests, touching his fingertips against each other, contemplatively, as would a chessman.

CHAPTER 64

AGAIN, THE DEPUTY turned and walked outside, the small of the back of his olive blouse already dark. As they waited, Judge Biltmore made a notation in a notebook. His courtroom was still. The voice of the deputy echoed down the corridor. He returned alone some minutes later and whispered to Judge Biltmore who held his hand over the microphone.

Though he was under subpoena, Ernest was not in the courthouse. Judge Biltmore asked Calvin and Thompson to approach the bench. He asked Calvin if he wished for him to issue a bench warrant. Calvin walked back and spoke to Alexander. Alexander drummed his fingers on counsel's table and looked down.

"Mr. Samuels," Judge Biltmore said.

Alexander shook his head, not looking up.

For the rest of the week, Calvin called his other witnesses.

His two experts criticized the state's recovery of the bodies. While there was no doubt the bodies recovered were those of Bonner and Heath, the state in excavating them with a backhoe may well have destroyed significant forensic evidence that might have exculpated Alexander.

He also put his character witnesses on the stand, and they all testified that Alexander's alleged engagement in such a heinous crime was a notion beyond credulity. One frustrated Thompson almost to tears because he was a Pan-American Airlines mechanic working out of the Pittsburgh airport who taught Sunday school when he was not out on rides with the gang. When Calvin and Thompson met in the men's room during a break, Thompson grumbled about the lengths to which some dealers went in constructing a cover.

Late on Saturday afternoon Judge Biltmore announced they would break for the day. Deputy Smith walked back from the front courtroom door to second counsel's table and asked Alexander if he was ready to go back up for the evening or if he required a few minutes. Calvin shook his head, and Alexander said he was ready.

Deputy Smith checked the front of the courtroom. The jurors were gone, and Judge Biltmore had returned to his chambers. Thompson was nowhere to be seen. He took an envelope from inside his blouse and laid it on the table before Calvin.

"Come on, Mark," he said. "Fried chicken and ice cream on Saturday nights, you know. Wouldn't want to miss that treat would you?"

CHAPTER 65

JUDGE BILTMORE CALLED a rare Sunday session. So rare that none of the old-time gallery handicappers could recall any judge calling a Sunday session. Ever. That morning before Alexander's trial picked up again, they stood on the dewy courthouse lawn, talking it over. While most said it was of no consequence, a few were not so certain. They said it seemed as odd as the weather they'd been suffering through that summer.

As was now his custom, Calvin came to the courthouse early. While he waited for the deputies to bring down Alexander, he prepared for the day's session, his papers stacked across the table from one end to the other in three neat rows. The bailiff came in not long after Calvin, and, first thing, he opened all of the windows as wide as they would go. He walked to second counsel's table and turned and looked back at the limp courtroom curtains, shaking his head.

"Going to be a long one," he said. "Long and merciless."

The gallery filled early, and Calvin remarked to Deputy Smith it seemed more crowded that day than it had been any other all week. The deputy laughed and told Calvin a prisoner they'd picked up the night before had told them that even the Sunday-morning cockfights outside of Goshen had been cancelled so the regulars could attend the county's other Sunday spectacle for the week.

"Hell, Calvin, you should be right proud of yourself. They don't even cancel the cockfights for the Super Bowl."

"Really?"

"No, sir. Come to think of it, they didn't neither for that time Miss Dolly Parton sang and strutted and showed what she had out at the fairgrounds when she was there with one of them TV preachers. I seen her and you believe me when I tell you she's a whole lot better put together than you or Mark, if you don't mind my saying so."

"I don't mind much you're saying so, Smitty."

"Now what was the name of that preacher? You re-member. The one they sent off to prison down in Georgia a few month back for raiding the till and groping some of the younger members of his congregation. Was in all the papers. You must of read about it. Every time I see you, you're read-ing something. Excepting the *Racing News*."

To gain some purchase on the heat, Judge Biltmore had scheduled the day's session to begin an hour early. At a minute before eight o'clock, the spectators' buzzing ceased when a pair of deputies escorted in Alexander, the first-timers asking the veterans if that was sure enough him. "Kind of fancies himself, don't he?" one of them said. "All dressed up in his suit and all."

Alexander had no more than taken his seat next to Calvin when Judge Biltmore came out of his chambers and ordered the bailiff to bring in the jury.

"Court will come to order. Defense will call its next witness."

Calvin stood. "Your Honor, the defense calls Mark Alexander."

Alexander rose and walked to where the bailiff waited, Bible in hand. Calvin stood behind the podium. When he finished administering the oath, the bailiff nodded to Calvin to begin.

During his first five minutes on the stand, Alexander skirted over his boyhood up until his meeting Peter Bonner. Calvin led him through the summer of 1980, detail by detail, beginning with his meeting Allison Morris at the racetrack and continuing until the first time they visited her stepbrother out at the abandoned farm off of the Old Church Road.

"And about when did you first visit the farm?"

"I'd have to say it was sometime in June."

"Was anyone living there at the time?"

"Walters was."

As he was making a notation, Calvin's antique fountain pen from Italy dried up, and even after shaking it, he could not get his pen to write.

"Better get another, Mr. Samuels," Judge Biltmore said.

Calvin walked to second counsel's table, knelt, and opened his brief bag. He found a spare pen, but as he stood his eyes met those of Reverend Barnhouse who was standing along the back wall, just beneath the clock, its hands pointing down. The minister nodded toward the witness stand. Calvin turned. Of all the curtains in the courtroom, only those hanging from the window adjacent to Alexander were not still.

Calvin returned to the podium. "What about John Rogers?"

"Jolly Rogers?" Alexander grinned. "What about him?"

"Wasn't he living there too?"

At the tenor of the question, the jurors turned from Alexander to Calvin. Lawyer and client studied one another.

"Yes, he was living there," Alexander said. "He and Walters were cousins or something. They were hanging out at the farm that summer after Walters's old lady threw him out."

The window curtain rippled. Calvin moved on.

"How familiar did you become with the farm?"

"I would have to say I became somewhat familiar with it."

"Why was that?"

"Allison and I would sometimes stay there, sometimes for two or even three days at a time."

"Did you ever live out at the farm?"

"No. I kept a change of clothes there. And I did move out a stereo system for when we had some friends up from

Weirton, but I never lived there."

"What was the big attraction?" Calvin said. "An abandoned farmhouse out in the middle of nowhere with no electricity. No plumbing."

"I had always liked camping as a kid, Mr. Samuels, and the farm reminded me of some of trips I had taken with my folks."

"A little bit like a rustic cabin?"

"Yes, and it was a place to invite my friends to come and relax. A place for them and their children to picnic. To take a swim in Bear Cross Creek. It was quiet. Peaceful. You've been there. I find it to be very restful."

The woman who had fallen into the outhouse pit during the jury view rolled her eyes.

Calvin continued eliciting Alexander's version of the events of that summer. "It had been a good summer. At least it had been so up until his car accident. After that, everything seemed to slide downhill for him. For almost a week he was confined to the hospital. While he was in the hospital, he lost his trailer. After his discharge, he and Allison had gone to his uncle's, but she had stayed with him only for the first night before leaving the next day all in a tizzy just because of Jocelyn's unexpected appearance."

"Did Ms. Morris visit you again after leaving?"

"Once, but by then we were pretty shaky."

Calvin nodded and flipped to the next page of his notes. Alexander watched him, his eyes gleaming like a cat toying with a mouse.

"We'd started arguing because she was seeing Rogers."

Calvin's head snapped up. "Allison was seeing . . ."

"Yes. They started up when I was in the hospital. Perhaps even before, I think, because they always seemed awfully friendly even if they were distant cousins. I asked her about it once, and she told me they were only friends." Alexander shook his head. "I didn't believe it, and that was when Jocelyn and I started getting serious. I was getting ready to tell Allison to move out just about the time I had my accident."

Calvin stared at Alexander so long Judge Biltmore found it necessary to tell him to put another question.

"Yes, Your Honor. Sorry. Just gathering my thoughts." Alexander scratched at his mustache and smiled.

"Why did you suspect Allison of seeing John Rogers?" Judge Biltmore raised his eyebrows.

"Objection, Your Honor," Thompson said. "I don't see the relevance."

"Yes, sustained. Please move on, Mr. Samuels. We'd like to finish this trial before Christmas if you don't mind."

Calvin and Alexander looked at one another. Judge Biltmore cleared his throat. Calvin flipped to another page of his notes.

"Were you dealing drugs that summer, Mark?"

"No, I was not."

"Were you using?"

"Oh, I definitely was using," Alexander said. "As was everyone else who came there. One of the prices of youth is youthful stupidity, I guess. And I've got to say I manifested some significant amounts that summer."

"What kind of drugs?"

"I smoked some marijuana. Sniffed a little cocaine."

"Why do you think Bonner and Heath were spending so much time in Goshen that summer?"

"Boy, I've got no idea, Mr. Samuels. They told me they were having some problems in Michigan, but they didn't say what. And I never asked. I figured they'd tell me when they were good and ready and not before."

"Were they dealing?"

"I couldn't say for sure."

"And you never suspected?"

"Oh, I took Taylor to the airport a few times, and he'd always be reluctant to tell me where he was going."

"You never suspected?"

"I suppose if I'd given it any thought I should have guessed, but like I said, I was being especially stupid that summer. Dope will do that to you, which is why I've stopped."

On it went into midafternoon, Alexander contradicting each assertion made by Walters and Morris. Sometimes convincingly, other times not.

Shortly before three o'clock, Calvin asked Alexander if he could recall the last time he saw Bonner and Heath.

"Yes. Yes, I can."

"When was that?"

"It was when they came to visit me in the hospital." Alexander looked down at his hands. "Didn't mean much to me at the time. It didn't because they were always going out of their way to be nice to someone. It means a lot to me now, though."

"Did you murder Peter Bonner?"

"No, I did not, Mr. Samuels. I couldn't have murdered him. Peter was my best friend."

"Did you murder Taylor Heath?"

"No, he was my friend, too."

"No further questions, Your Honor."

"State may cross-examine."

During his cross-examination of Alexander, Thompson asked one seemingly innocuous question after another, seeking a misstatement here, a contradiction there. The answer to any one question meaningless, but the sum total of which he would make damning in his closing argument. His cross-examination lasted until early evening. Four o'clock. Five o'clock. Six.

"Mr. Alexander, you testified earlier today that you drove Taylor Heath to the Pittsburgh airport more than once."

"Yes, yes, I did."

And that would be all Thompson would ask Alexander on the subject, and he would move on to the next question, only to return to it an hour later.

Did Alexander know Tony Mason? For how long? Didn't the two of them regularly correspond? Wasn't Mason serving a prison term for drug trafficking stemming from a police raid at the Club Paddock in Weirton? Then Thompson moved on to the next series of questions, looking to hammer in one more nail. Sometimes missing, but just as often driving his point home.

How had Alexander been employed since leaving college? Just how long had he been employed as a structural-steel painter? For which trucking company had he worked as a driver? What type of license was needed for that type of driving? What crew had employed him as a carpenter? Was it rough or finish carpentry? Thompson would continue onward to another equally detailed and devilishly probing topic.

And so forth through the early evening until Thompson looked to the bench.

"The state has no more questions for Mr. Alexander, Your Honor."

Judge Biltmore looked down to second counsel's table. Calvin looked at the questions he had prepared for redirect examination. He looked at the faces of the jurors. He looked again at his questions.

"No redirect, Your Honor."

Judge Biltmore turned to Alexander and told him he was excused. As Alexander stepped down, Judge Biltmore announced that court was adjourned for the day and, owing to the lateness of the hour, they would not reconvene tomorrow until one o'clock. He nodded to the jurors and told them they could go home.

Alexander and Calvin stood side by side as they waited

for the jurors to leave and for the gallery to empty.

"What do you think, counselor? Where do we stand?"

Calvin regarded for a moment the door by which the jurors were leaving the courtroom.

"It's close, Mark. Real close. Right now, I'd say the jury could go either way. The witnesses are about equally balanced."

"Yes, that's how it looks to me, too."

"So tomorrow, when we re-call Walters, should decide it in your favor if he sticks to what he wrote me in his letter."

Alexander nodded and turned, looking back toward the gallery where the last of the spectators were making their way toward the doors. After a minute Calvin also turned and saw he was watching Allison, who had sat in the back all day and was now speaking to Deputy Smith.

Alexander shook his head and spoke, not to Calvin, but softly to her. "If I knew then what I know now, sweetheart, I surely would have burned your bitch eyes out, too, when I had the chance."

Alexander did not turn back to Calvin. Calvin did not turn away from Alexander. Another deputy walked over and asked Alexander if he wanted to use the restroom before they drove back up to County, and he said he did.

As Alexander and the deputy were leaving, Deputy Smith saw his partner leaving with their prisoner and hurried after them. When Calvin turned to Allison, she was looking at him. Calvin pursed his lips and nodded. Allison nodded that yes, she would.

CHAPTER 66

A T ONE O'CLOCK on the following afternoon, Judge Biltmore told Calvin to call his next witness. Calvin stood.

Lines furrowed the judge's forehead, and half-moons darkened beneath his eyes. He was not alone. Not only judge, but lawyers, jurors, and even spectators, were drained. Drained from listening to irreconcilable versions from two summers ago, hearing them replayed over and over at night while they slept. From a week in a country courtroom at the end of a queer summer, with their only relief from the heat coming from open windows through which no breeze blew, and an old, clicking overhead fan which had stopped turning just past noon.

"Defense re-calls James Walters," Calvin said.

Deputy Smith crossed the hall to the sheriff's court-house office where Walters had been waiting since being driven down from the jail. Not long after his arrival, an approaching thunderstorm had blown a transformer somewhere in the electrical grid along Lake Erie, and Hanna had darkened as at dusk. Before Judge Biltmore called the court to order, some in the gallery had speculated he would extend the trial to the following day, but he had ordered the lawyers to proceed, the midday twilight notwithstanding.

The deputy returned with Walters, who wore again his Goodwill Store suit. When he was brought to the witness stand, Walters hesitated and looked at Thompson for guidance, but Judge Biltmore told him that since he had already been sworn in once before, he could just be seated. He reminded Walters he was still under oath, still sworn to tell the truth. As Walters stepped up to be seated, he stumbled, and he would have cracked his head on the chair had the deputy not caught hold of him by his coat collar.

"Easy there, boy," he told Walters.

Calvin stood waiting at the podium. He looked down at the legal tablet before him and closed his eyes.

He had wakened at two o'clock that morning screaming, "Not again. Not this time. No," and his scream seemed to echo on and on through his open window and on out into the night. He had been back at the farm again. Out the kitchen window he saw it was winter. Standing beside him was Elizabeth Barnhouse, and on a table laid a woman, her face indistinct, but her throat was slit open, and it smiled up at him, wide and agape.

Mrs. Barnhouse looked at him. "You failed her, Calvin," she said. "You were the last friend she had. She was depending upon you to save her, and you failed."

Outside the courthouse, the wind, which had risen with the approach of the storm, ceased, and the window curtains stood centurion-still. Calvin opened his eyes and nodded.

"Mr. Walters."

"Yes, sir."

"A week ago you testified you were being held up at the Creek County Jail while awaiting transport to the Lucasville Correctional Facility for Men, is that correct?"

"Yes, sir. I am."

"You also testified that you'd been sentenced to Lucasville upon your entering a plea of guilty to a charge of aiding and abetting in the murders of Peter Bonner and Taylor Heath, is that also correct?"

"Yeah, that's right."

"Mr. Walters, how long have you been in the Creek County Jail?"

Walters looked down at his hand, whispering to himself as he counted on his fingers. He scratched his chin and looked up at the ceiling. "April. Maybe May. I ain't quite sure exactly when."

"Of this year?"

"Yes, sir. This year. Nineteen eighty-one."

"You mean nineteen eighty-two?"

"Eighty-two?" Walters looked down again and frowned

and flapped his hand. "Yeah, I guess it is eighty-two, ain't it?" He shrugged. "I ain't no lawyer, you know."

"You also testified you watched Mark Alexander murder Peter Bonner."

"Yes, sir."

"And you then watched him murder Taylor Heath."

"Yes, sir," Walters said. "I did."

"Is that true? Did you, in fact, watch Mark Alexander first murder Peter Bonner and then Taylor Heath?"

Walters did not answer. Calvin repeated the question.

"No, sir," Walters finally said. "Alexander didn't murder them."

"Who did then?"

"Me."

The handheld fans in the gallery stopped, frozen in midmotion.

"Before their murders, did you know Bonner and Heath?"

"Yes, sir. I did." He wetted his lips. "I knowed both of them."

"And you killed both of them?"

"Yes, sir. Sorry to say so now, but I'm the one who done it." Walters nodded toward second counsel's table. " 'Twasn't him."

"Please go on," Calvin said. "Tell us how you murdered them."

"It was back in July or August, two summers ago. I ain't completely certain which month it was. I'm not real good with dates and stuff."

"Do the best you can."

Walters was looking only at the floor. Not at the jurors, not at Calvin.

"I was at one of the bars in Goshen. I ain't exactly sure which one, but we's only got two down there. Might of been Ernest's. Probably was, but I can't swear to it. I was pretty well messed up."

"Messed up how?"

"I was there getting loaded on beer and 'ludes."

"Quaaludes?"

"Yeah, Mr. Samuels. Quaaludes."

"Go on."

"I was in the bar getting loaded on beer and 'ludes when my cousin, John Rogers, comes in."

"Did the two of you speak?"

"Yes, sir."

"About what?"

"He sits down at my table and tells me he's just picked up some angel dust that morning and I says to him, 'Angel dust. You know, man, I love that stuff.' So we went back in shitter and he gives me a couple of lines, and we snorted some off the top of one of the pissers."

"What happened after the two of you snorted the angel dust?"

"We went back out and drank some beer. After a while I told him I sure would like to buy some more dust, and he said he didn't have no more, but we could go back to the farm and get us all of the dust in the world. So after we had us another couple of beers, we sashayed on out and got into Taylor's van, and John drove us back to the farm."

"What happened when you got back?" Calvin said.

"Bonner and Heath was there."

"Was anything said to them?"

"Yeah, some stuff was said."

"What was said, Jimmy?"

"I told them I sure would like to deal their dust for them in Goshen. Told them I thought I could pick up a fair piece of change for them if I did."

"And?"

"And then we all talked the deal over while they was getting us high on their dust. Shooting up with some Demerol, too."

He shook his head. "I gotta tell you, Mr. Samuels, the higher we got, the cooler they acted. Those two. Those two just thought they was so cool, they did—but we showed them. Showed them they wasn't nothing."

"Really?"

Walters paused. He looked over at the water pitcher and asked if it would be all right if he had a drink. Judge Biltmore nodded to the deputy who was standing beside Walters. The deputy poured and handed Walters the glass.

Distant thunder rumbled through the courtroom. The wind blew in through the window. The curtain next to Walters reached out, brushing his shoulder, and Walters jerked around and spilled the water on his trousers. Walters turned back around, his face the color of the curtain, and he could not steady his hand even when he grabbed onto it with his other, and the deputy finally had to take the glass from him.

"You okay, Jimmy?"

Walters nodded.

"Please go on then."

"I, I, was messed up—I mean really, really messed up—but I started saying to myself that these guys were just clowns."

"Where was Rogers during all this?"

"John was just about out of it. He was lying there in the corner of the room with a needle sticking out of his arm."

"Go on."

"Sometime later that night, Bonner and Heath decided to drive to Ernest's to get some more beer."

"What happened after they left?"

"A while later John started coming out of it, and we talked. He said he didn't like the way these Michigan guys was treating him. Said they was always making fun of him and didn't treat him right."

"Go on."

"We talked some more, and we snorted some more dust, and we talked some more. We decided we was going to rip these guys off for their dope and cash. I got to tell you, Mr. Samuels, we was out of our heads."

"What sort of plan did you work out?"

"I says to John that I should be the one to rob them

because they didn't know me as good as they knew him. Then me and him could split up the dope and cash later."

"So how did all this transpire?"

"No, we wasn't transpiring much, Mr. Samuels. We was barely sweating."

"How did the rip-off go down?"

"I had a .45 John give me that he'd found in Bonner's sleeping bag. When I saw the truck pull up, I told him to stay in the bedroom while I waited there in the living room. Heath come in and stretches out on the couch with a can of beer sitting on his stomach, but Bonner, he just stood in the doorway. Like he knew something was up. After we talked for a minute, I pulled out the .45 and put it on Bonner. Told them both that me and my cousin was taking their dope and their money, and then we was going to go. Told them not to try nothing stupid so no one would get hurt."

"What happened then?"

"I'd no more than told them to stay put than Heath pulls out a goddamn pistol." Walters shook his head. "He had more goddamn pistols than anybody else I ever knowed of. Bonner jumps toward me, and I shot him square in the mouth. I heard a shotgun blast, and I turned. It was John. He'd shot Heath. Blew him clean across the room and out into the kitchen."

"Go on," Calvin said.

"We just went crazy. Shot up that whole house. Me and John did. When we ran out of ammunition, we decided to throw the bodies down the shitter."

"How did you get them there?"

"Just dragged them out on their sleeping bags. John was still pretty well messed up, but I got him to help me get them out."

"Did you have any difficulties dumping the bodies in?"

Walters nodded. "Bonner was too big to just dump down the hole. John had to tear off the seats with a crowbar we found in one of the sheds. After we dumped them in, we went back in the house and got the drugs and cash."

"How much was there?"

"They had about three thousand between them and a pound of dust. I kept the dust, and me and John split up the cash. Then we just partied 'til the sun come up."

"What happened in the morning?"

"We drove into Goshen and bought some lime. When we got back, we dumped it in, and we busted the shitter up and set it on fire. By the end of the day, it had pretty well burnt down, but some of their bones was sticking up. We had to kick them off and throw them to the dogs they kept there."

"Anything happen after you burned down the outhouse?"

"John said Alexander had told him the Pagans was coming out in a few days to party. So I told him to be quiet and not say nothing about what we done. He dropped me off in Weirton and took the truck. Said he'd get rid of it."

Calvin looked down at his notes. Save for the wind rustling papers at the two counsel's tables, the courtroom was still.

"Anything else?" Calvin said.

"No, there ain't nothing else. That's all."

Outside the courtroom windows there was a flash, but no thunder.

"Jimmy," Calvin said. "What's the length of sentence you'll be serving in Lucasville?"

"Seven to twenty-five years, sir."

"And that sentence is for aiding and abetting Mark Alexander in the murders of Peter Bonner and Taylor Heath?"

"Yes, sir."

"And another two to five years for the auto theft."

"Yes, sir," Walters said.

"Both sentences to be served concurrently."

"Yeah. That's it. Both to be served at the same time."

"Jimmy," Calvin said, "if you should be tried and convicted for murdering both Peter Bonner and Taylor Heath, you could receive two life sentences."

"Yes, sir."

"To be served consecutively."

"Yes, sir," Walters said.

"After your auto-theft sentence."

"I know it."

"One right after the other," Calvin said.

"Yes, sir."

"Meaning you'd be a very old man before you were paroled. If you ever were."

"Yes, sir," Walters said.

"Before you testified today, you could've been paroled in another four years."

"Yes, sir."

"So why confess?" Calvin asked. "Confess to the murders of Bonner and Heath when you didn't have to."

Walters squinted. "Sir?"

"Why confess and risk not being paroled until you're a very old man, if then?"

Walters looked at Alexander a moment. He looked back. "Well, I know Alexander, Mr. Samuels. He's good people."

"Good people?"

"Oh sure, he might of ridden that summer with a gang and done some stuff, but he ain't no killer."

Walters swallowed. "Besides, I thought if I done the right thing, maybe Mr. Thompson would go easy on me."

"I see," Calvin said. "Have you told the truth here today?"

"Yes, sir."

"The whole and complete truth?"

"Yes, sir, Mr. Samuels. I sure have. The whole and complete and God-given truth."

Calvin looked at Judge Biltmore. "No further questions, Your Honor."

"State may cross-examine."

Calvin sat down. Alexander beamed and patted him on the shoulder, but Calvin only stared straight ahead.

Thompson studied Walters a moment, tapping his pen up and down on the table. Walters would not look up at him, but only stared down at the abyssal cracks in floor-boards. Another rumble of thunder, this one louder than the last, rolled through the courtroom. The calm had passed, and the window curtains twisted and danced in the wind. Thompson rose and walked to the podium.

"Mr. Walters."

"Yes, sir."

"Do you know Ms. Morris? Allison Morris, who testified in this trial, in this very courtroom, just last week."

"Yes, sir. You know that, Mr. Thompson. She's my stepsister. Same moms, different dads."

"Since you've been up in the county jail, have you ever written to her, your stepsister?"

Walters looked at Calvin, but Calvin would give him no guidance. He turned back slowly to Thompson. "Written, sir?"

"Yes. Written. You can write, can you not?"

"I'm not exactly sure what you mean."

"Well, Mr. Walters. It's a fairly easy question. Since you have been a guest of the citizens of Creek County up at the jail, have you ever written to Allison Morris? Yes or no?"

"Maybe. I can't really say. Can't really remember. I've written a lot of letters lately. To my friends. My family. Not much else to do up there."

Thompson smiled. He walked to first counsel's table where his assistant handed him several pages of yellow, lined paper.

"Let me ask you once more, Mr. Walters, if you have

within the past week written to Allison Morris?"

"No, sir. I don't believe I have there."

"No, Mr. Walters?" Thompson taunted.

"No."

"Let me show you what's been marked as State's Exhibit Number Thirty-Seven, and let me ask if you recognize it."

Thompson walked to the witness stand and handed the pages to Walters, who stared down at them a moment before he took them.

"It looks like mine," he said.

"It looks like your what?"

Walters didn't answer.

"It looks like your what, Mr. Walters?"

"It looks like . . . it looks like a letter of mine I might of started." Walters looked up. "But I never mailed it, Mr. Thompson." He looked behind at Deputy Smith, but the deputy was studying the storm outside.

"Nevertheless, it is a letter from you to Ms. Morris that you wrote while you've been in the Creek County Jail."

Walters shook his head.

"It's in your own handwriting, is it not?"

"I . . . I have to say I don't remember writing no letter."

Thompson stood there, weighing Walters's words; but he ultimately erased them with a slow, waving motion of his index and middle fingers in the air before him.

"In that case, let me read it to you. Just to refresh your memory. 'Dear Allison,' you begin. 'Okay, just relax, please.

Miza told me that you are worried. But me and Alexander are getting ready to have some fun now. Smile. Yeah. I did sign the letter to his attorney you heard about and, no, my life is in no danger and, no, I haven't been threatened in any way'."

Walters closed his eyes.

" 'I know it's hard on you to understand, and I'm sorry if all this hurts you. But I couldn't tell you what I was up to before because I couldn't take the chance of any of this getting out'."

Alexander turned to Calvin, but Calvin only looked at Walters.

" 'Just trust me. We've spent a whole lot of time on this, honey, and believe me, we know what we're doing. I won't be charged, although I hope I am. I know I'm not the brightest man around, but I'm far from stupid. Do you realize how much Thompson will be squirming around? Smile! This case is at the top of his list, and yeah, a whole lot of publicity is on this case.

" 'Allison, when you talk to Thompson, don't tell him what I'm telling you. Just tell him I won't talk about it to you or to Mom or Dad and leave it at that. Understand? Please don't ruin this for me. I have everything under control.

" 'Babe, no matter what I say or sign, they can't do nothing to me. Naturally, I'm being called as a witness against Alexander. But after I switch my story, Thompson will tell the jury I didn't do it, that I'm trying to get Alexander off and that he's been threatening me or Miza or something.

Now that would look pretty funny on Thompson, wouldn't it, if he turns around after the jury lets Alexander go and tries to charge me? Do you see what I'm saying? There's a lot more to it, but I'm sure you get my point.

" 'Hell, Allison, do you think I'm so stupid as to do something like this and not have my own tracks covered? We've been working on this. We know what we're doing.

" 'Now you're wondering, why are we doing this, right? Think baby, just think. I don't feel like doing no more time for these people. Do you know how much I'll do this go-round? About until nineteen eighty-six, but I'll probably do longer the way this whole thing is rigged against me.

" 'So don't ruin it for us. Me and Alexander have an escape all worked out that will work. I know we're talking about my life, babe, which is all the more reason to trust me. It's a very touchy situation right now; they know we're going to be doing something, so it's going be hard enough the way it is. Watch what you say when and if you write back. I know my mail is read. Love, Jimmy'."

Walters was staring down at his hands. It had started to rain into the courtroom while Thompson had been reading, but the bailiff and the deputies had made no move to close the windows.

"Mr. Walters," Thompson said, "does that letter refresh your memory?"

"Yes," Walters said. Though he whispered his answer, none in the courtroom failed to hear it.

"Did you, in fact, write this letter that I've just read?"
Walters nodded.

CHAPTER 67

ALEXANDER'S TRIAL WAS all but over. Calvin presented no more testimony. The Pagans and Alexander's supporters from Ernest's, who had sat in the courtroom or stood and waited in the hallway, vanished. Thompson's two rebuttal witnesses testified on a few minor issues concerning the reliability of the forensic evidence, but added little. The jurors fidgeted and kept looking back at the clock.

The lawyers' closing arguments were short. Thompson spoke for thirty minutes, Calvin for just twenty. The gallery handicappers said later they knew it was his last. The fire, the passion for the underdog, was emasculated. When Calvin stood at the podium, his head bowed, it was difficult for the older spectators to hear. Those who could, said his summation sounded more like an apology, a farewell. A shame, they said. After he had worked so hard for so long to become a trial lawyer.

The jury deliberated for just two hours before they returned with their verdict. The jury foreman, a woman who
had shaken her head at Jocelyn's engagement to Alexander,
handed the verdict form to the bailiff who in turn handed it
to Judge Biltmore, who took some time to study it. After a
minute, he looked up.

"Mark Alexander, please rise."

The storm had let up enough so that, toward the end
of the jury's deliberations, the bailiff had cracked open the
courtroom windows. Reverend Barnhouse, sitting near
an open window, was shivering and had wrapped his arms
around himself, but no one else in the gallery seemed bothered. The electricity was again on, and the overhead fan
turned, but it did so without clicking like a clock.

Alexander and Calvin rose together. Judge Biltmore
read aloud from the jury verdict.

"We the jury, in the above entitled case, do find the
defendant, Mark M. Alexander, guilty of the crime of the
aggravated murder of Peter Bonner on or about July thirty-
first, nineteen eighty, in Creek County, Ohio."

"You bastard," Alexander whispered.

"We the jury, in the above entitled case, do also find the
defendant, Mark M. Alexander, guilty of the crime of the
aggravated murder of Taylor Heath on or about July thirty-
first, nineteen eighty, in Creek County, Ohio."

After Judge Biltmore polled the jury to confirm its

verdict, he turned again to Alexander.

"Do you have anything to say why the judgment of this court should not be passed upon you at this time?"

Alexander shook his head, the temples behind his eyes creased and his fists clenched. When he spoke, his voice broke. "Thompson did his job, I guess. If you can call convicting an innocent man his job. But I was innocent, and I'm still innocent."

Alexander was quiet a moment, but he turned from Judge Biltmore to Calvin, and his iron-gray eyes narrowed. "And I'll be innocent when judgment day comes."

Judge Biltmore sentenced Alexander to life imprisonment and ordered his immediate transportation to Lucasville. Calvin turned to Alexander, but the line of deputies who sat behind them during the trial quickly circled Alexander, and they moved him to the courtroom door where Walters waited just outside in the corridor with Deputy Smith. The deputies manacled their wrists and legs together and moved them down the flight of steps, out the front courthouse door.

Calvin watched until they were gone and the courtroom doors again closed. He packed up his briefcase. He walked up to Thompson, who stood at first counsel's table talking to McLain, and the two shook hands.

"You had me worried there toward the end, Calvin."

He walked out the front courtroom door and up the back flight of stairs to the Public Defender's Office, where he looked out his window. In front of the courthouse, the newspaper reporters and some of the spectators stood and watched as the deputies and a contingent of state police surrounding Alexander and Walters escorted them through the rain to the third cruiser of a five-cruiser convoy that would carry them to Lucasville. In the back stood Mrs. Bonner and Mr. Heath. After a while, Mrs. Bonner leaned toward Mr. Heath who nodded as she spoke, and the two walked together back into the courthouse.

Calvin watched as the convoy drove out of Hanna, lights flashing, and he continued to look down the street and over the rooftops even after they had disappeared. There was a knock at his locked door, but he just stood at the window, watching. After a while he looked to Cemetery Hill.

"God speed John Rogers."

Three and a half hours into the six-hour trip, the convoy pulled into a highway patrol post so the troopers and deputies could stretch their legs and drink coffee. They left Alexander and Walters handcuffed in the cruiser and still manacled to one another. A trooper and a deputy stood at attention in their rain gear on either side of the car, each holding a twelve-gauge pump shotgun with the safeties off.

Both prisoners sat in silence for a quarter-hour, each looking out their own window, until Alexander finally spoke, spoke as quietly as a father might to his errant child.

"Why, Psycho? Just tell me why. Why would you write such a letter? And why would you give it to Allison? Her, of all people."

Walters was looking out his window to Interstate 71 a mile away. "What can I say? She took me in, Mark. She took me in. I can't believe it. My own stepsister. God, she's good. Played me like a banjo." He shook his head. "Just played me like a five-string banjo."

Alexander said nothing.

"She must of given Thompson that letter I give Smitty after Miza visited me last Sunday."

"Miza visited you?"

"Yeah. Told me Allison was saying you was thinking about turning on me for John's murder 'cause she testified against you. Miza said maybe I just better write a letter to get me off the hook and get it to her just in case you did."

Neither spoke for a minute. Finally Walters said, "Jesus, Mark. Your own lawyer must of knowed about that letter."

"Yes," Alexander said. "He must have, and now Allison has us both on the way to Lucasville."

"You know what's funny? Or what would be if it weren't the two of us on our way there?"

"I can't imagine."

"It was her that set up wasting John to begin with," Walters said.

Alexander looked at him. "I thought it was all your doing."

"Nope," Walters said.

"Really?"

"After she dropped you off at the airport, Allison and Miza drove back to Goshen. She walks into Ernest's and sees

John talking to Rock. A little while later she sees John on the phone and figures maybe he's trying to tip off the cops, and she didn't want to take no chances. Rock was tending bar that night, and I was shooting pool. She saw him on the phone and waits for him to get off and then sits down with him. Talks to him for a couple, three hours. When he gets up and goes to the pisser, she comes over and tells me what might be going down. Told me that when they goes to leave, I should follow and we'd find out for sure."

"You mean it wasn't John who called the cops to begin with?" Alexander said.

"No way. He was too scared and too doped to do nothing. But by the time Allison was satisfied he hadn't said nothing to the cops, he was so bad off after what she'd done to make him talk, we had to finish him off. Kind of felt bad about it. My cousin and all."

Alexander looked back out at the foggy mist that grew closer as night fell.

"I don't care if I'm a hundred when I get out. I don't. But when I do, I'm going to hunt her down and when I find her, I'm going to burn her. I'm going to burn her bitch eyes out. Just like she did to Jolly Rogers."

CHAPTER 68

1992

RENATE THOMPSON CIRCLED her husband's shoulder with her arm as they danced to the same Cole Porter tune to which they had danced their first dance at their wedding reception. If she held him a little closer than was her custom, it may have been because of the music or because she still felt unsteady from the three glasses of champagne from earlier that evening. Or she may have been seeking solace.

Thompson felt her pensiveness, but said nothing. So for a while longer they danced, each within their own silences. The living room where they danced was dark save for the fireplace embers, which threw outsized shadows of silhouetted dancers against the walls and upon the ceiling. They vanished and reappeared and vanished again like moths. Renate rested her cheek on her husband's shoulder and hummed as she watched their shadows, watched their patterns cross back and forth. After a while, she pulled away and looked up at him.

"I just can't believe it."

"What is it you just can't believe?"

"What you told me when you came home."

"Oh?"

"Do you mean to tell me that ever since she was murdered, he's been traveling the country in search of Alexander?"

"That's why he came to see me. Said he thought maybe I'd heard something or maybe I might hear something and I could get word to him if I did. Assuming I could even find him."

Renate frowned. "Where would Calvin even begin to look?"

"He told me that when he needs money, he'll pump gas or tend bar. He likes tending bar better."

"The free drinks, I bet."

"That, and it's warm. He can hear a lot, and he can ask questions without being obvious."

She laid her cheek back against his shoulder, and they danced for another minute before she again pulled away.

"What was that car explosion during Alexander's trial all about? Down at that bar in Goshen. 'Ed's' or something."

"Ernest's."

"That's the one. I've always wondered about that. At the time you said you couldn't discuss it."

"No, I couldn't."

"Why can't you now?"

"I suppose now there's no longer a need for secrecy."

Thompson looked for a moment into the dying embers. "The Michigan mobsters who employed Bonner and Heath to run their drugs up from Miami were not at all happy about their deaths."

"Why's that? I would think guys like them would be a dime a dozen."

"Not even a dime, but if word got around any small town punk could mess with their runners, they might as well go back to stealing hubcaps."

"I suppose that's so."

"Not long after the murders, Alexander and his old girlfriend had a falling out."

"Over what?"

"Most likely over his new girlfriend."

Renate shook her head. "Men. They never seem to learn."

"At about this same time, the old girlfriend killed, or had killed, John Rogers, who'd been hanging out at the farm with them."

"I remember John."

"That's right. He was one of your early charges."

"That's how we first met. When I came up to see you about going after his mother. But why did she kill him?"

"Probably because he'd been talking, or because he knew too much and might be talking."

"Have you known this all along?" Renate asked.

Thompson shook his head.

"Since when?"

"A year or so after the trial, at a meeting of Midwestern prosecutors, the D.A. from Detroit and I were sitting up at the hotel bar one midnight and got to telling each other our war stories."

"You told me you always went to bed early when you attended those things."

"I usually do, except that night we went to a strip club."

"You what?"

Thompson grinned. "Purely for professional reasons, honey."

"Wasn't that when I was pregnant with Sarah?"

"Might've been."

"We'll come back to your professional reasons, but first tell me about the car bombing."

"A year before, the FBI arrested a small-time Detroit wiseguy who spilled his guts in exchange for placement in their witness-protection program. He told them Rogers had been talking, but not to the police."

"Then who?"

"He'd been at Ernest's one night not long after the murders and drinking too much and ended up telling everything to John Allen Rock. When Rogers turned up dead some days later after leaving Ernest's with Alexander's old girlfriend and Walters not far behind them, Rock put two and two together."

"Who's Rock?"

"He'd been the president of the Pagans before we sent him to prison, which was when Alexander took over. When Rock got out, he wanted his old gang back, but Alexander wasn't giving, and he had the muscle to make it stick after he knifed one of Rock's flunkies at Club Paddock."

"What did Rock do then?"

"He bided his time, and when the opportunity presented itself, he checked in with the mobsters who remembered him from the old days."

"What did they do?"

"They thought about it for a few months, talked it over with the folks in Miami, and finally told Rock they thought it was a good idea."

"A good way to get out the message, I guess."

"After they gave Rock the go ahead, he called in the tip. When the Goshen police dug up the bodies, they went to Walters first because it was his granduncle's farm. You remember about his granduncle? Harry Katz."

"I don't know that you ever told me," Renate said.

"Disappeared not long before Alexander's trial started."

"Was he ever found?"

"The next spring the Goshen PD found him floating in the cistern across the road from where he lived."

"Good Lord."

"Strangest thing. No sign of foul play. Just seemed to have fallen in."

"What about Walters?"

"The police knew he'd been staying there the summer before, and they figured they could crack him."

"Did they?"

Thompson nodded. "Then Rock blackmailed Alexander's old girlfriend into stepping forward, but also promising her a piece of the run if they could put away her old boyfriend."

"What'd she do?"

"She came to us and named Alexander as the killer."

"Why did you believe her?"

"She proved herself by directing us to Heath's van at the airport. Then Walters agreed to testify against Alexander in exchange for a reduced charge of conspiracy instead of murder."

"She and Rock were going to get the run?"

"Not a chance. The mobsters already had someone else in mind, someone a bit more reliable, but they needed to send a message to anyone foolish enough to interfere with their runners."

"Why not simply kill Alexander?"

"Because Creek County already had more than its share of grisly murders for a rural county. Murder him and maybe the FBI or DEA might begin to take notice. So they told Rock that if he could take out Alexander without bloodshed, the run was his."

"So she turned on him."

"She came in, told us about the murders and of Walters's

involvement and where we could find Heath's van."

"When are you going to get to the car bombing?"

"Rock got nervous after the trial began. He stood in the back of the courtroom the first day, and he must have thought Calvin had a chance of actually proving up Alexander's alibi defense. The night before she was to testify, Jocelyn Murphy was at Ernest's. While she was inside, Rock walked outside with three sticks of dynamite, which he tried to connect to the distributor cap of her car."

"The old Youngstown tune-up," Renate said.

"Never actually having dynamited someone's car before—or even ever having watched it done—he caught the wrong wire and blew himself up. He nonetheless succeeded in frightening Jocelyn into testifying less than enthusiastically, and in frightening Alexander's uncle out of the state altogether. No one's seen him since."

"What about the old girlfriend?"

"After she lost her partner, she suspected the mob of duplicity. She had, maybe, one friend left, and definitely one enemy."

Renate lifted her head and turned toward the French doors leading out to what would again be their garden in the spring. "Listen. It's calm outside."

"Storm's passed," Thompson said. "The night's cleared."

The courthouse clock struck midnight. Thompson bent forward and kissed his wife. "Happy engagement anniversary."

She looked up and drew his face down to hers. "Happy nineteenth engagement anniversary, sweetheart."

She smiled and laid her cheek back on her husband's shoulder. "Funny."

"What's funny?"

"I haven't thought of her for years, but ever since you came home, I've been trying to remember the name of the woman Calvin married."

Thompson smiled. "Why, Renate. I'm surprised at you. You're such a smut monger. It was all the scandal at the time."

"I remember her. And of course I remember the scandal. I just can't recall her name. Must be too much champagne."

"Her name was Allison. Allison Morris."

"And Alexander murdered her?"

Thompson didn't answer.

"Well, didn't he?"

"After Calvin left this afternoon, I called the sheriff," Thompson said.

"And?"

"He's still in prison."

"I thought I read in the paper where he'd been paroled?"

"You read in the paper where Walters had been paroled. Allison's stepbrother. Alexander's still sitting in Lucasville."

"Was it Walters then who murdered her?"

"I don't think so." said Thompson.

"Why not?"

"Sheriff says that when he called this afternoon, they

told him Walters had definitely been out there, but he'd been picked up on a new drug charge and was in jail for over a week before her murder."

"There's something else, isn't there?" Renate said.

"Calvin wasn't the one who called in the murder."

"Who did?"

"Neighbors. After Allison had been dead a week."

"Where was Calvin?"

"Police went to his jobsite and found he'd been gone a week. Didn't even pick up his last paycheck. They showed members of his roofing crew some mug shots and two of them picked out Walters as having been at the jobsite talking to Calvin his last day on the job. Until today, no one's seen him since he disappeared."

"I don't understand."

Thompson didn't answer.

After a while Renate said, "You'd think the police investigating her murder would have contacted someone back here to keep an eye out for Calvin if they wanted to talk to him. If they thought he knew something of her murder. Why didn't you hear that they were looking for him?"

"Her parents moved away soon after Alexander's trial. No one's heard from them since. They weren't even at her funeral."

"Why weren't you contacted?"

"The police back there did contact the Sheriff's Office after her murder."

"Why didn't they come to you?"

"Sheriff Wilson's only been on the job for a little over two years. He was living on the other side of Ohio during Alexander's trial."

"That's right. He was."

"And after they cleaned house up at the jail and arrested Smitty and some of that crew, there was no one left who remembered Alexander's trial and so no one thought to say anything to me. I didn't even know they were looking for him until I called the sheriff after Calvin left."

"Strange he should disappear after speaking to Walters."

"Yes. Very strange."

"I wonder what Walters told him."

"I don't know, but I can guess."

"I wonder why Calvin believed him."

"We may never know."

"What else is bothering you?"

"Calvin's fingers."

"His fingers?"

"When he was in my chambers this afternoon, I asked him about his fingers, and he said he'd injured them at work."

"Well, you said he'd been working as a roofer. Maybe he hit them with a hammer."

Thompson shook his head.

"Why not?"

"Do you remember when Sarah knocked over the skillet of hot grease and burned her hand?"

"Yes, of course I do."

"How she had to wait six months before she could begin the skin grafts? And while we waited she had that seeping scar tissue that smelled awful."

"Yes, Ben. Of course I do, but what's that to do with Calvin?"

"That's how his fingertips looked. Like Sarah's, after she had those third-degree burns to her fingers, and they had scabbed over some months later. They looked as though some months ago he'd held something burning in his hand that seared the tips of his fingers."

Calvin rose on wobbling-whiskey legs and stood a moment in the alley until he thought he could walk without falling. He had waited in the cemetery until long after dark before walking back down the hill to Simpson's State Store and using the last of his change and a half-dozen empty Coke bottles found in a trashcan along the way to buy a pint bottle of Four Roses.

When the alley stopped spinning, he capped the empty bottle and crossed to the hill of debris behind his old cottage house and tossed it on top. The owner was gutting the inside. A sign out front promised an antique and gift shop would be opening by spring. Sticking out of the debris was the handle to the fishing pole Maude Ferguson had bought for him.

It looked like someone, maybe Gregg Ferguson, had divided the Hanna Mansion into ten or twelve apartments. In one flat the tenants were still celebrating the New Year. Gone was the stained-glass window through which he had once looked out onto her front porch.

"Ah, Maude," Calvin said. "God damn it. Just God damn it to hell, anyway."

He staggered down the alley, first on one side, then the other, toward the courthouse. At the intersection with Court Street, he turned toward Goshen. There was no traffic, and he walked fast to stay warm. A half-mile outside of Hanna a pickup truck finally came on, and when Calvin held out his thumb, it slowed, and stopped.

Inside the truck sat a woman with crow-black hair seated between two men who looked only a little older than she. A burned crack pipe coruscated in the ashtray. The passenger next to the door rolled down the window.

"Where you headed to, fella?"

"Goshen. Ernest's."

The passenger looked back toward the driver, who shook his head and smirked.

"There ain't no place called Ernest's," the passenger said. "Not in Goshen there ain't."

"Bar just outside the village limits?"

"Nah. Not in Goshen. Only bar we got anymore is Jocelyn's."

"That'll do."

Calvin did not speak to the woman sitting in the middle, who only stared straight ahead.

"Ain't got no room up front for you," the driver said. He pointed with his thumb. "You'll need to ride in back."

"Thanks."

Calvin climbed up into the bed. As the truck picked up speed, he shivered from the wind. He took the oil-stained tarpaulin covering the spare tire and wrapped it around himself and looked out into the passing darkness. After a while he said, "You think Alexander might be holding up at Jocelyn's?"

"Don't know, Mr. Samuels," John Rogers said. "Guess we'll just have to go there and have us a look-see." Then he laughed. "Maybe I should of said, *You'll just have to go there and have a look-see for the both of us.*"

Calvin nodded. He pulled the tarpaulin in a half-shroud over the back of his head. "I sure was glad to see you when you finally showed up again. Where'd you go to for all that time?"

"Oh, I was around. I was always around."

"You're not going to take off on me again, are you?"

John shook his head. "Now, Mr. Samuels. What kind of question's that? Ain't I been with you for the last five months? The last twenty-five hundred miles? You remember. It was right after Jimmy come to see you."

The passenger inside the truck turned around from watching Calvin. "Go a little bit faster there, will you, Paul? The old alky we got back there is talking to hisself." He shook his head. "God damn it, I told you we shouldn't of stopped for him."

"Couldn't just drive by him, Terry. He'd of frozen to death for sure long before he ever got to Goshen no matter how much antifreeze he's had tonight."

The passenger turned back around to watch Calvin's conversation with the night. "I'm telling you, you don't know what you're dealing with back there. My uncle come down with the DTs once and I'll tell you what, they ain't nothing to mess with."

After a while, the truck gathered speed.

EPILOGUE

The heart is deceitful above all things
and desperately wicked. Who can know it?
—Jeremiah 17:9

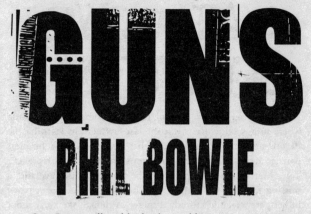

"Fast, engaging – a fine debut."
— Lee Child, NY Times bestselling author of *One Shot*

GUN'S
PHIL BOWIE

Sam Bass is tall and lanky, loves old western movies, wears cowboy boots and drives a beat-up Jeep Wrangler. He has a gorgeous girlfriend, Valerie, a Cherokee widow with a young son, and he's a hot shot pilot. A hot shot pilot with a past. And when Sam makes a daring and dangerous rescue of a couple lost at sea in a storm, he gets publicity he definitely doesn't need.

The Cowboy, as he's known in certain circles, has finally been located and a hit team is dispatched to take care of unfinished business. A bomb is planted in the beat-up Jeep. But it isn't Sam who drives it that day.

Grief stricken, Sam visits Valerie's grandfather in the North Carolina mountains to tell him he plans to avenge Valerie in the ancient Native American way of members of a wronged family seeking justice — with no help from the law. With only the old man's help, Sam trains his mind and body for the task ahead. And then the bloody hunt is on . . .

ISBN#1932815597
ISBN#9781932815597
Gold Imprint
US $6.99 / CDN $8.99
Available Now
www.philbowie.com

LORI G. ARMSTRONG
HALLOWEd GROUNd

Grisly murders are rocking the small county of Bear Butte where Julie Collins has spent the last few months learning the PI biz without the guidance of her best friend and business partner, Kevin Wells. Enter dangerous, charismatic entrepreneur Tony Martinez, who convinces Julie to take a case involving a missing five-year-old Native American girl, the innocent pawn in her parents' child custody dispute. Although skeptical about Martinez' motives in hiring her, and confused by her strange attraction to him, Julie nevertheless sees the opportunity to hone her investigative skills outside her office.

But something about the case doesn't ring true. The girl's father is foreman on the controversial new Indian casino under construction at the base of the sacred Mato Paha, and the girl's mother is secretly working for a rival casino rumored to have ties to an east coast crime family. Local ranchers — including her father — a Lakota Holy group, and casino owners from nearby Deadwood are determined to stop the gaming facility from opening.

With the body count rising, the odds are stacked against Julie to discover the truth behind these hidden agendas before the murderer buries it forever. And when Julie unwittingly attracts the attention of the killer, she realizes no place is safe . . . not even hallowed ground.

ISBN#1932815740
ISBN#9781932815740
Gold Imprint
US $6.99 / CDN $8.99
Available Now
www.loriarmstrong.com

NATURAL SELECTION

A Liz Wolfe Novel

Paige Blackwell needs a vacation. She's been working hard as a partner in Shelby Parker's PI agency. When she's offered a chance to be on a survival type reality television show that takes place on a tropical island, she jumps at the opportunity.

On the island Paige meets her fellow competitors, including one it might be fun to share a sleeping bag with, should things work out. It looks like the week is going to be even more enjoyable than she had thought. And then the first shots are fired. At them.

There's no reality TV show. Just reality. They're being hunted. Survival takes on a whole new meaning. But Paige and her companions are not the only ones in jeopardy.

Back home, Shelby and new associate Zoe are racing against the clock to stop a plot by the shadowy and sinister Dominion Order to control the U.S. guided missile system.

Who wants the carefully selected contestants on the island dead? What do they all have in common? And why are Shelby and Zoe now targets, too?

Clearly, only the fittest will survive.

ISBN#1932815228
ISBN#9781932815221
Gold Imprint
US $6.99 / CDN $8.99
Available Now
www.lizwolfe.net

For more information

about other great titles from

Medallion Press, visit

www.medallionpress.com